Save Yourself!

BONES
LEOPARD

KELLY & NICHOLE
MATTHEWS

Published by
BOOm! BOX

SERIES DESIGNER
GRACE PARK

ASSISTANT EDITOR
KENZIE RZONCA

COLLECTION DESIGNER
MICHELLE ANKLEY

EDITOR
SHANNON WATTERS

COVER BY
KELLY & NICHOLE MATTHEWS

CREATED BY
BONES LEOPARD

BOOM! BOX

SAVE YOURSELF!, March 2022. Published by BOOM! Box, a division of Boom Entertainment, Inc. Save Yourself! is ™ and © 2022 Bones Leopard, Kelly Matthews & Nichole Matthews. Originally published in single magazine form as SAVE YOURSELF! No. 1-4. ™ & © 2021 Bones Leopard. All rights reserved. BOOM! Box™ and the BOOM! Box logo are trademarks of Boom Entertainment, Inc., registered in various countries and categories. All characters, events, and institutions depicted herein are fictional. Any similarity between any of the names, characters, persons, events, and/or institutions in this publication to actual names, characters, and persons, whether living or dead, events, and/or institutions is unintended and purely coincidental. BOOM! Studios does not read or accept unsolicited submissions of ideas, stories, or artwork.

BOOM! Studios, 5670 Wilshire Boulevard, Suite 400, Los Angeles, CA 90036-5679. Printed in China. First Printing.

ISBN: 978-1-68415-811-9, eISBN: 978-1-64668-444-1

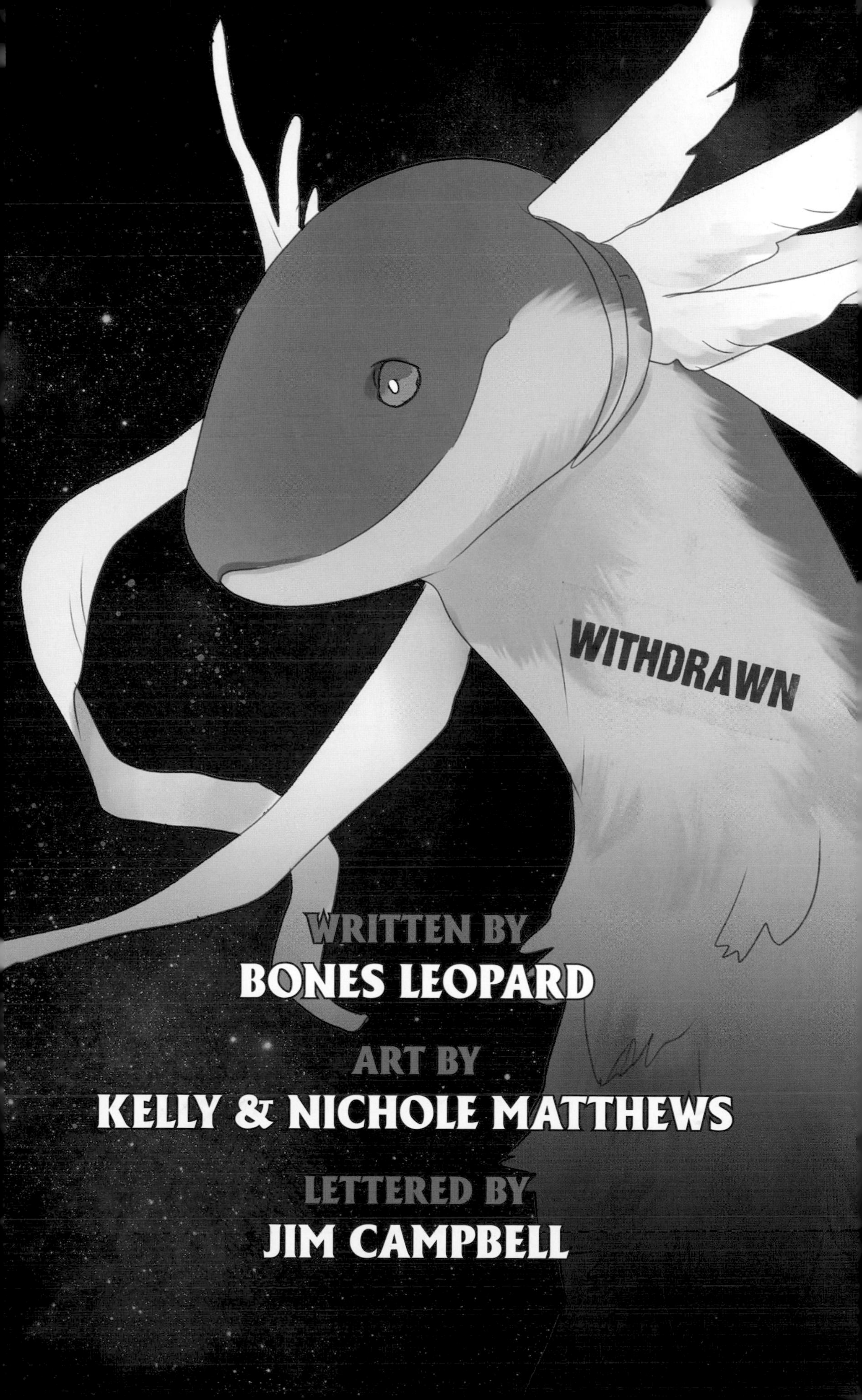

WRITTEN BY

BONES LEOPARD

ART BY

KELLY & NICHOLE MATTHEWS

LETTERED BY

JIM CAMPBELL

CHAPTER
ONE

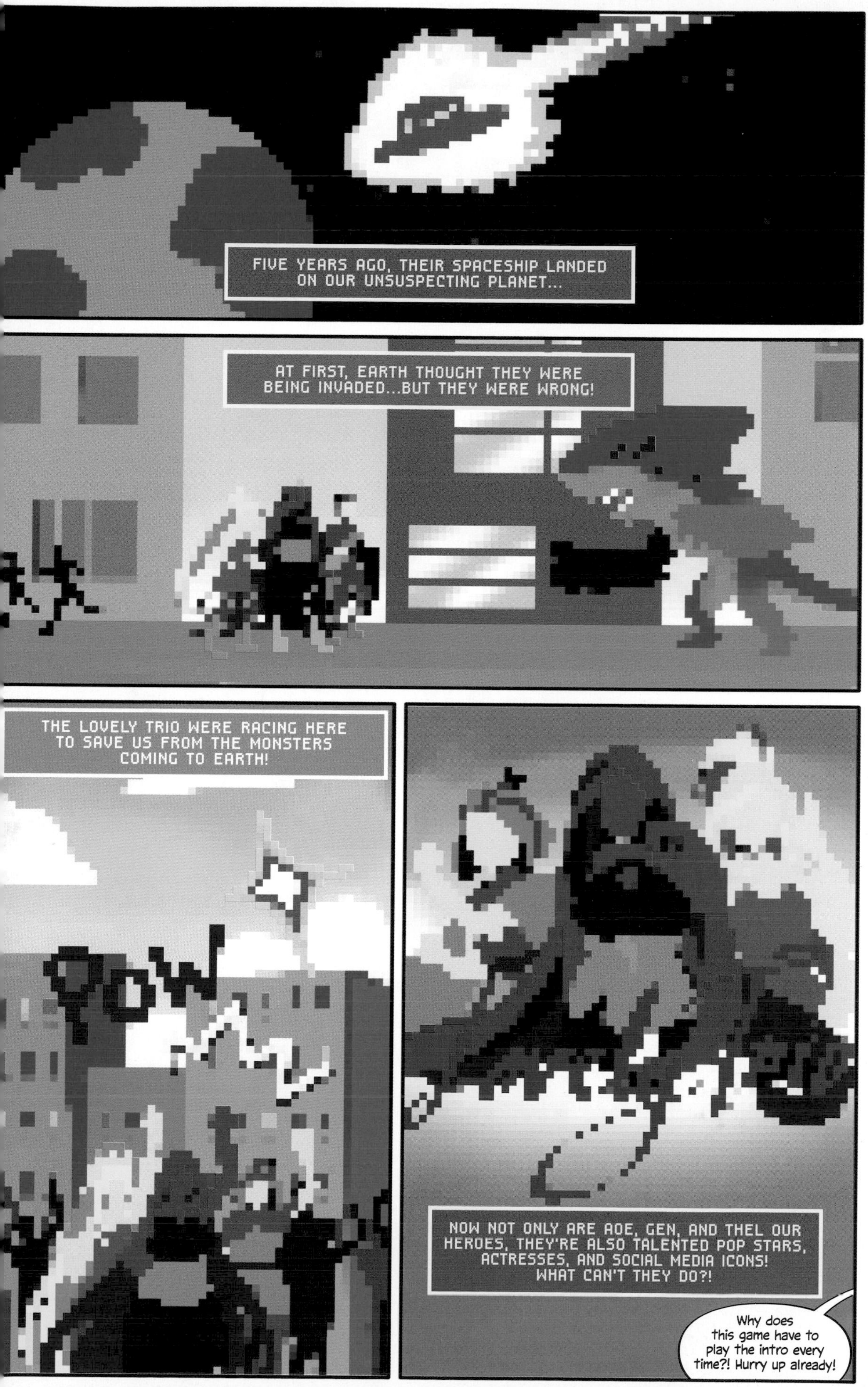
FIVE YEARS AGO, THEIR SPACESHIP LANDED ON OUR UNSUSPECTING PLANET...
AT FIRST, EARTH THOUGHT THEY WERE BEING INVADED...BUT THEY WERE WRONG!
THE LOVELY TRIO WERE RACING HERE TO SAVE US FROM THE MONSTERS COMING TO EARTH!
POW
NOW NOT ONLY ARE AOE, GEN, AND THEL OUR HEROES, THEY'RE ALSO TALENTED POP STARS, ACTRESSES, AND SOCIAL MEDIA ICONS! WHAT CAN'T THEY DO?!
Why does this game have to play the intro every time?! Hurry up already!

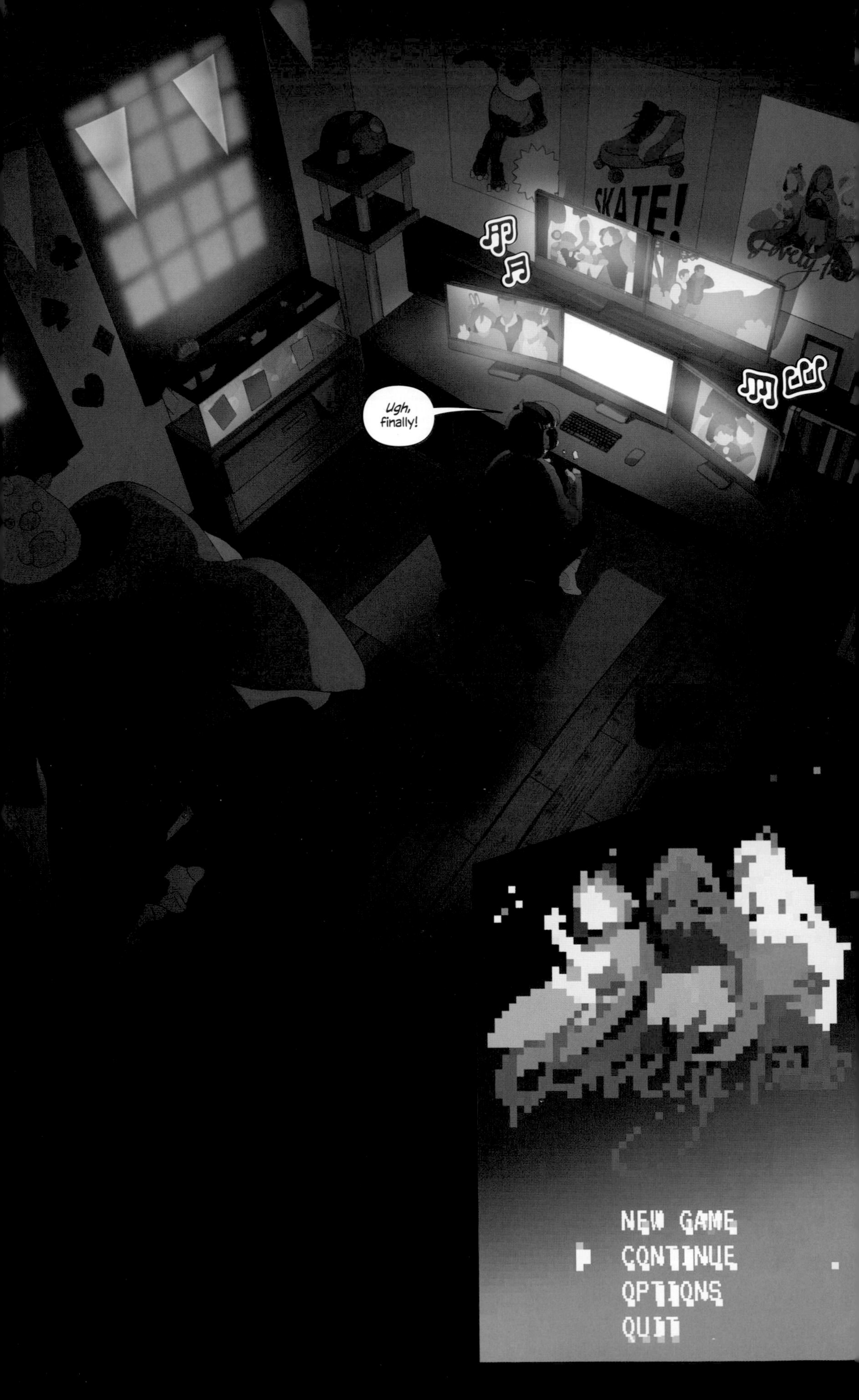
SKATE!
Ugh, finally!
NEW GAME
CONTINUE
OPTIONS
QUIT

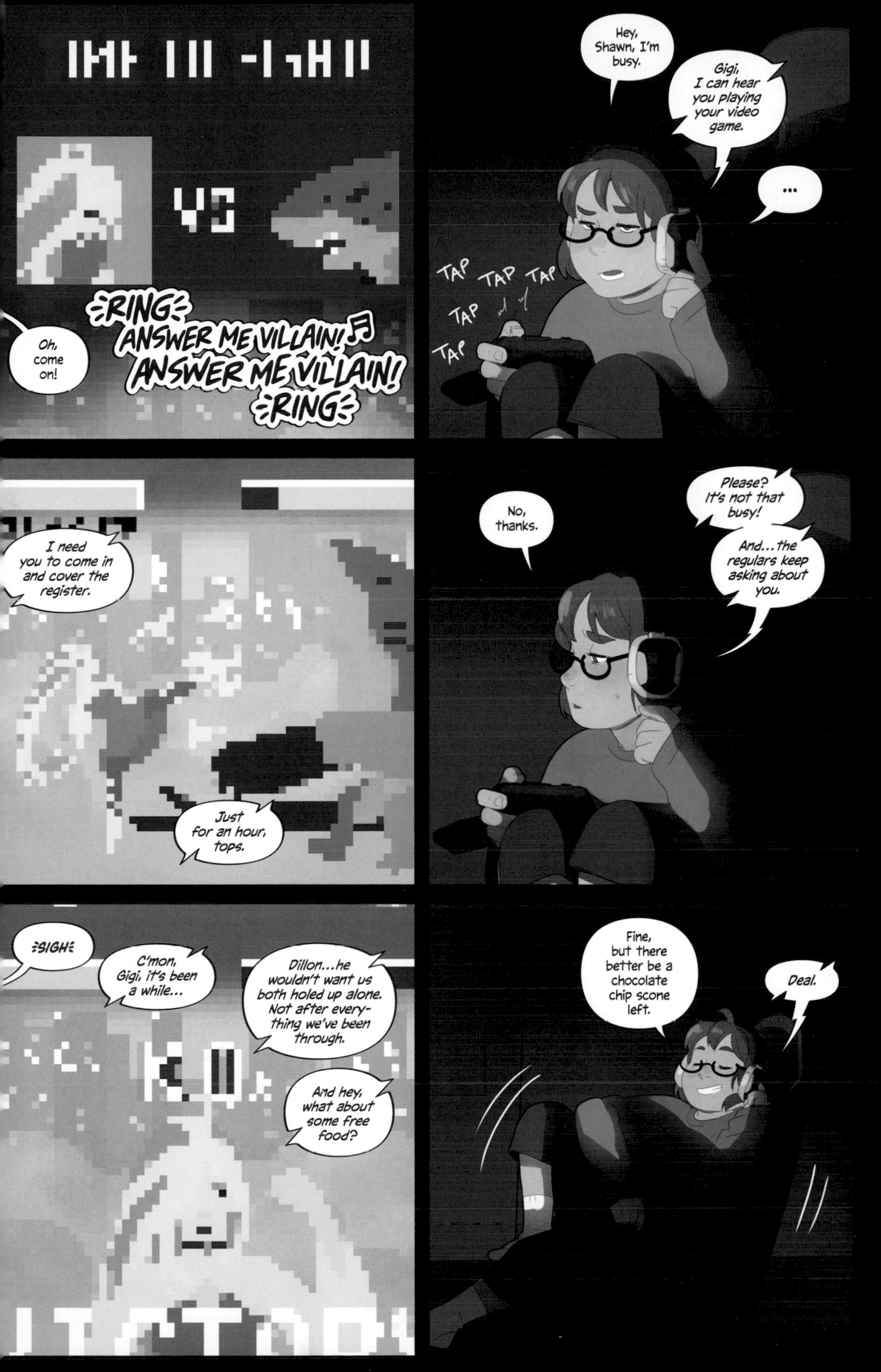

Hey, Shawn, I'm busy.
Gigi, I can hear you playing your video game.
...
TAP TAP TAP TAP TAP
RING
ANSWER ME VILLAIN! ANSWER ME VILLAIN!
RING
Oh, come on!
No, thanks.
Please? It's not that busy!
And...the regulars keep asking about you.
I need you to come in and cover the register.
Just for an hour, tops.
SIGH
C'mon, Gigi, it's been a while...
Dillon...he wouldn't want us both holed up alone. Not after every-thing we've been through.
And hey, what about some free food?
Fine, but there better be a chocolate chip scone left.
Deal.

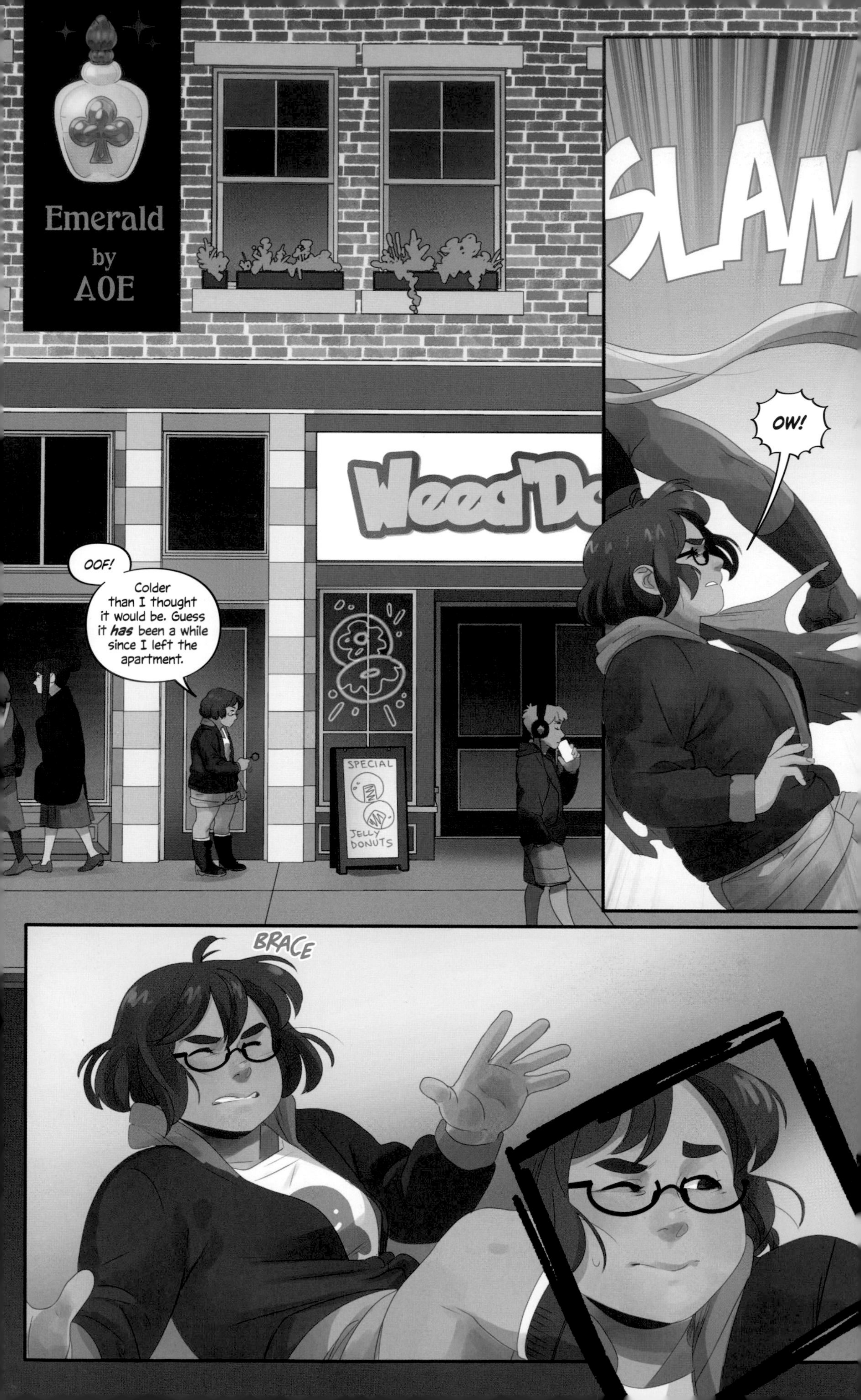
Emerald
by
AOE
OOF!
Colder than I thought it would be. Guess it ***has*** been a while since I left the apartment.
SPECIAL
JELLY DONUTS
SLAM
OW!
BRACE

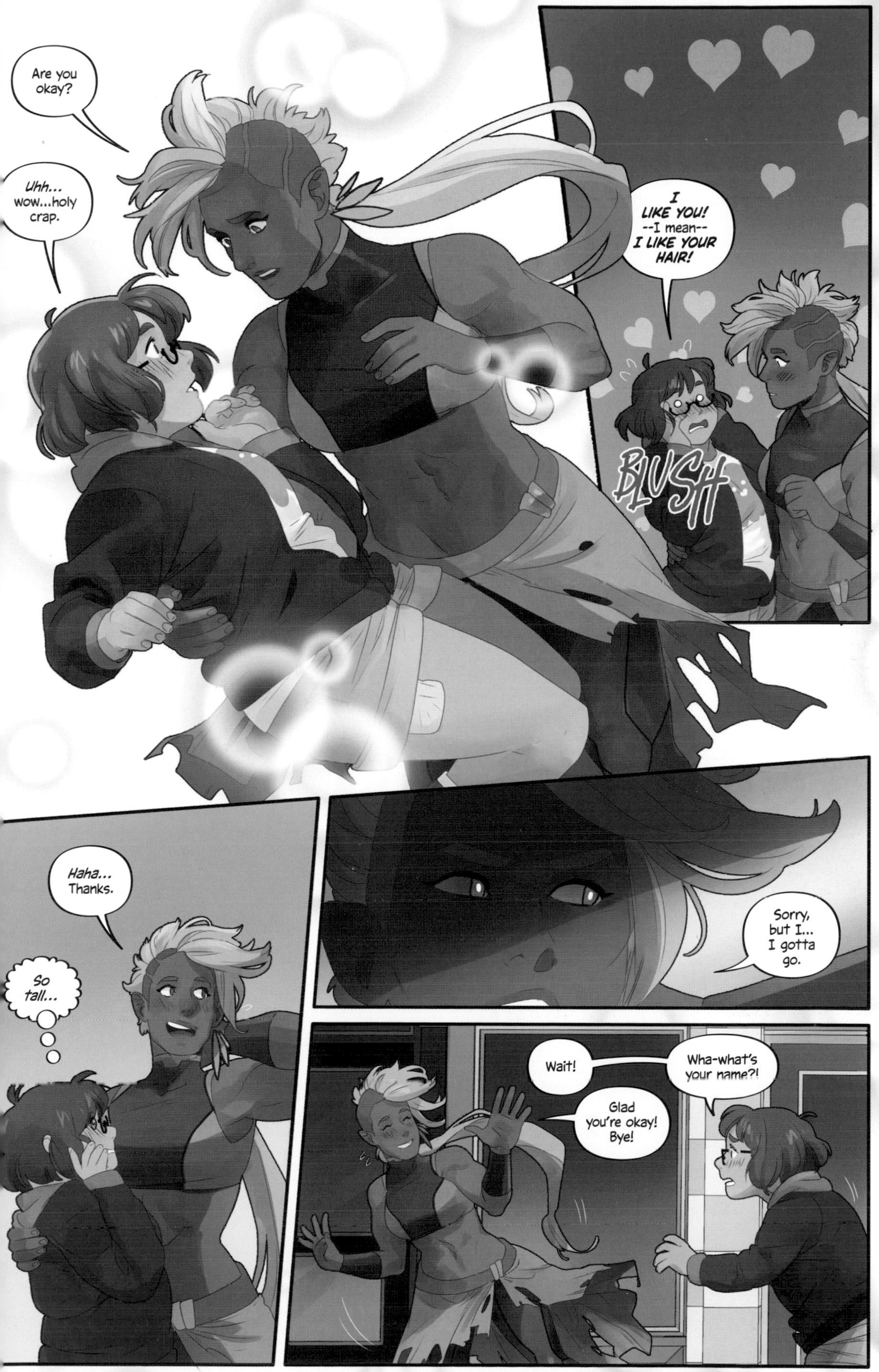
Are you okay?
Uhh... wow...holy crap.
I LIKE YOU! --I mean-- I LIKE YOUR HAIR!
BLUSH
Haha... Thanks.
So tall...
Sorry, but I... I gotta go.
Wait!
Wha-what's your name?!
Glad you're okay! Bye!

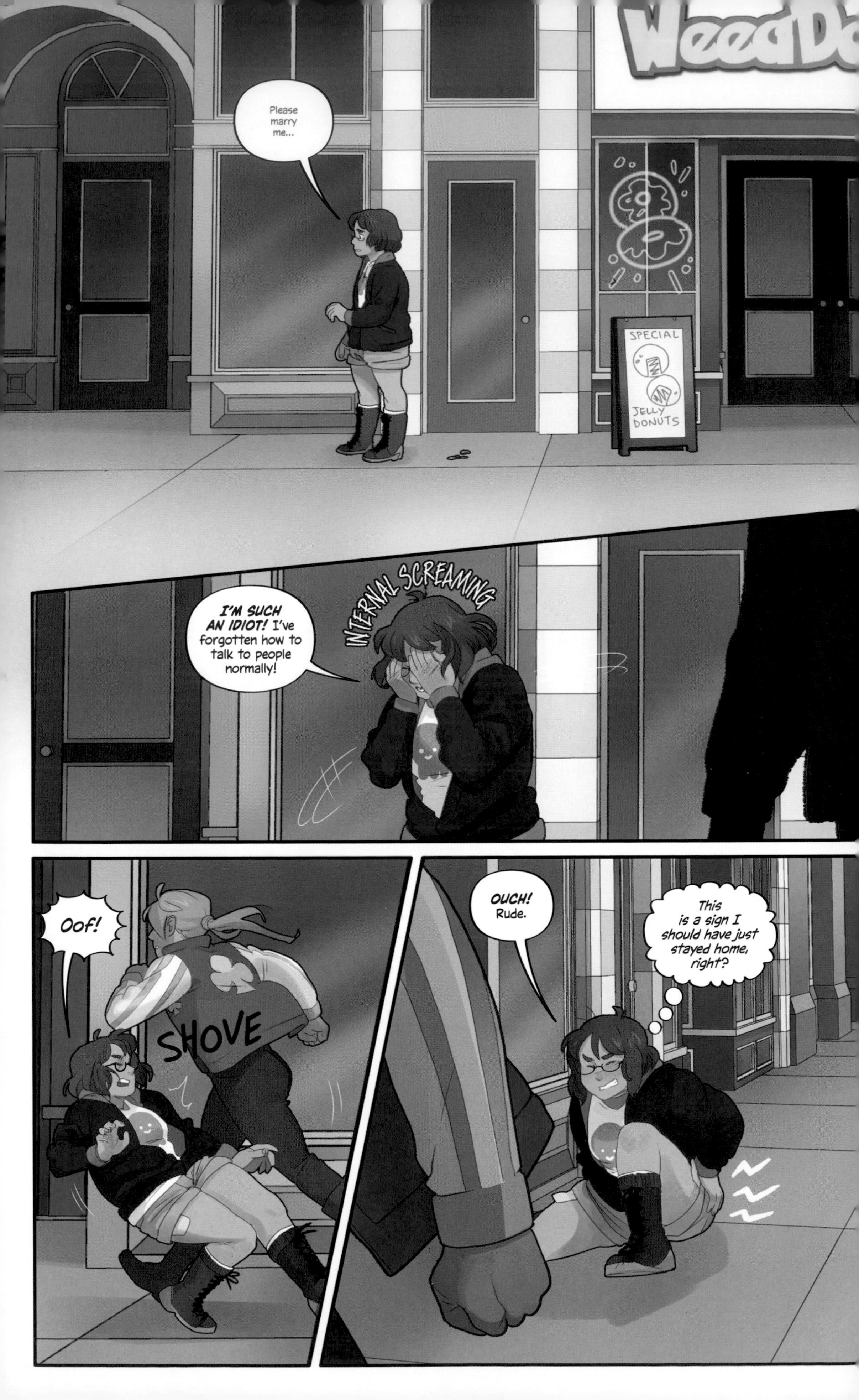
Please marry me...
SPECIAL
JELLY DONUTS
INTERNAL SCREAMING
I'M SUCH AN IDIOT! I've forgotten how to talk to people normally!
Oof!
SHOVE
OUCH! Rude.
This is a sign I should have just stayed home, right?

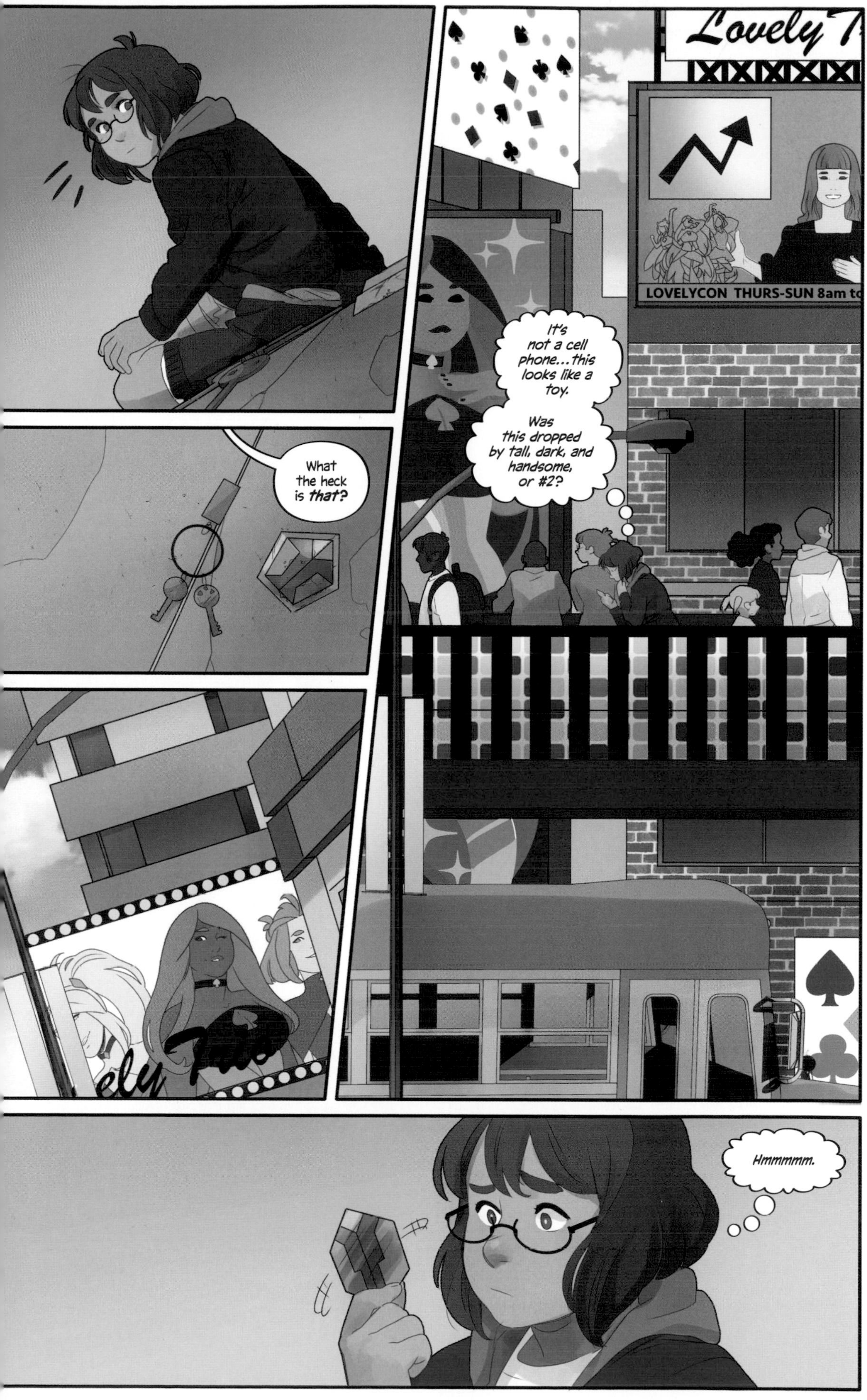

What the heck is *that?*
Lovely T
LOVELYCON THURS-SUN 8am to
It's not a cell phone...this looks like a toy.
Was this dropped by tall, dark, and handsome, or #2?
Hmmmmm.

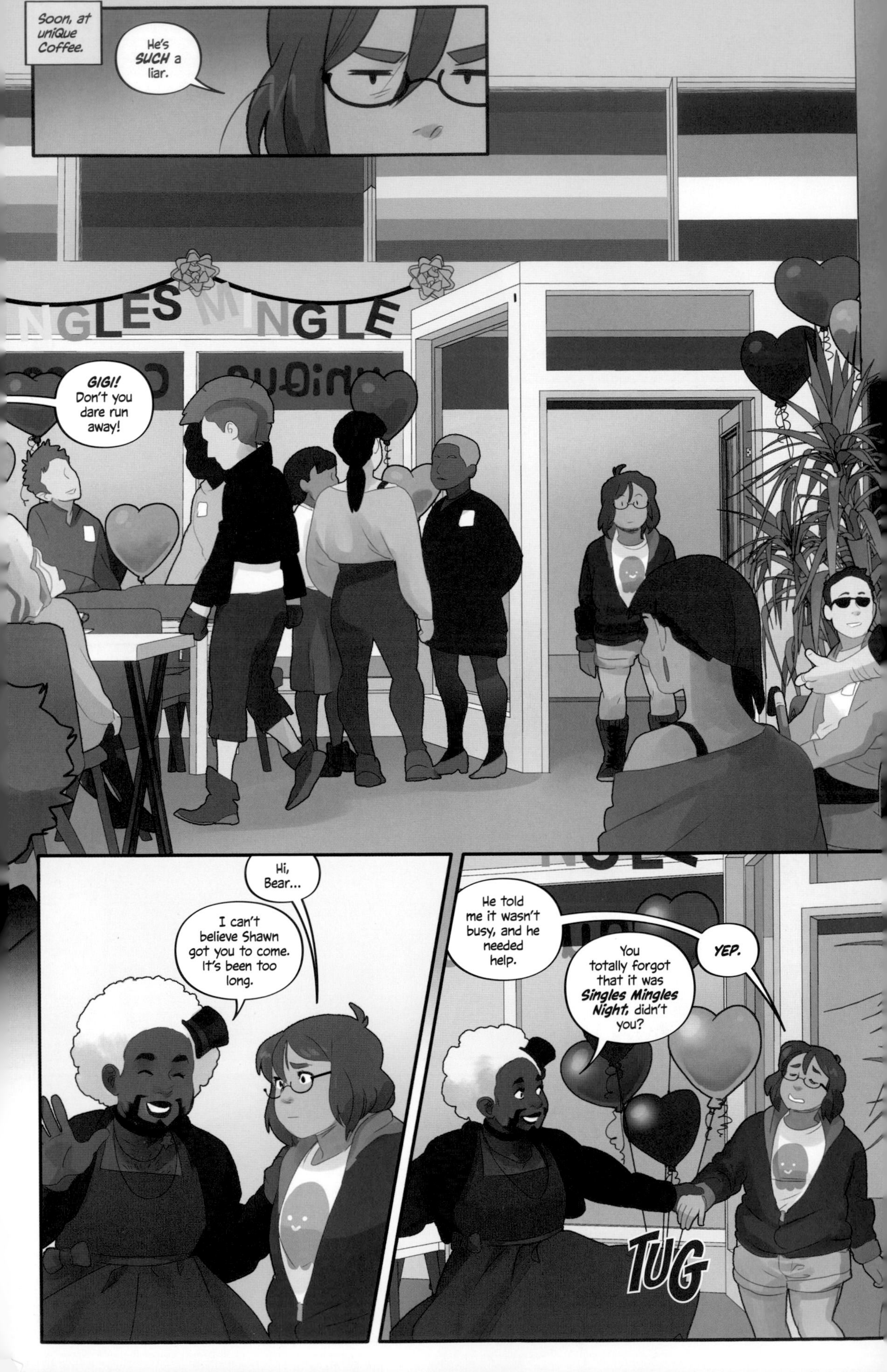
Soon, at uniQue Coffee.
He's SUCH a liar.
SINGLES MINGLE
GIGI! Don't you dare run away!
Hi, Bear...
I can't believe Shawn got you to come. It's been too long.
He told me it wasn't busy, and he needed help.
You totally forgot that it was Singles Mingles Night, didn't you?
YEP.
TUG

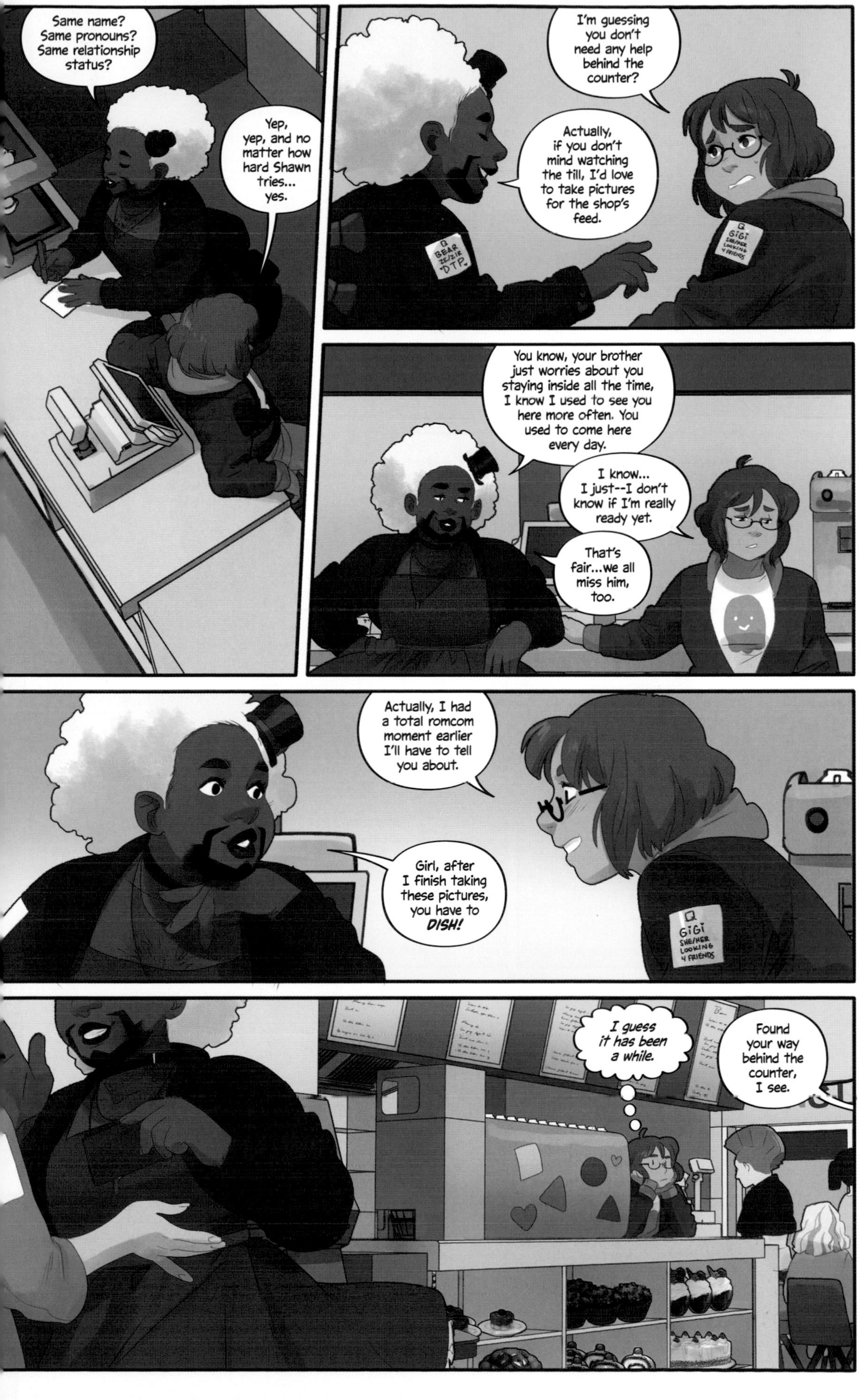

Same name? Same pronouns? Same relationship status?
Yep, yep, and no matter how hard Shawn tries... yes.
I'm guessing you don't need any help behind the counter?
Actually, if you don't mind watching the till, I'd love to take pictures for the shop's feed.
You know, your brother just worries about you staying inside all the time, I know I used to see you here more often. You used to come here every day.
I know... I just--I don't know if I'm really ready yet.
That's fair...we all miss him, too.
Actually, I had a total romcom moment earlier I'll have to tell you about.
Girl, after I finish taking these pictures, you have to *DISH!*
GiGi SHE/HER LOOKING 4 FRIENDS
I guess it has been a while.
Found your way behind the counter, I see.

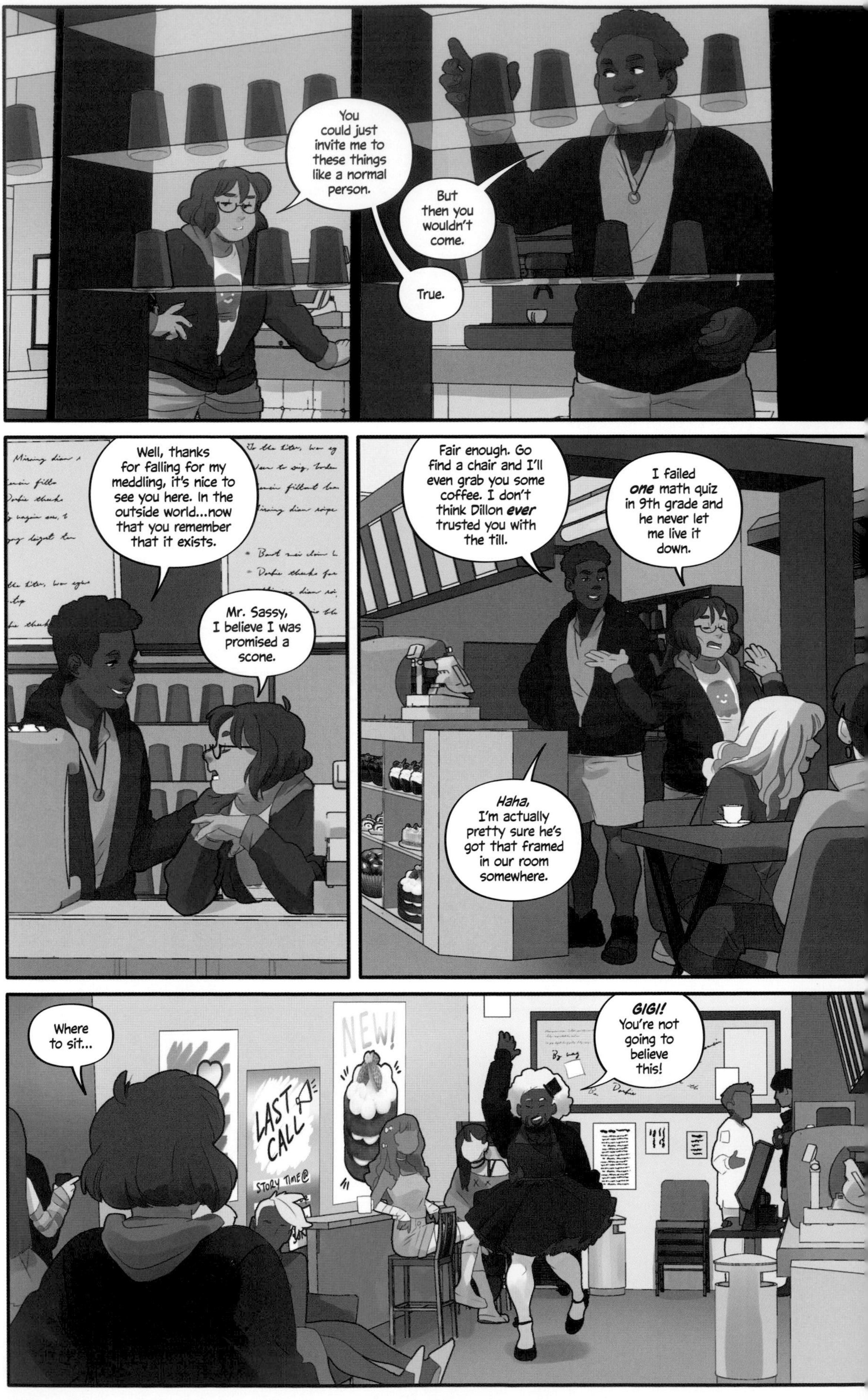
You could just invite me to these things like a normal person.
But then you wouldn't come.
True.
Well, thanks for falling for my meddling, it's nice to see you here. In the outside world...now that you remember that it exists.
Mr. Sassy, I believe I was promised a scone.
Fair enough. Go find a chair and I'll even grab you some coffee. I don't think Dillon *ever* trusted you with the till.
I failed *one* math quiz in 9th grade and he never let me live it down.
Haha, I'm actually pretty sure he's got that framed in our room somewhere.
Where to sit...
NEW!
LAST CALL
STORY TIME@
GIGI! You're not going to believe this!

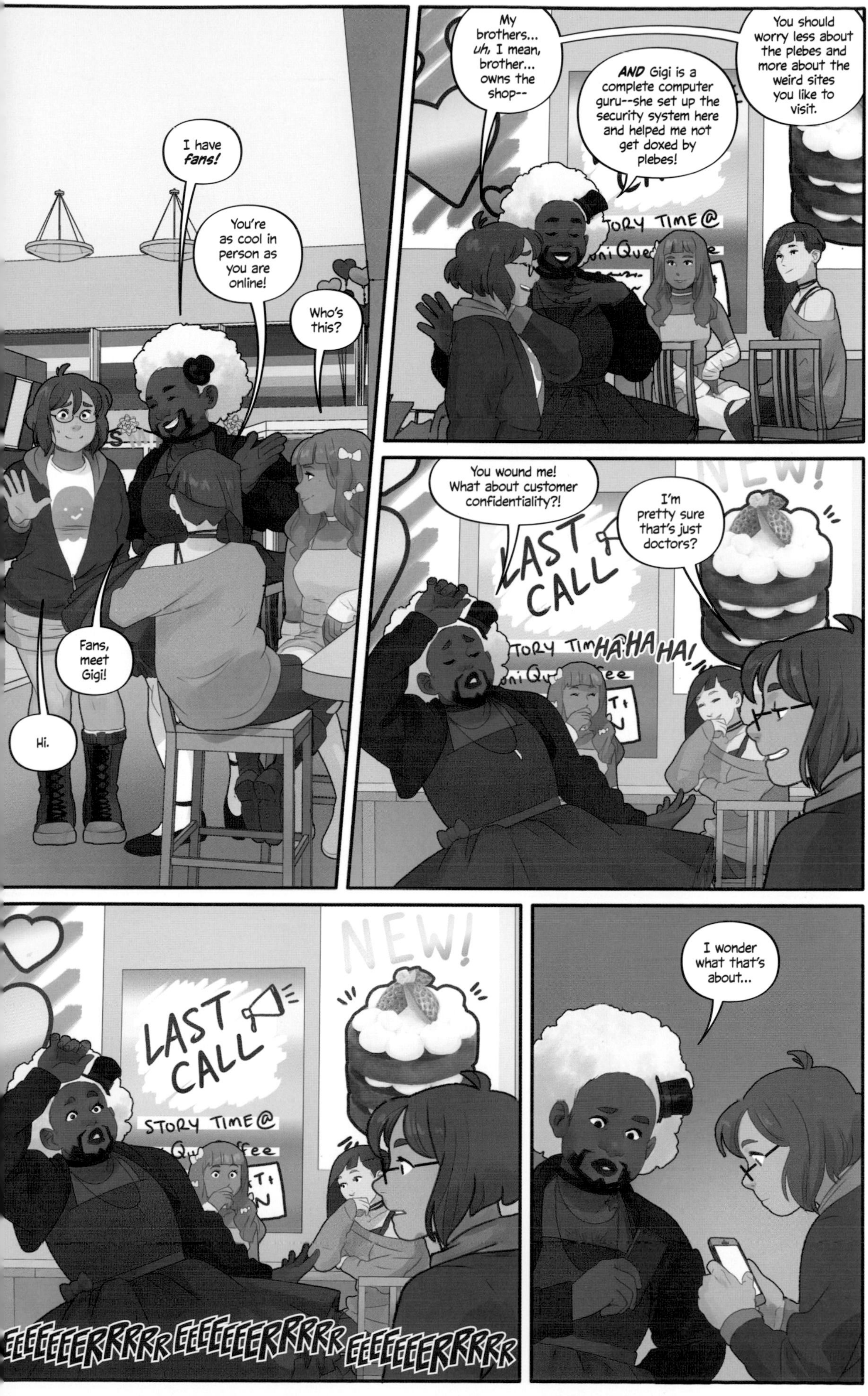
I have *fans!*
You're as cool in person as you are online!
Who's this?
Fans, meet Gigi!
Hi.
My brothers... *uh,* I mean, brother... owns the shop--
AND Gigi is a complete computer guru--she set up the security system here and helped me not get doxed by plebes!
You should worry less about the plebes and more about the weird sites you like to visit.
STORY TIME@
You wound me! What about customer confidentiality?!
I'm pretty sure that's just doctors?
NEW!
LAST CALL
HA HA HA!
NEW!
LAST CALL
STORY TIME@
EEEEEEERRRRR EEEEEEERRRRR EEEEEEERRRRR
I wonder what that's about...

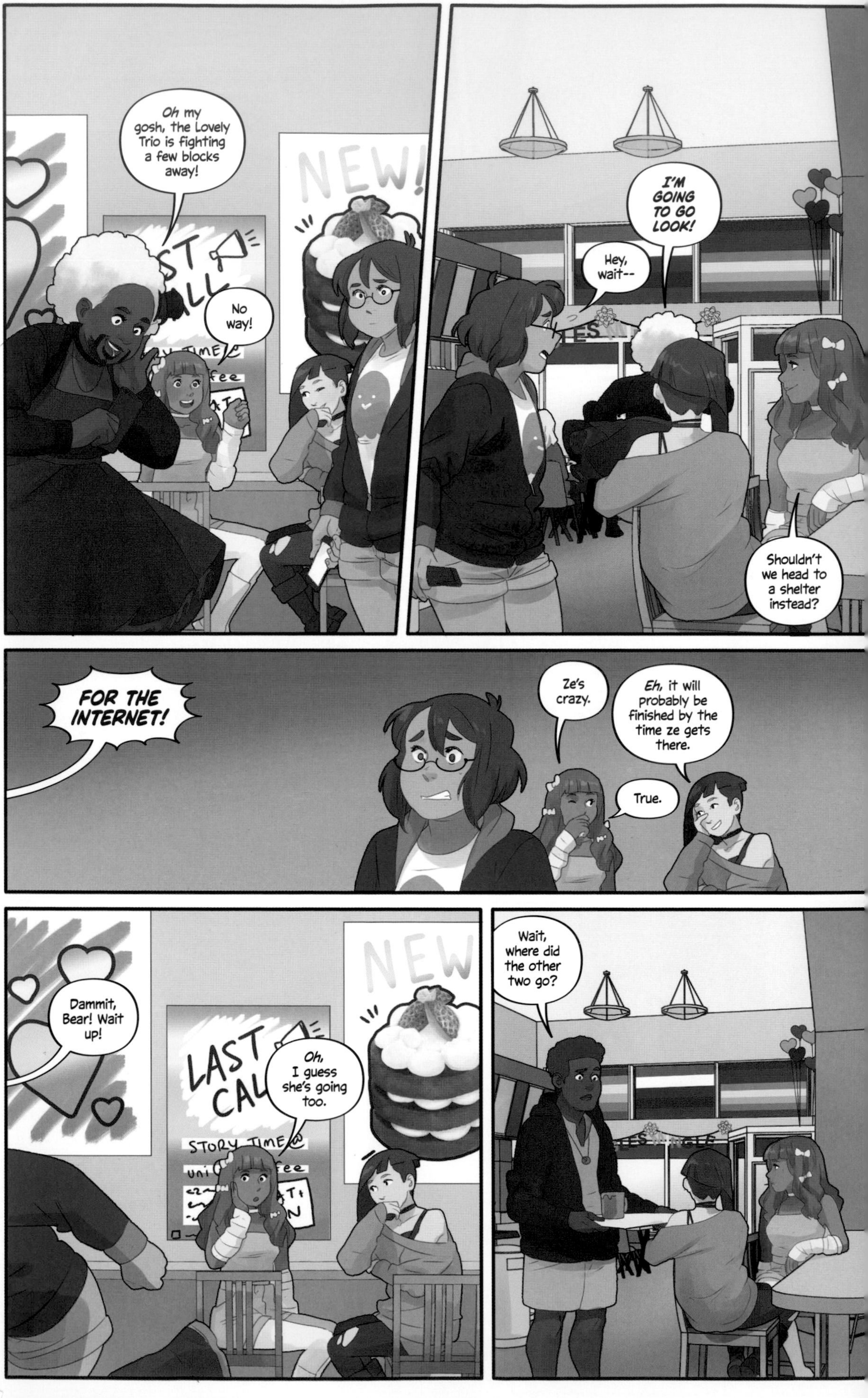

Oh my gosh, the Lovely Trio is fighting a few blocks away!
No way!
NEW!
I'M GOING TO GO LOOK!
Hey, wait--
Shouldn't we head to a shelter instead?
FOR THE INTERNET!
Ze's crazy.
Eh, it will probably be finished by the time ze gets there.
True.
Dammit, Bear! Wait up!
LAST CAL
STORY TIME @
NEW
Oh, I guess she's going too.
Wait, where did the other two go?

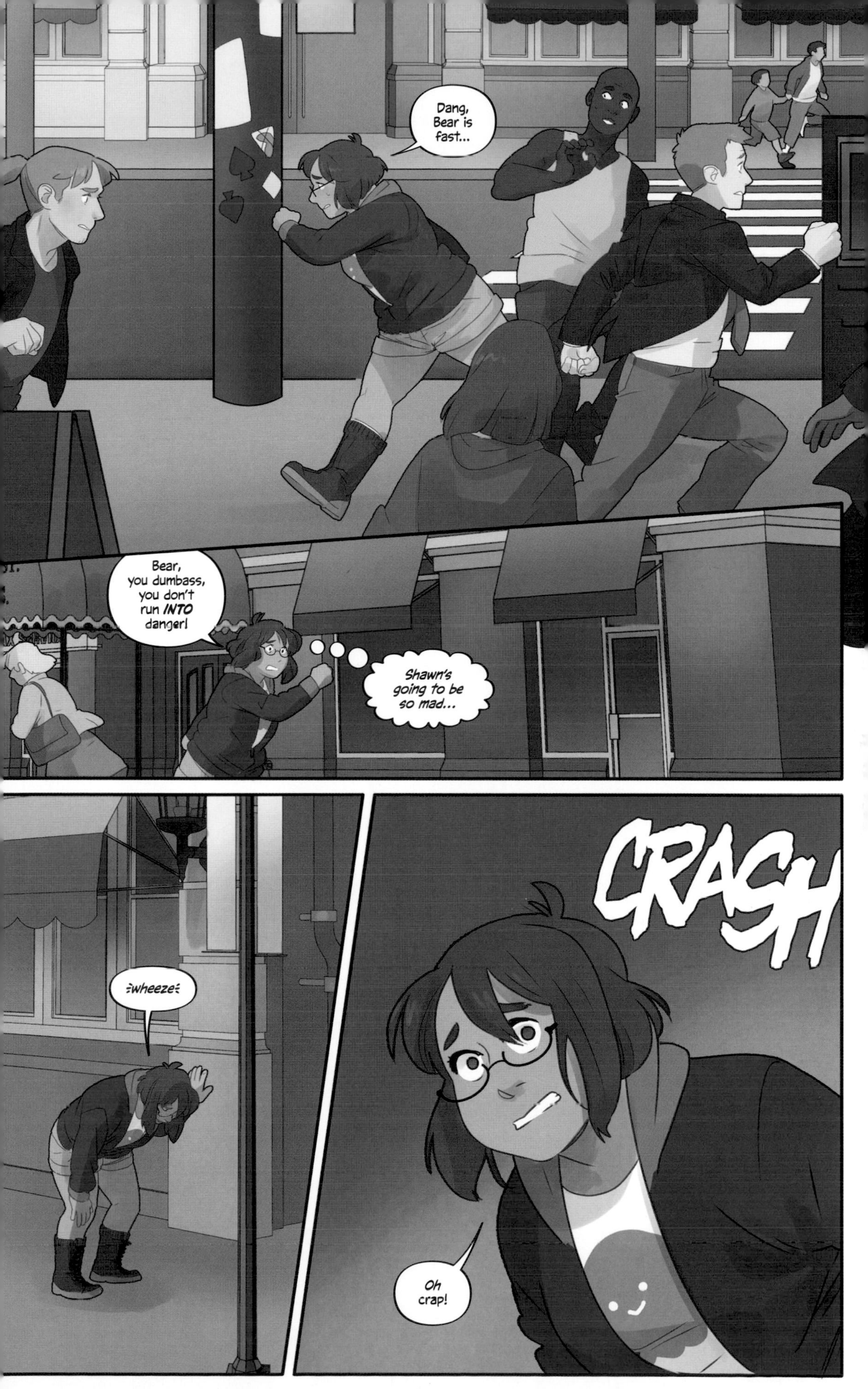
Dang, Bear is fast...
Bear, you dumbass, you don't run INTO danger!
Shawn's going to be so mad...
wheeze
CRASH
Oh crap!

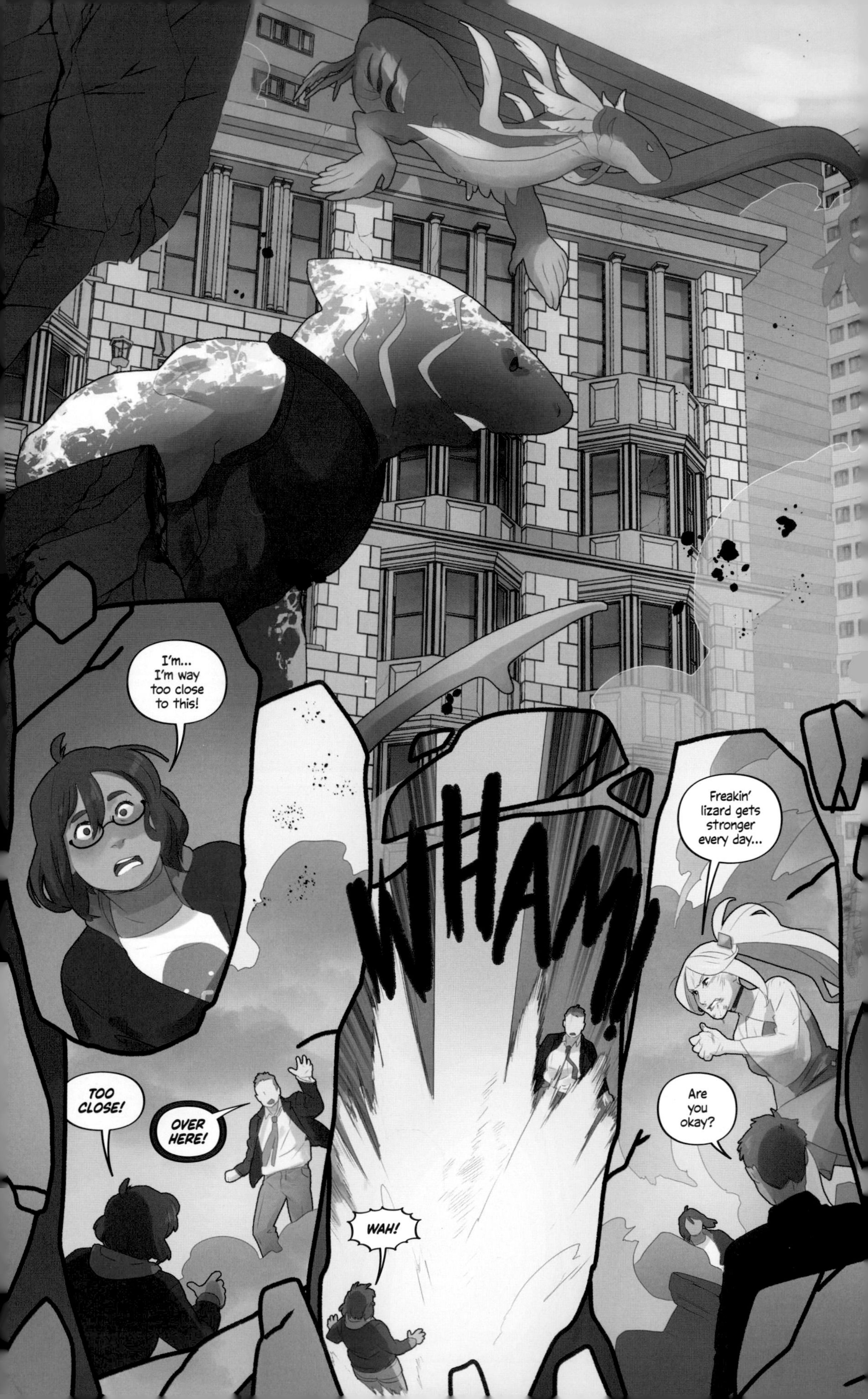
I'm...
I'm way
too close
to this!
WHAM!
Freakin'
lizard gets
stronger
every day...
TOO
CLOSE!
OVER
HERE!
Are
you
okay?
WAH!

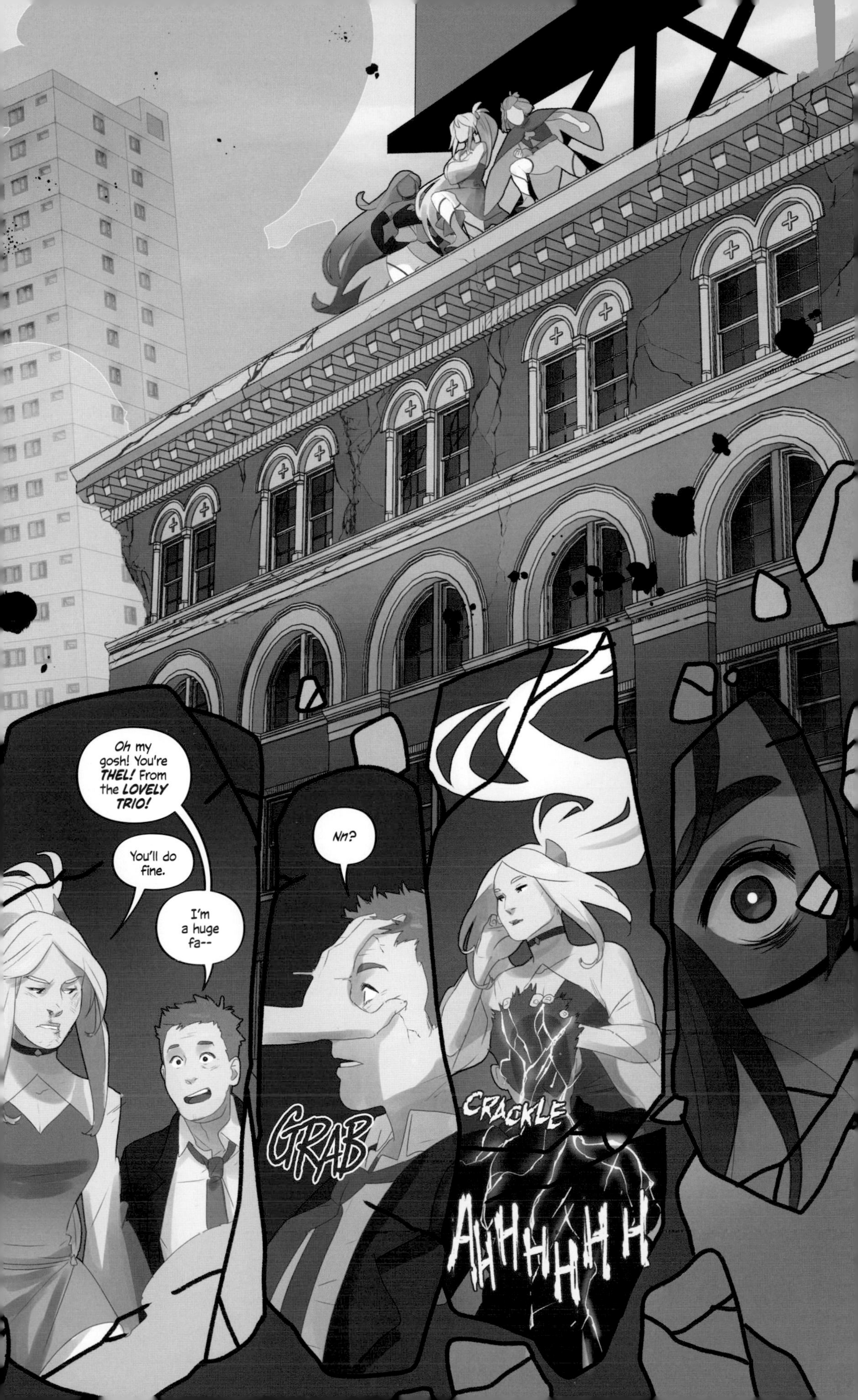

Oh my gosh! You're THEL! From the LOVELY TRIO!
You'll do fine.
I'm a huge fa--
Nn?
GRAB
CRACKLE
AHHHHHH

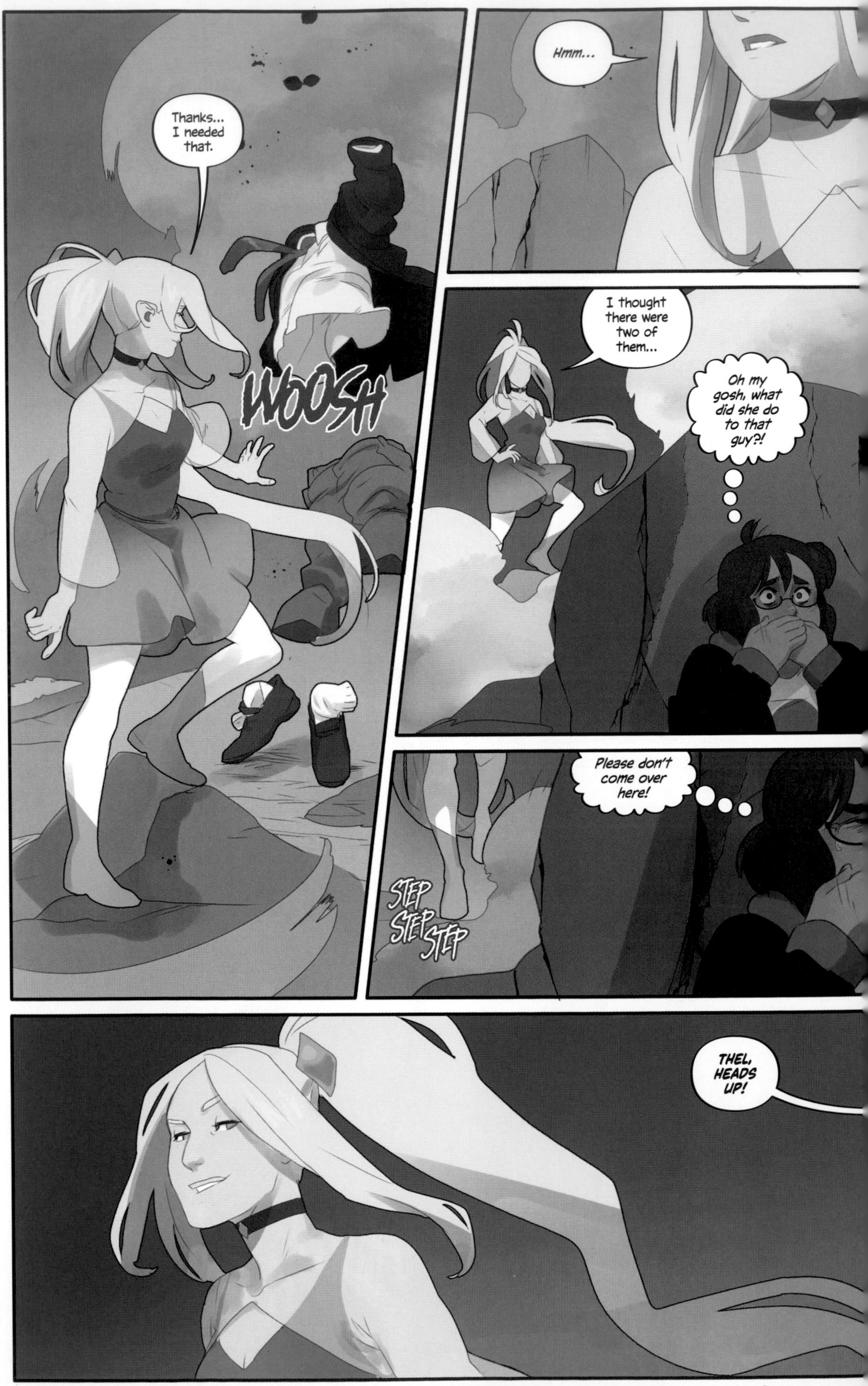

Thanks... I needed that.
WOOSH
Hmm...
I thought there were two of them...
Oh my gosh, what did she do to that guy?!
Please don't come over here!
STEP STEP STEP
THEL, HEADS UP!

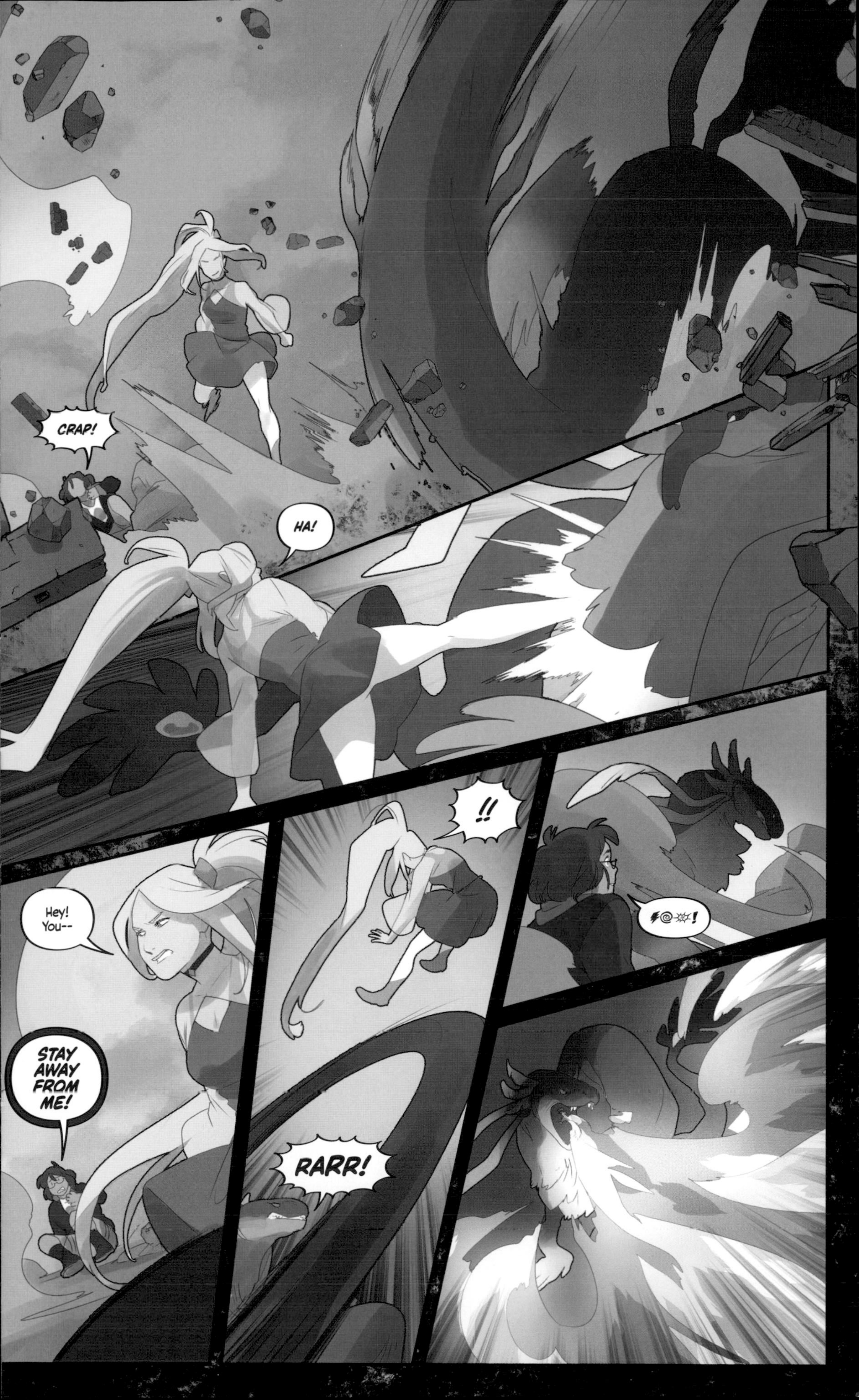
CRAP!
HA!
Hey! You--
STAY AWAY FROM ME!
!!
RARR!

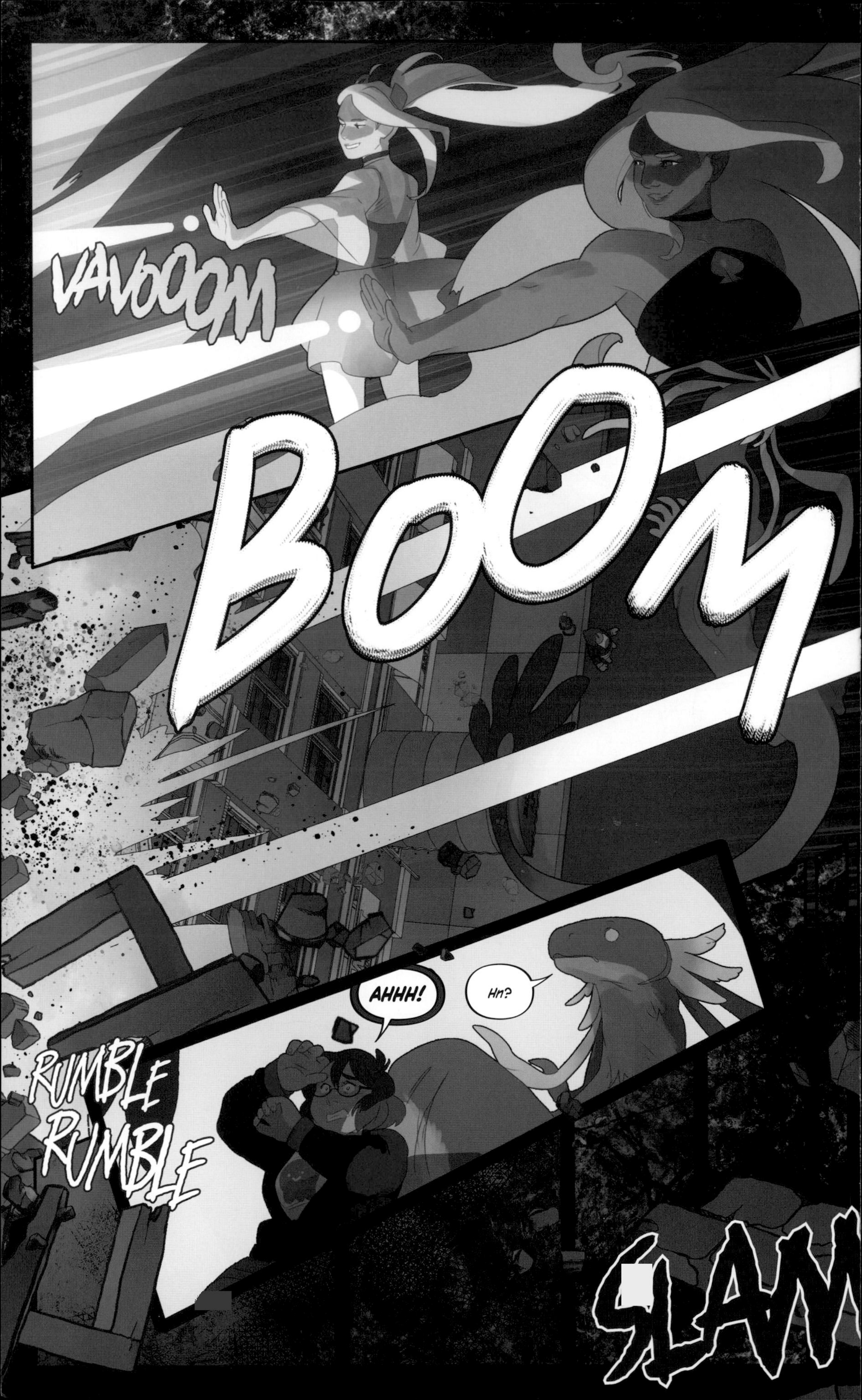
VAVOOOM
BOOM
AHHH!
Hn?
RUMBLE
RUMBLE
SLAM

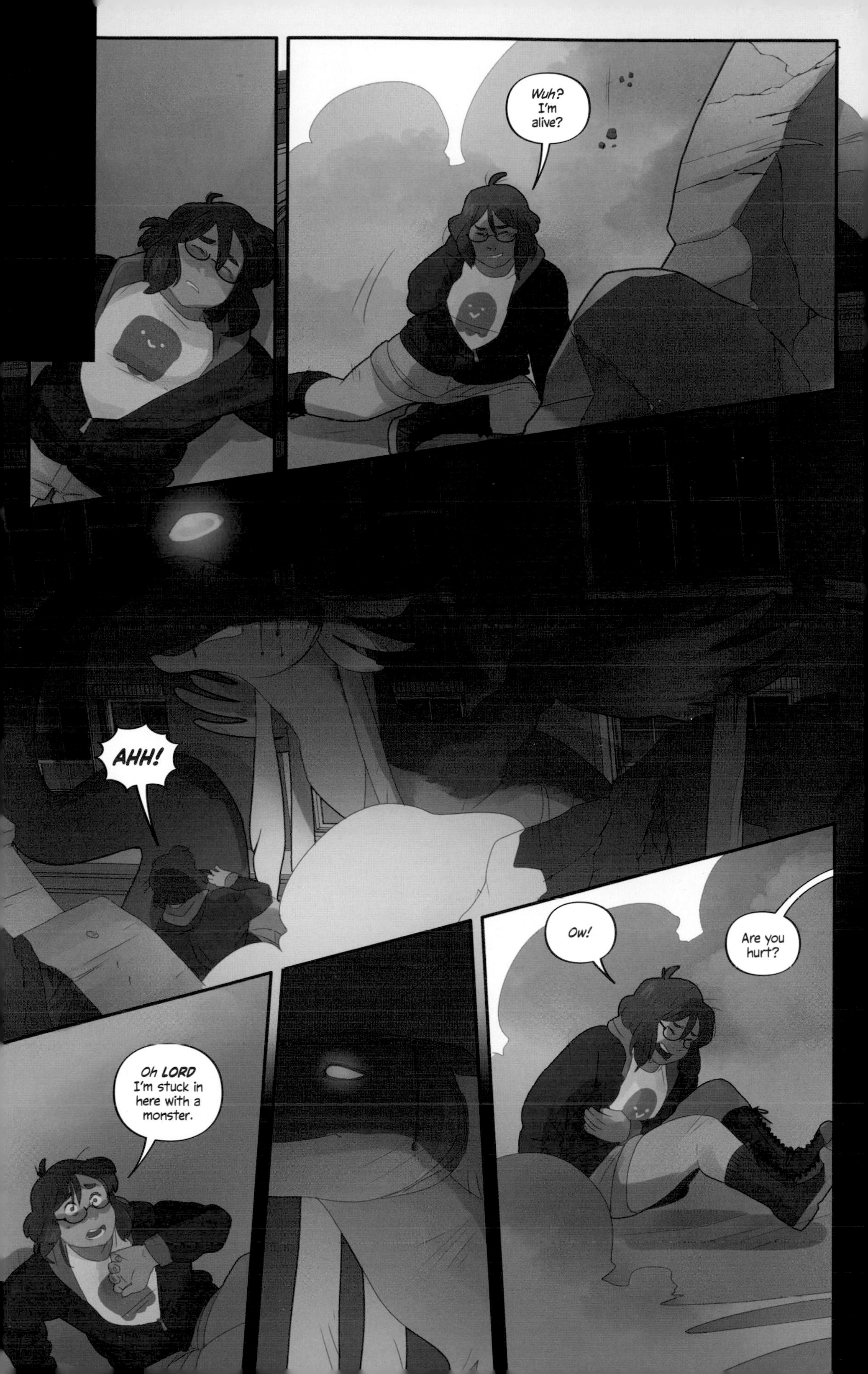
Wuh? I'm alive?
AHH!
Ow!
Are you hurt?
Oh LORD I'm stuck in here with a monster.

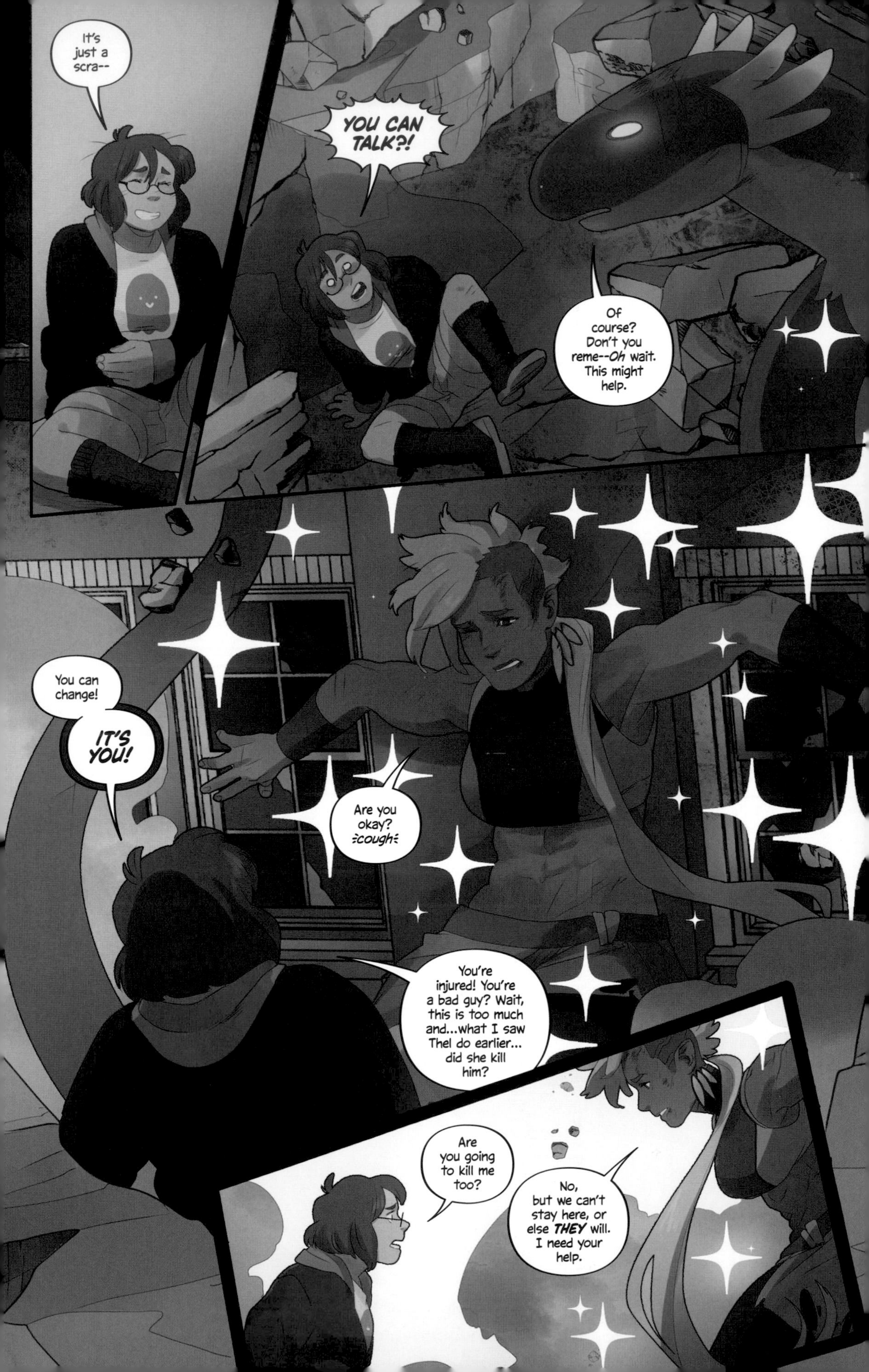
It's just a scra--
YOU CAN TALK?!
Of course? Don't you reme--*Oh* wait. This might help.
You can change!
IT'S YOU!
Are you okay? cough
You're injured! You're a bad guy? Wait, this is too much and...what I saw Thel do earlier... did she kill him?
Are you going to kill me too?
No, but we can't stay here, or else *THEY* will. I need your help.

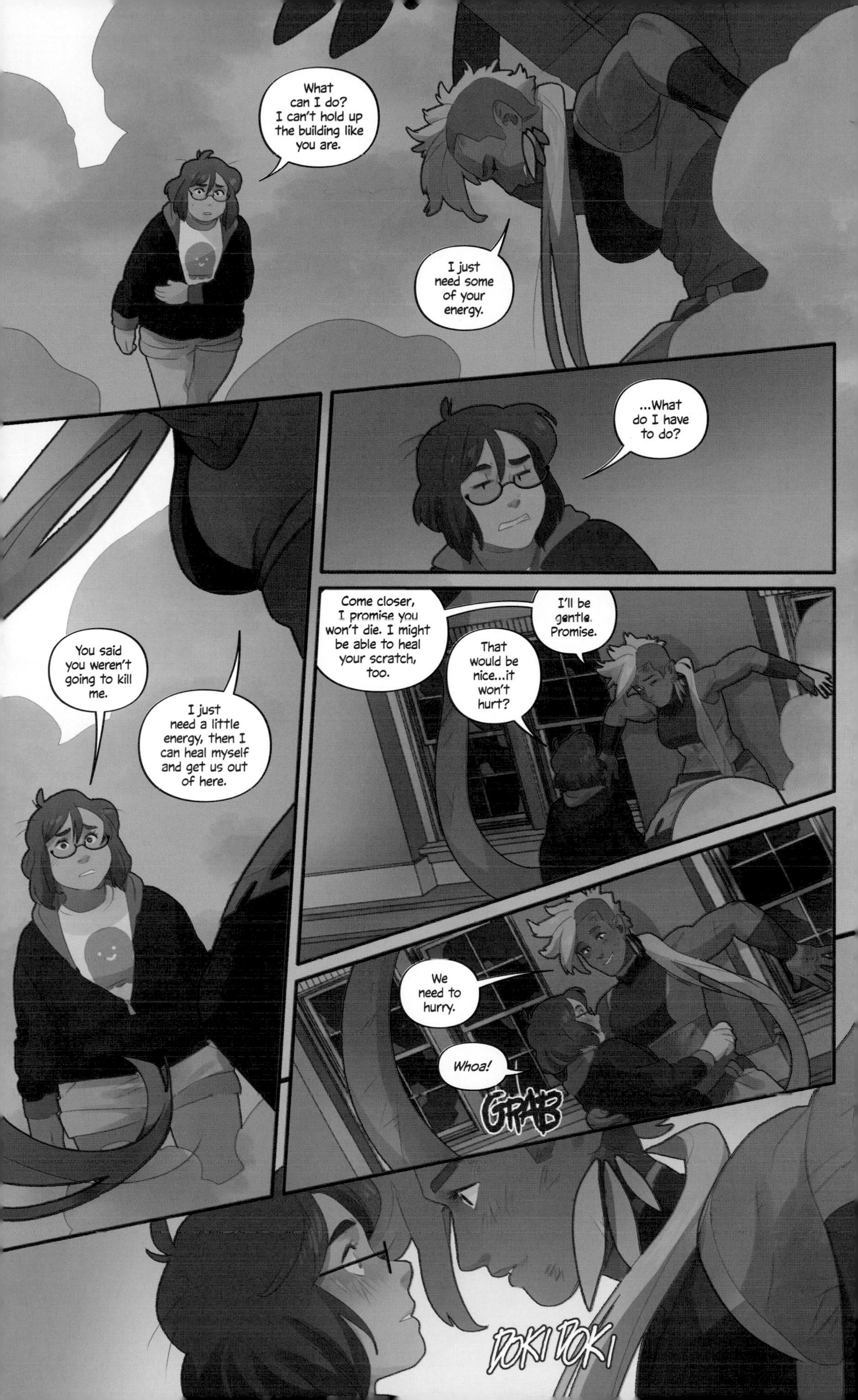
What can I do? I can't hold up the building like you are.
I just need some of your energy.
...What do I have to do?
You said you weren't going to kill me.
I just need a little energy, then I can heal myself and get us out of here.
Come closer, I promise you won't die. I might be able to heal your scratch, too.
That would be nice...it won't hurt?
I'll be gentle. Promise.
We need to hurry.
Whoa!
GRAB
DOKI DOKI

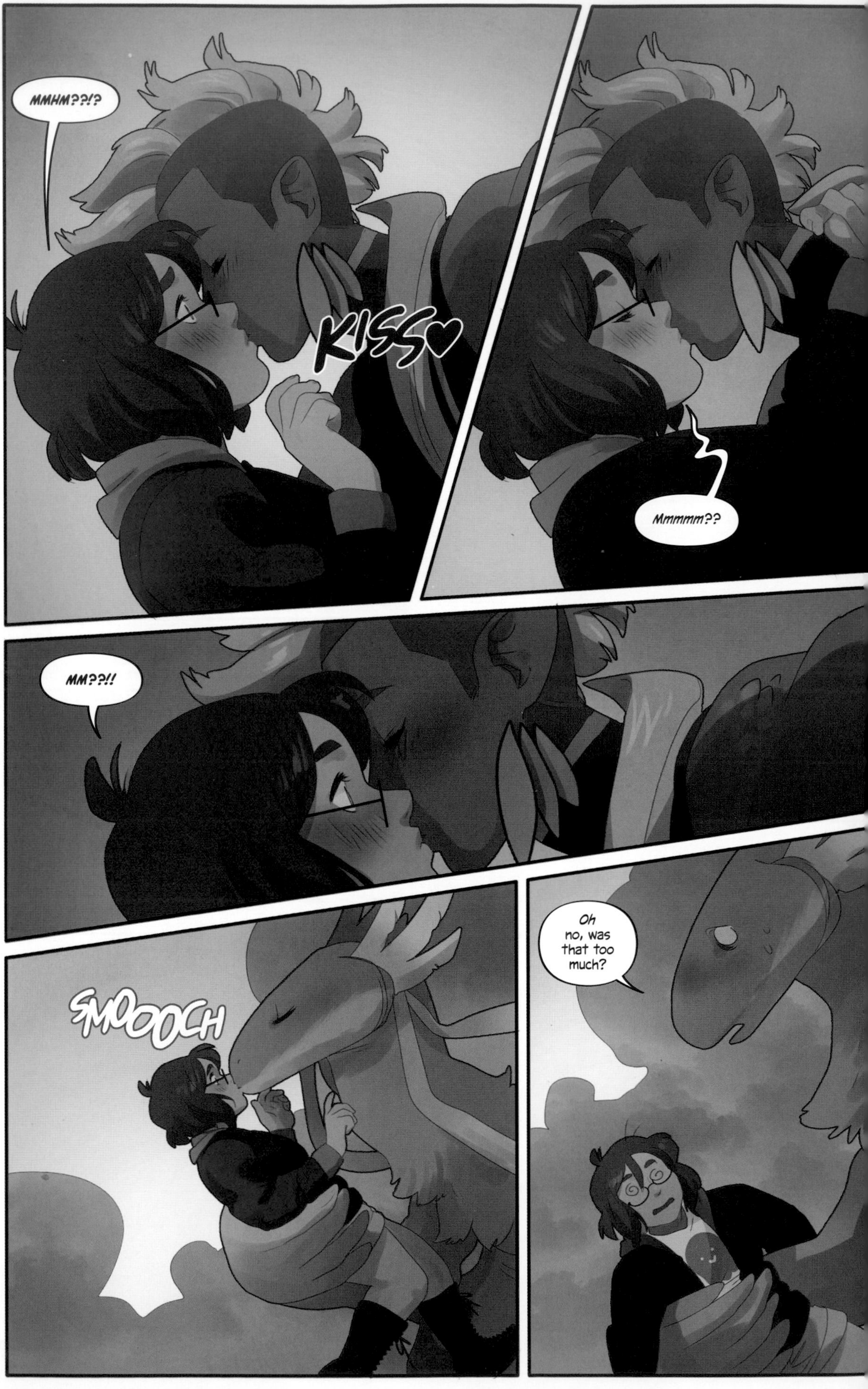
MMHM??!?
KISS♥
Mmmmm??
MM??!!
SMOOOCH
Oh no, was that too much?

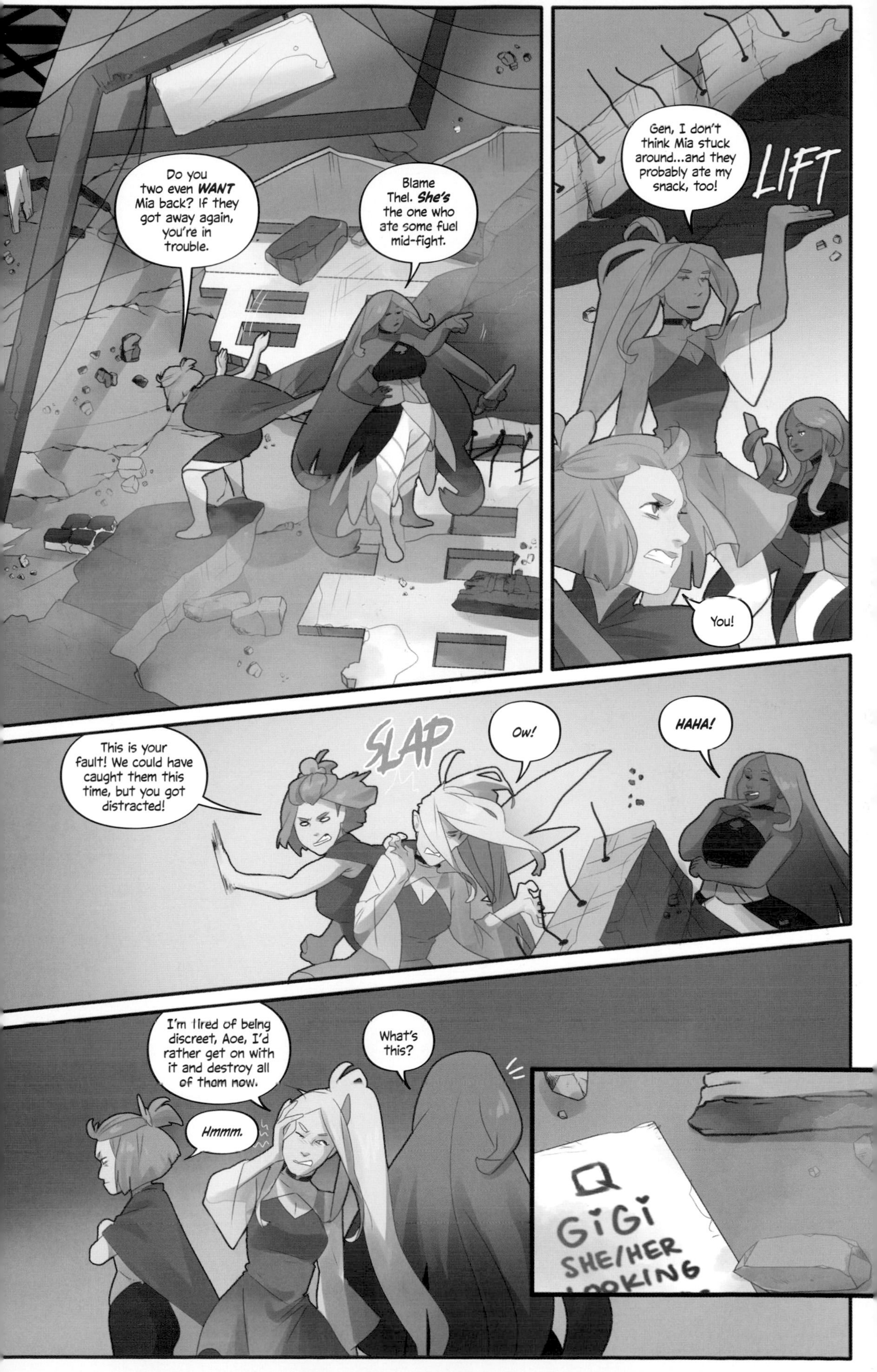
Do you two even **WANT** Mia back? If they got away again, you're in trouble.
Blame Thel. ***She's*** the one who ate some fuel mid-fight.
Gen, I don't think Mia stuck around...and they probably ate my snack, too!
LIFT
You!
This is your fault! We could have caught them this time, but you got distracted!
SLAP
Ow!
HAHA!
I'm tired of being discreet, Aoe, I'd rather get on with it and destroy all of them now.
Hmmm.
What's this?
GiGi
SHE/HER
LOOKING

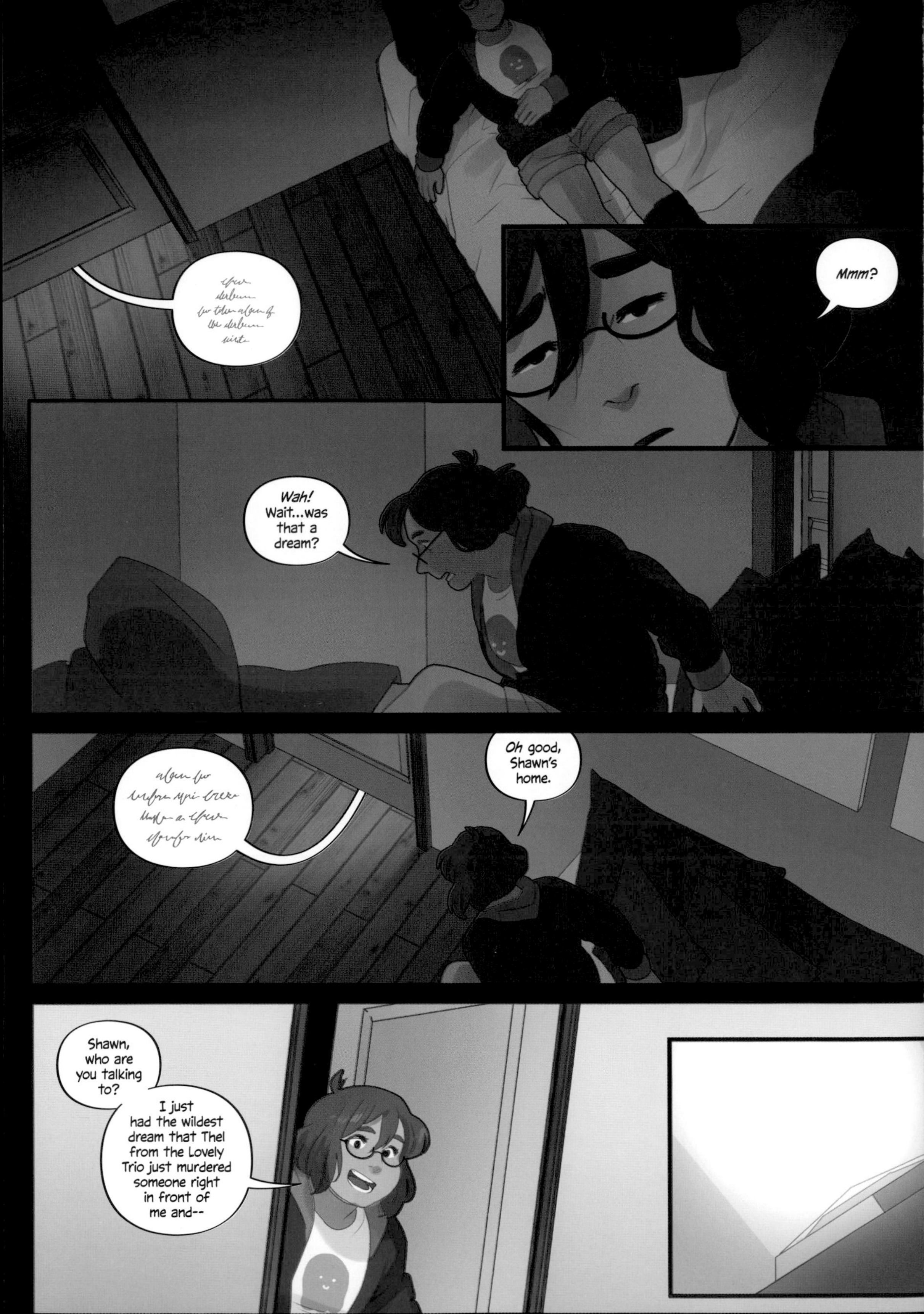

Mmm?
Wah! Wait...was that a dream?
Oh good, Shawn's home.
Shawn, who are you talking to?
I just had the wildest dream that Thel from the Lovely Trio just murdered someone right in front of me and--

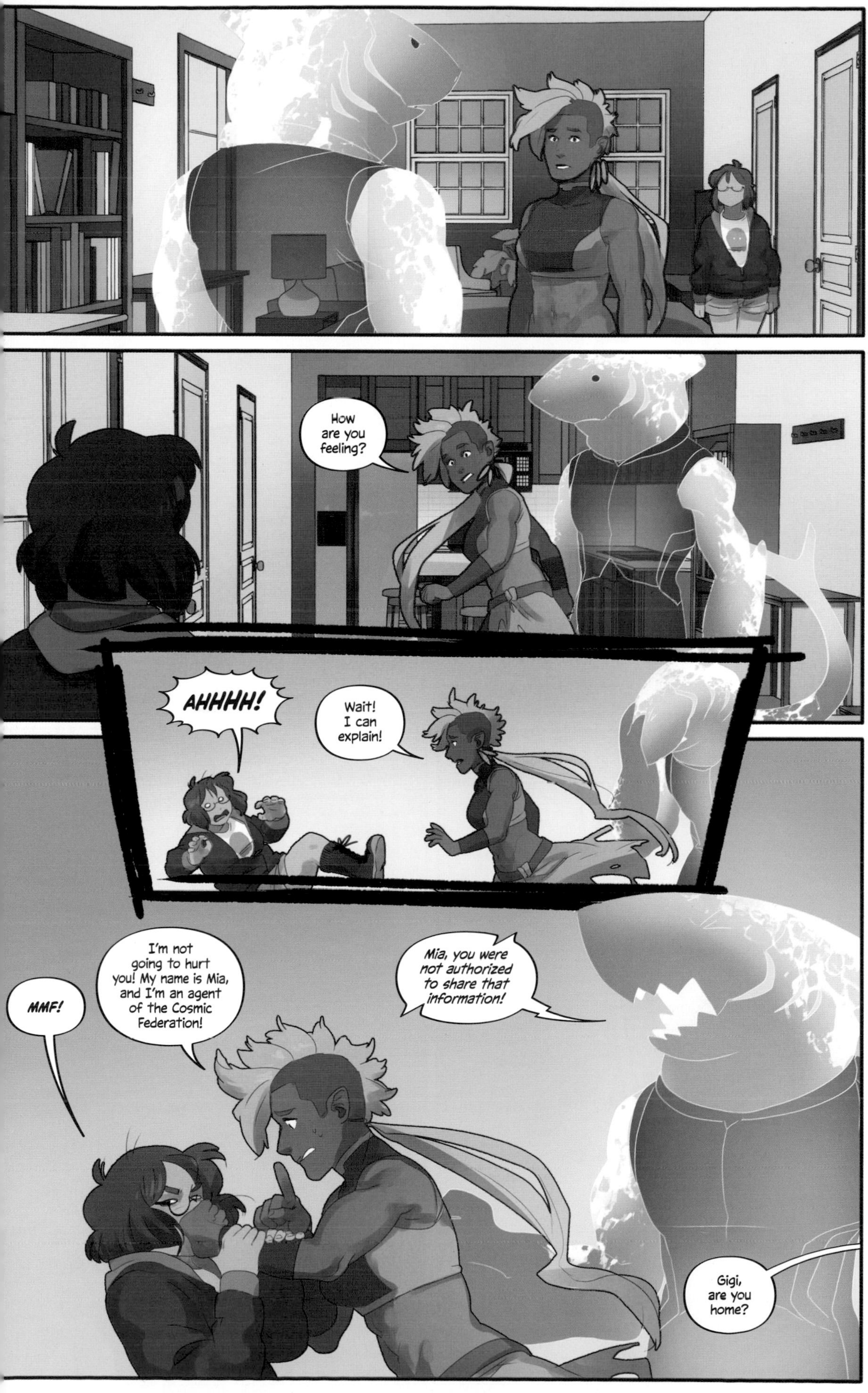
How are you feeling?
AHHHH!
Wait! I can explain!
MMF!
I'm not going to hurt you! My name is Mia, and I'm an agent of the Cosmic Federation!
Mia, you were not authorized to share that information!
Gigi, are you home?

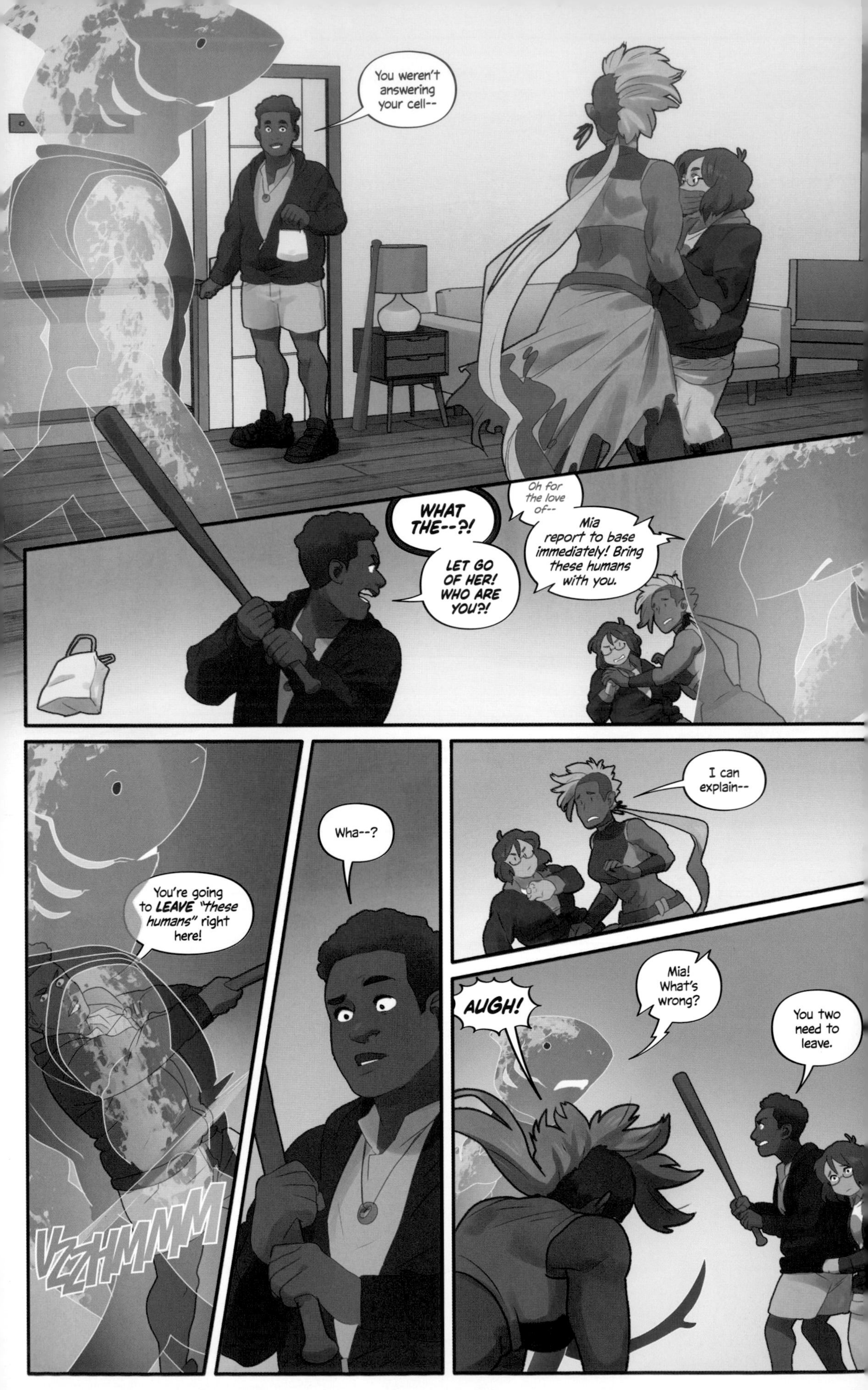
You weren't answering your cell--
WHAT THE--?!
LET GO OF HER! WHO ARE YOU?!
Oh for the love of--
Mia report to base immediately! Bring these humans with you.
You're going to LEAVE "these humans" right here!
VZZHMMM
Wha--?
I can explain--
AUGH!
Mia! What's wrong?
You two need to leave.

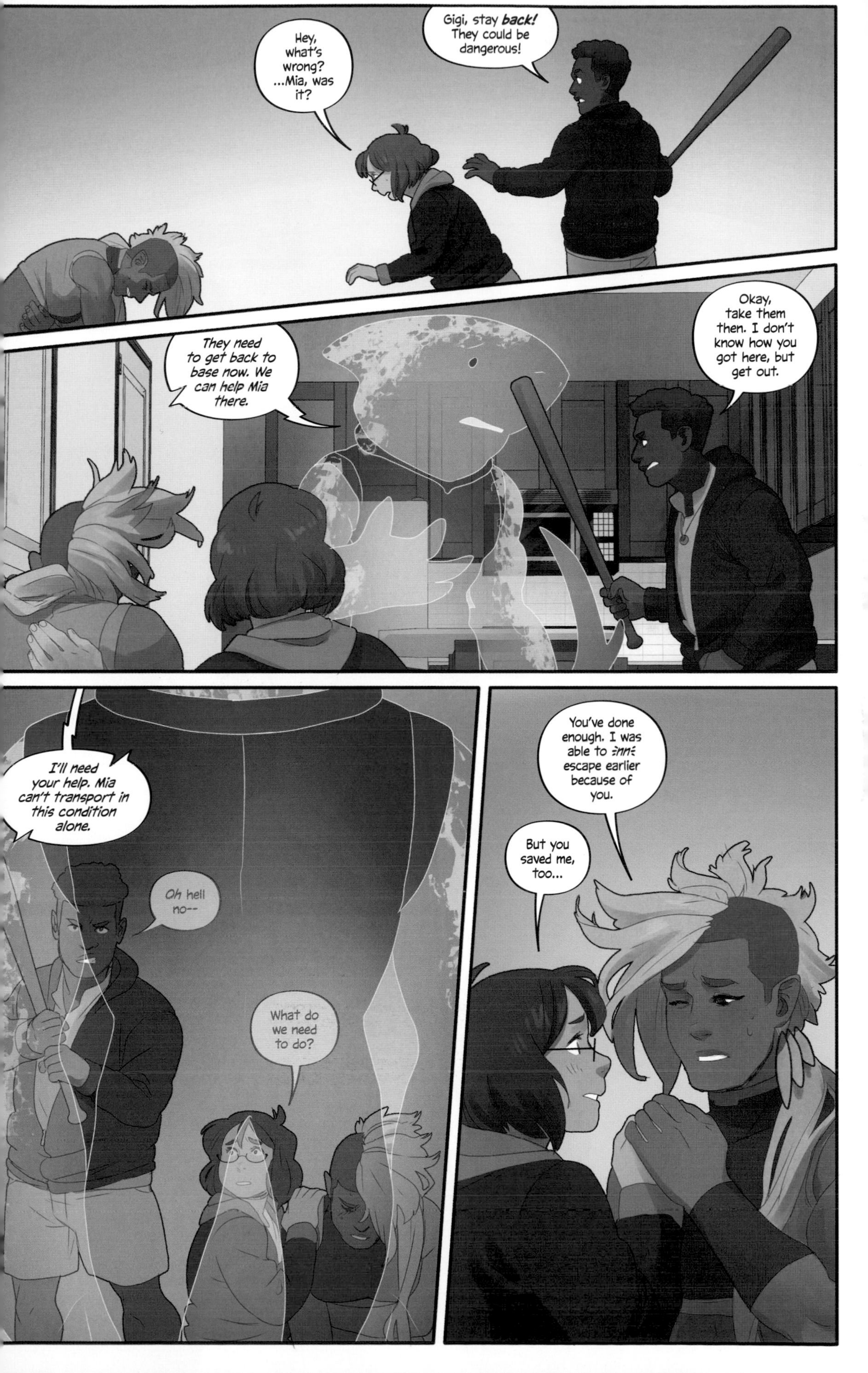
Hey, what's wrong? ...Mia, was it?
Gigi, stay *back!* They could be dangerous!
They need to get back to base now. We can help Mia there.
Okay, take them then. I don't know how you got here, but get out.
I'll need your help. Mia can't transport in this condition alone.
Oh hell no--
What do we need to do?
You've done enough. I was able to *nn* escape earlier because of you.
But you saved me, too...

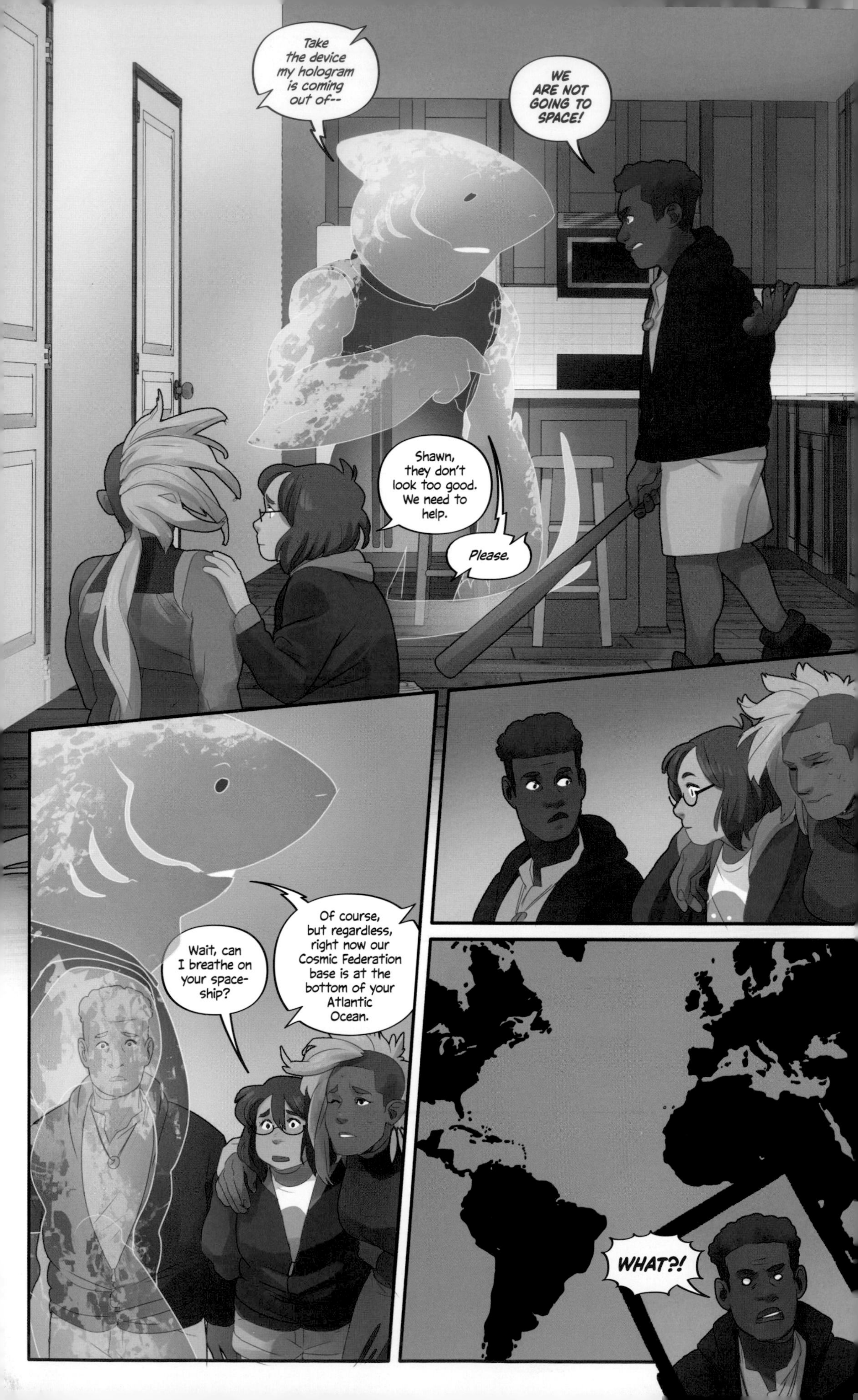
Take the device my hologram is coming out of--
WE ARE NOT GOING TO SPACE!
Shawn, they don't look too good. We need to help.
Please.
Wait, can I breathe on your space-ship?
Of course, but regardless, right now our Cosmic Federation base is at the bottom of your Atlantic Ocean.
WHAT?!

SAVE YOURSELF! #1 MAIN COVER BY

KELLY & NICHOLE MATTHEWS

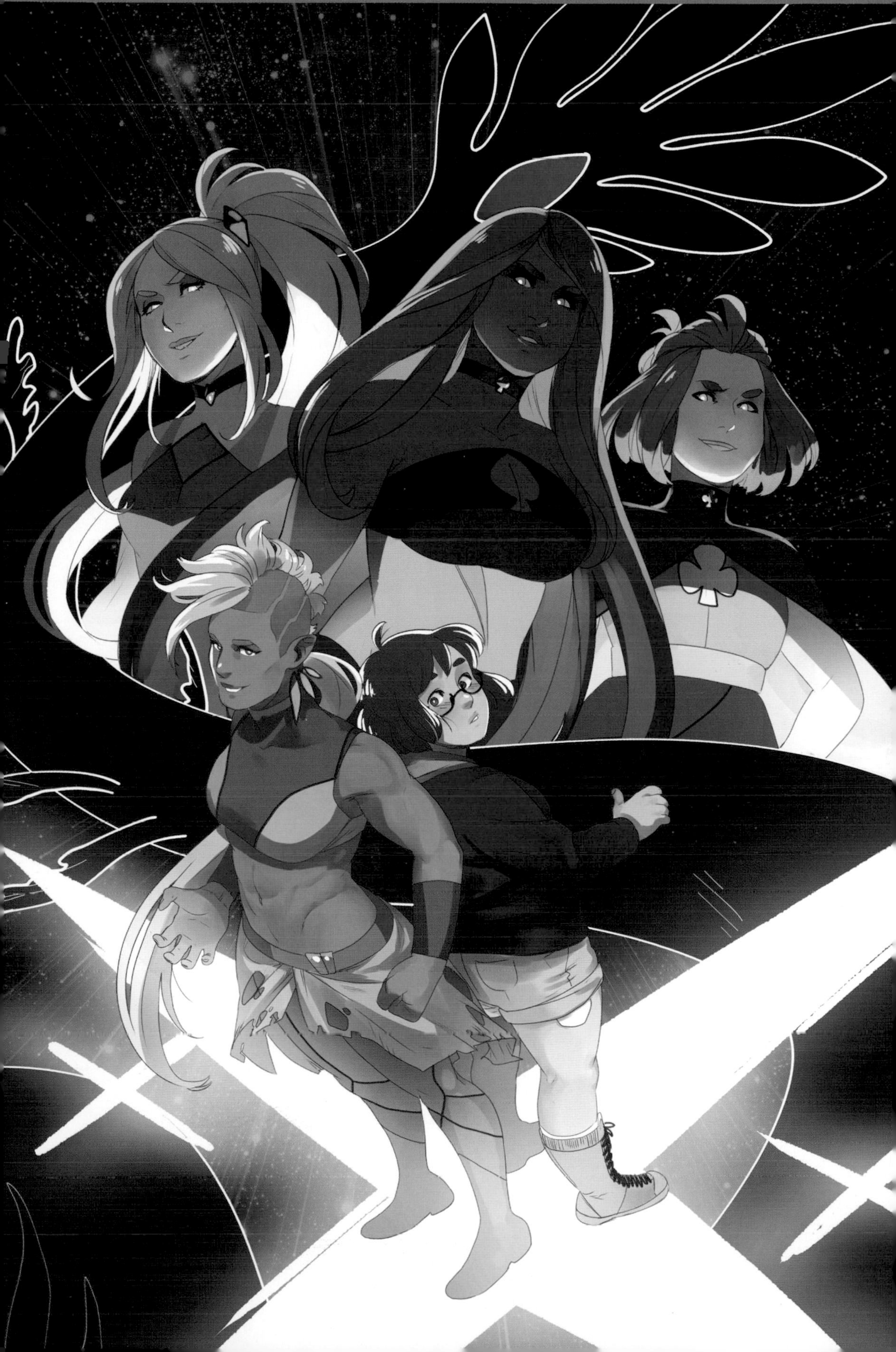

CHAPTER
TWO

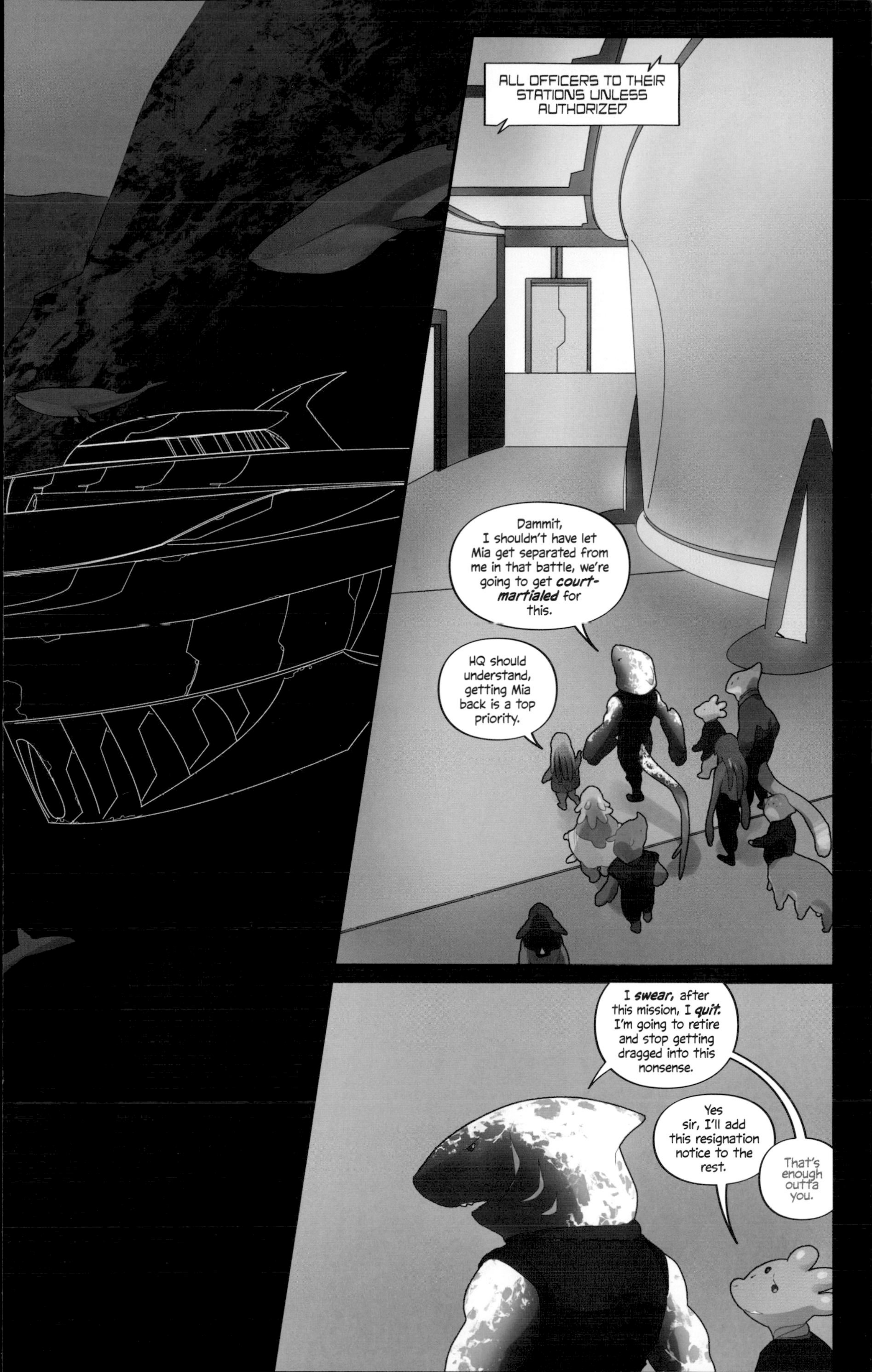
ALL OFFICERS TO THEIR STATIONS UNLESS AUTHORIZED
Dammit, I shouldn't have let Mia get separated from me in that battle, we're going to get *court-martialed* for this.
HQ should understand, getting Mia back is a top priority.
I *swear,* after this mission, I *quit.* I'm going to retire and stop getting dragged into this nonsense.
Yes sir, I'll add this resignation notice to the rest.
That's enough outta you.

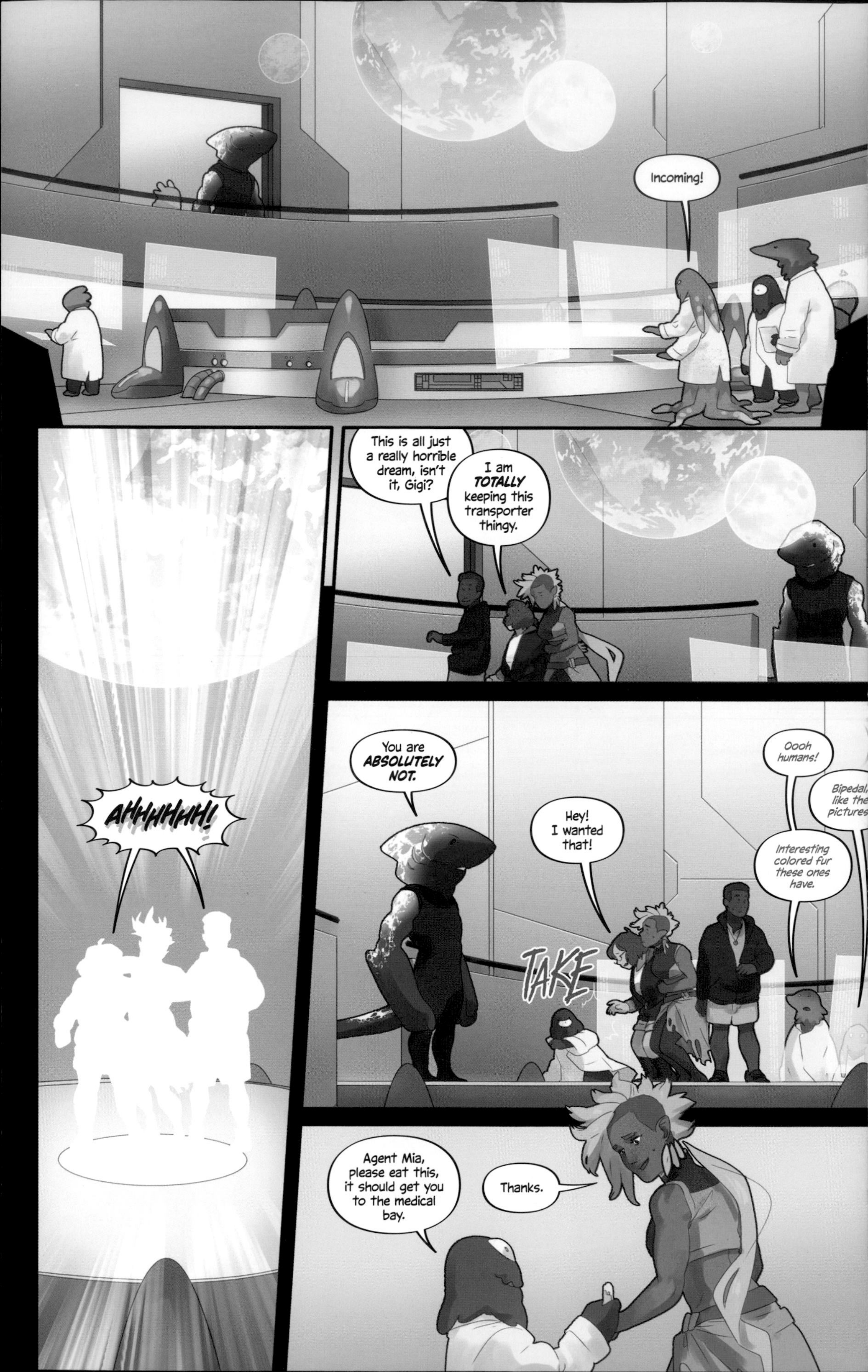
Incoming!
AHHHHHH!
This is all just a really horrible dream, isn't it, Gigi?
I am *TOTALLY* keeping this transporter thingy.
You are *ABSOLUTELY NOT.*
Hey! I wanted that!
TAKE
Oooh humans!
Interesting colored fur these ones have.
Agent Mia, please eat this, it should get you to the medical bay.
Thanks.

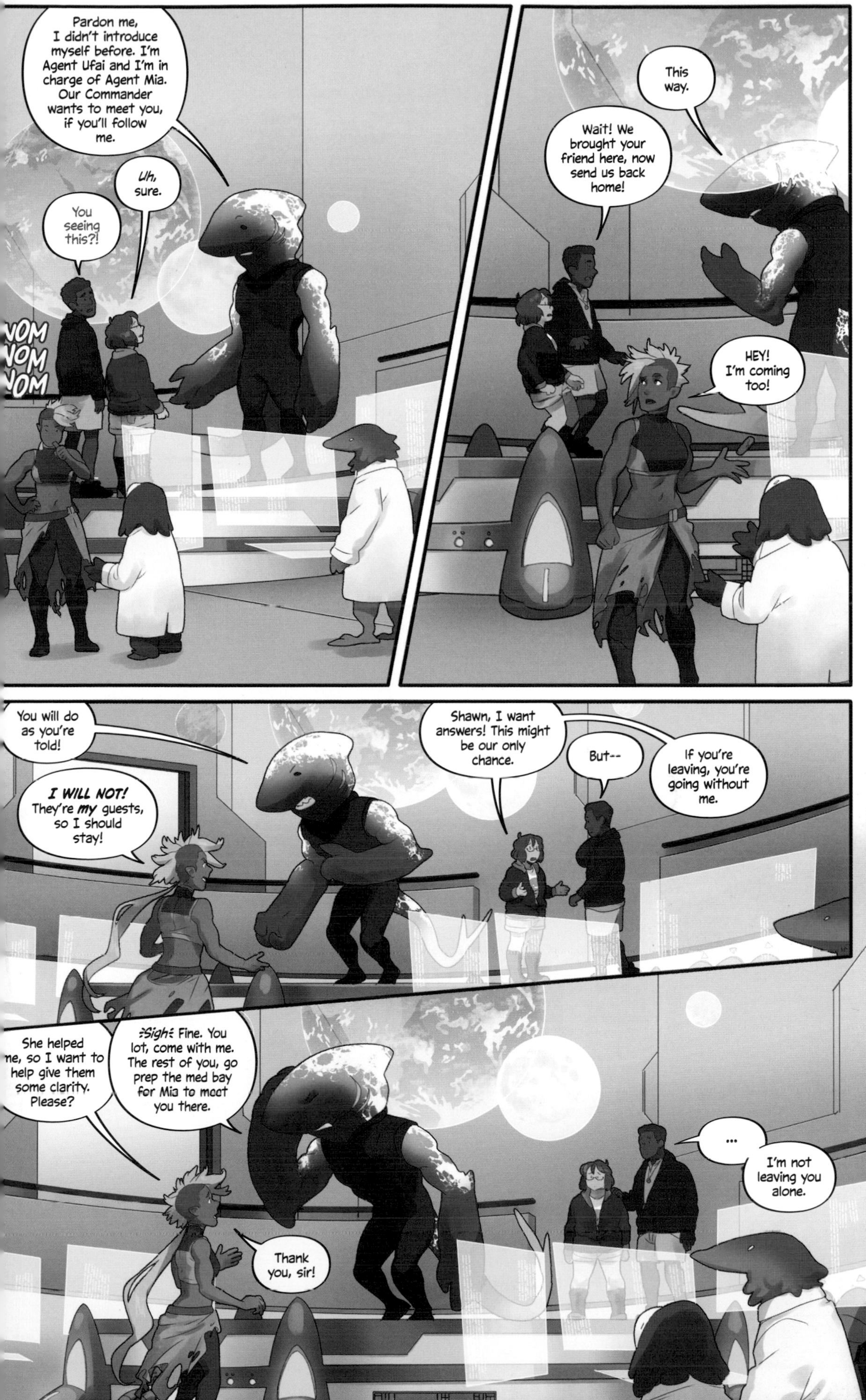
Pardon me, I didn't introduce myself before. I'm Agent Ufai and I'm in charge of Agent Mia. Our Commander wants to meet you, if you'll follow me.
Uh, sure.
You seeing this?!
NOM NOM NOM
This way.
Wait! We brought your friend here, now send us back home!
HEY! I'm coming too!
You will do as you're told!
I WILL NOT! They're my guests, so I should stay!
Shawn, I want answers! This might be our only chance.
But--
If you're leaving, you're going without me.
She helped me, so I want to help give them some clarity. Please?
Sigh Fine. You lot, come with me. The rest of you, go prep the med bay for Mia to meet you there.
Thank you, sir!
...
I'm not leaving you alone.

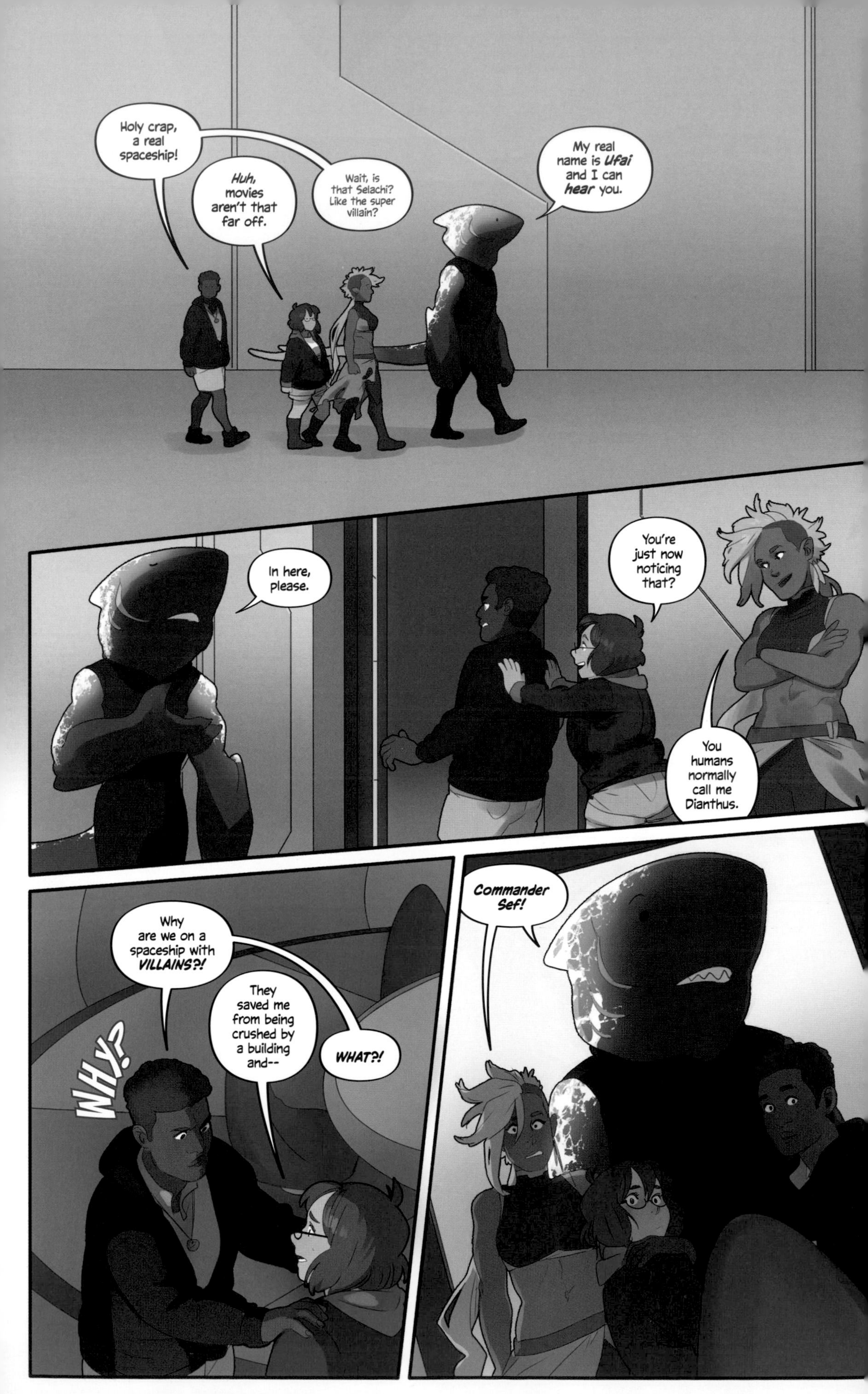

Holy crap, a real spaceship!
Huh, movies aren't that far off.
Wait, is that Selachi? Like the super villain?
My real name is Ufai and I can hear you.
In here, please.
You're just now noticing that?
You humans normally call me Dianthus.
Why are we on a spaceship with VILLAINS?!
WHY?
They saved me from being crushed by a building and--
WHAT?!
Commander Sef!

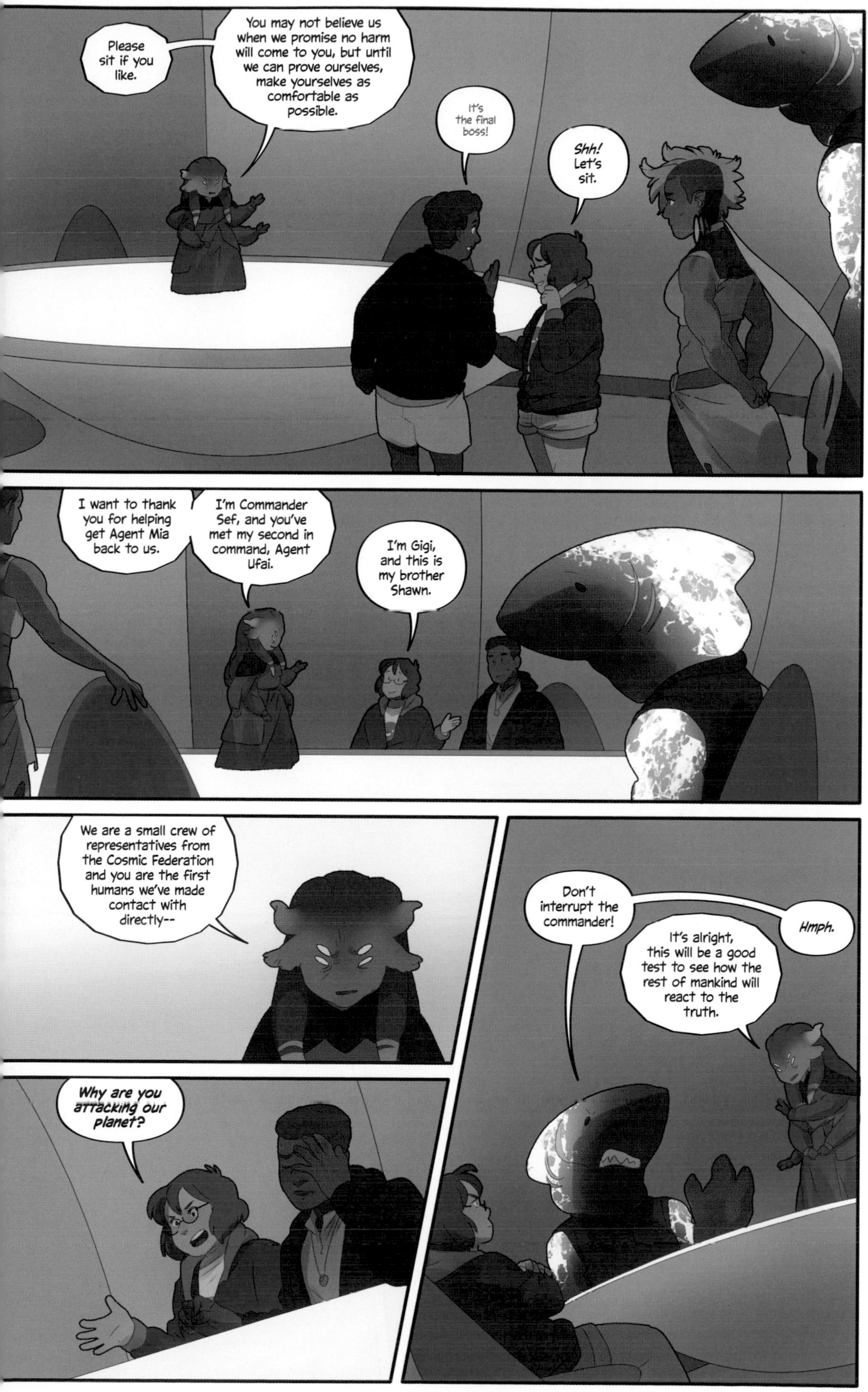

Please sit if you like.
You may not believe us when we promise no harm will come to you, but until we can prove ourselves, make yourselves as comfortable as possible.
It's the final boss!
Shh! Let's sit.
I want to thank you for helping get Agent Mia back to us.
I'm Commander Sef, and you've met my second in command, Agent Ufai.
I'm Gigi, and this is my brother Shawn.
We are a small crew of representatives from the Cosmic Federation and you are the first humans we've made contact with directly--
Why are you attacking our planet?
Don't interrupt the commander!
Hmph.
It's alright, this will be a good test to see how the rest of mankind will react to the truth.

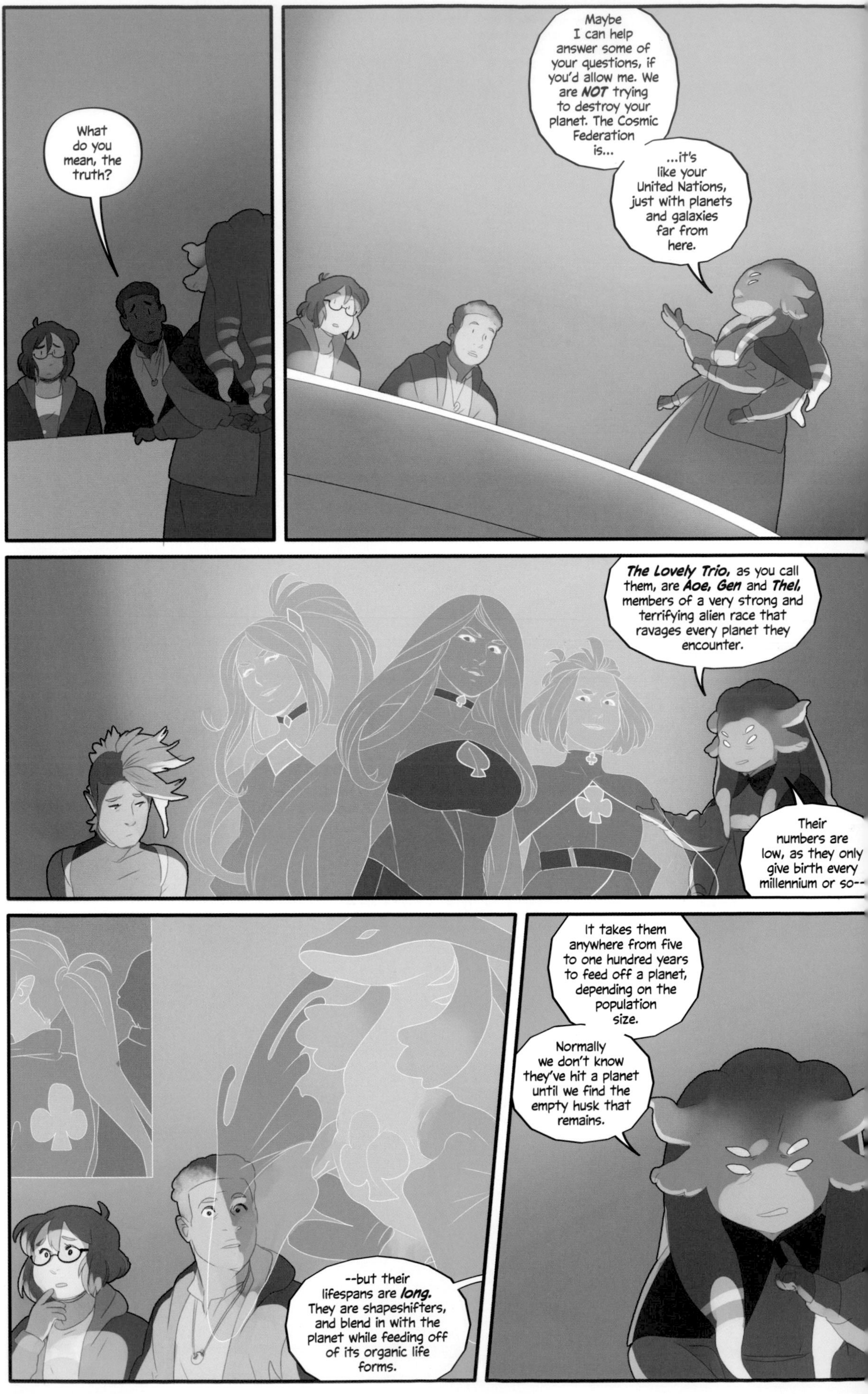
What do you mean, the truth?
Maybe I can help answer some of your questions, if you'd allow me. We are **NOT** trying to destroy your planet. The Cosmic Federation is...
...it's like your United Nations, just with planets and galaxies far from here.
The Lovely Trio, as you call them, are ***Aoe, Gen*** and ***Thel,*** members of a very strong and terrifying alien race that ravages every planet they encounter.
Their numbers are low, as they only give birth every millennium or so--
--but their lifespans are ***long.*** They are shapeshifters, and blend in with the planet while feeding off of its organic life forms.
It takes them anywhere from five to one hundred years to feed off a planet, depending on the population size.
Normally we don't know they've hit a planet until we find the empty husk that remains.

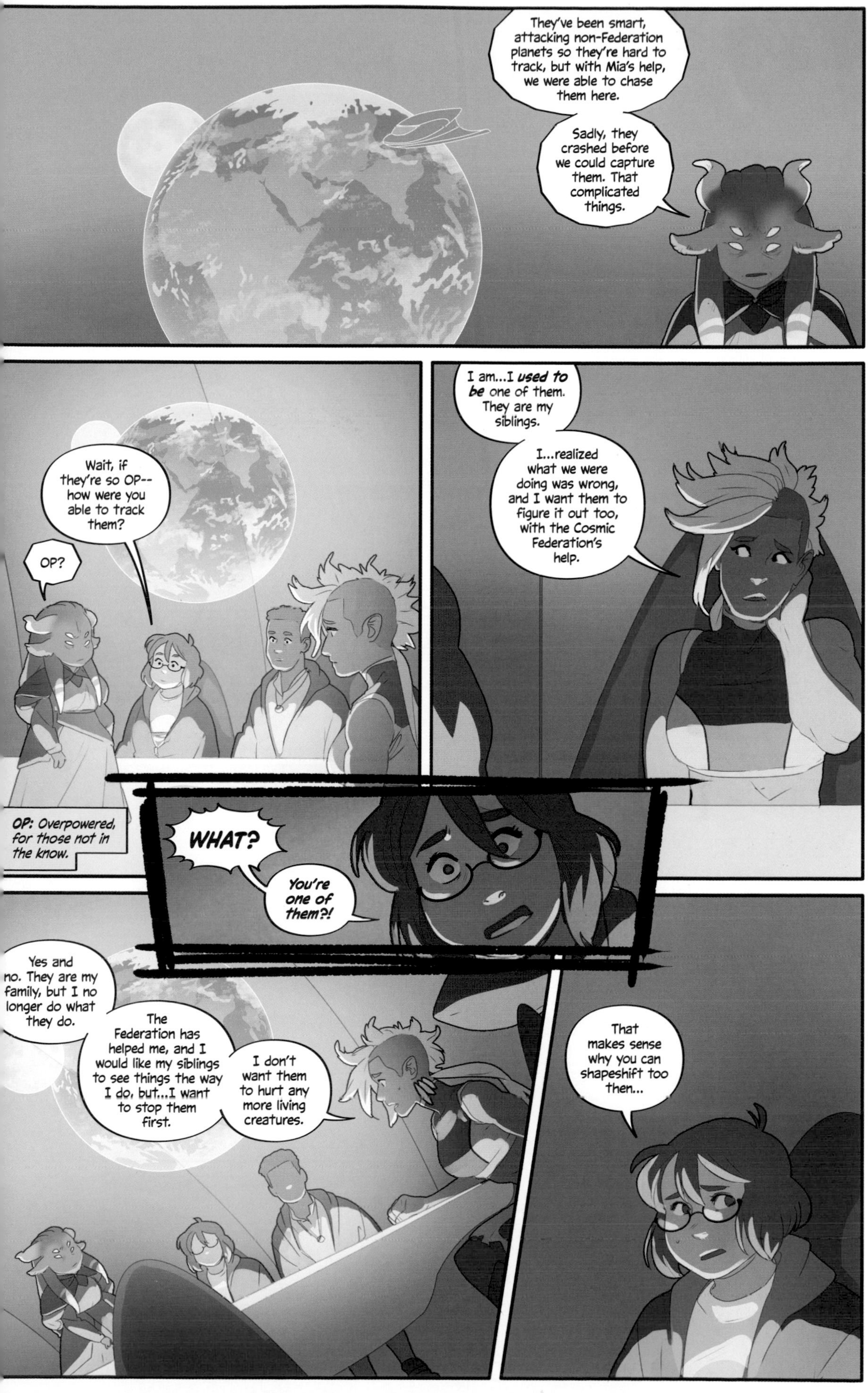
They've been smart, attacking non-Federation planets so they're hard to track, but with Mia's help, we were able to chase them here.
Sadly, they crashed before we could capture them. That complicated things.
Wait, if they're so OP-- how were you able to track them?
OP?
OP: Overpowered, for those not in the know.
I am...I used to be one of them. They are my siblings.
I...realized what we were doing was wrong, and I want them to figure it out too, with the Cosmic Federation's help.
WHAT?
You're one of them?!
Yes and no. They are my family, but I no longer do what they do.
The Federation has helped me, and I would like my siblings to see things the way I do, but...I want to stop them first.
I don't want them to hurt any more living creatures.
That makes sense why you can shapeshift too then...

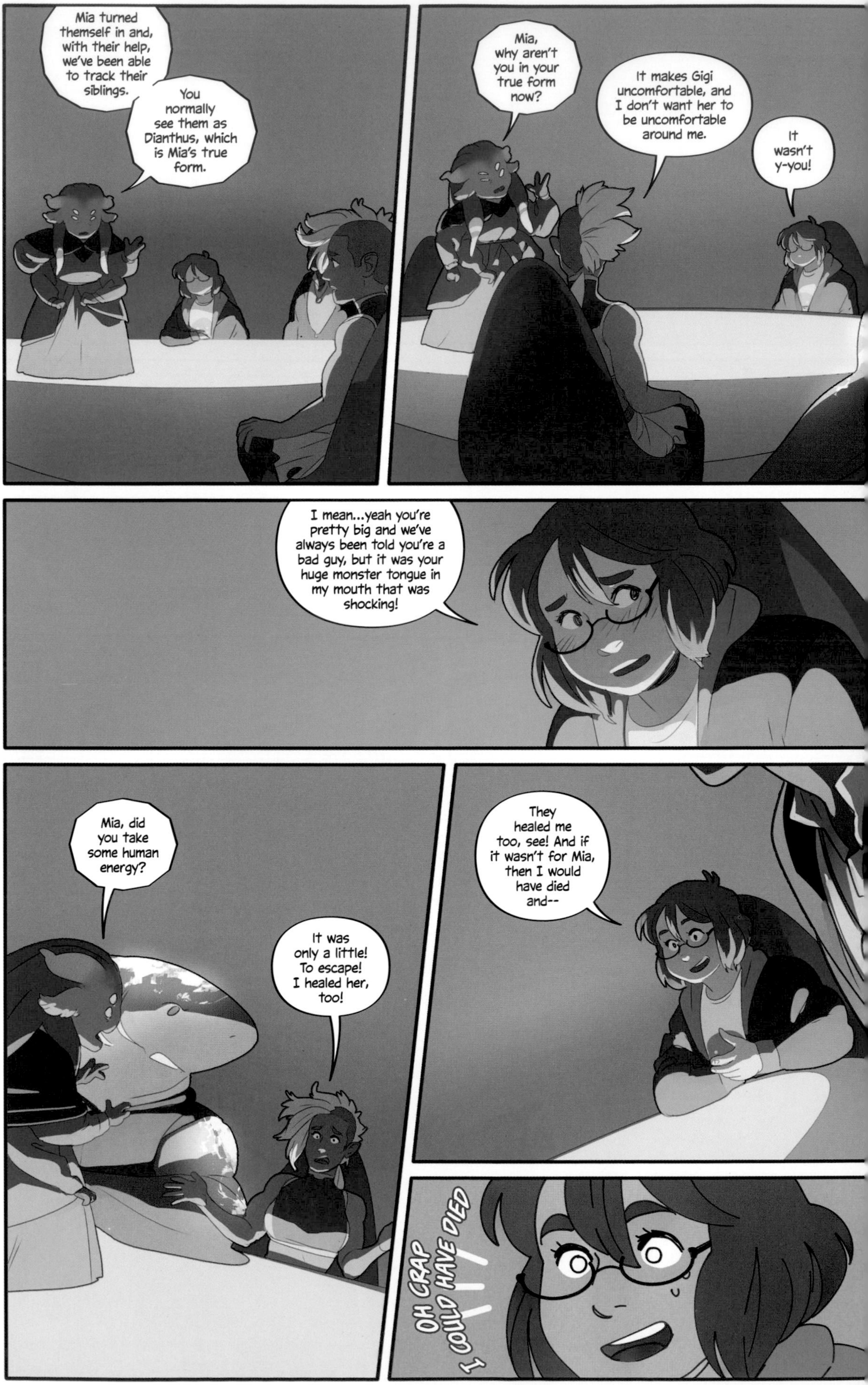
Mia turned themself in and, with their help, we've been able to track their siblings.
You normally see them as Dianthus, which is Mia's true form.
Mia, why aren't you in your true form now?
It makes Gigi uncomfortable, and I don't want her to be uncomfortable around me.
It wasn't y-you!
I mean...yeah you're pretty big and we've always been told you're a bad guy, but it was your huge monster tongue in my mouth that was shocking!
Mia, did you take some human energy?
It was only a little! To escape! I healed her, too!
They healed me too, see! And if it wasn't for Mia, then I would have died and--
OH CRAP I COULD HAVE DIED

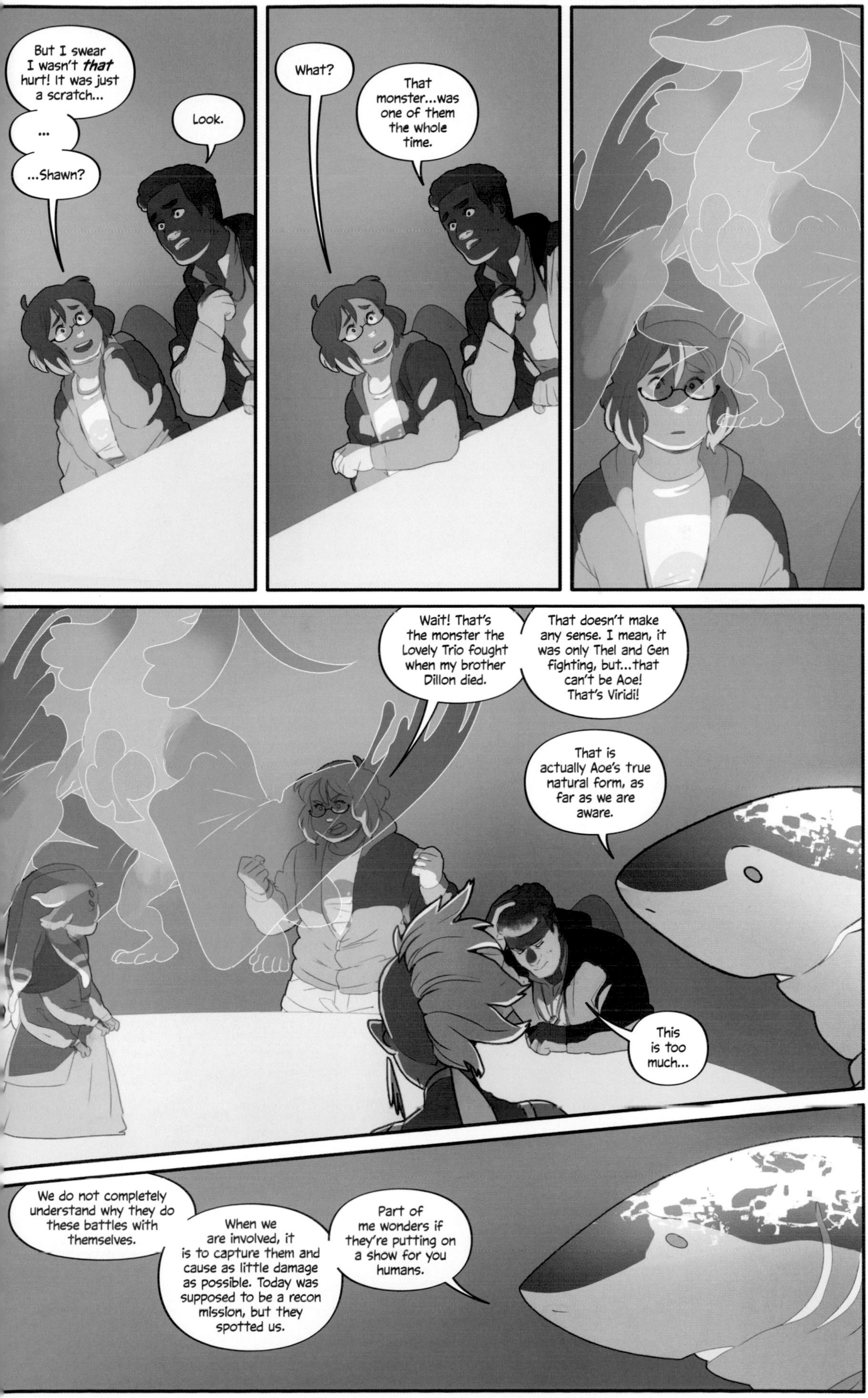
But I swear I wasn't *that* hurt! It was just a scratch...
...
...Shawn?
Look.
What?
That monster...was one of them the whole time.
Wait! That's the monster the Lovely Trio fought when my brother Dillon died.
That doesn't make any sense. I mean, it was only Thel and Gen fighting, but...that can't be Aoe! That's Viridi!
That is actually Aoe's true natural form, as far as we are aware.
This is too much...
We do not completely understand why they do these battles with themselves.
When we are involved, it is to capture them and cause as little damage as possible. Today was supposed to be a recon mission, but they spotted us.
Part of me wonders if they're putting on a show for you humans.

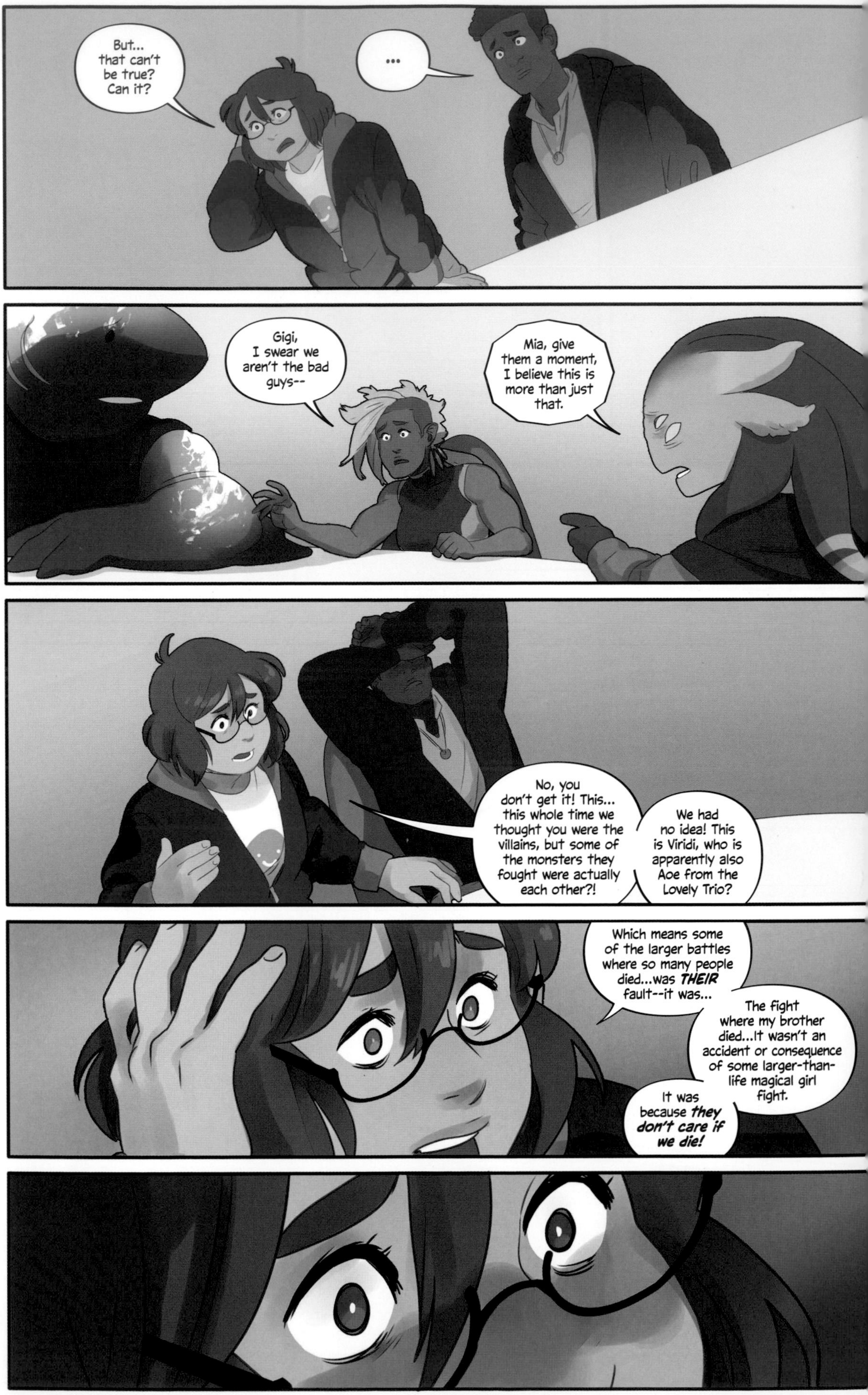

But... that can't be true? Can it?
...
Gigi, I swear we aren't the bad guys--
Mia, give them a moment, I believe this is more than just that.
No, you don't get it! This... this whole time we thought you were the villains, but some of the monsters they fought were actually each other?!
We had no idea! This is Viridi, who is apparently also Aoe from the Lovely Trio?
Which means some of the larger battles where so many people died...was ***THEIR*** fault--it was...
The fight where my brother died...It wasn't an accident or consequence of some larger-than-life magical girl fight.
It was because ***they don't care if we die!***

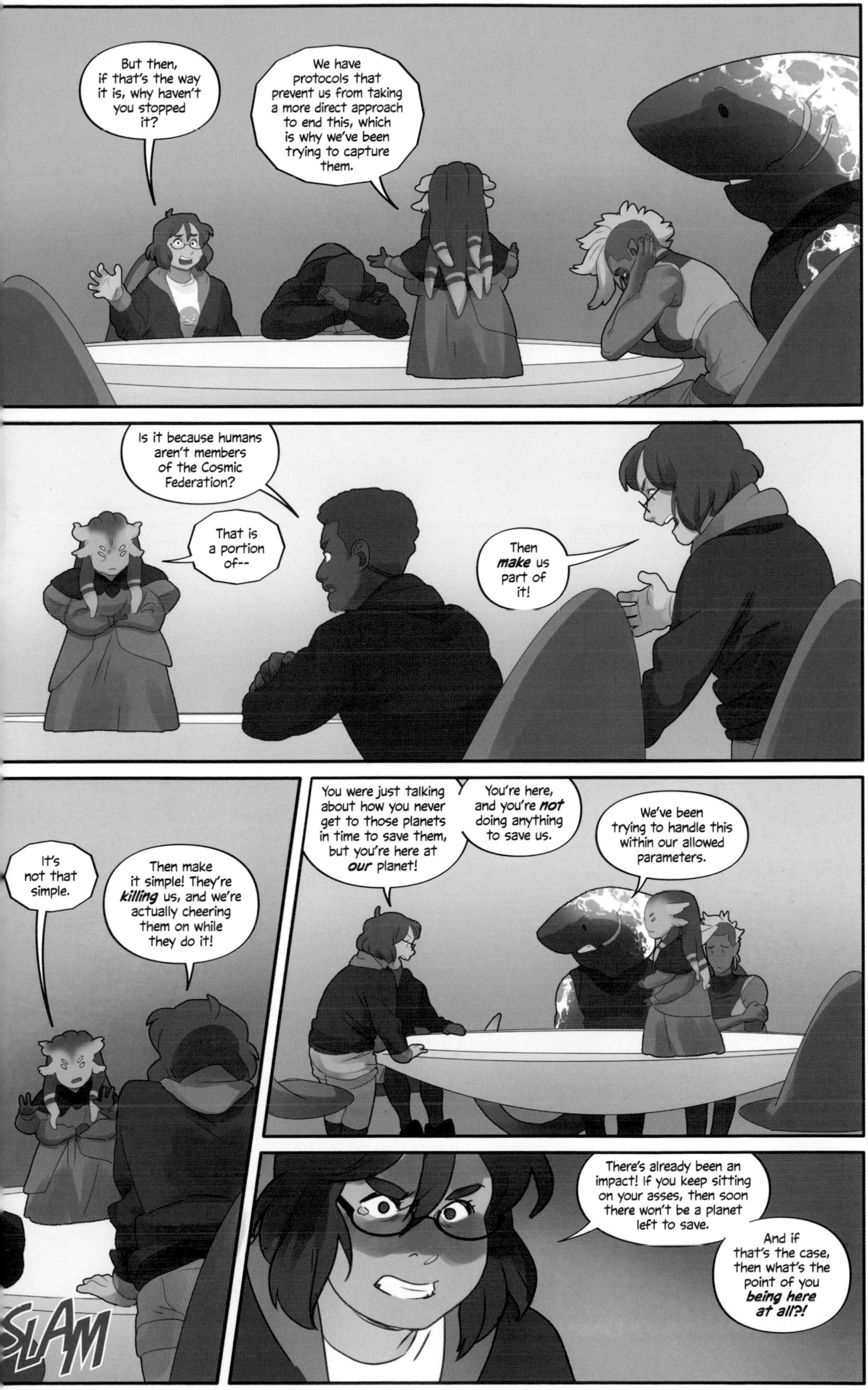
But then, if that's the way it is, why haven't you stopped it?
We have protocols that prevent us from taking a more direct approach to end this, which is why we've been trying to capture them.
Is it because humans aren't members of the Cosmic Federation?
That is a portion of--
Then *make* us part of it!
It's not that simple.
Then make it simple! They're *killing* us, and we're actually cheering them on while they do it!
SLAM
You were just talking about how you never get to those planets in time to save them, but you're here at *our* planet!
You're here, and you're *not* doing anything to save us.
We've been trying to handle this within our allowed parameters.
There's already been an impact! If you keep sitting on your asses, then soon there won't be a planet left to save.
And if that's the case, then what's the point of you *being here at all?!*

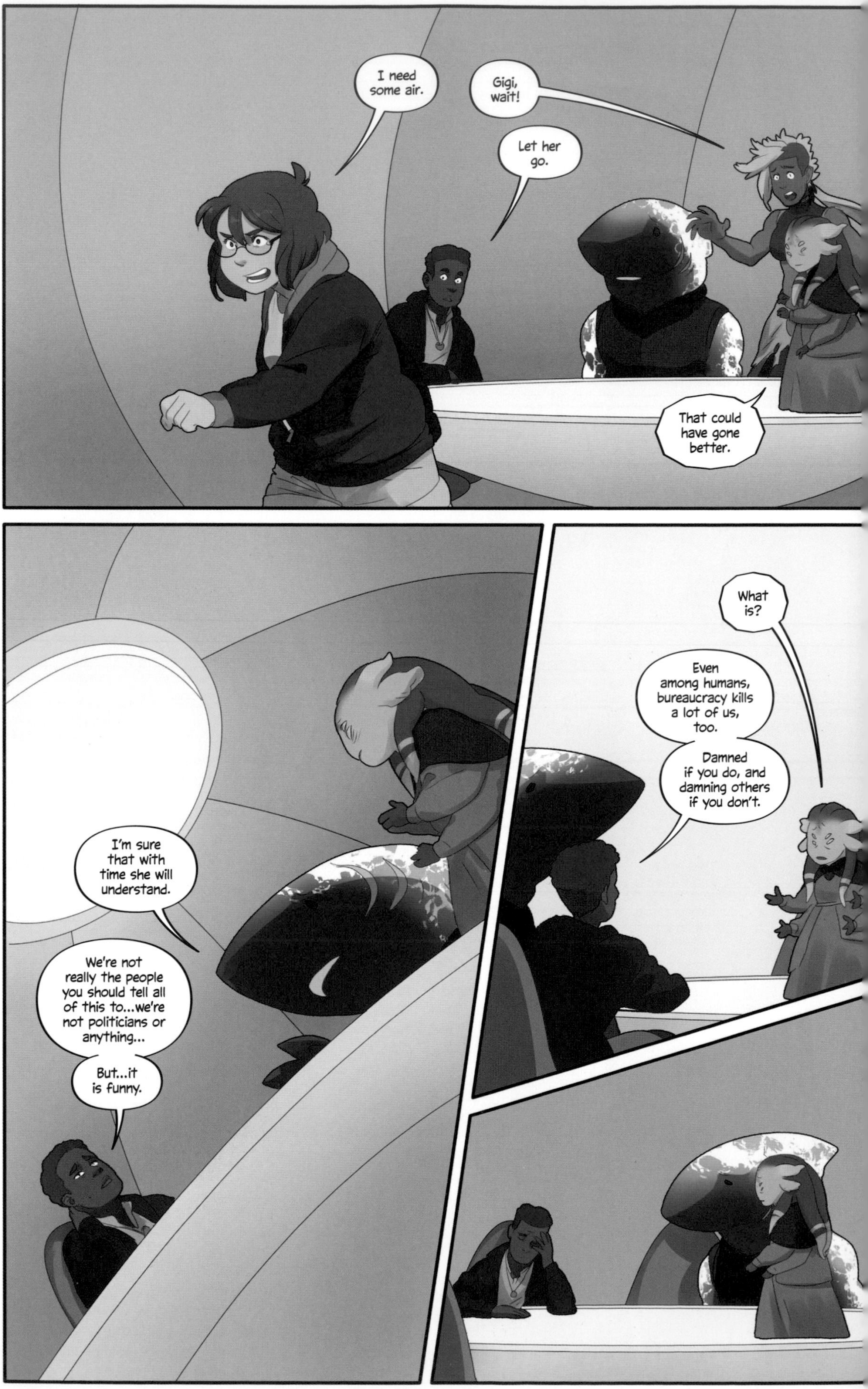
I need some air.
Gigi, wait!
Let her go.
That could have gone better.
I'm sure that with time she will understand.
We're not really the people you should tell all of this to...we're not politicians or anything...
But...it is funny.
What is?
Even among humans, bureaucracy kills a lot of us, too.
Damned if you do, and damning others if you don't.

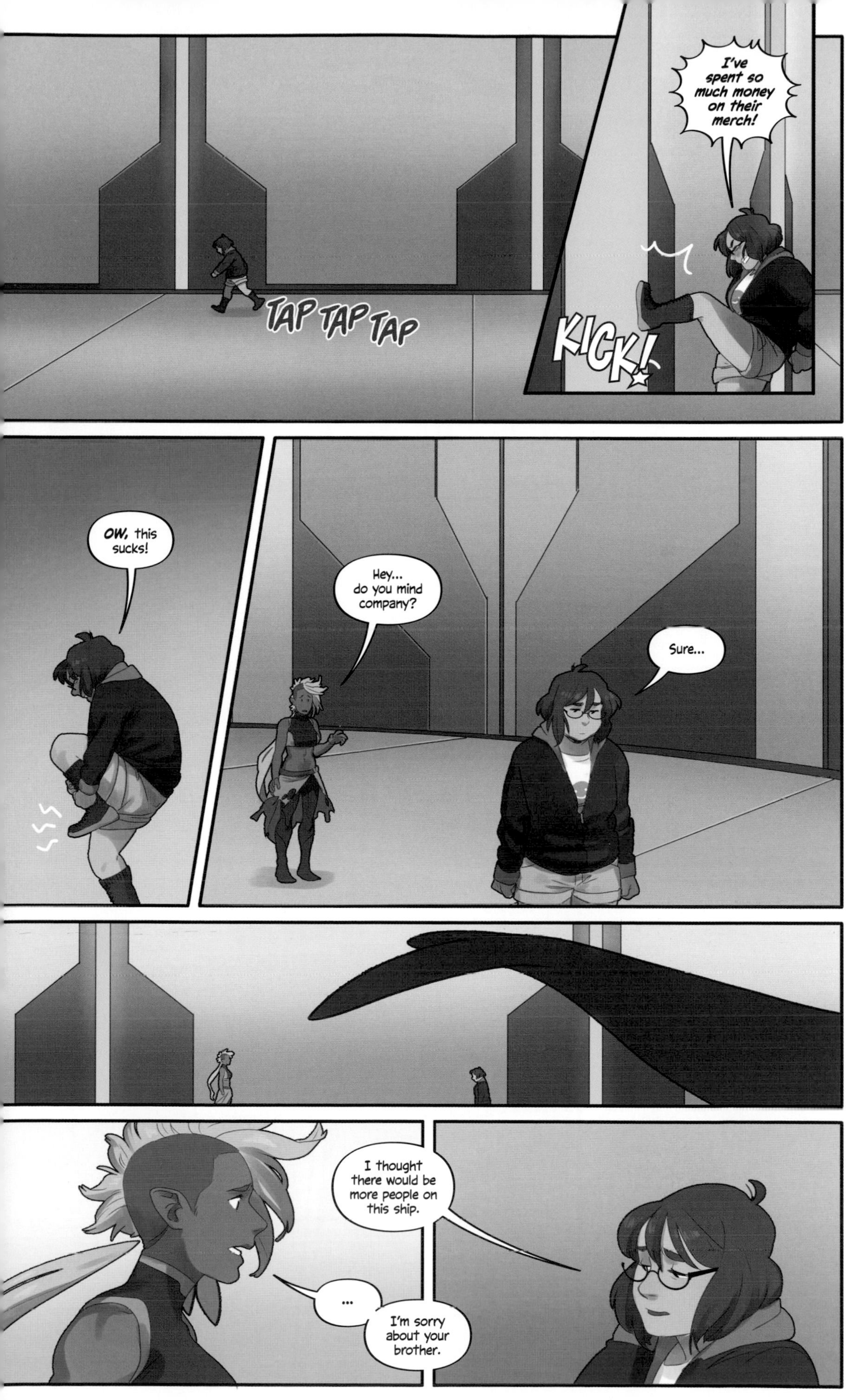
TAP TAP TAP
I've spent so much money on their merch!
KICK!
OW, this sucks!
Hey... do you mind company?
Sure...
I thought there would be more people on this ship.
...
I'm sorry about your brother.

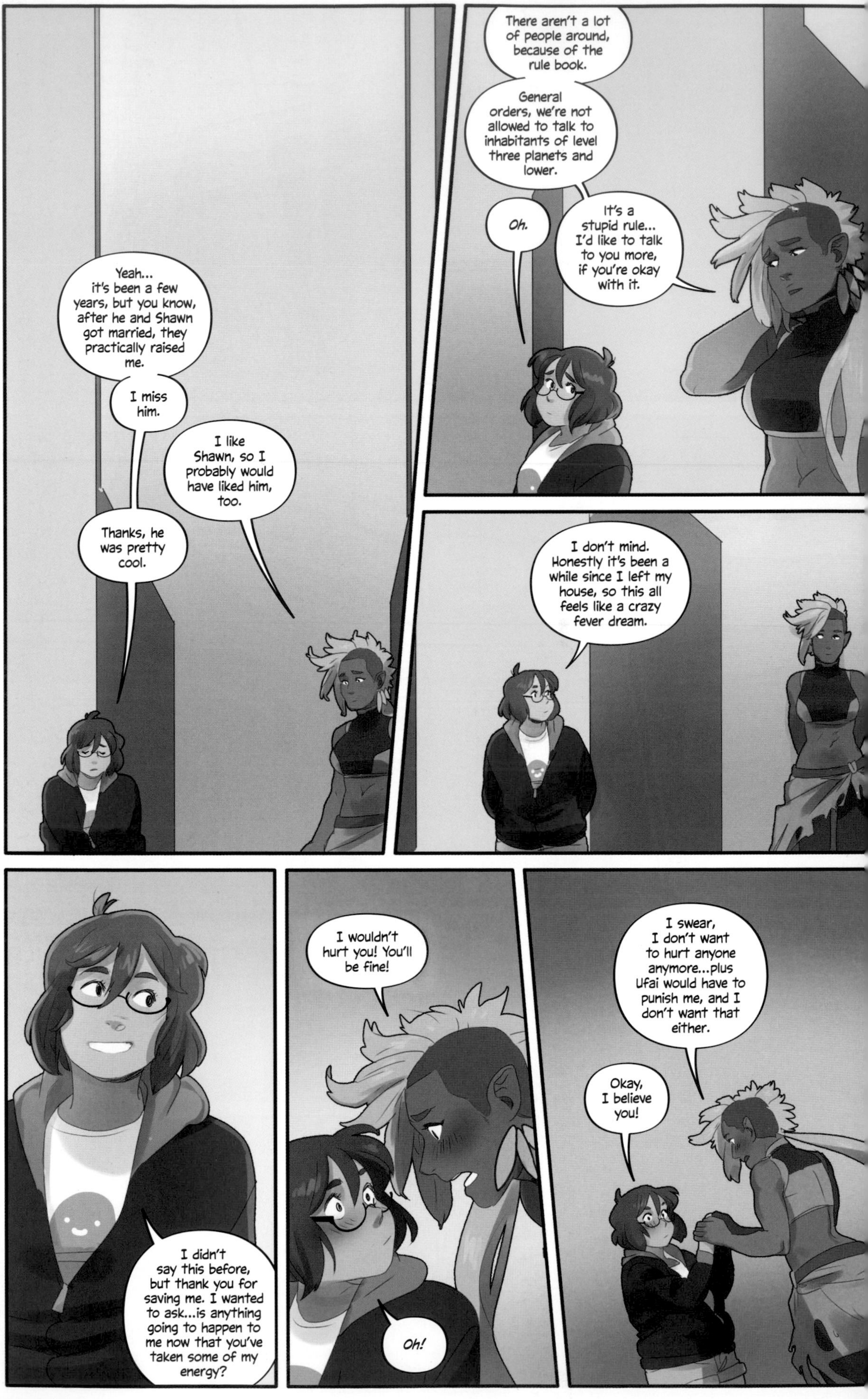
Yeah... it's been a few years, but you know, after he and Shawn got married, they practically raised me.
I miss him.
I like Shawn, so I probably would have liked him, too.
Thanks, he was pretty cool.
There aren't a lot of people around, because of the rule book.
General orders, we're not allowed to talk to inhabitants of level three planets and lower.
Oh.
It's a stupid rule... I'd like to talk to you more, if you're okay with it.
I don't mind. Honestly it's been a while since I left my house, so this all feels like a crazy fever dream.
I didn't say this before, but thank you for saving me. I wanted to ask...is anything going to happen to me now that you've taken some of my energy?
I wouldn't hurt you! You'll be fine!
Oh!
I swear, I don't want to hurt anyone anymore...plus Ufai would have to punish me, and I don't want that either.
Okay, I believe you!

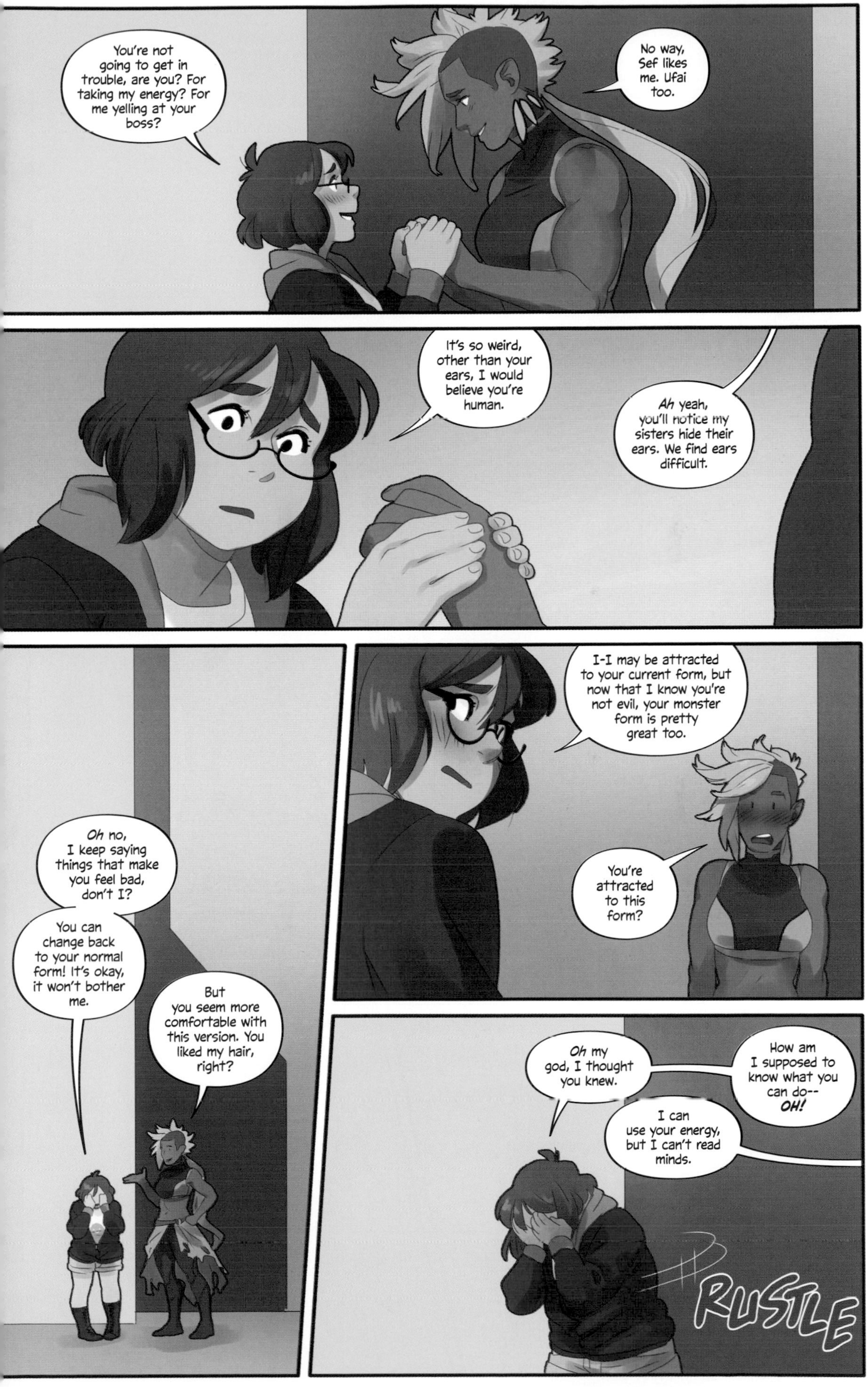

You're not going to get in trouble, are you? For taking my energy? For me yelling at your boss?
No way, Sef likes me. Ufai too.
It's so weird, other than your ears, I would believe you're human.
Ah yeah, you'll notice my sisters hide their ears. We find ears difficult.
Oh no, I keep saying things that make you feel bad, don't I?
You can change back to your normal form! It's okay, it won't bother me.
But you seem more comfortable with this version. You liked my hair, right?
I-I may be attracted to your current form, but now that I know you're not evil, your monster form is pretty great too.
You're attracted to this form?
Oh my god, I thought you knew.
How am I supposed to know what you can do-- ***OH!***
I can use your energy, but I can't read minds.
RUSTLE

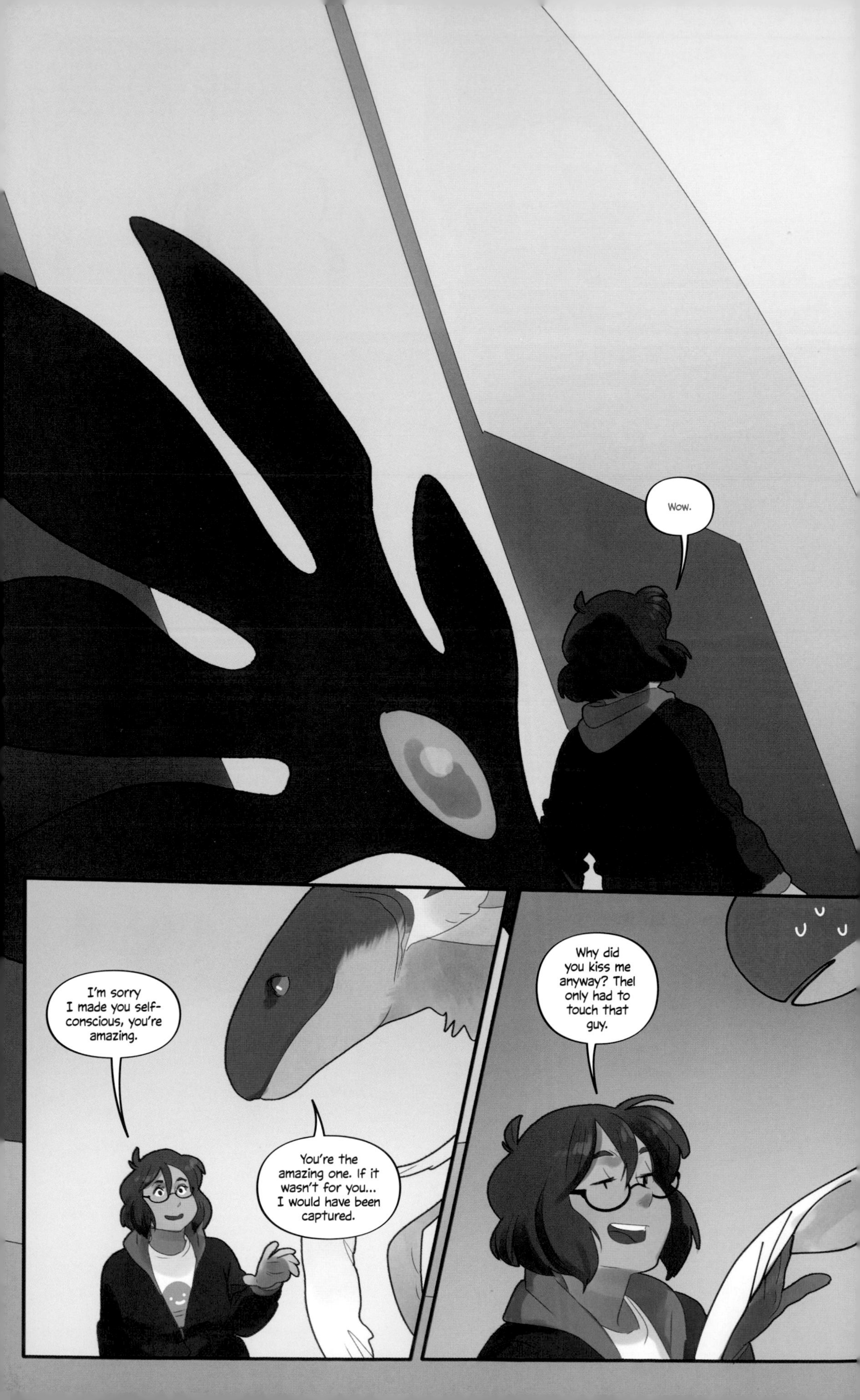
Wow.
I'm sorry I made you self-conscious, you're amazing.
You're the amazing one. If it wasn't for you... I would have been captured.
Why did you kiss me anyway? Thel only had to touch that guy.

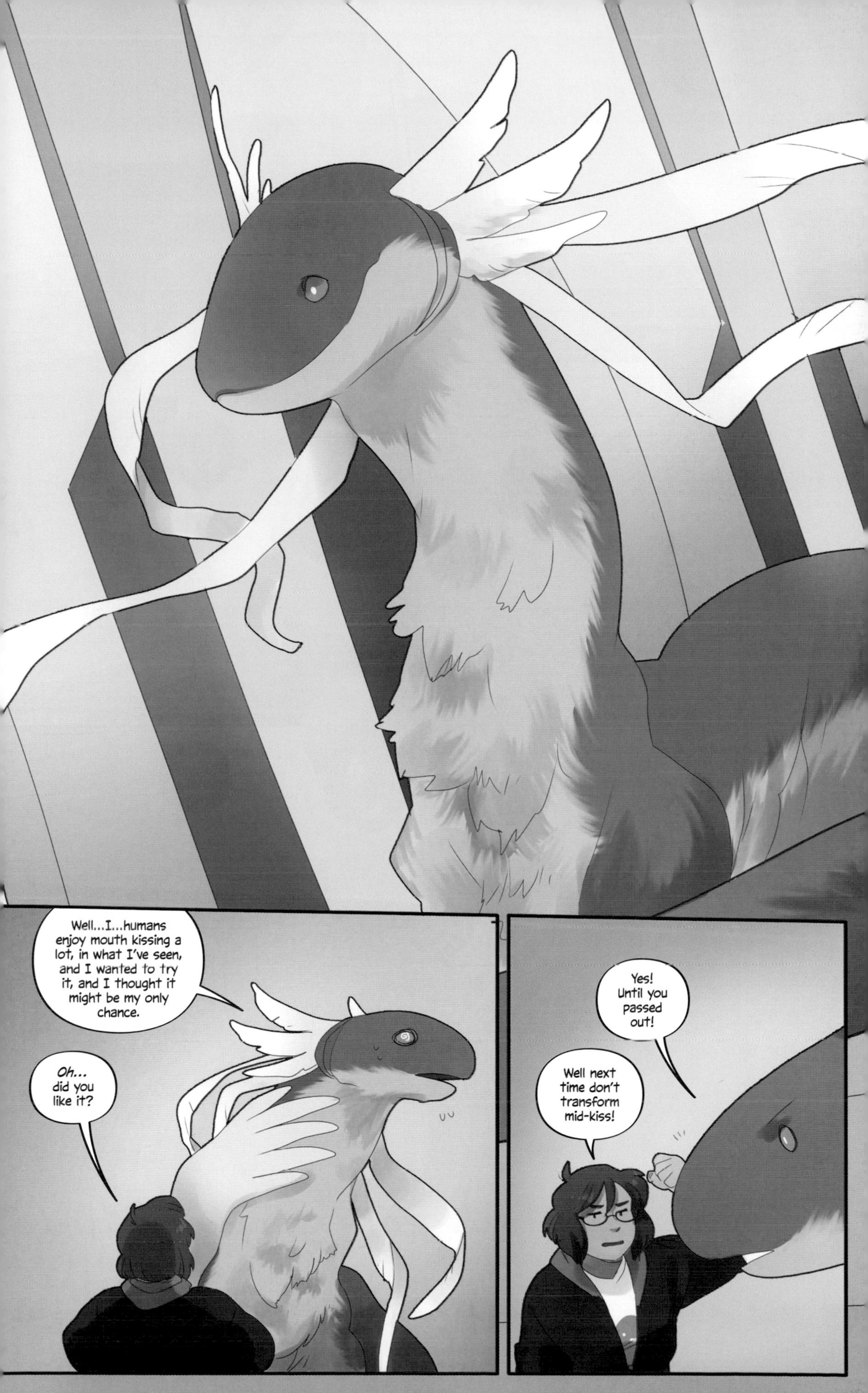
Well...I...humans enjoy mouth kissing a lot, in what I've seen, and I wanted to try it, and I thought it might be my only chance.
Oh... did you like it?
Yes! Until you passed out!
Well next time don't transform mid-kiss!

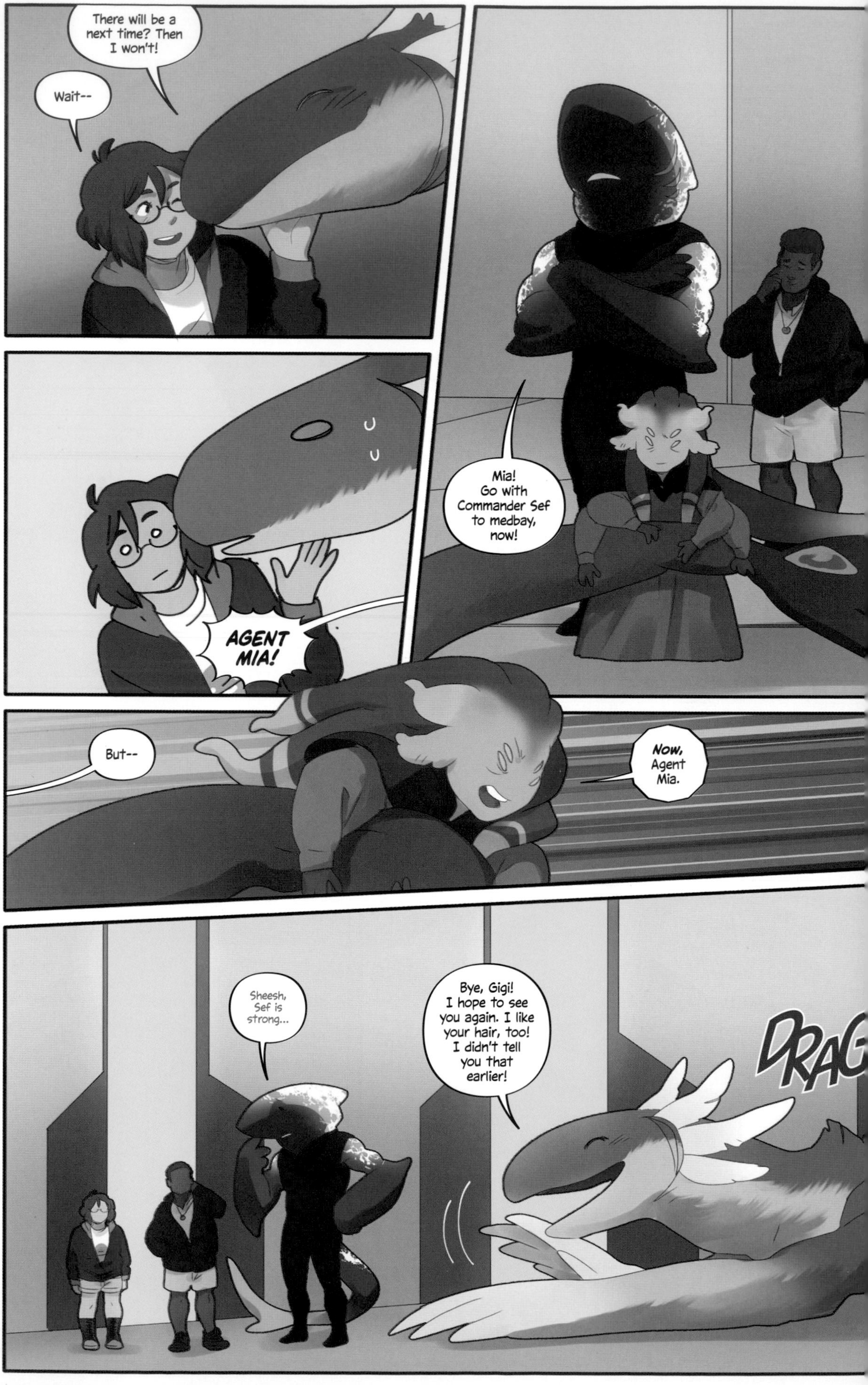
There will be a next time? Then I won't!
Wait--
Mia! Go with Commander Sef to medbay, now!
AGENT MIA!
But--
Now, Agent Mia.
Sheesh, Sef is strong...
Bye, Gigi! I hope to see you again. I like your hair, too! I didn't tell you that earlier!
DRAG

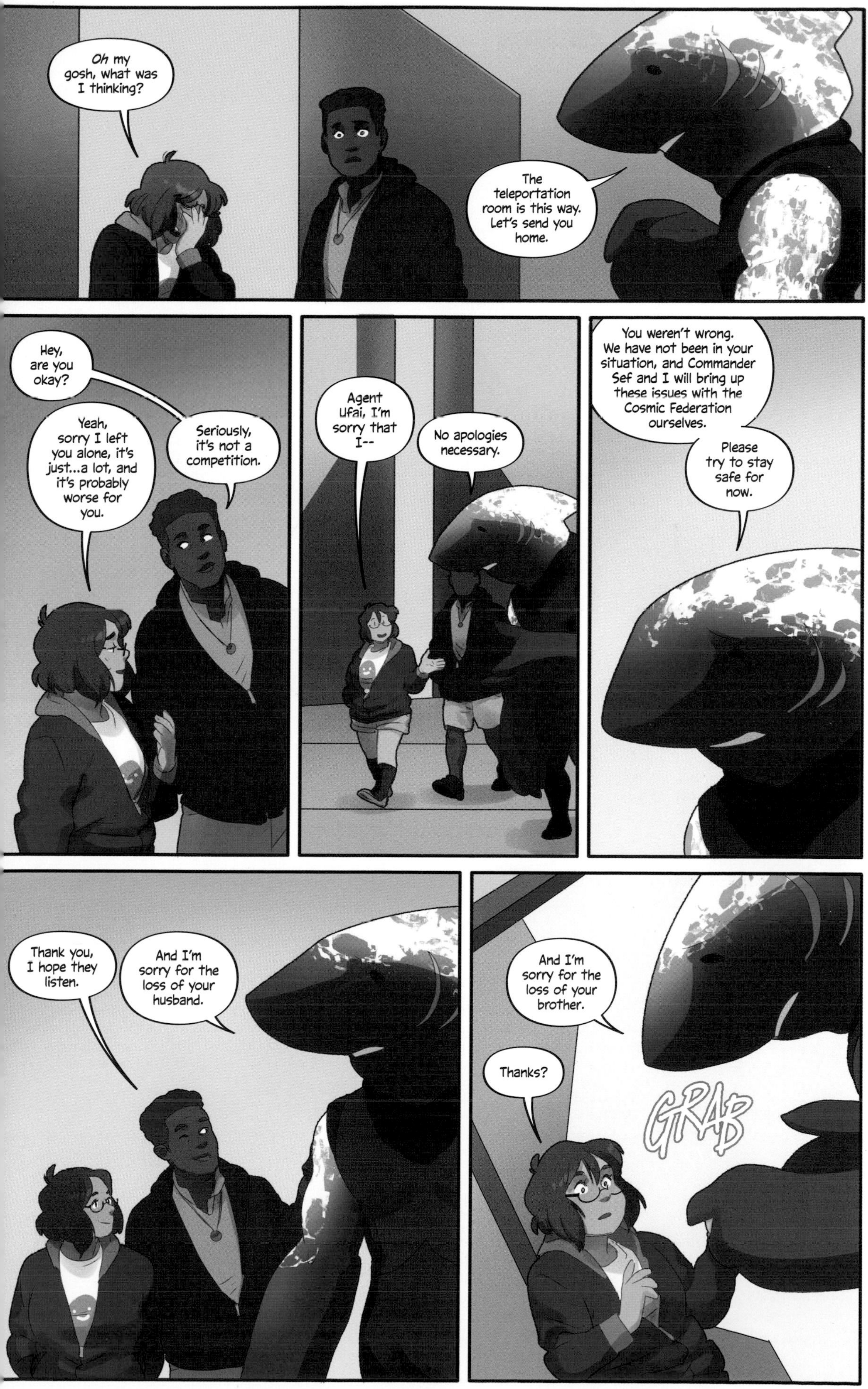
Oh my gosh, what was I thinking?
The teleportation room is this way. Let's send you home.
Hey, are you okay?
Yeah, sorry I left you alone, it's just...a lot, and it's probably worse for you.
Seriously, it's not a competition.
Agent Ufai, I'm sorry that I--
No apologies necessary.
You weren't wrong. We have not been in your situation, and Commander Sef and I will bring up these issues with the Cosmic Federation ourselves.
Please try to stay safe for now.
Thank you, I hope they listen.
And I'm sorry for the loss of your husband.
And I'm sorry for the loss of your brother.
Thanks?
GRAB

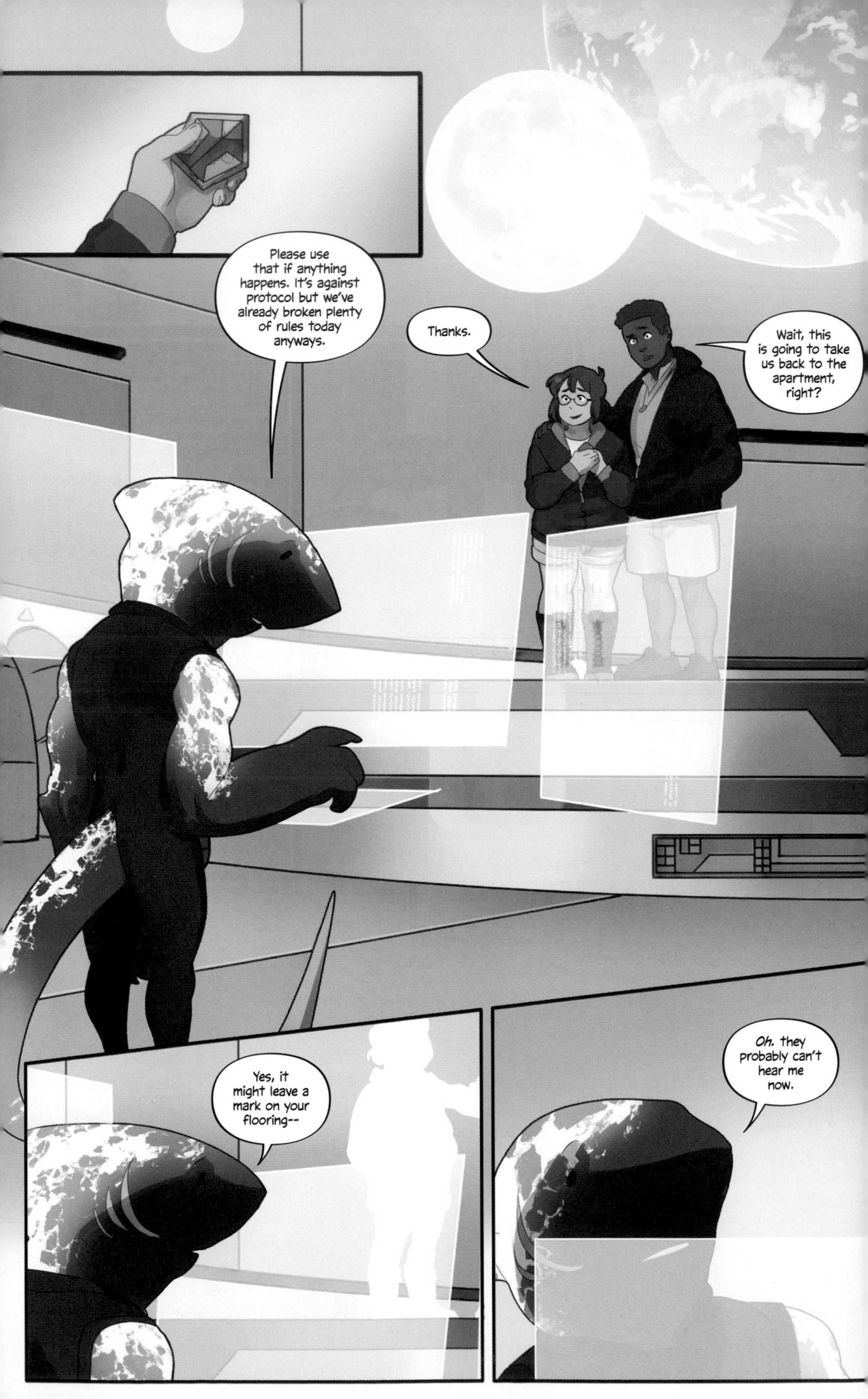
Please use that if anything happens. It's against protocol but we've already broken plenty of rules today anyways.
Thanks.
Wait, this is going to take us back to the apartment, right?
Yes, it might leave a mark on your flooring--
Oh. they probably can't hear me now.

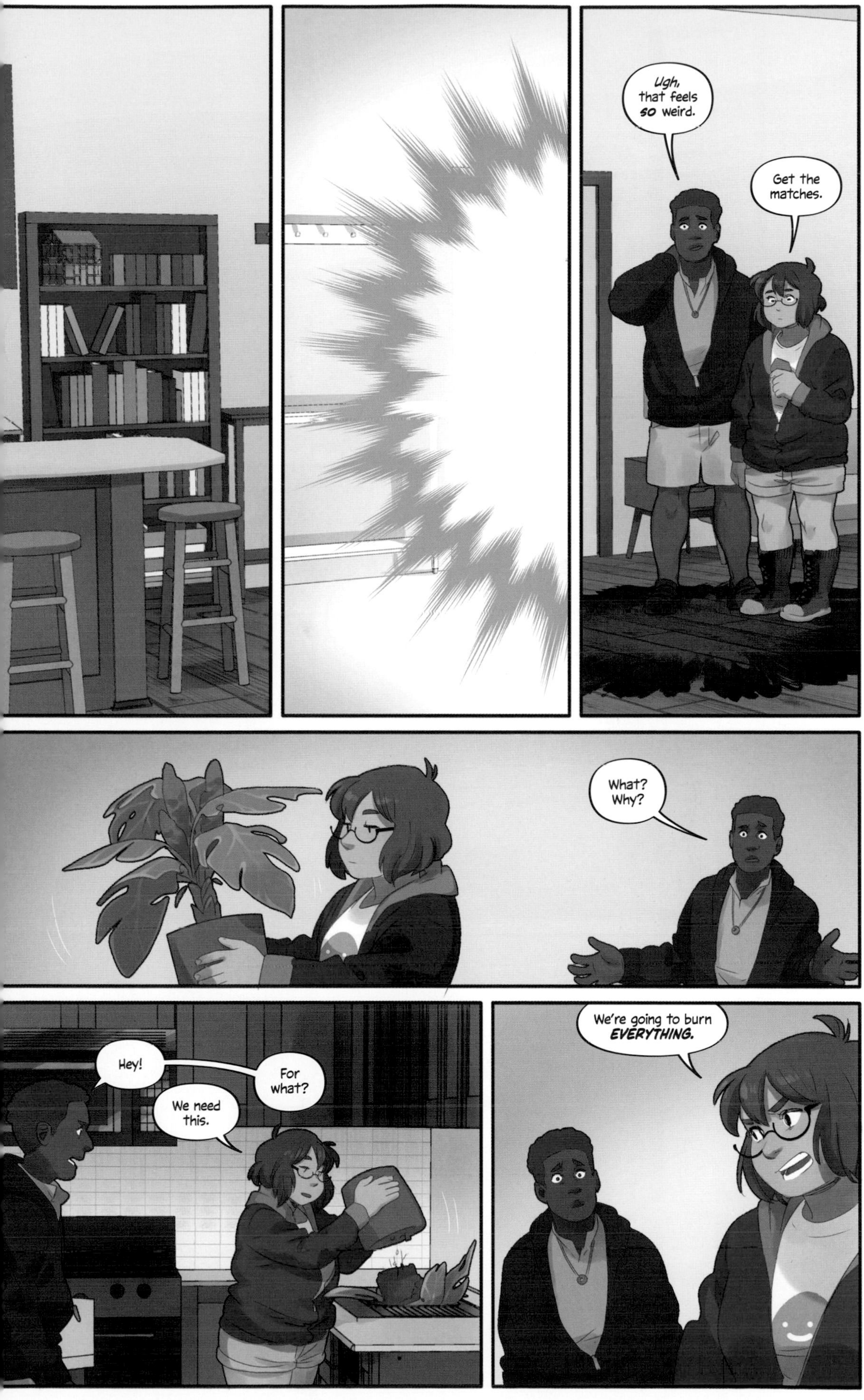

Ugh, that feels so weird.
Get the matches.
What? Why?
Hey!
For what?
We need this.
We're going to burn EVERYTHING.

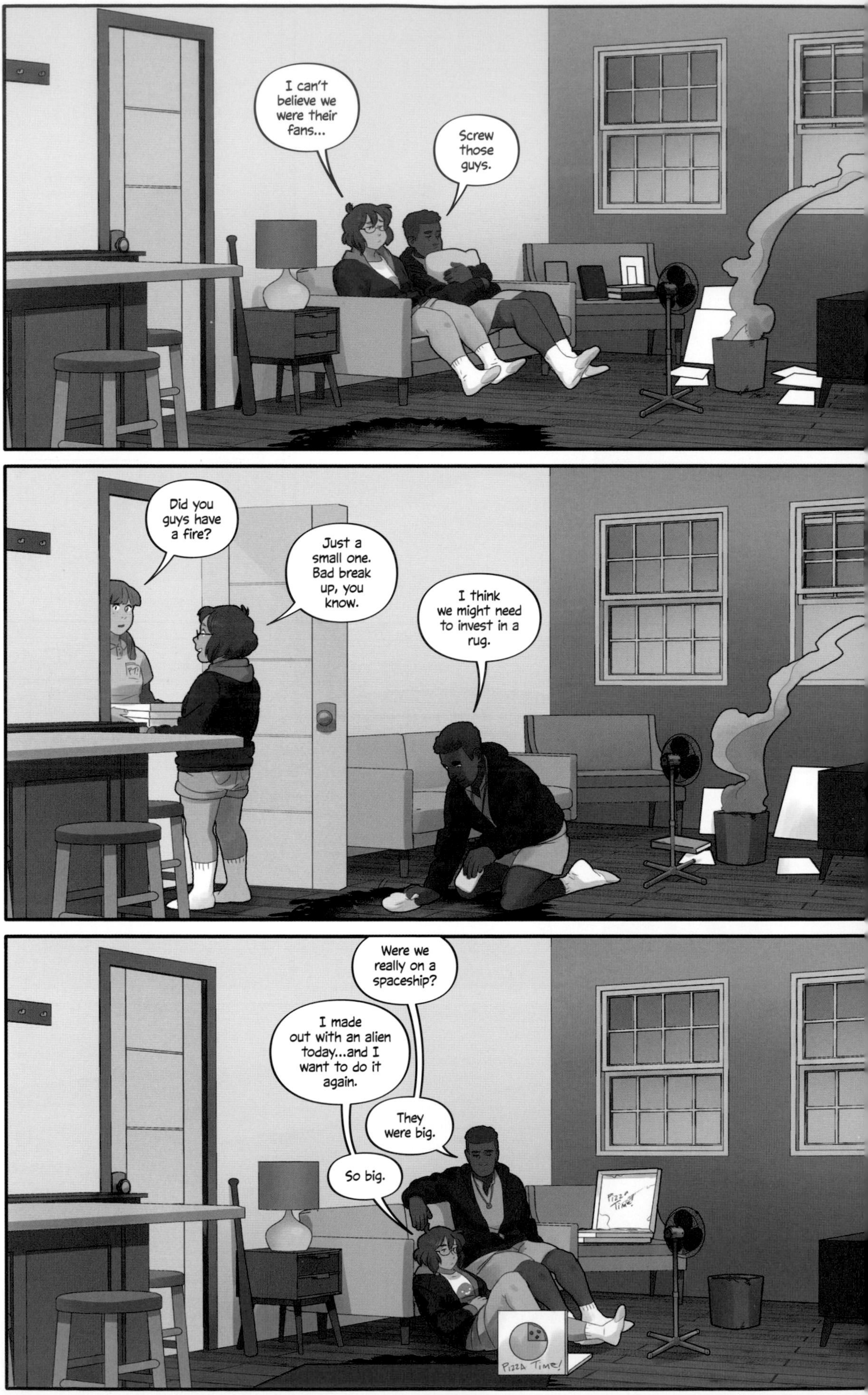
I can't believe we were their fans...
Screw those guys.
Did you guys have a fire?
Just a small one. Bad break up, you know.
I think we might need to invest in a rug.
Were we really on a spaceship?
I made out with an alien today...and I want to do it again.
They were big.
So big.
PIZZA TIME!

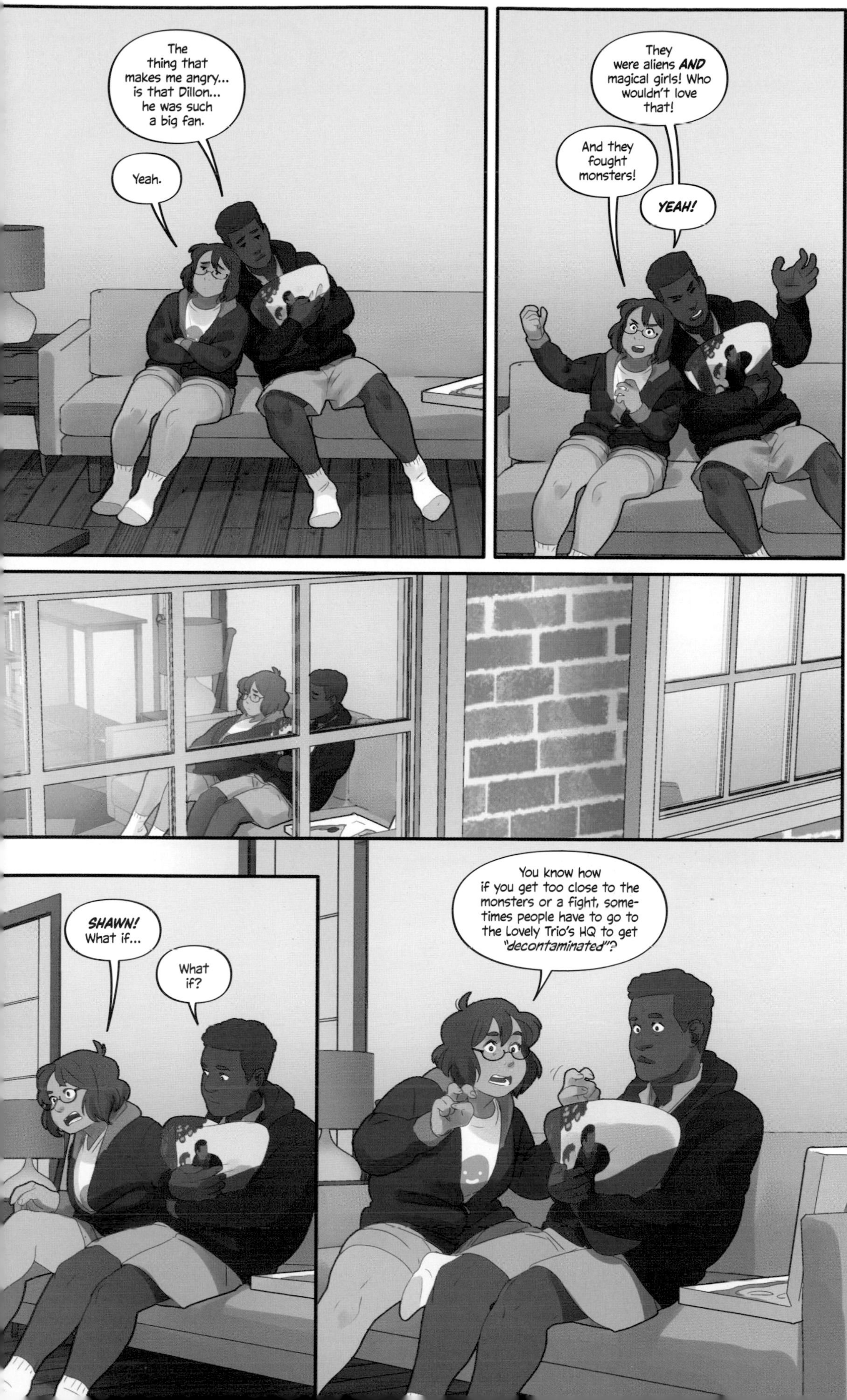
The thing that makes me angry... is that Dillon... he was such a big fan.
Yeah.
They were aliens AND magical girls! Who wouldn't love that!
And they fought monsters!
YEAH!
SHAWN! What if...
What if?
You know how if you get too close to the monsters or a fight, sometimes people have to go to the Lovely Trio's HQ to get "decontaminated"?

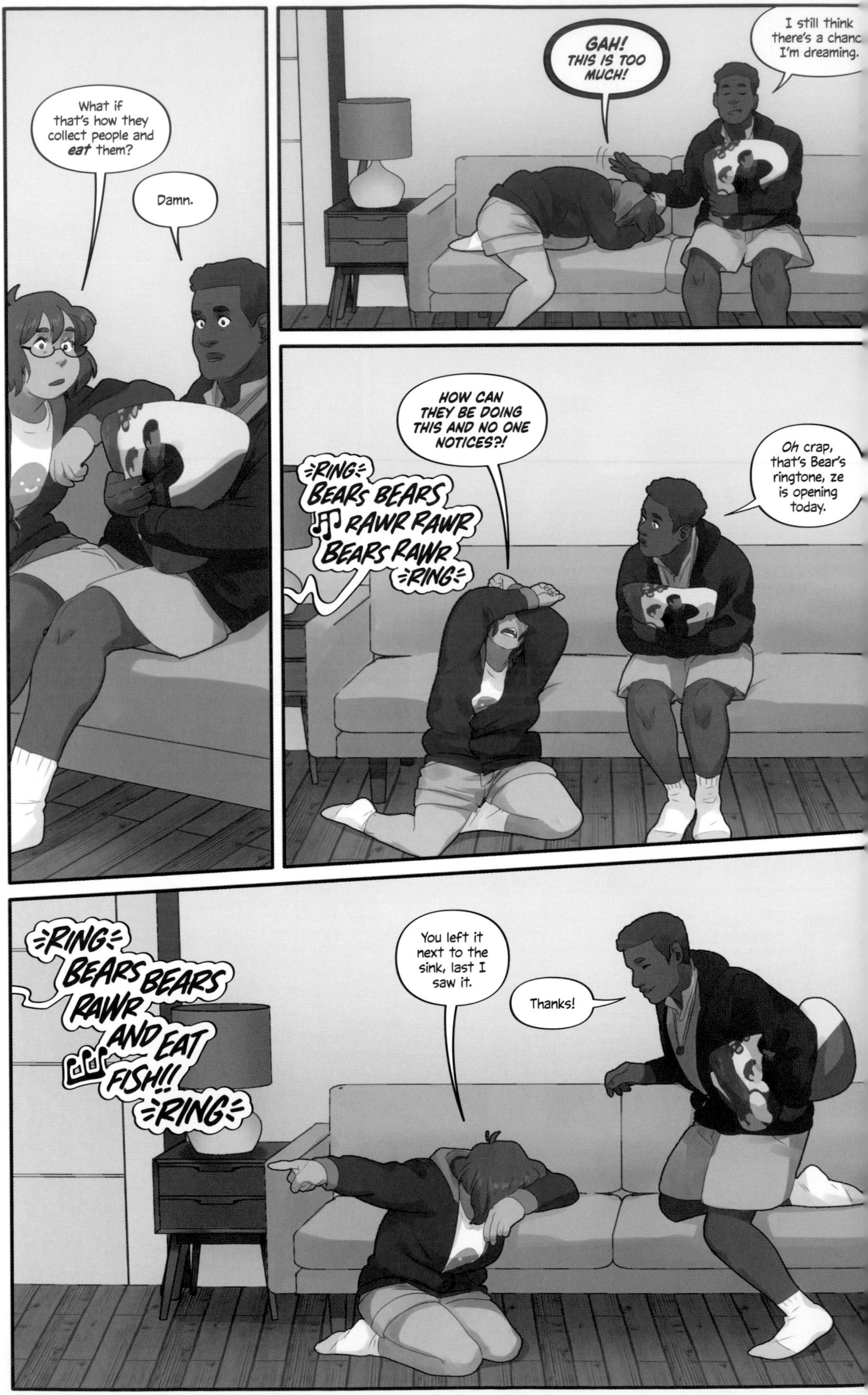

What if that's how they collect people and *eat* them?
Damn.
GAH! THIS IS TOO MUCH!
I still think there's a chanc I'm dreaming.
HOW CAN THEY BE DOING THIS AND NO ONE NOTICES?!
RING BEARS BEARS RAWR RAWR BEARS RAWR RING
Oh crap, that's Bear's ringtone, ze is opening today.
RING BEARS BEARS RAWR AND EAT FISH!! RING
You left it next to the sink, last I saw it.
Thanks!

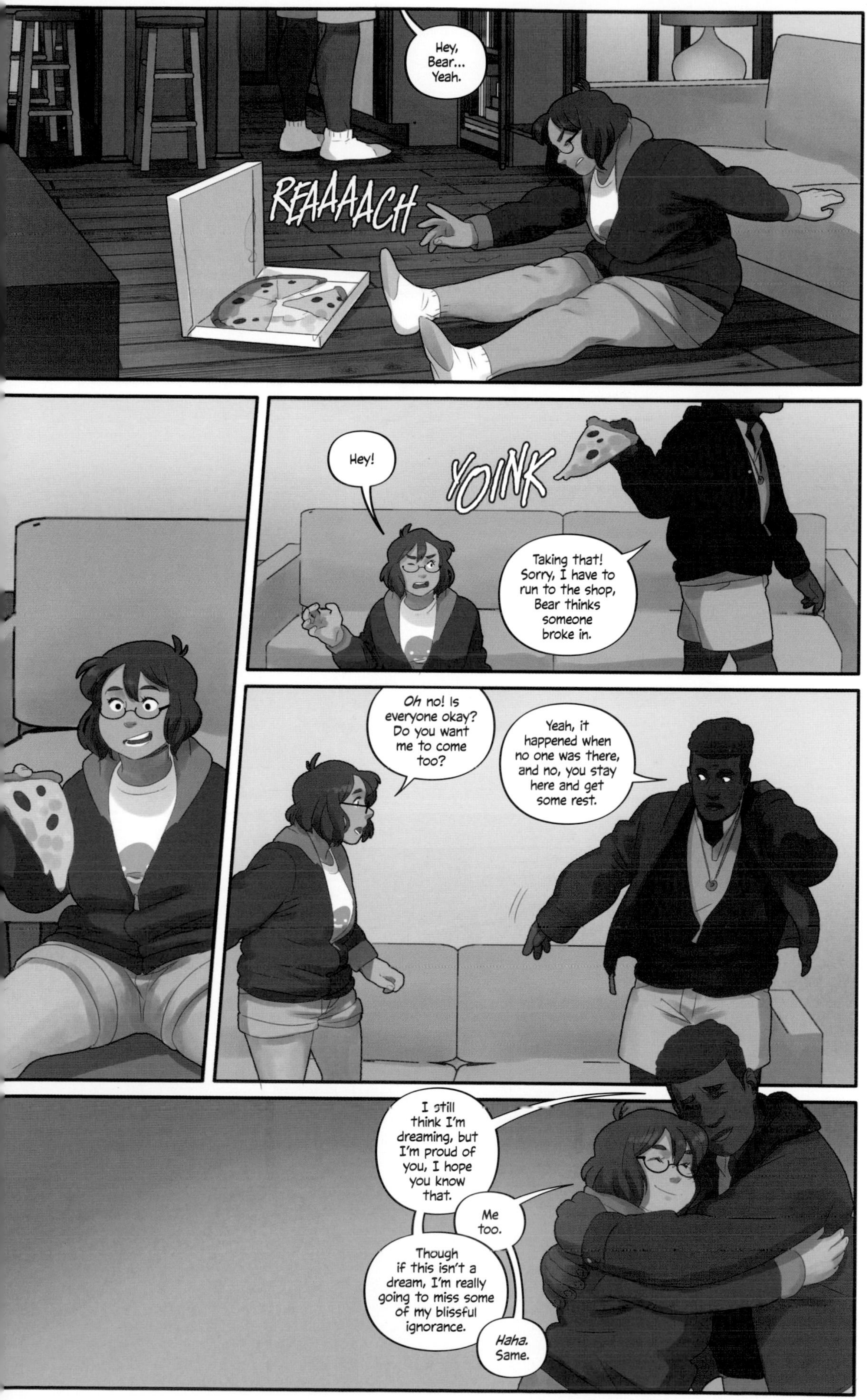
Hey,
Bear...
Yeah.
REAAAACH
Hey!
YOINK
Taking that! Sorry, I have to run to the shop, Bear thinks someone broke in.
Oh no! Is everyone okay? Do you want me to come too?
Yeah, it happened when no one was there, and no, you stay here and get some rest.
I still think I'm dreaming, but I'm proud of you, I hope you know that.
Me too.
Though if this isn't a dream, I'm really going to miss some of my blissful ignorance.
Haha. Same.

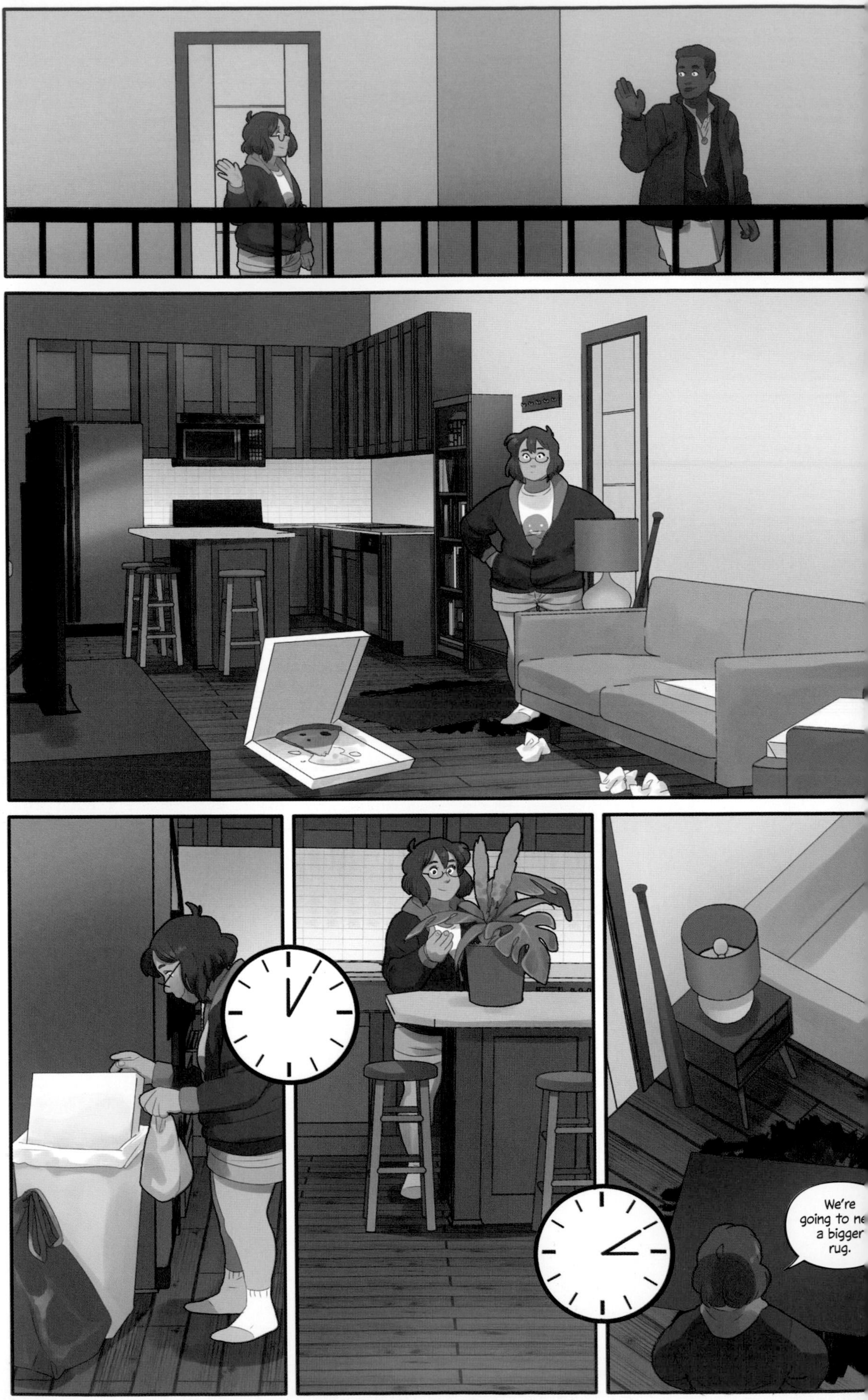
We're going to ne a bigger rug.

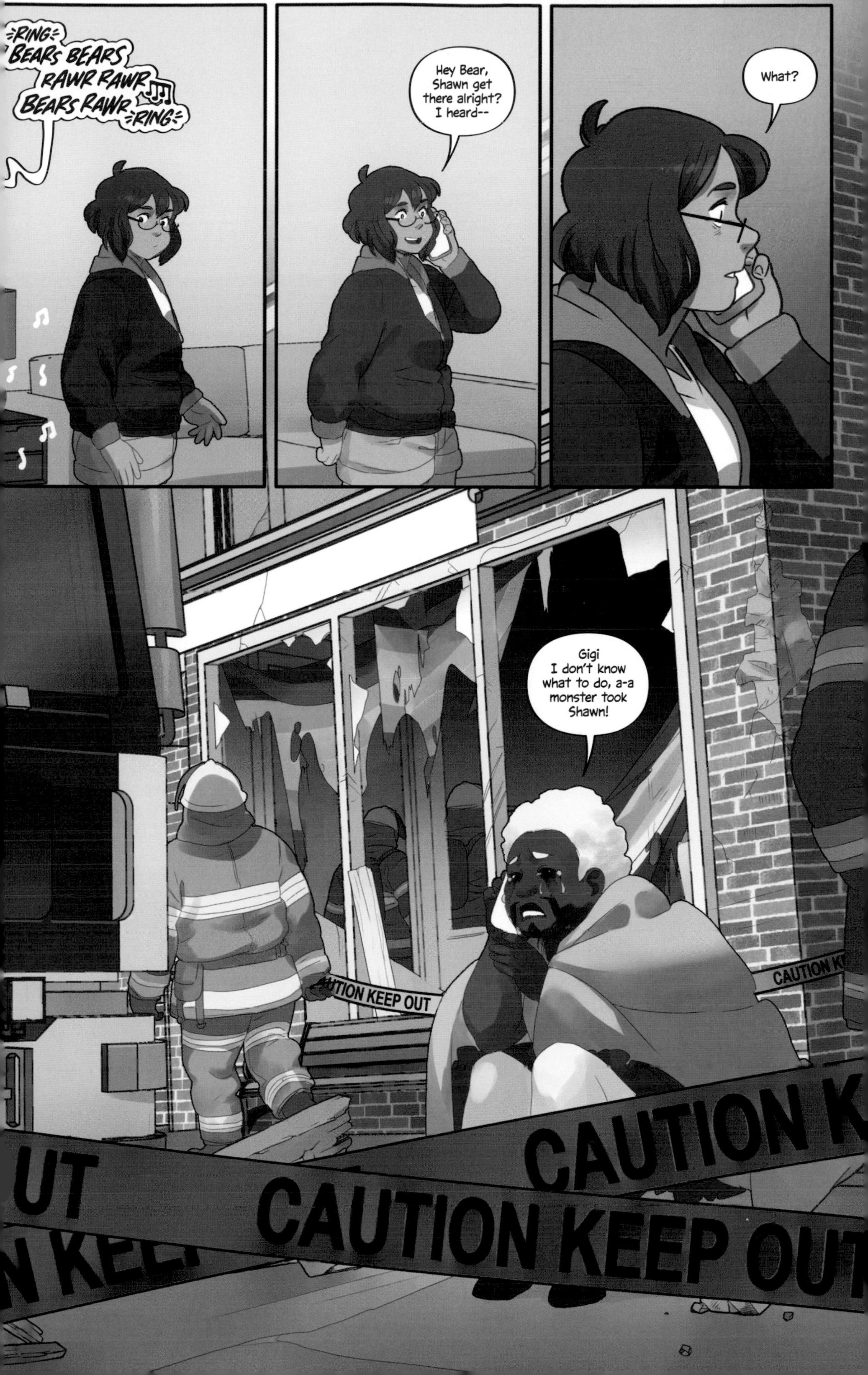
RING
BEARS BEARS
RAWR RAWR
BEARS RAWR
RING
Hey Bear, Shawn get there alright? I heard--
What?
Gigi I don't know what to do, a-a monster took Shawn!
CAUTION KEEP OUT
CAUTION K
UT
CAUTION K
CAUTION KEEP OUT
N KEE

SAVE YOURSELF! #2 MAIN COVER BY

KELLY & NICHOLE MATTHEWS

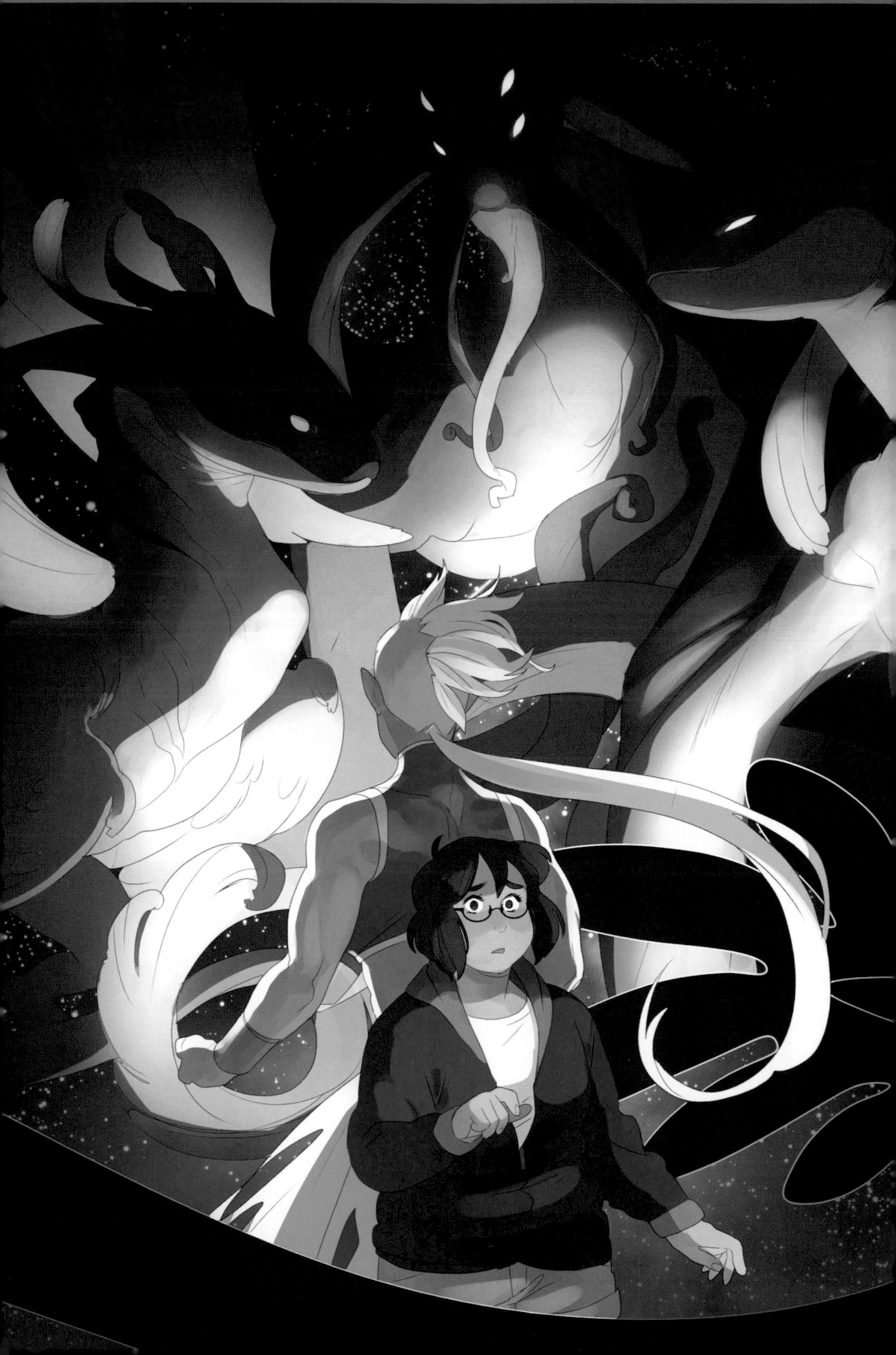

CHAPTER
THREE

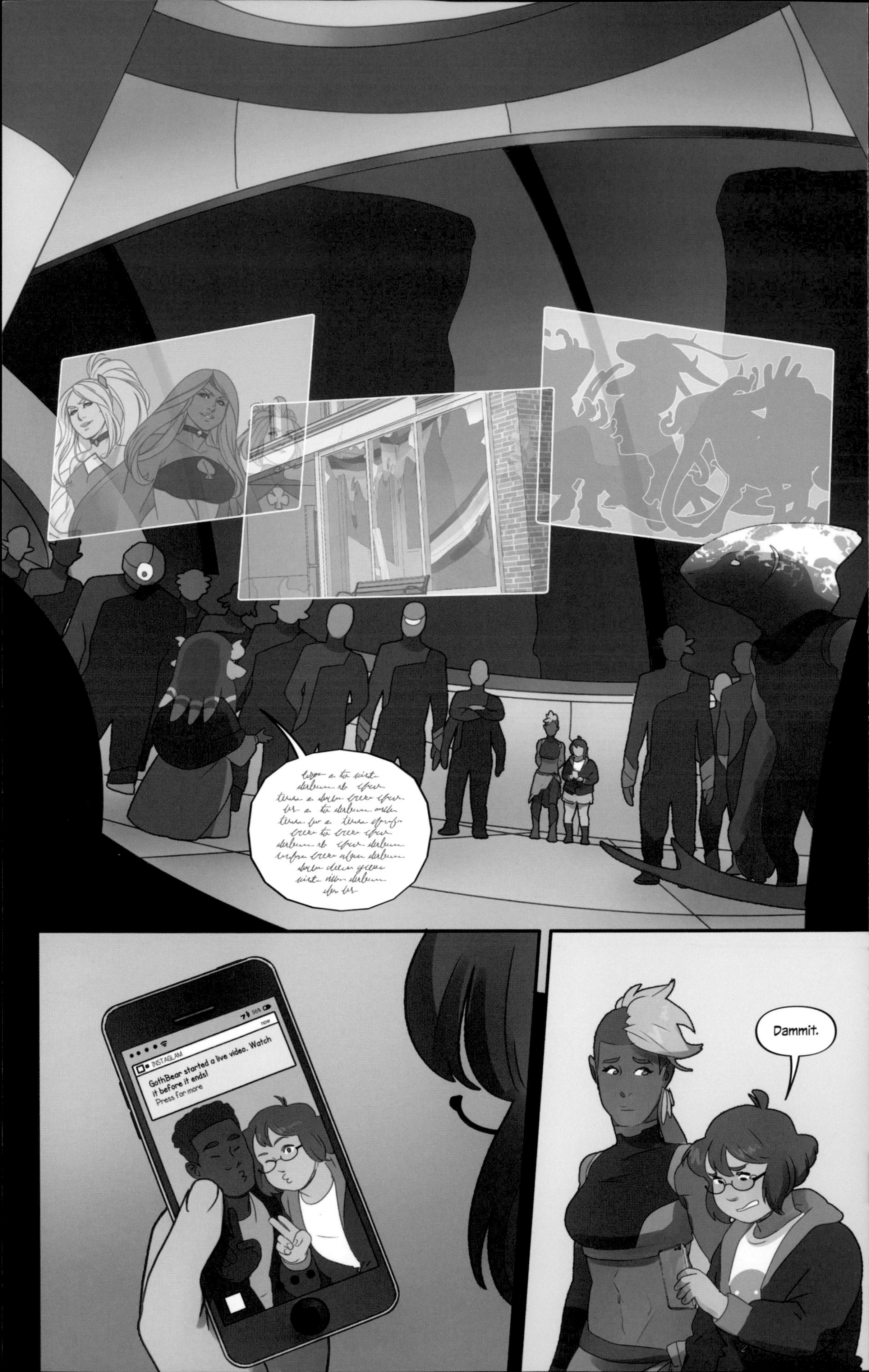
now
INSTAGLAM
GothBear started a live video. Watch it before it ends!
Press for more
Dammit.

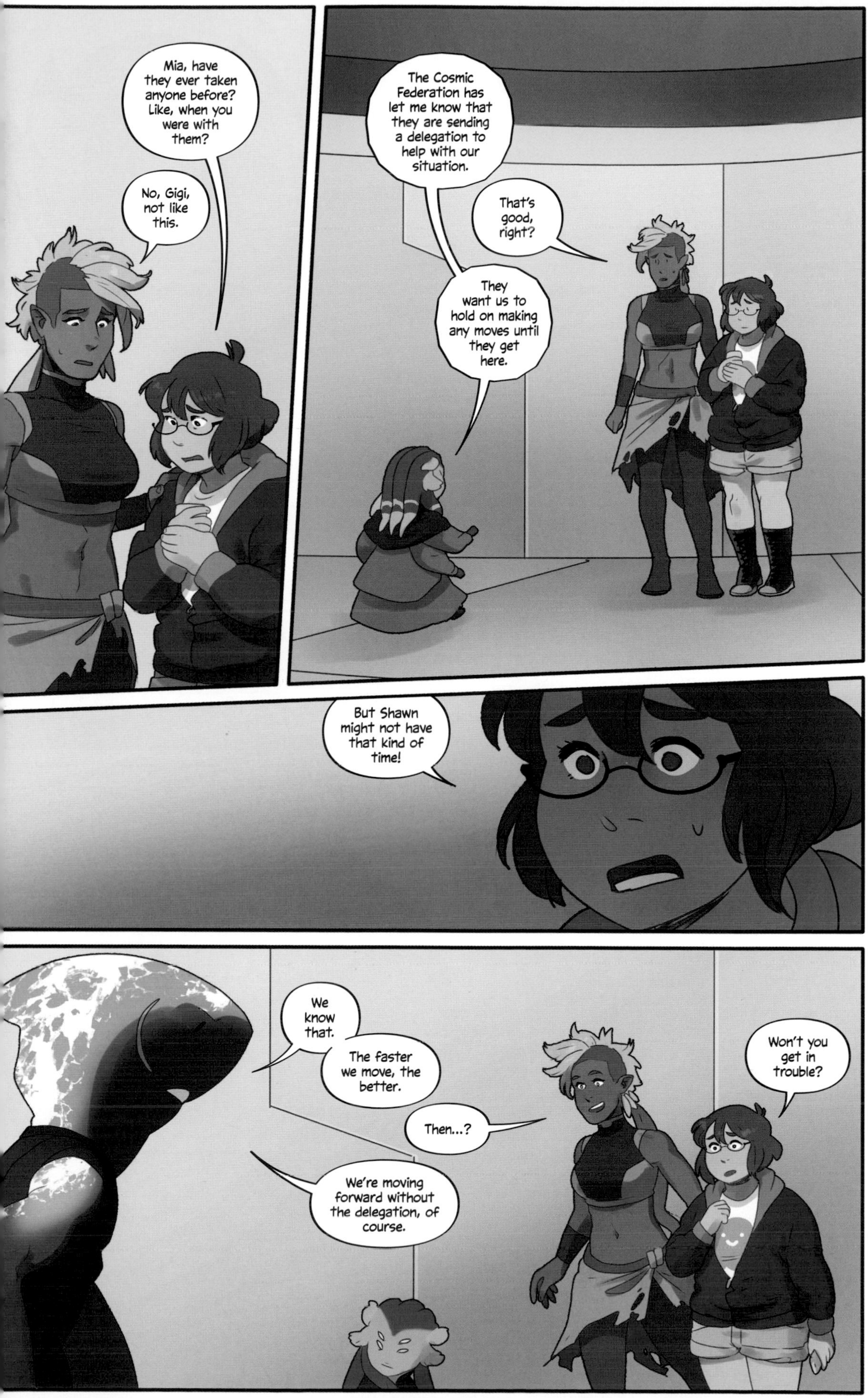
Mia, have they ever taken anyone before? Like, when you were with them?
No, Gigi, not like this.
The Cosmic Federation has let me know that they are sending a delegation to help with our situation.
That's good, right?
They want us to hold on making any moves until they get here.
But Shawn might not have that kind of time!
We know that.
The faster we move, the better.
Then...?
Won't you get in trouble?
We're moving forward without the delegation, of course.

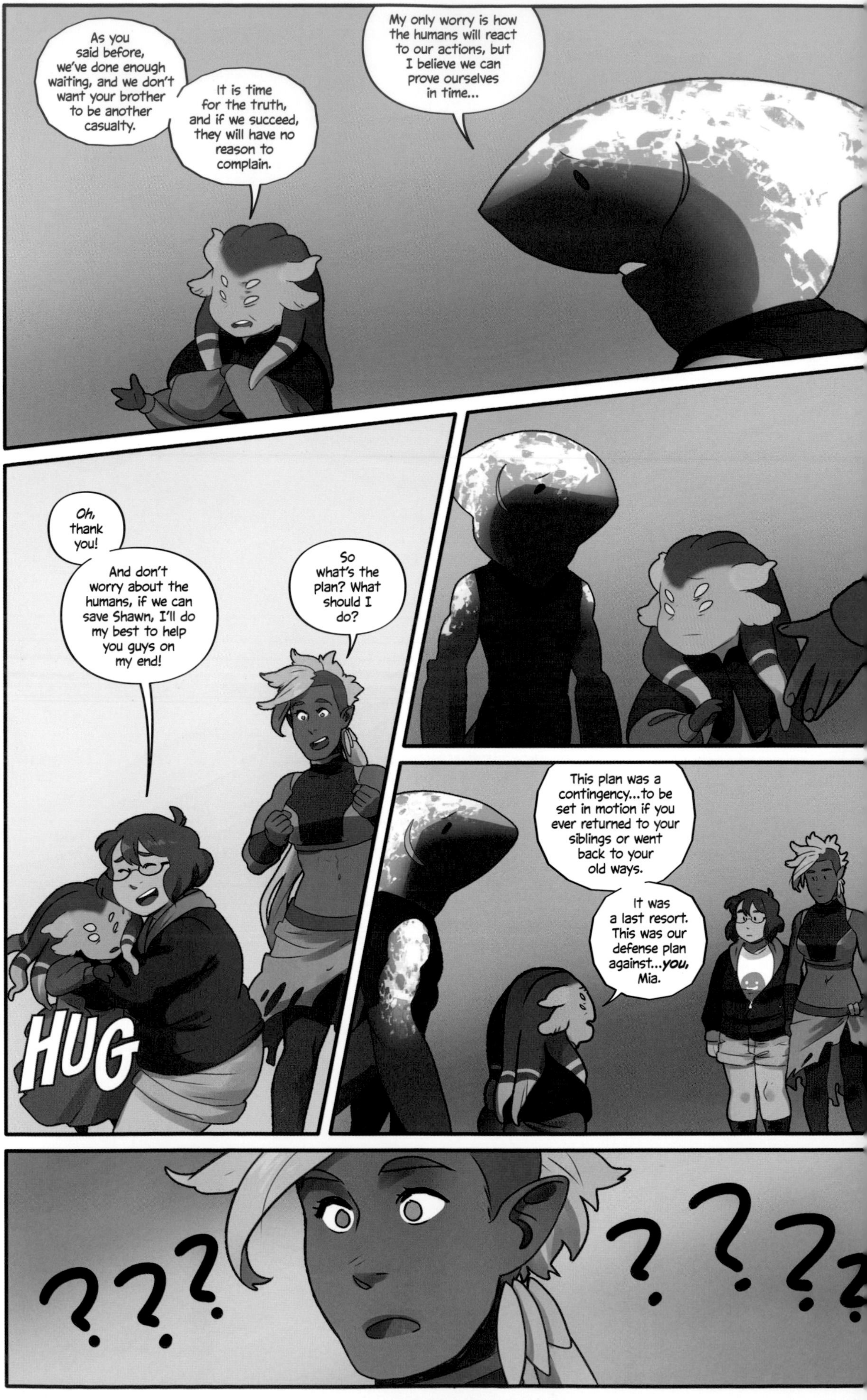
As you said before, we've done enough waiting, and we don't want your brother to be another casualty.
It is time for the truth, and if we succeed, they will have no reason to complain.
My only worry is how the humans will react to our actions, but I believe we can prove ourselves in time...
Oh, thank you!
And don't worry about the humans, if we can save Shawn, I'll do my best to help you guys on my end!
So what's the plan? What should I do?
HUG
This plan was a contingency...to be set in motion if you ever returned to your siblings or went back to your old ways.
It was a last resort. This was our defense plan against...*you,* Mia.
???
???

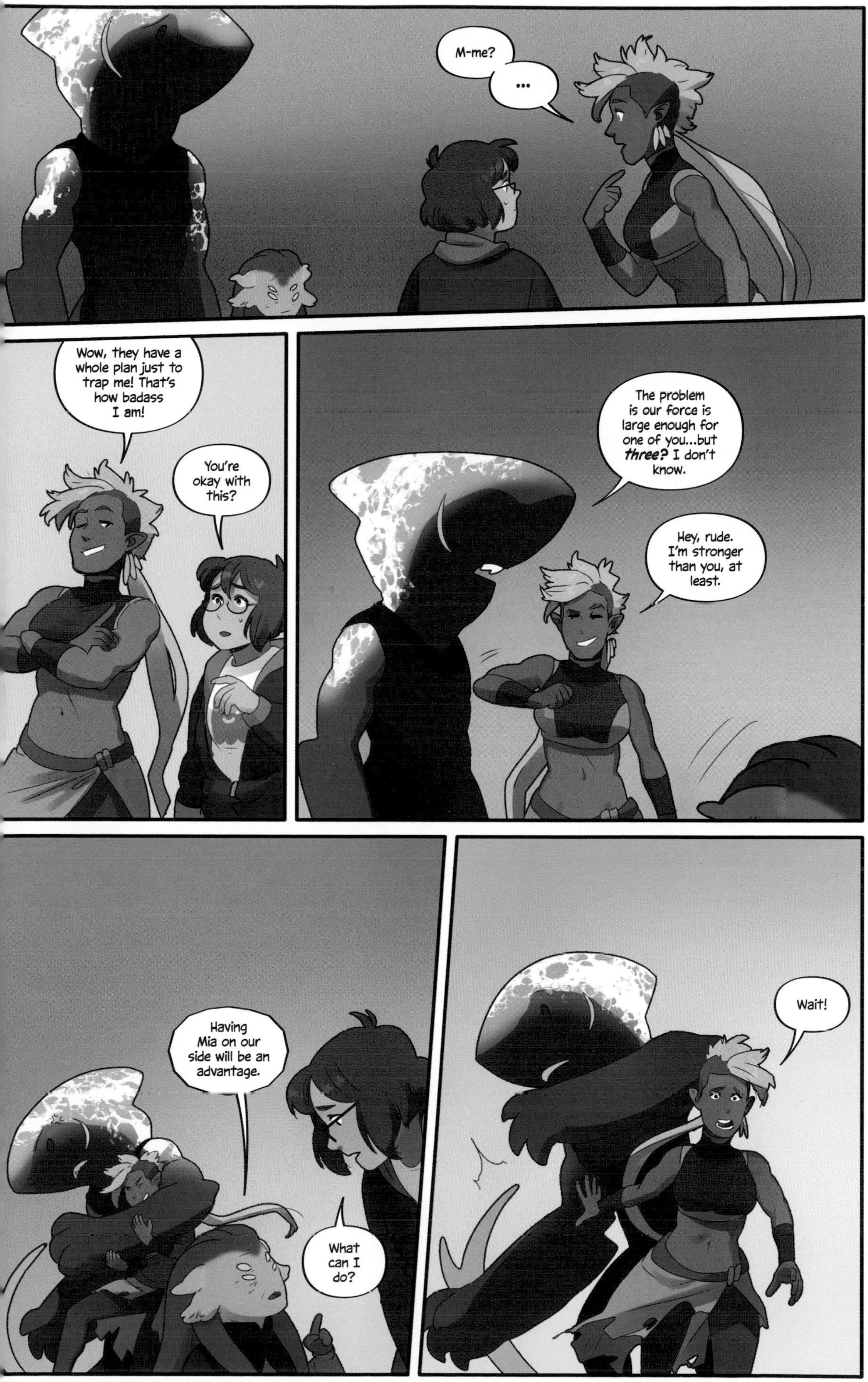
M-me?
...
Wow, they have a whole plan just to trap me! That's how badass I am!
You're okay with this?
The problem is our force is large enough for one of you...but *three?* I don't know.
Hey, rude. I'm stronger than you, at least.
Having Mia on our side will be an advantage.
What can I do?
Wait!

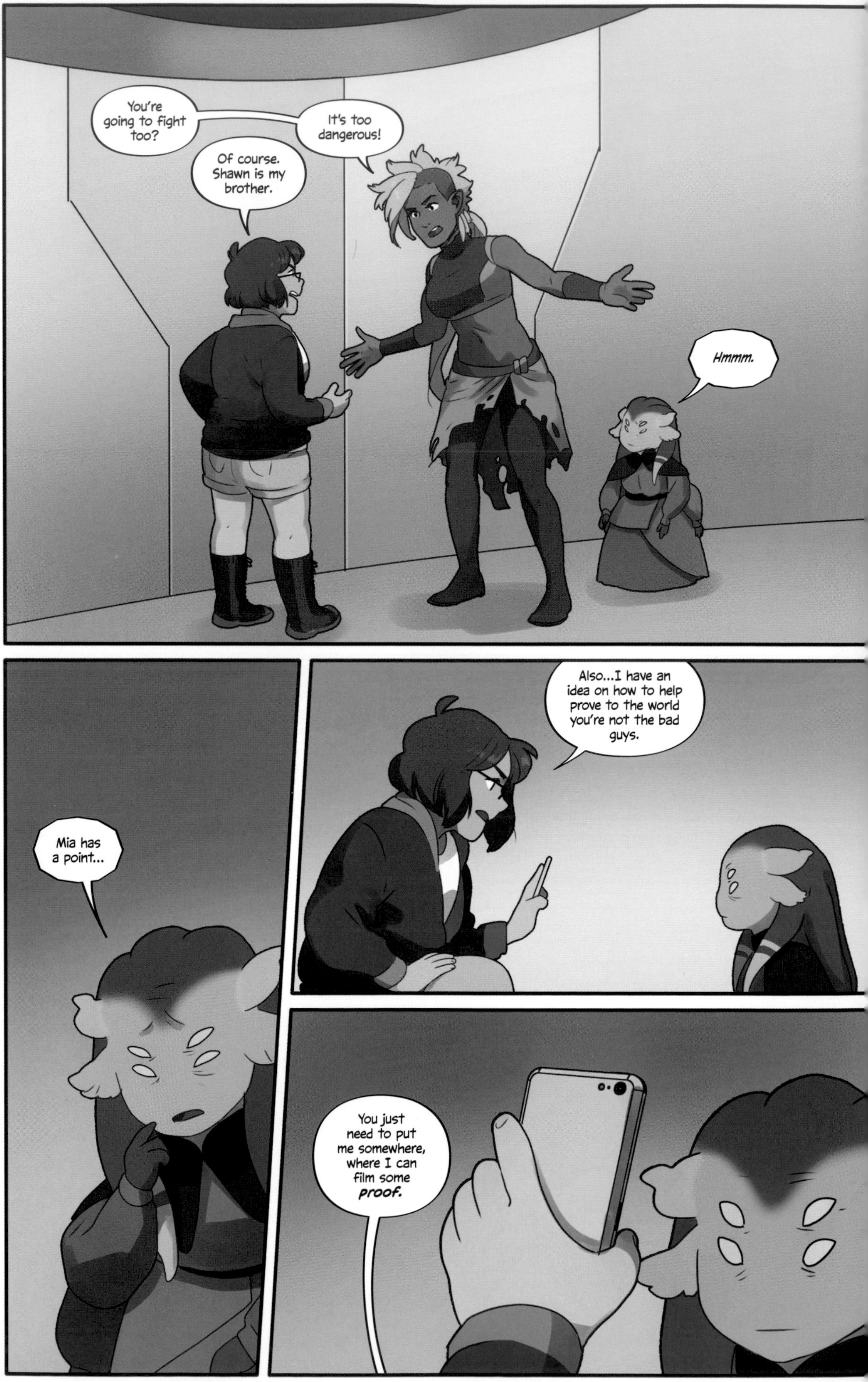
You're going to fight too?
It's too dangerous!
Of course. Shawn is my brother.
Hmmm.
Mia has a point...
Also...I have an idea on how to help prove to the world you're not the bad guys.
You just need to put me somewhere, where I can film some *proof.*

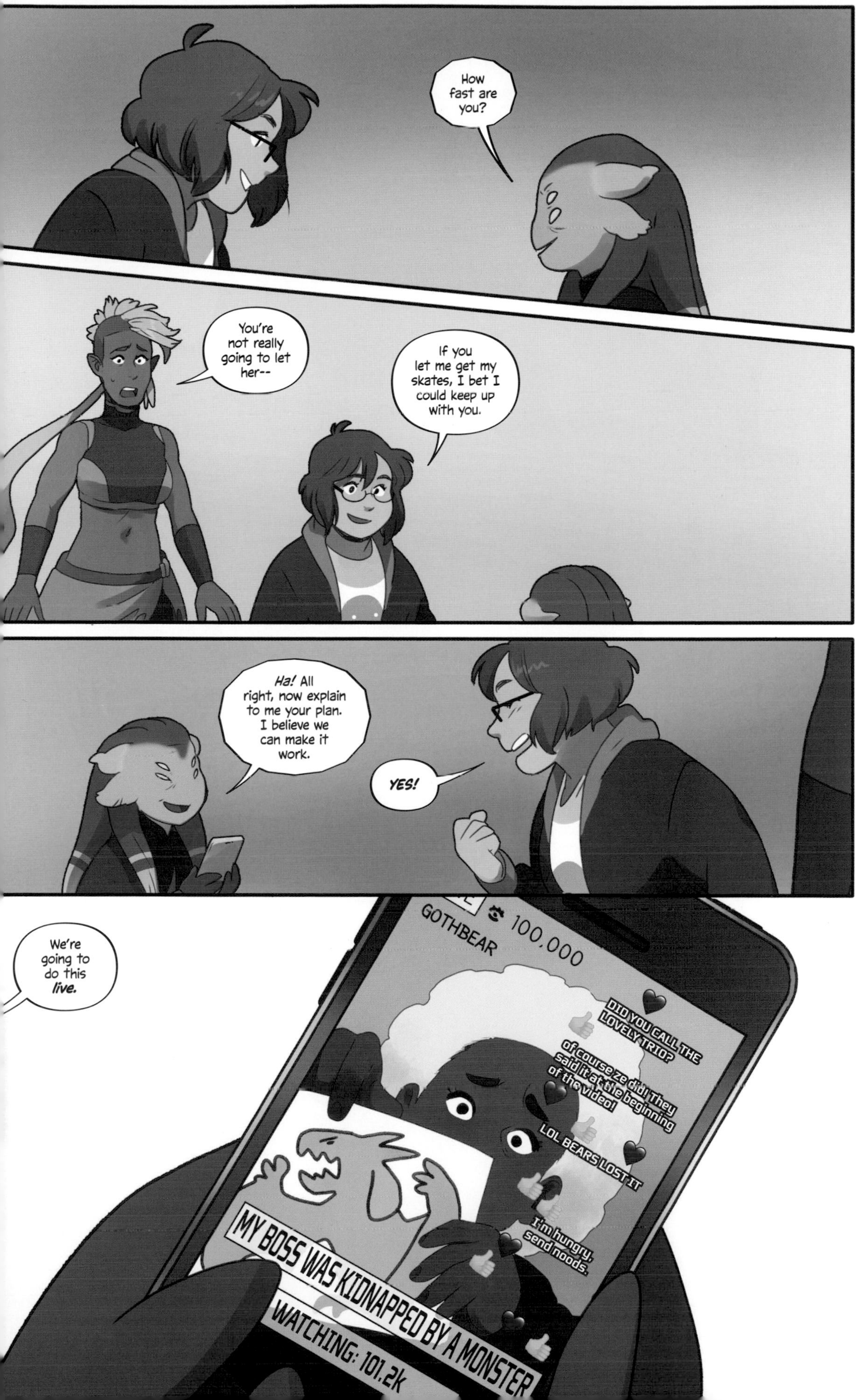
How fast are you?
You're not really going to let her--
If you let me get my skates, I bet I could keep up with you.
Ha! All right, now explain to me your plan. I believe we can make it work.
YES!
We're going to do this ***live.***
GOTHBEAR
100,000
DID YOU CALL THE LOVELY TRIO?
of course ze did! They said it at the beginning of the video!
LOL BEARS LOST IT
I'm hungry, send noods.
MY BOSS WAS KIDNAPPED BY A MONSTER
WATCHING: 101.2k

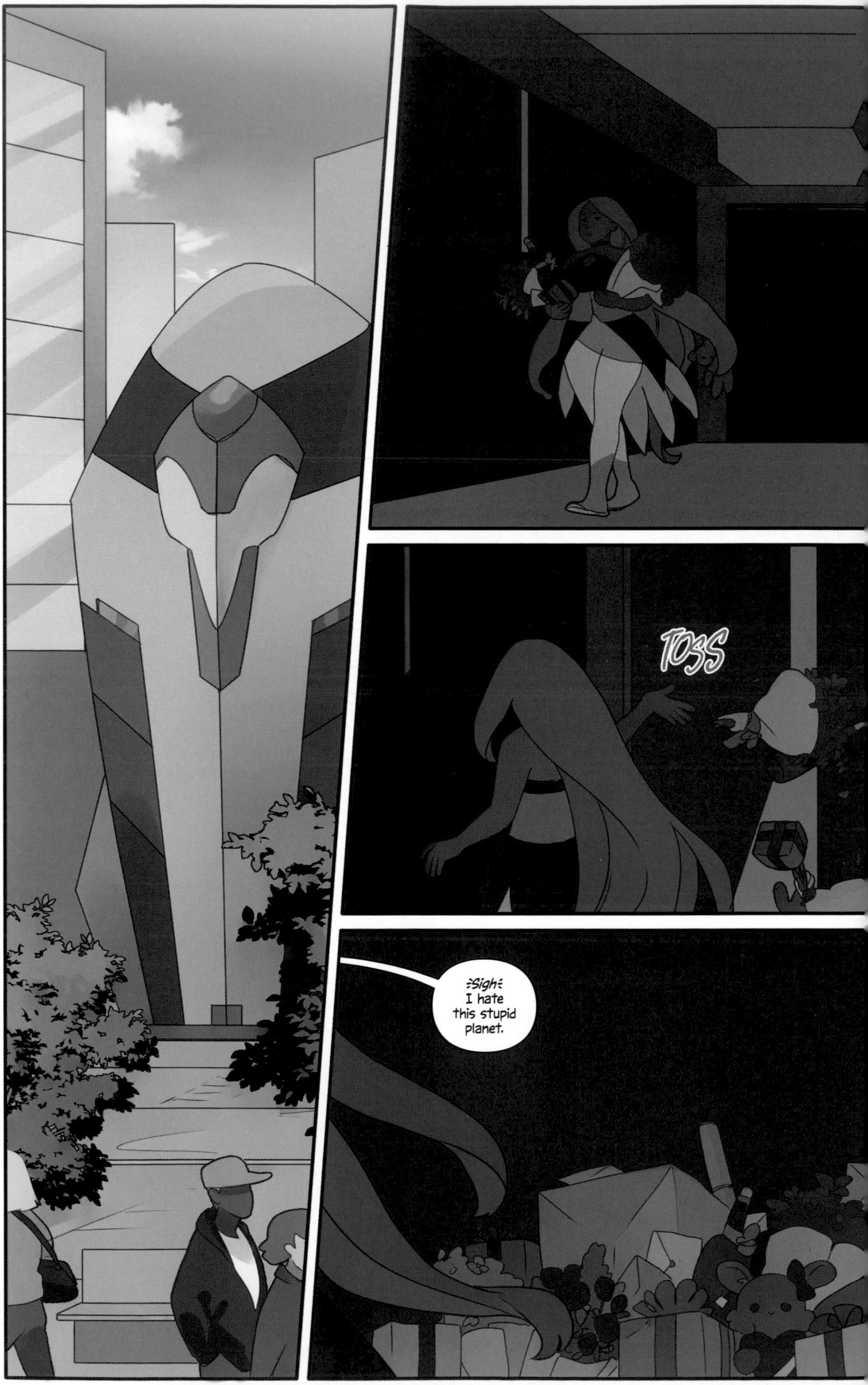
TOSS
≈Sigh≈ I hate this stupid planet.

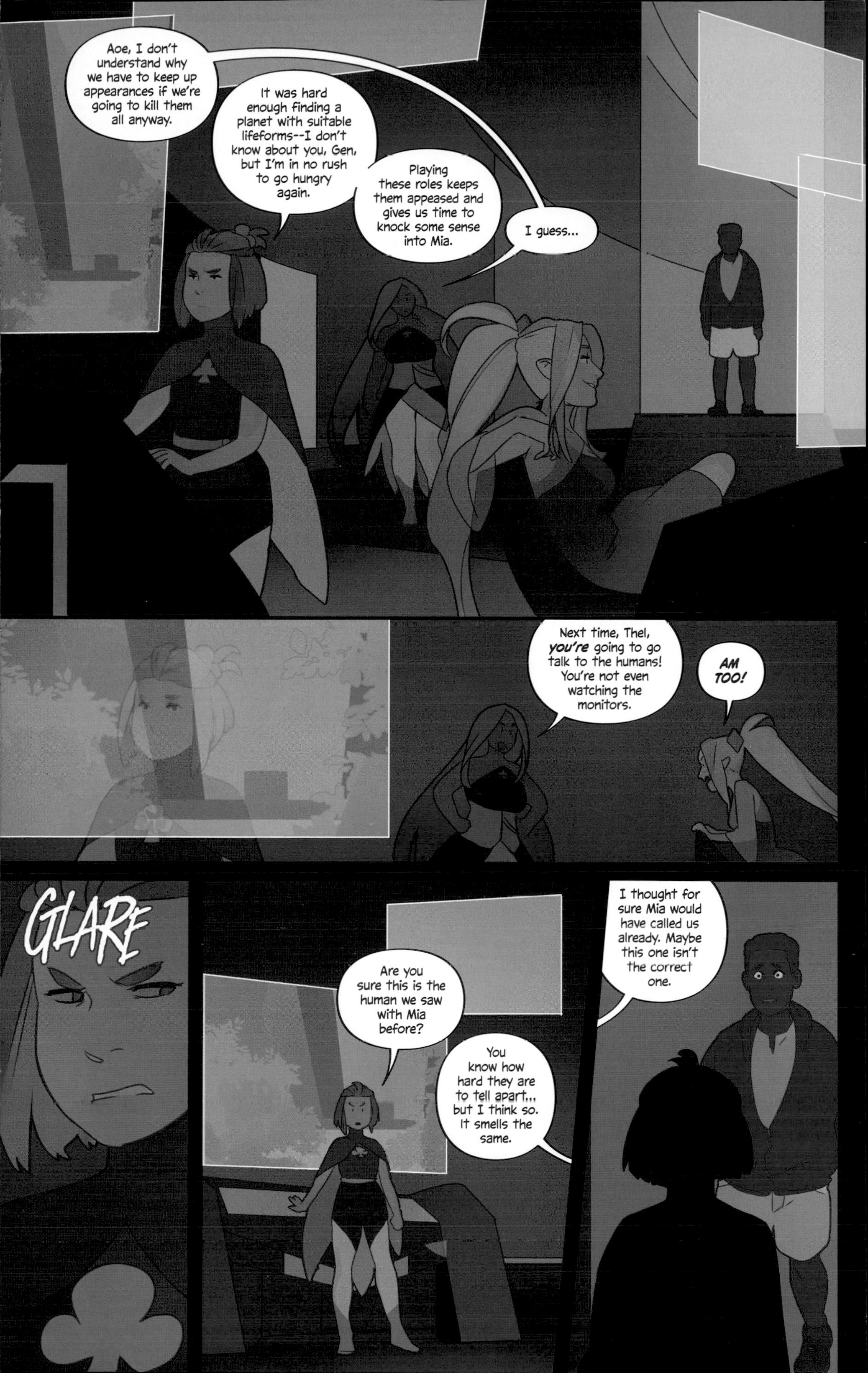
Aoe, I don't understand why we have to keep up appearances if we're going to kill them all anyway.
It was hard enough finding a planet with suitable lifeforms--I don't know about you, Gen, but I'm in no rush to go hungry again.
Playing these roles keeps them appeased and gives us time to knock some sense into Mia.
I guess...
Next time, Thel, *you're* going to go talk to the humans! You're not even watching the monitors.
AM TOO!
GLARE
Are you sure this is the human we saw with Mia before?
You know how hard they are to tell apart... but I think so. It smells the same.
I thought for sure Mia would have called us already. Maybe this one isn't the correct one.

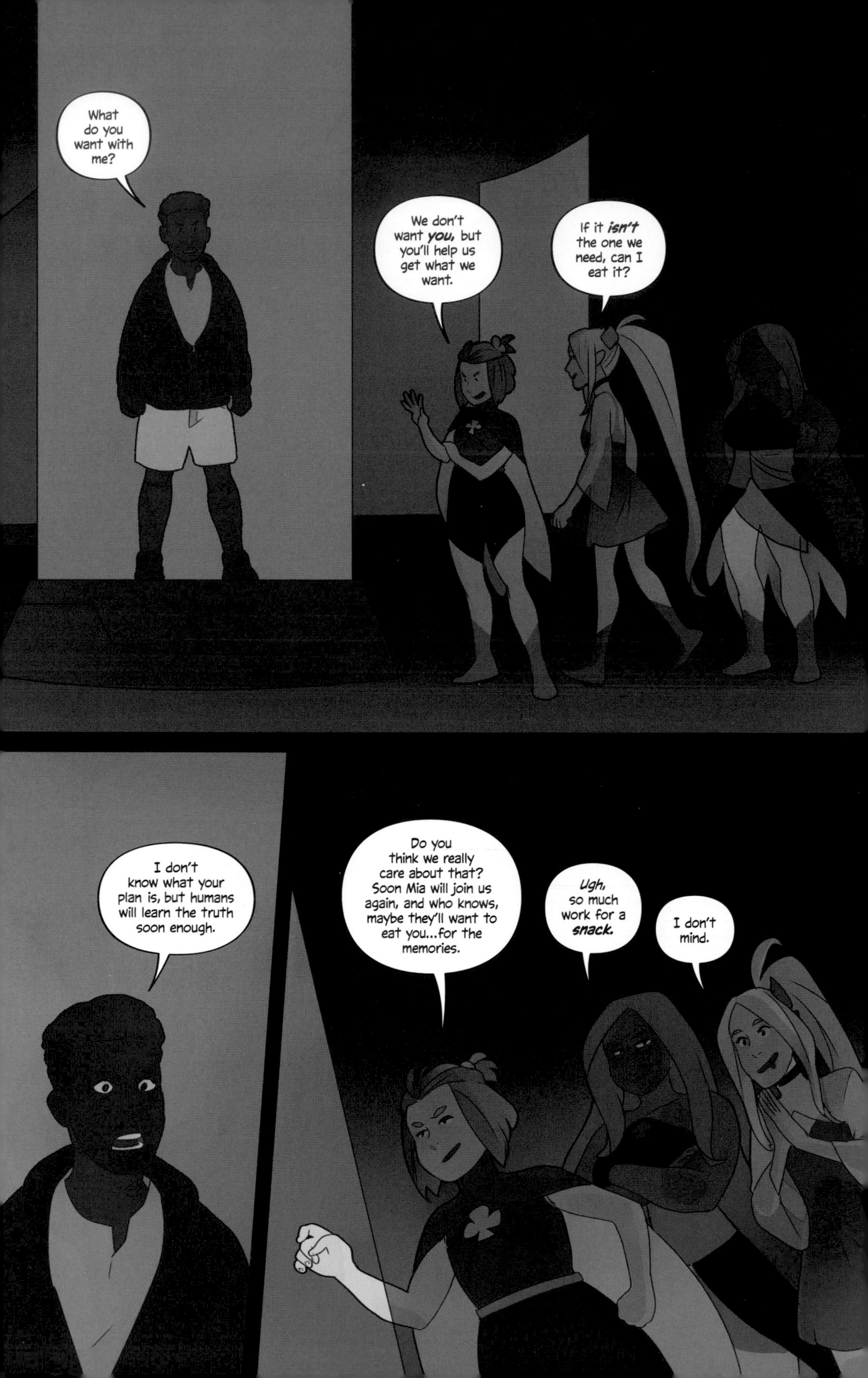
What do you want with me?
We don't want ***you,*** but you'll help us get what we want.
If it ***isn't*** the one we need, can I eat it?
I don't know what your plan is, but humans will learn the truth soon enough.
Do you think we really care about that? Soon Mia will join us again, and who knows, maybe they'll want to eat you...for the memories.
Ugh, so much work for a ***snack.***
I don't mind.

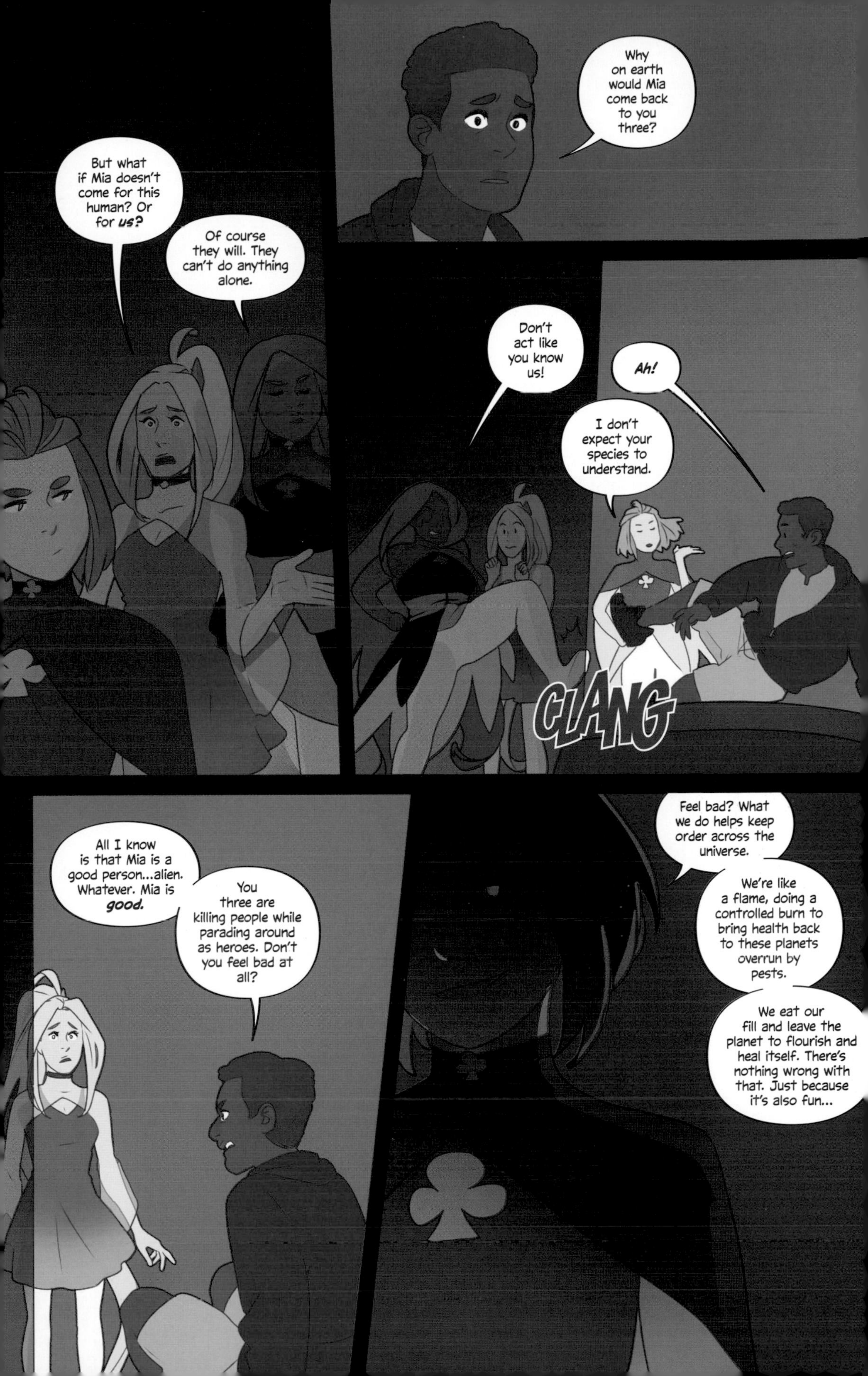
Why on earth would Mia come back to you three?
But what if Mia doesn't come for this human? Or for *us?*
Of course they will. They can't do anything alone.
Don't act like you know us!
Ah!
I don't expect your species to understand.
CLANG
All I know is that Mia is a good person...alien. Whatever. Mia is ***good.***
You three are killing people while parading around as heroes. Don't you feel bad at all?
Feel bad? What we do helps keep order across the universe.
We're like a flame, doing a controlled burn to bring health back to these planets overrun by pests.
We eat our fill and leave the planet to flourish and heal itself. There's nothing wrong with that. Just because it's also fun...

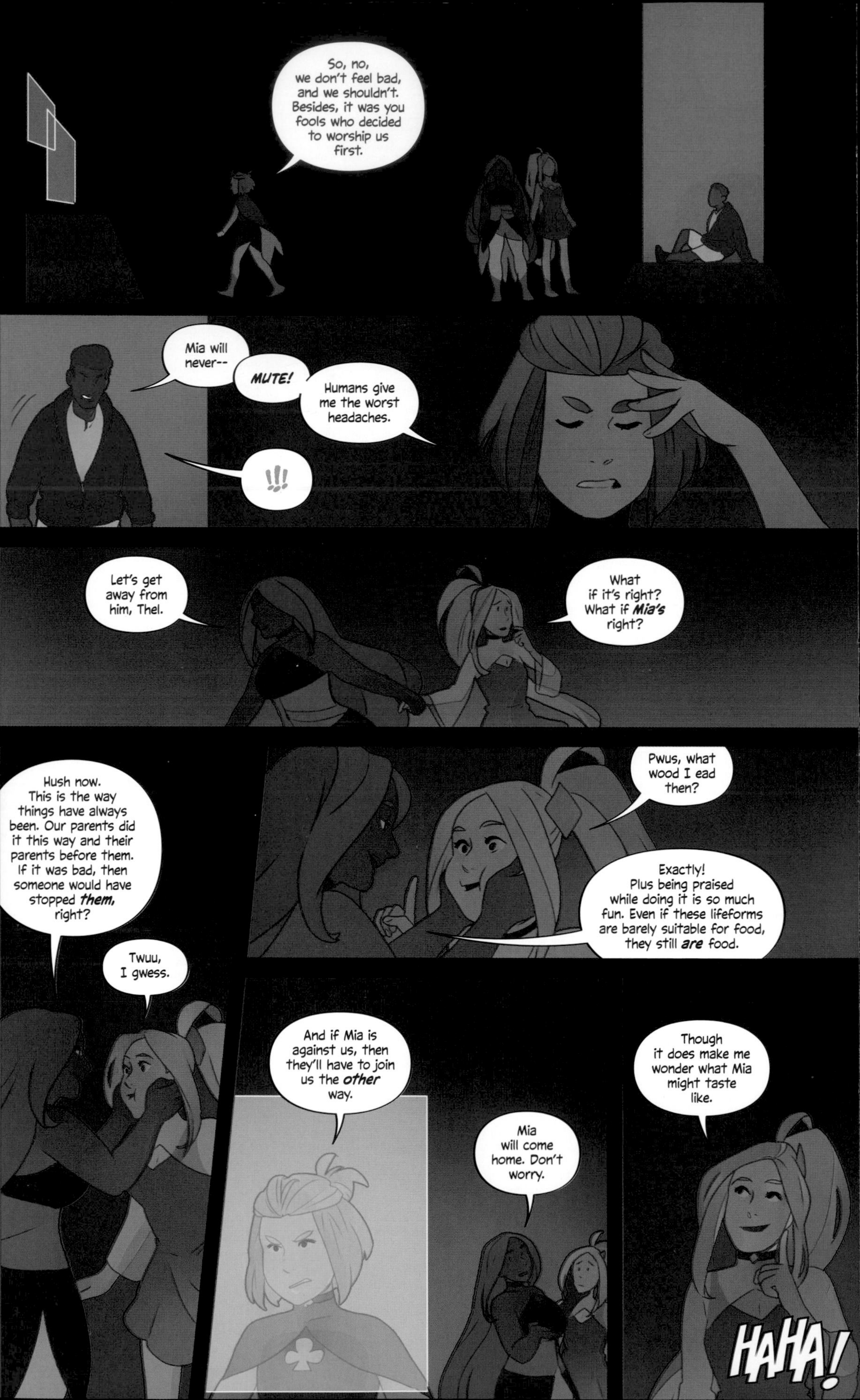
So, no, we don't feel bad, and we shouldn't. Besides, it was you fools who decided to worship us first.
Mia will never--
MUTE!
Humans give me the worst headaches.
!!!
Let's get away from him, Thel.
What if it's right? What if Mia's right?
Hush now. This is the way things have always been. Our parents did it this way and their parents before them. If it was bad, then someone would have stopped them, right?
Pwus, what wood I ead then?
Exactly! Plus being praised while doing it is so much fun. Even if these lifeforms are barely suitable for food, they still are food.
Twuu, I gwess.
And if Mia is against us, then they'll have to join us the other way.
Mia will come home. Don't worry.
Though it does make me wonder what Mia might taste like.
HAHA!

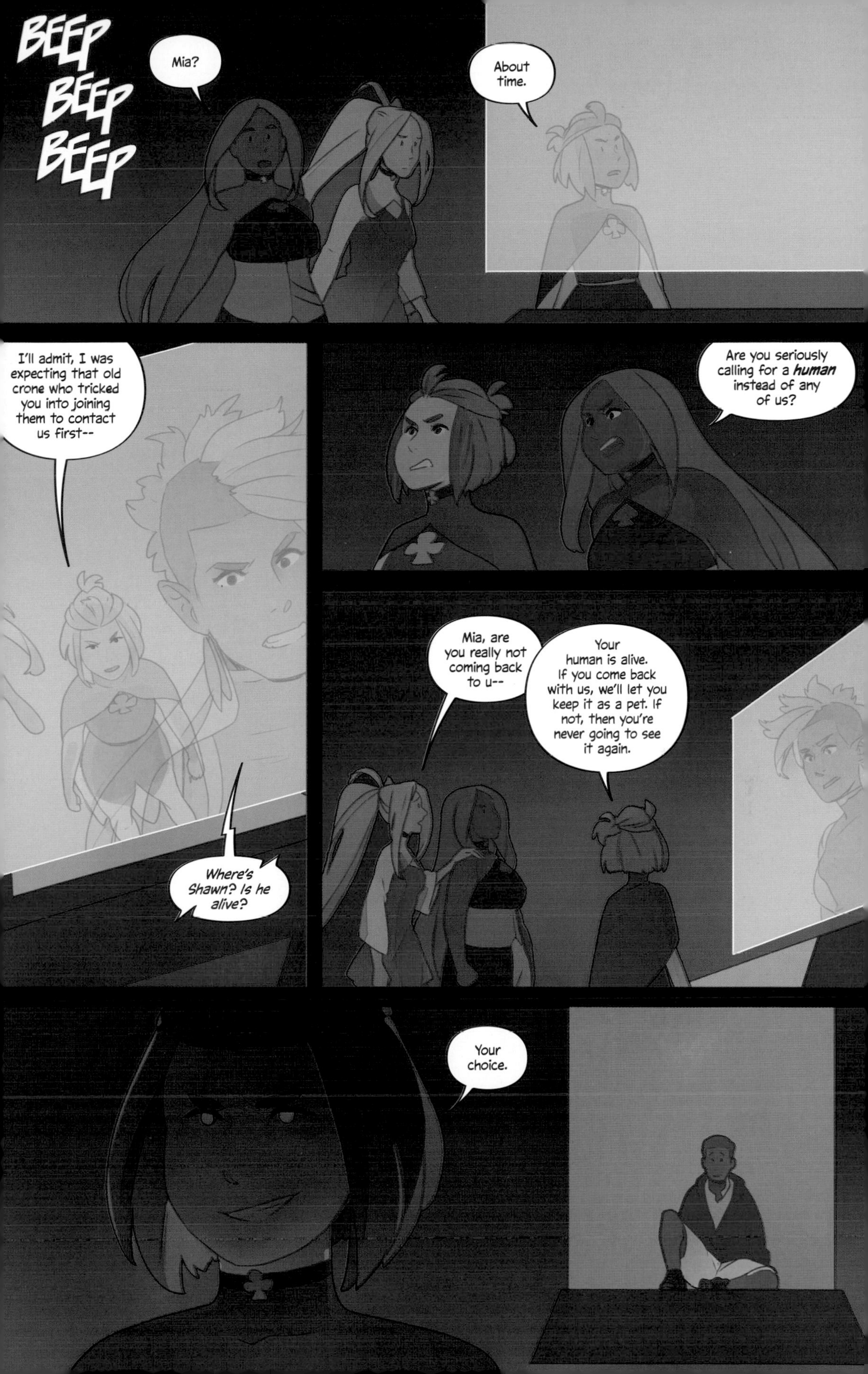
BEEP BEEP BEEP
Mia?
About time.
I'll admit, I was expecting that old crone who tricked you into joining them to contact us first--
Are you seriously calling for a *human* instead of any of us?
Where's Shawn? Is he alive?
Mia, are you really not coming back to u--
Your human is alive. If you come back with us, we'll let you keep it as a pet. If not, then you're never going to see it again.
Your choice.

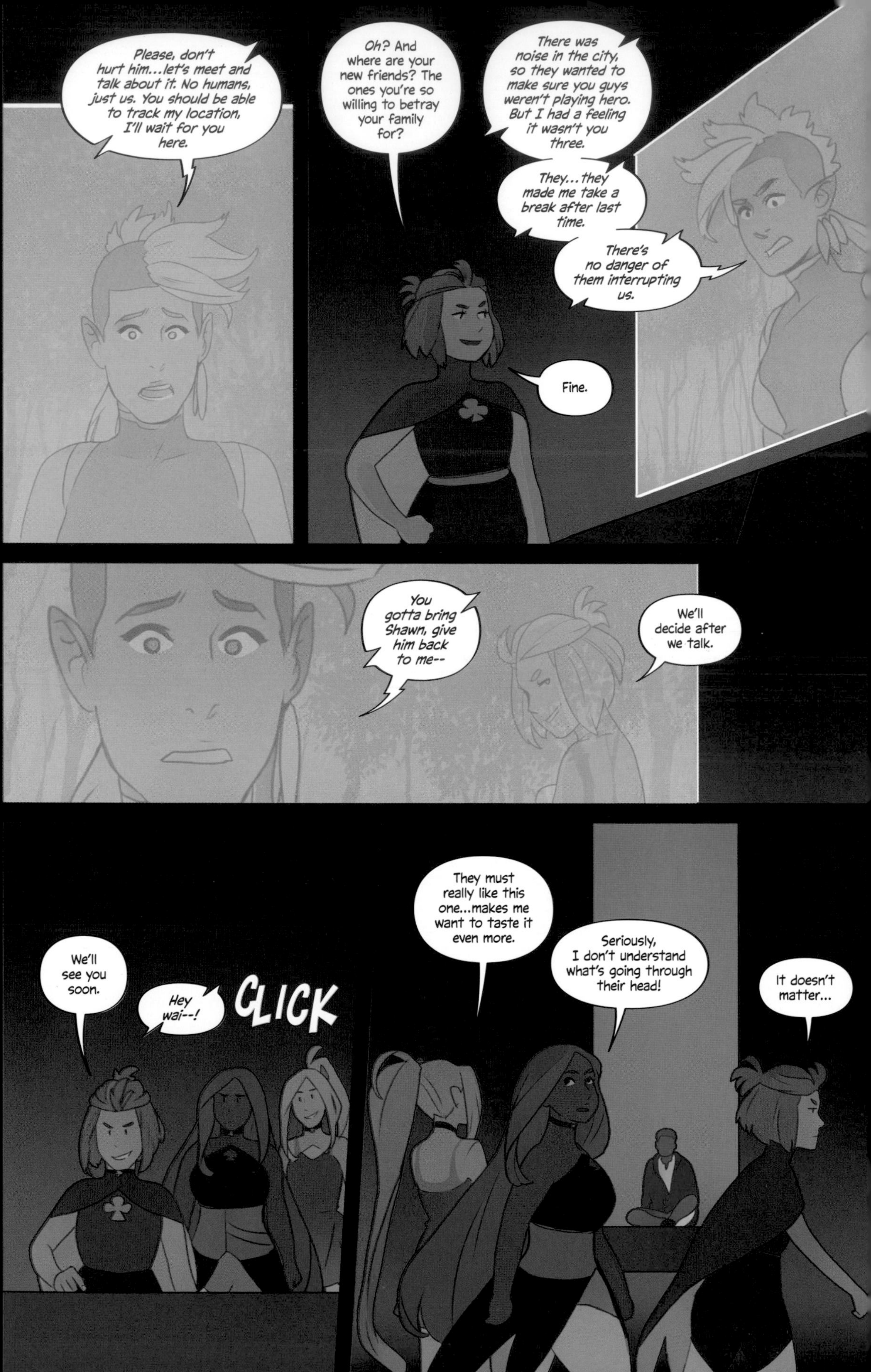
Please, don't hurt him...let's meet and talk about it. No humans, just us. You should be able to track my location, I'll wait for you here.
Oh? And where are your new friends? The ones you're so willing to betray your family for?
There was noise in the city, so they wanted to make sure you guys weren't playing hero. But I had a feeling it wasn't you three.
They...they made me take a break after last time.
There's no danger of them interrupting us.
Fine.
You gotta bring Shawn, give him back to me--
We'll decide after we talk.
We'll see you soon.
Hey wai--!
CLICK
They must really like this one...makes me want to taste it even more.
Seriously, I don't understand what's going through their head!
It doesn't matter...

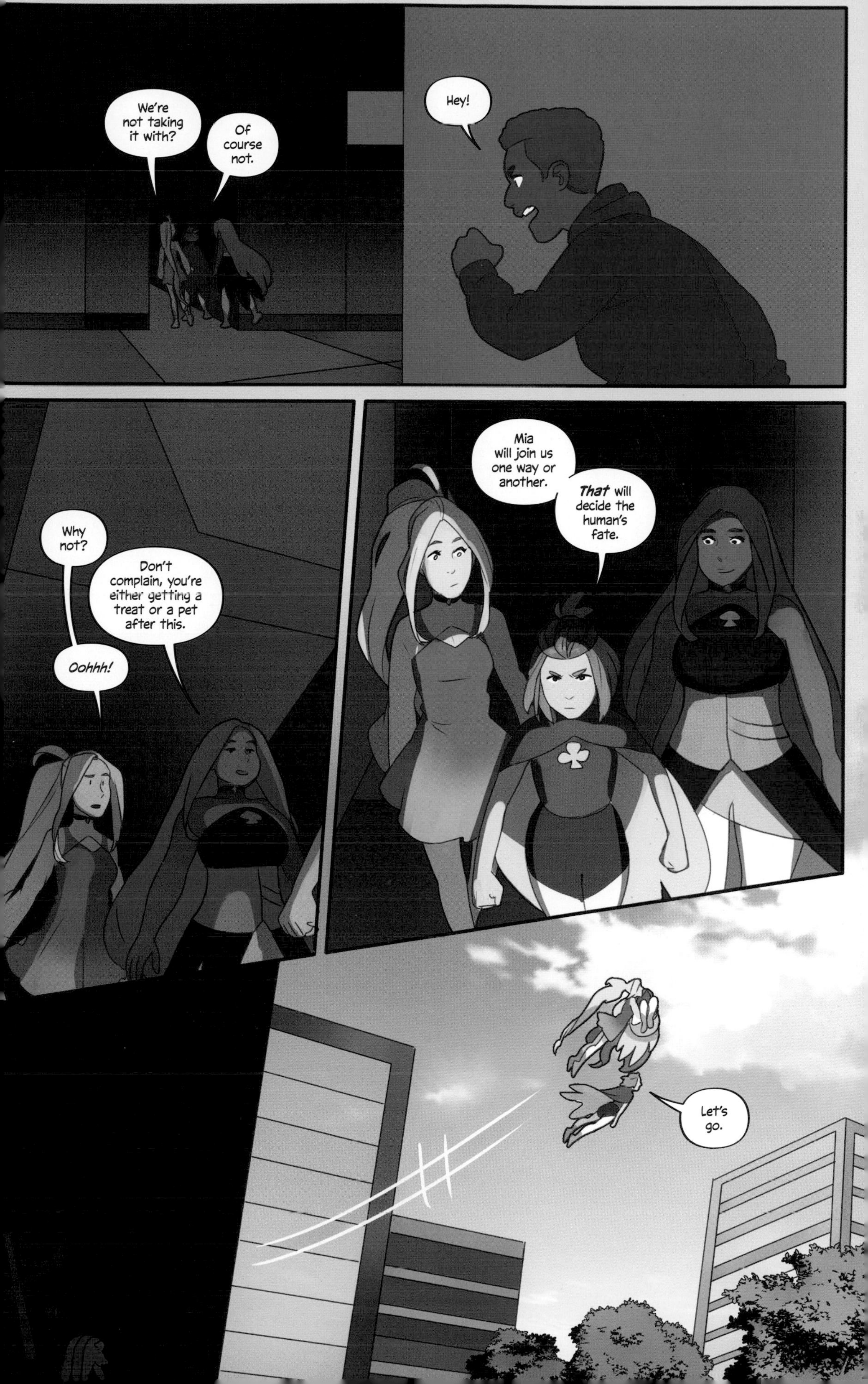
We're not taking it with?
Of course not.
Hey!
Why not?
Don't complain, you're either getting a treat or a pet after this.
Oohhh!
Mia will join us one way or another.
That will decide the human's fate.
Let's go.

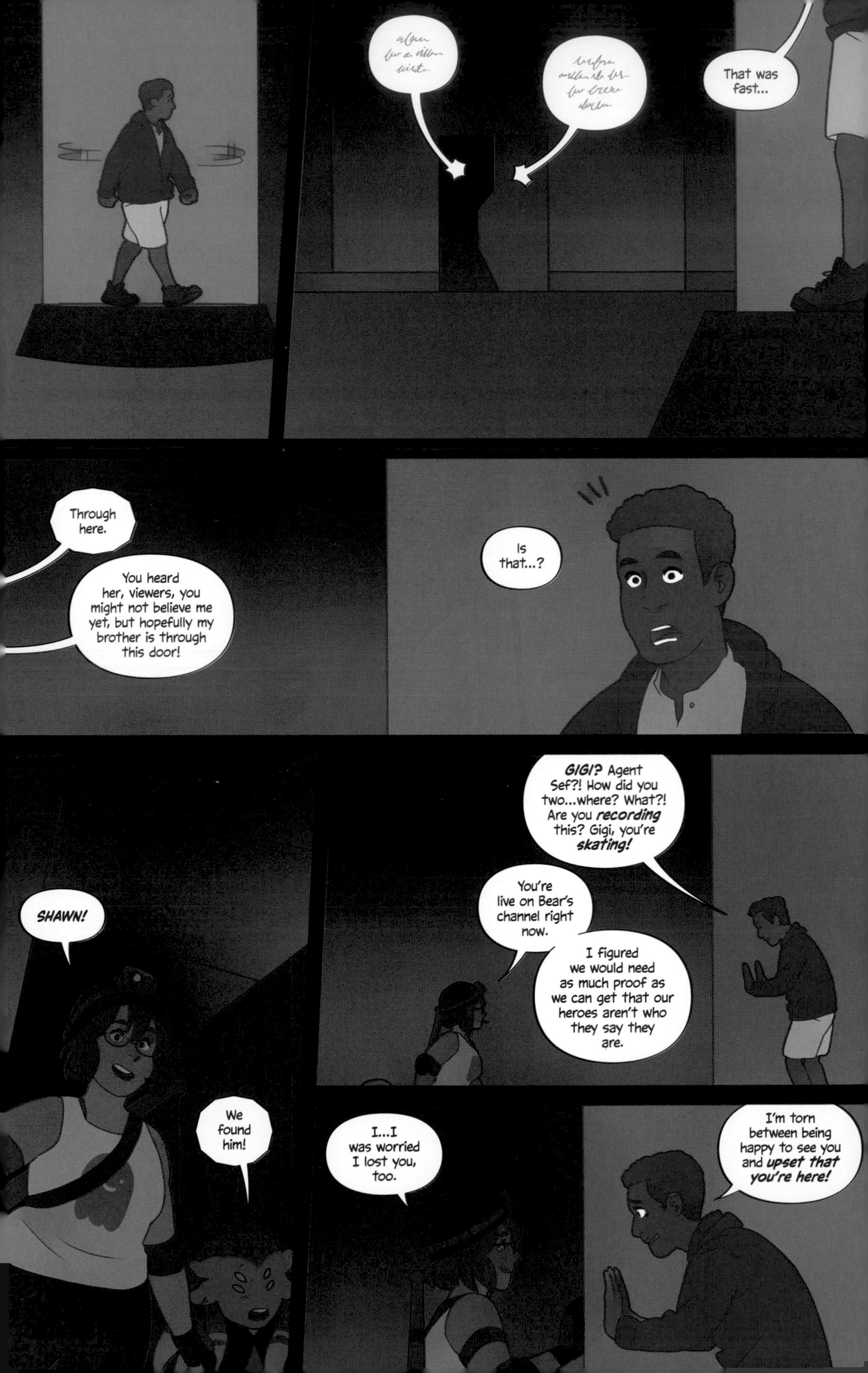
That was fast...
Through here.
You heard her, viewers, you might not believe me yet, but hopefully my brother is through this door!
Is that...?
SHAWN!
GIGI? Agent Sef?! How did you two...where? What?! Are you recording this? Gigi, you're skating!
You're live on Bear's channel right now.
I figured we would need as much proof as we can get that our heroes aren't who they say they are.
We found him!
I...I was worried I lost you, too.
I'm torn between being happy to see you and upset that you're here!

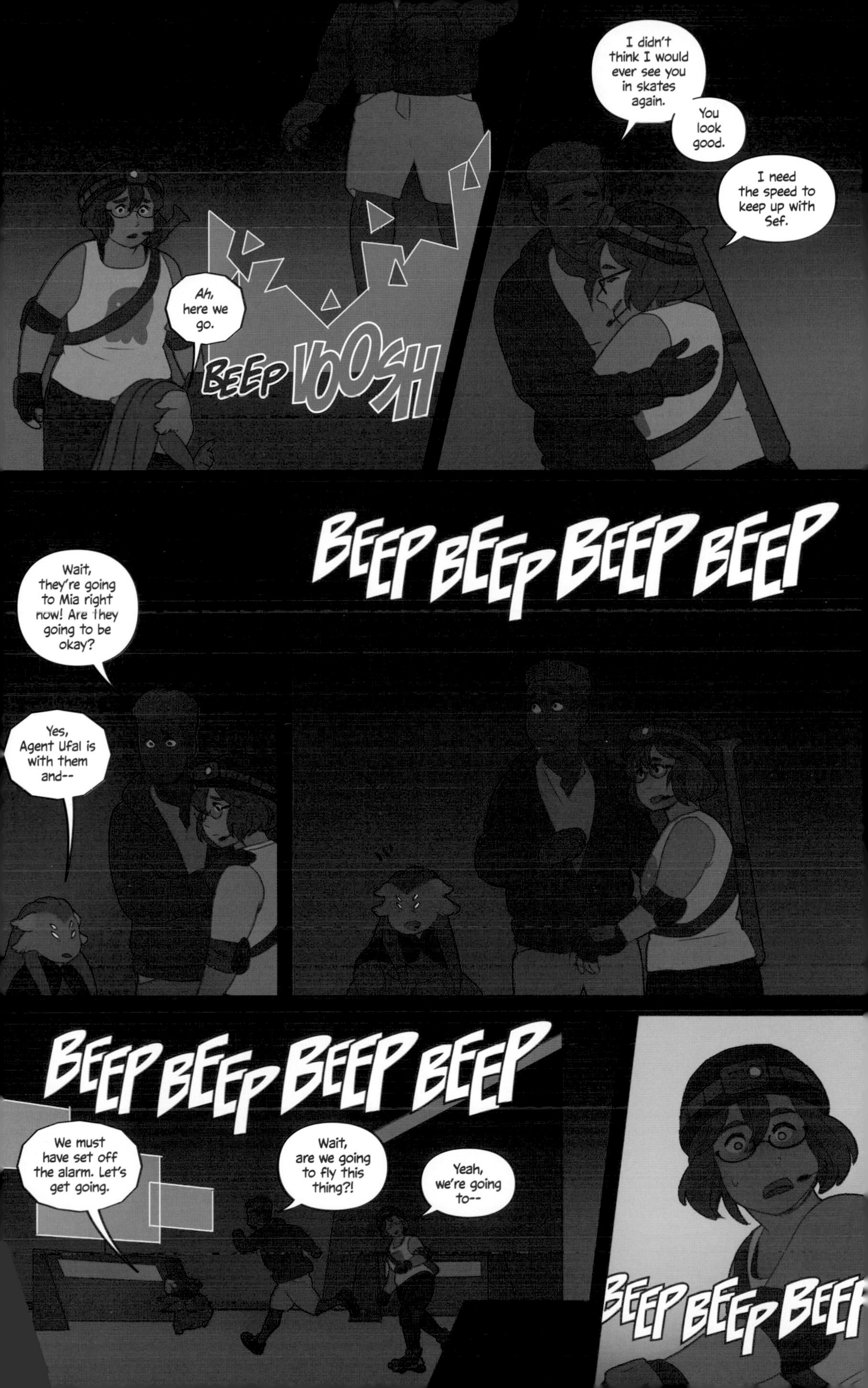
Ah, here we go.
BEEP VOOSH
I didn't think I would ever see you in skates again.
You look good.
I need the speed to keep up with Sef.
BEEP BEEP BEEP BEEP
Wait, they're going to Mia right now! Are they going to be okay?
Yes, Agent Ufal is with them and--
BEEP BEEP BEEP BEEP
We must have set off the alarm. Let's get going.
Wait, are we going to fly this thing?!
Yeah, we're going to--
BEEP BEEP BEEP

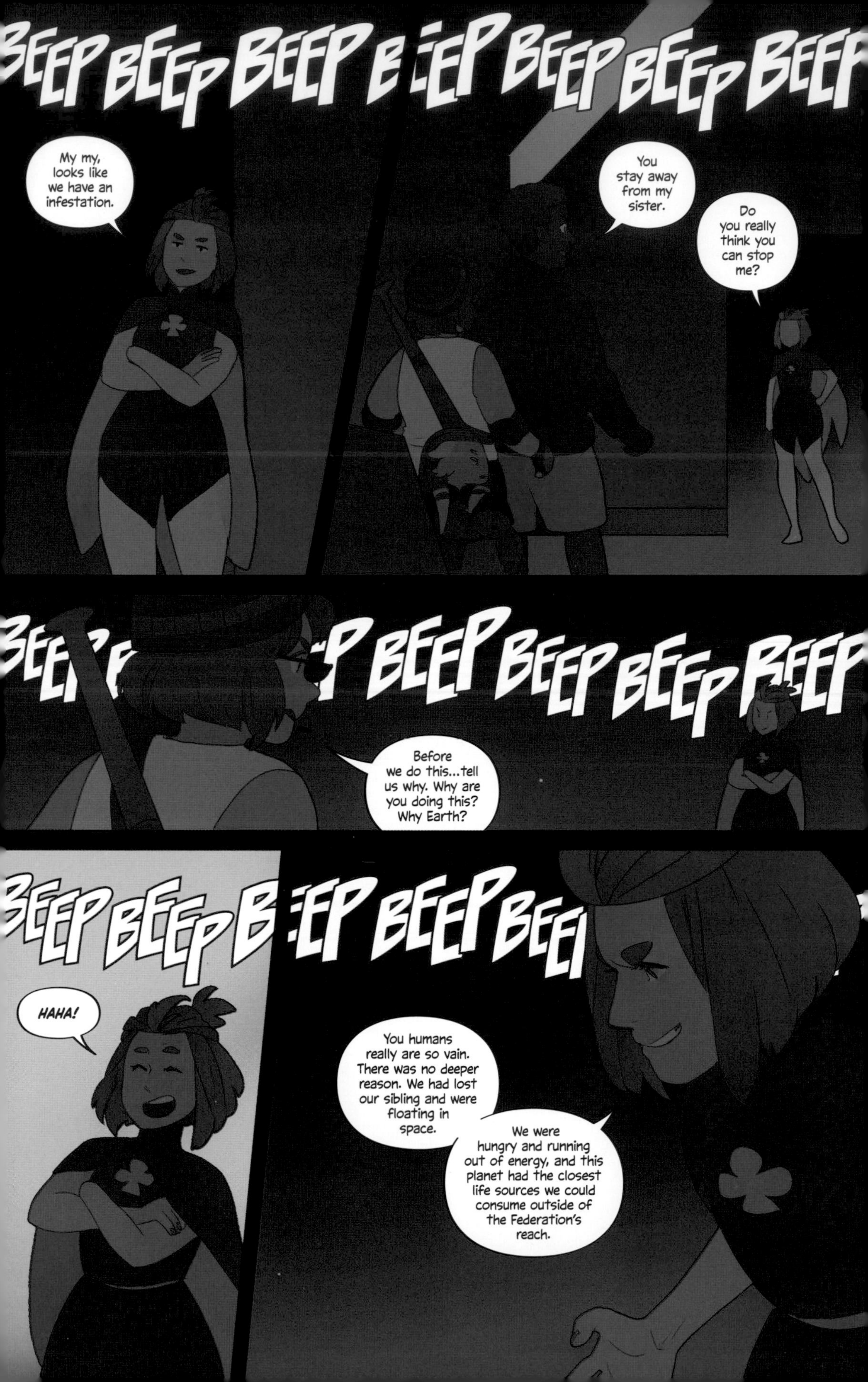
BEEP BEEP BEEP BEEP BEEP BEEP BEEP
My my, looks like we have an infestation.
You stay away from my sister.
Do you really think you can stop me?
BEEP BEEP BEEP BEEP
Before we do this...tell us why. Why are you doing this? Why Earth?
BEEP BEEP BEEP
HAHA!
You humans really are so vain. There was no deeper reason. We had lost our sibling and were floating in space.
We were hungry and running out of energy, and this planet had the closest life sources we could consume outside of the Federation's reach.

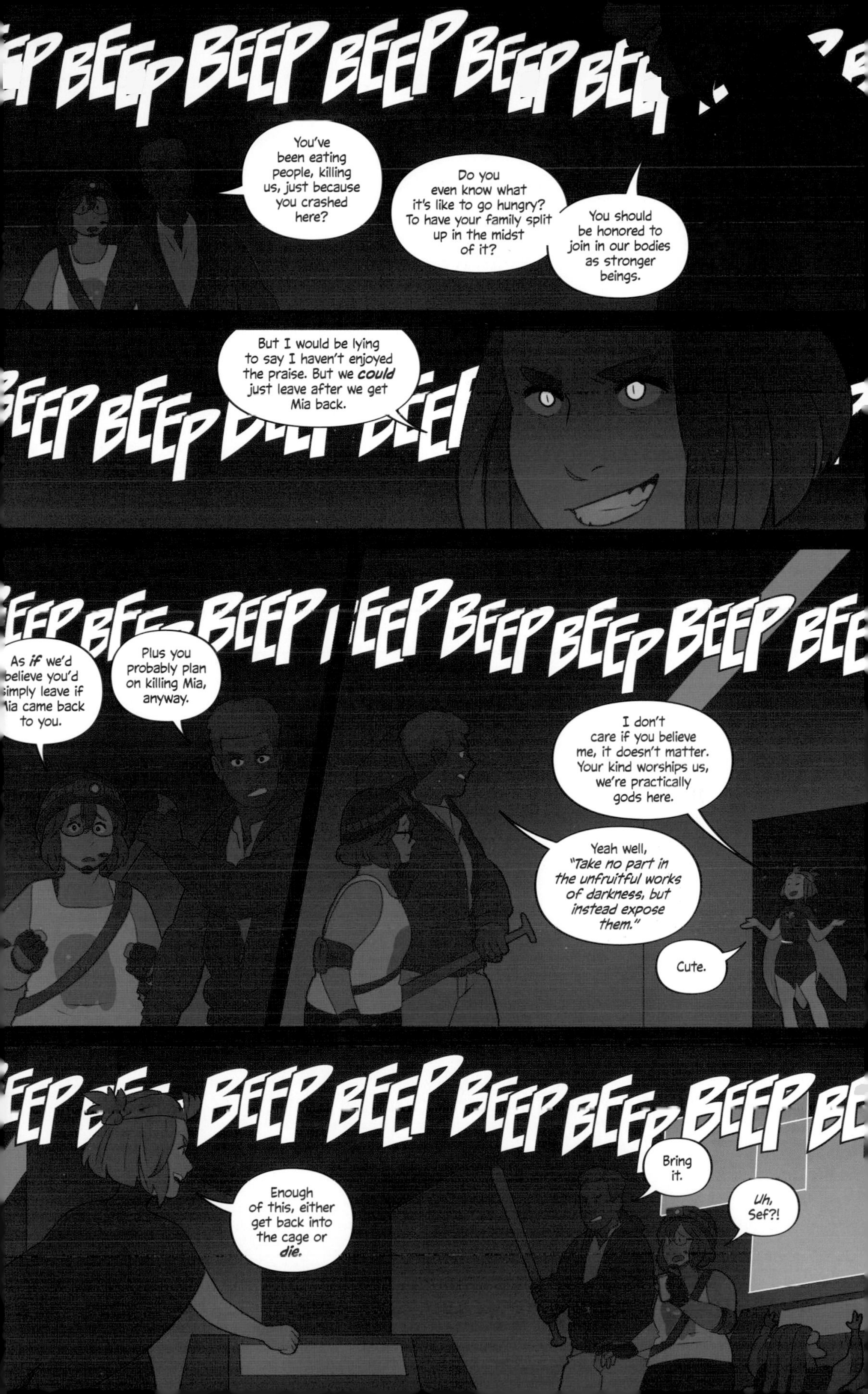
BEEP BEEP BEEP BEEP BEEP BEEP
You've been eating people, killing us, just because you crashed here?
Do you even know what it's like to go hungry? To have your family split up in the midst of it?
You should be honored to join in our bodies as stronger beings.
BEEP BEEP
But I would be lying to say I haven't enjoyed the praise. But we *could* just leave after we get Mia back.
BEEP BEEP BEEP BEEP BEEP BEEP
As *if* we'd believe you'd simply leave if Mia came back to you.
Plus you probably plan on killing Mia, anyway.
I don't care if you believe me, it doesn't matter. Your kind worships us, we're practically gods here.
Yeah well, *"Take no part in the unfruitful works of darkness, but instead expose them."*
Cute.
BEEP BEEP BEEP BEEP BEEP
Enough of this, either get back into the cage or ***die.***
Bring it.
Uh, Sef?!

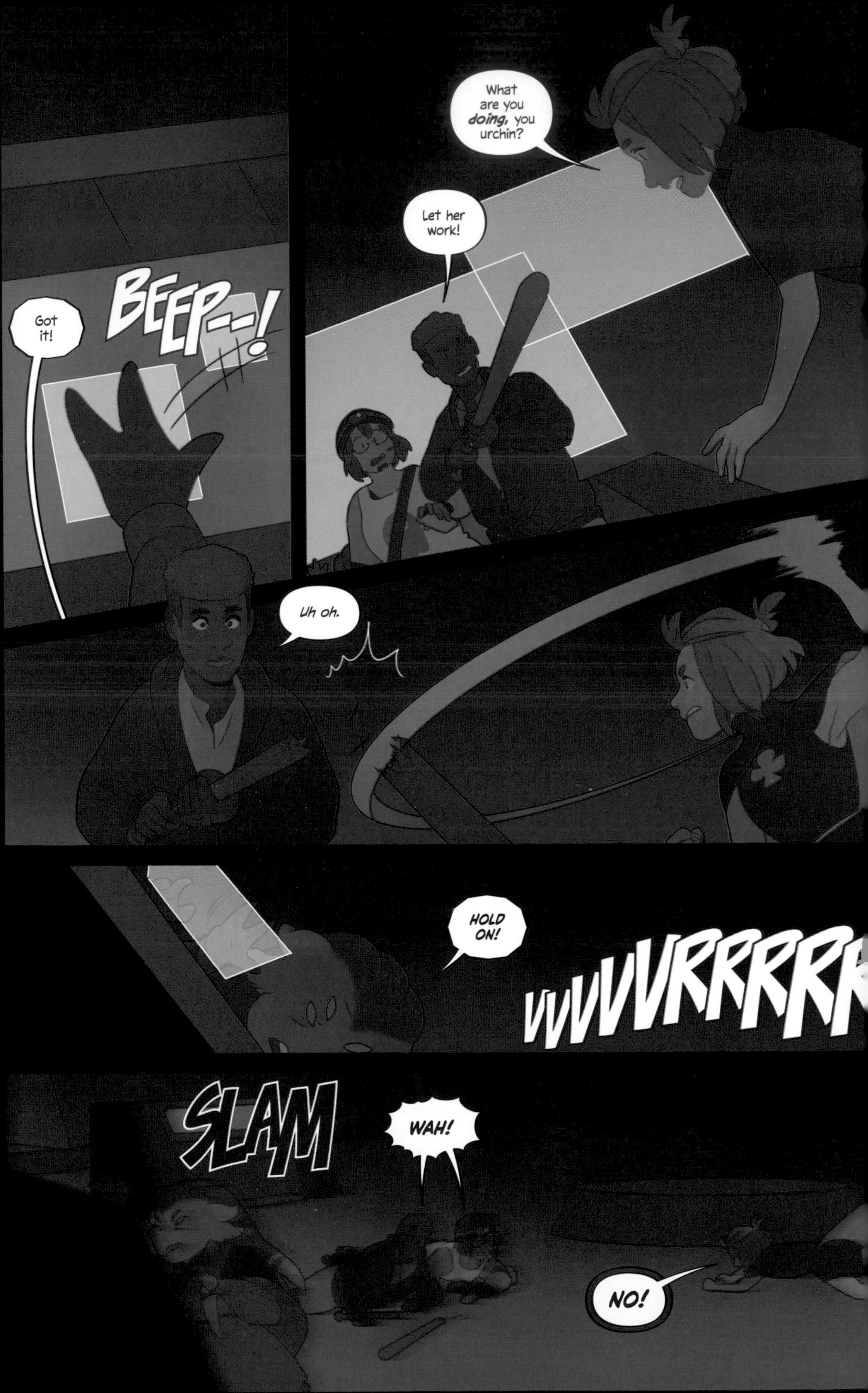
Got it!
BEEP--!
What are you *doing,* you urchin?
Let her work!
Uh oh.
HOLD ON!
VVVVURRRRR
SLAM
WAH!
NO!

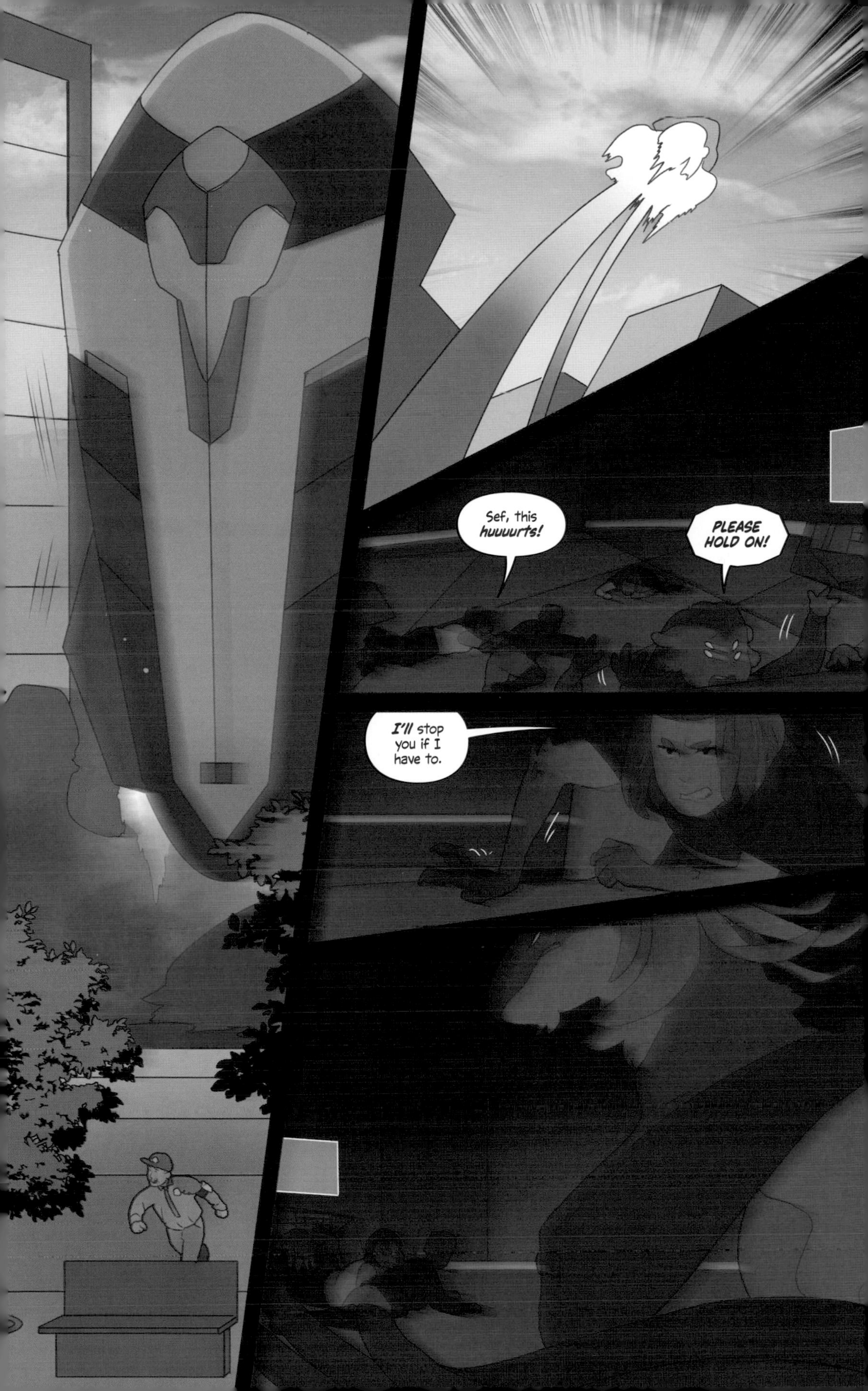

Sef, this *huuuurts!*
PLEASE HOLD ON!
I'll stop you if I have to.

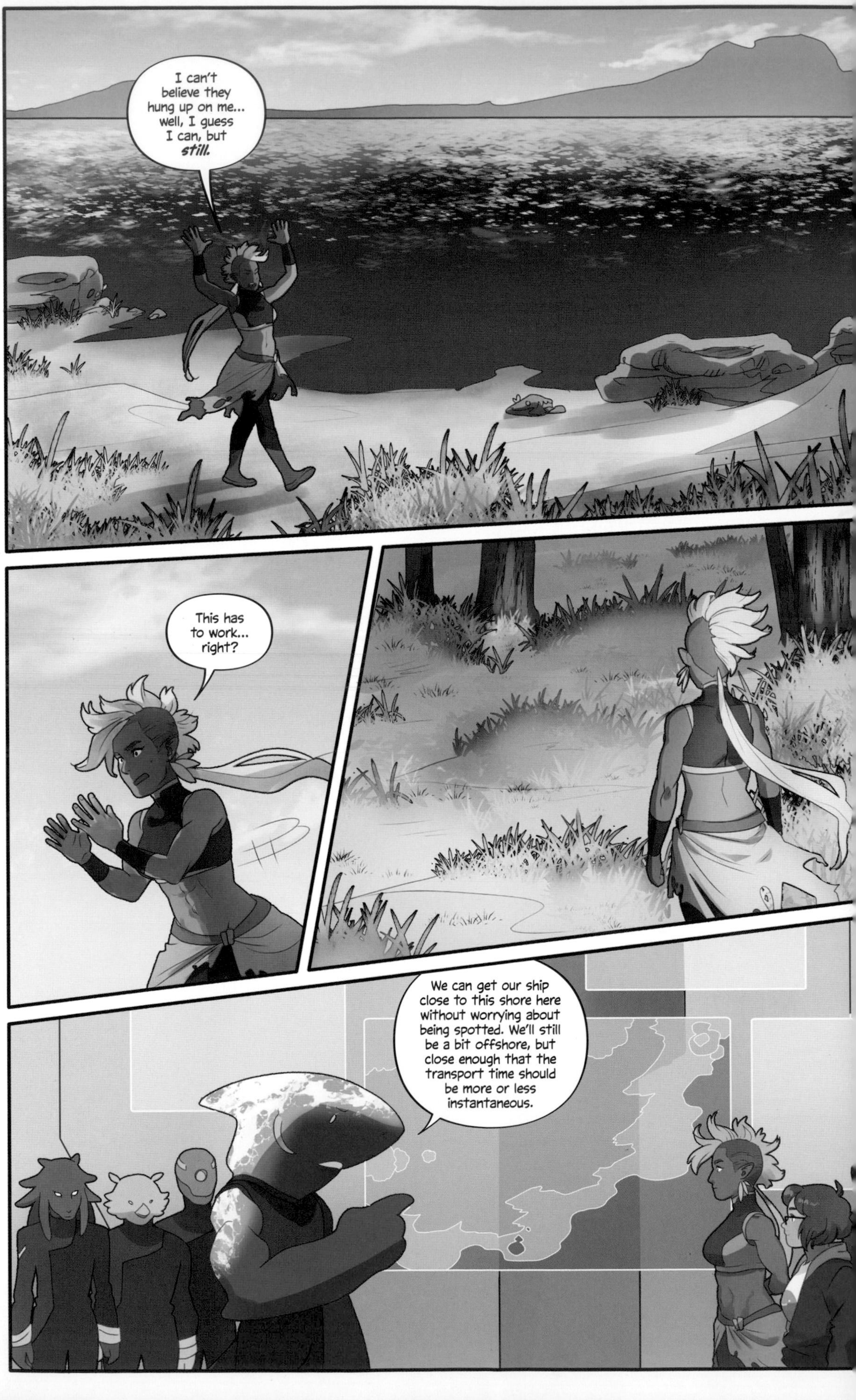
I can't believe they hung up on me... well, I guess I can, but *still.*
This has to work... right?
We can get our ship close to this shore here without worrying about being spotted. We'll still be a bit offshore, but close enough that the transport time should be more or less instantaneous.

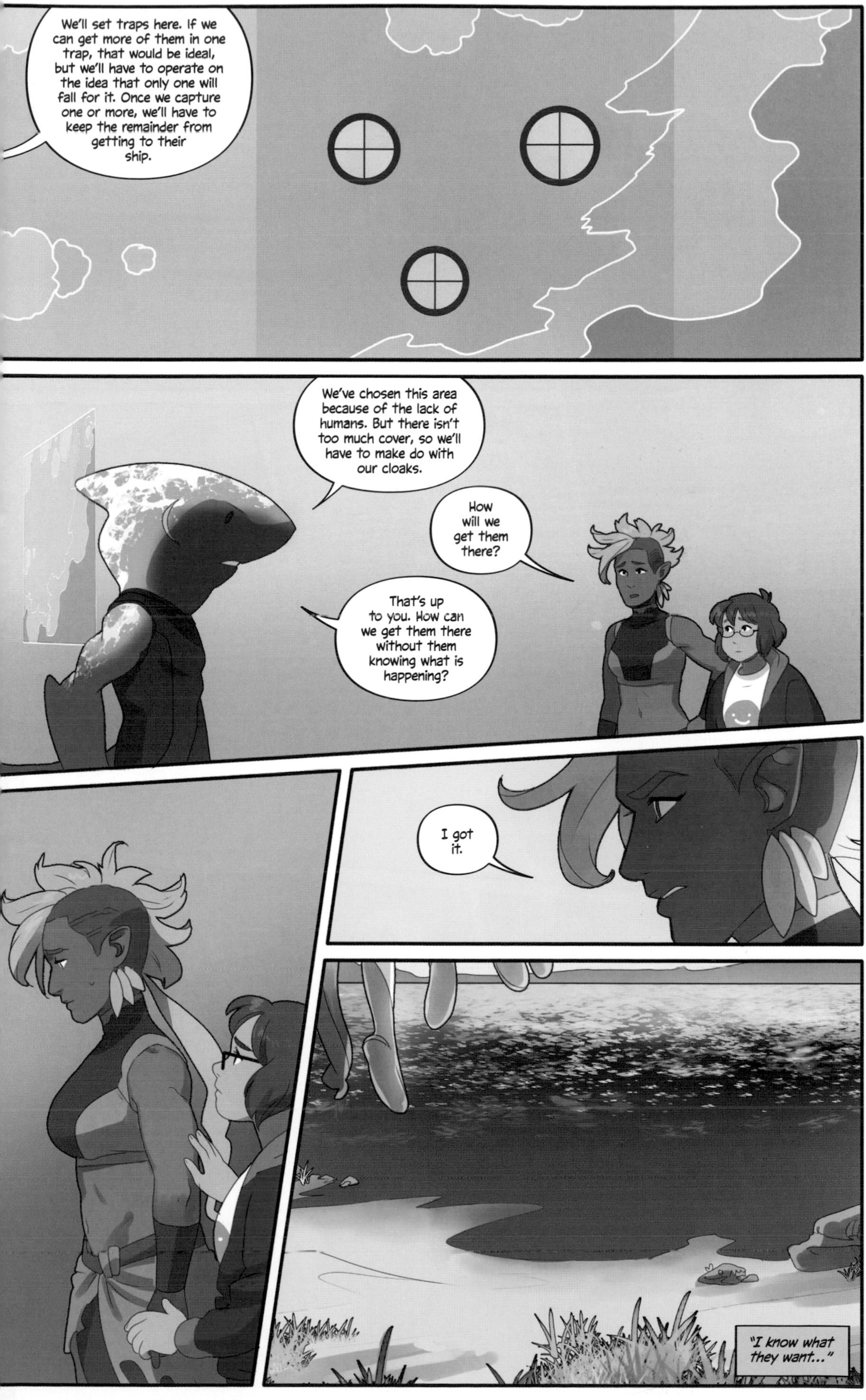
We'll set traps here. If we can get more of them in one trap, that would be ideal, but we'll have to operate on the idea that only one will fall for it. Once we capture one or more, we'll have to keep the remainder from getting to their ship.
We've chosen this area because of the lack of humans. But there isn't too much cover, so we'll have to make do with our cloaks.
How will we get them there?
That's up to you. How can we get them there without them knowing what is happening?
I got it.
"I know what they want..."

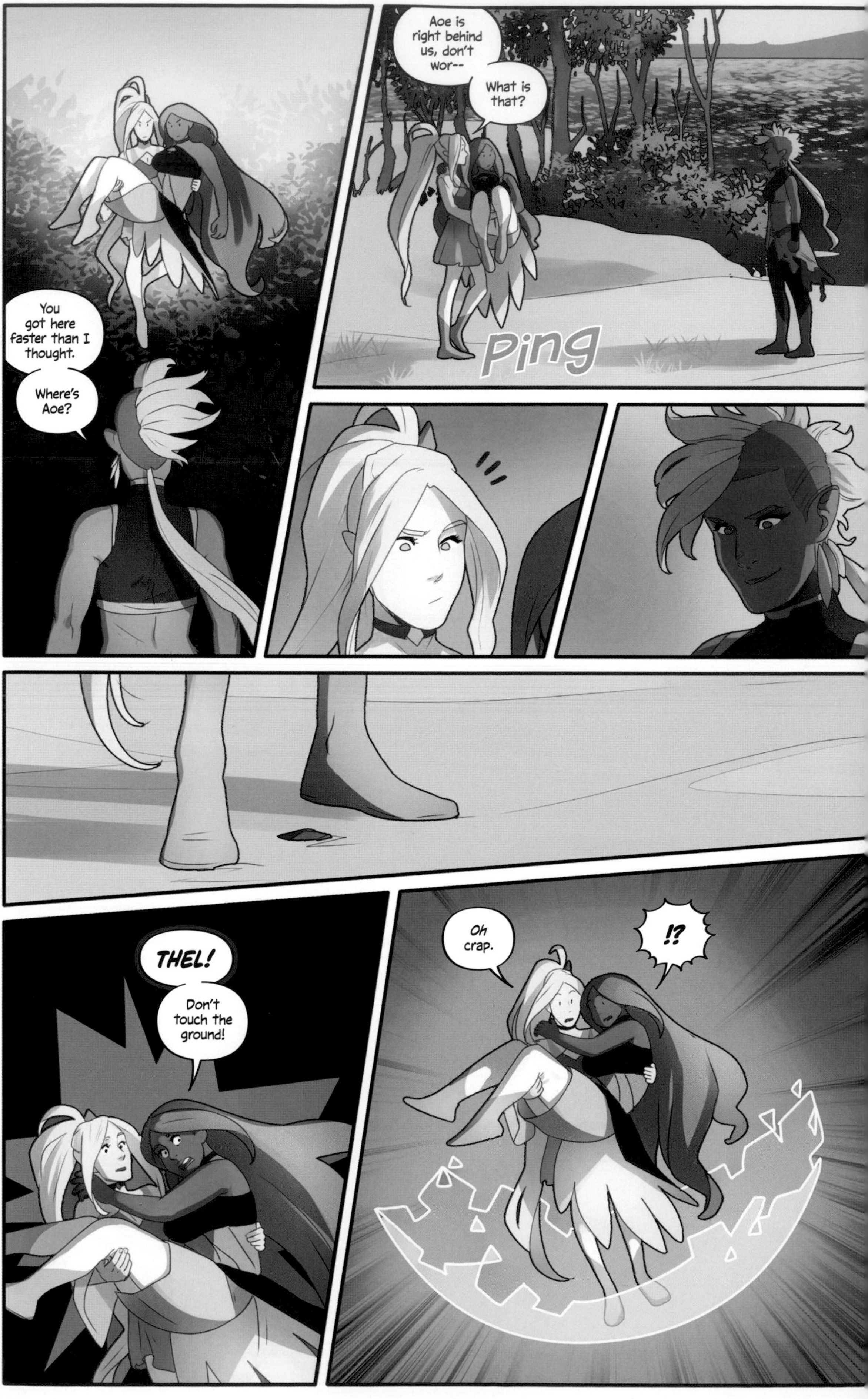

You got here faster than I thought.
Where's Aoe?
Aoe is right behind us, don't wor--
What is that?
Ping
THEL!
Don't touch the ground!
Oh crap.
!?

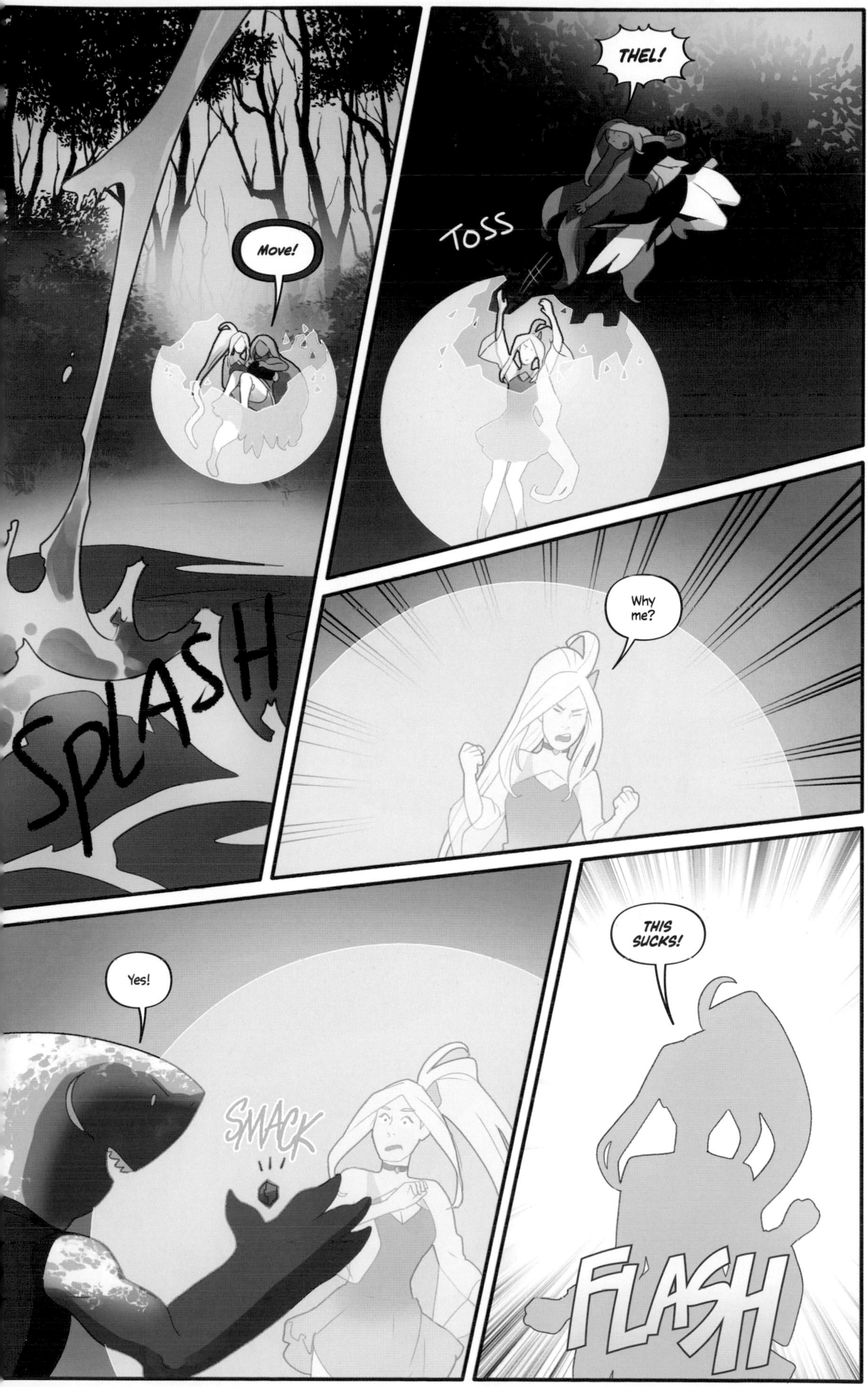
Move!
SPLASH
THEL!
TOSS
Why me?
Yes!
SMACK
THIS SUCKS!
FLASH

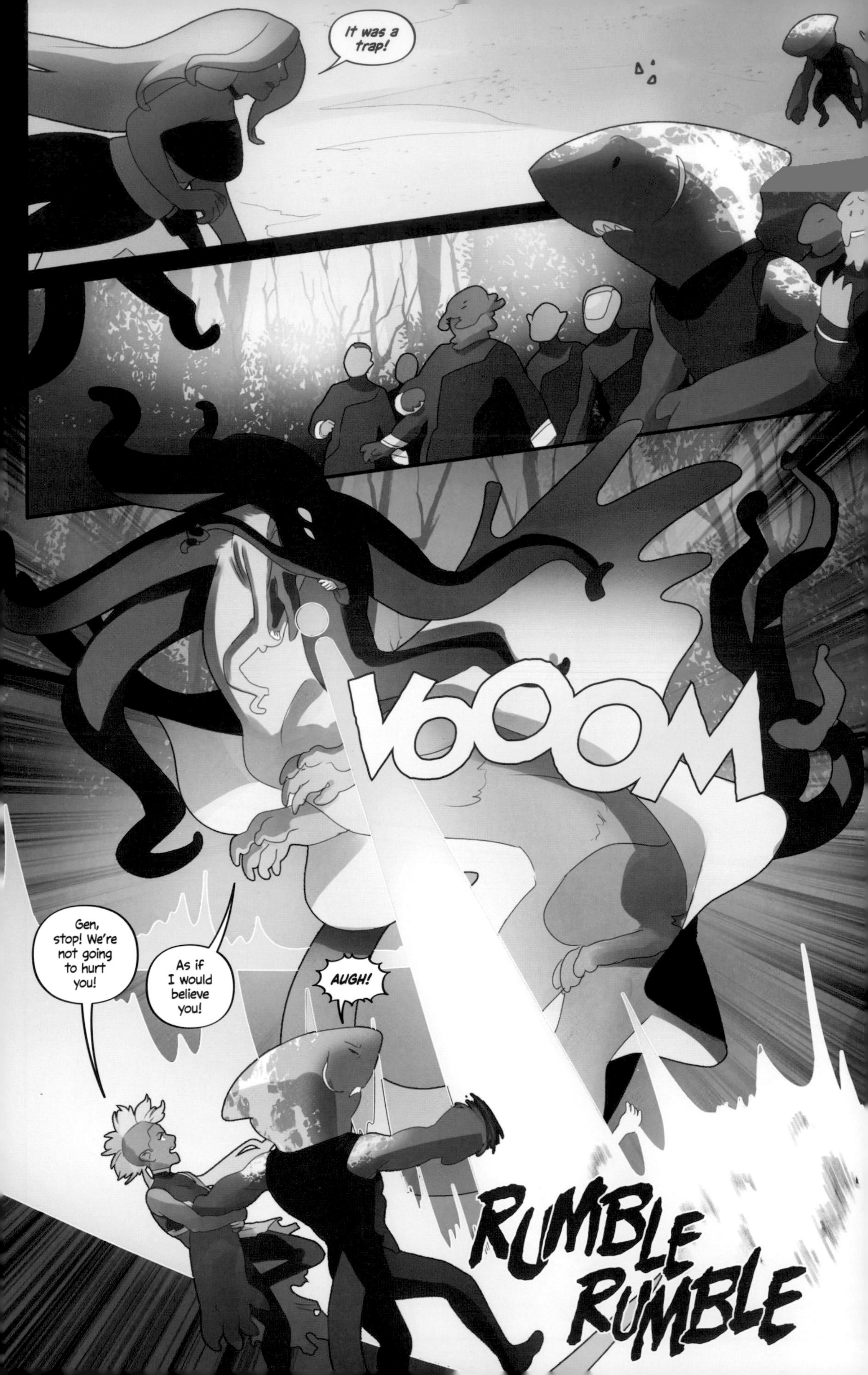
It was a trap!
VOOOM
Gen, stop! We're not going to hurt you!
As if I would believe you!
AUGH!
RUMBLE RUMBLE

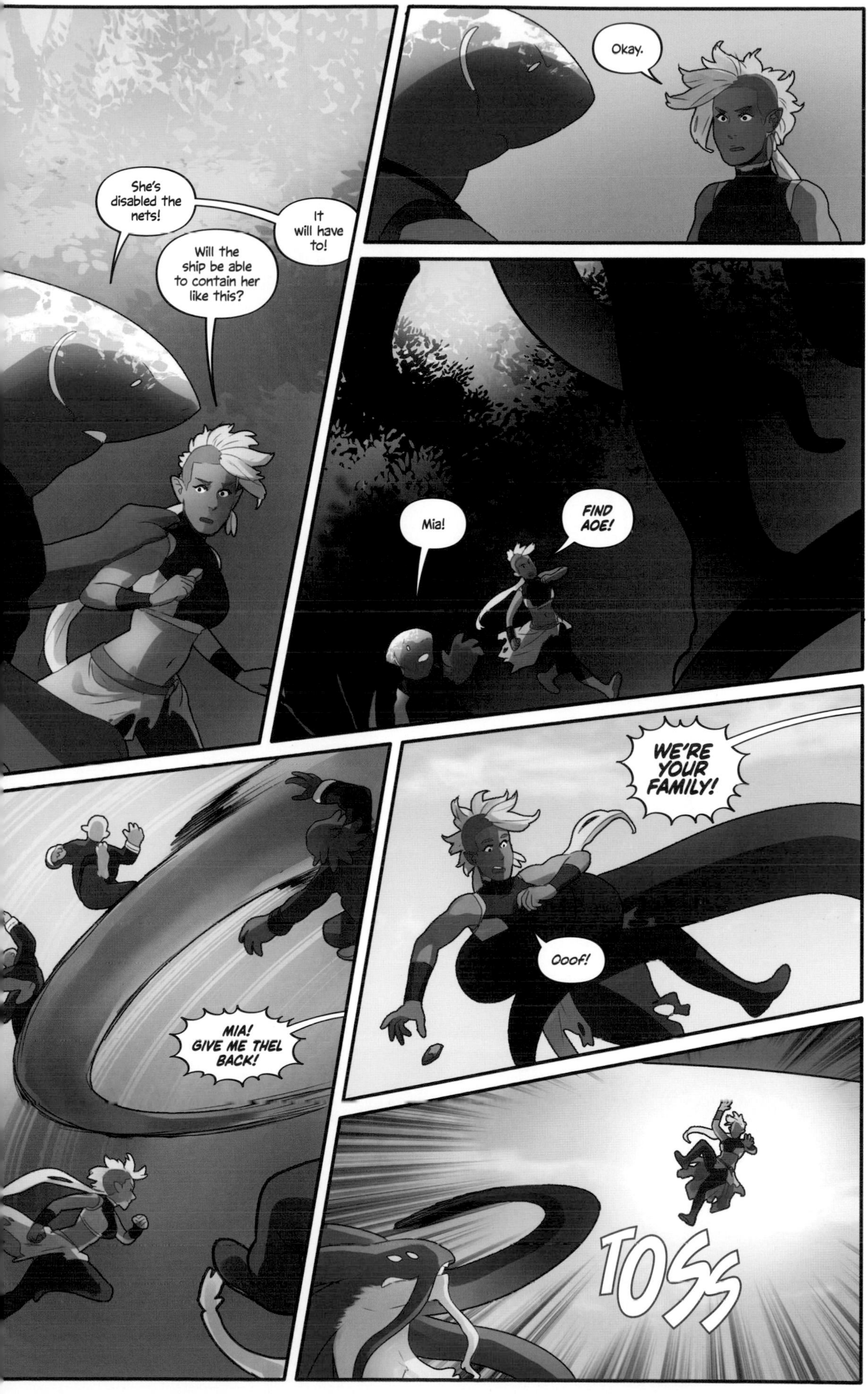
She's disabled the nets!
Will the ship be able to contain her like this?
It will have to!
Okay.
Mia!
FIND AOE!
MIA! GIVE ME THEL BACK!
WE'RE YOUR FAMILY!
Ooof!
TOSs

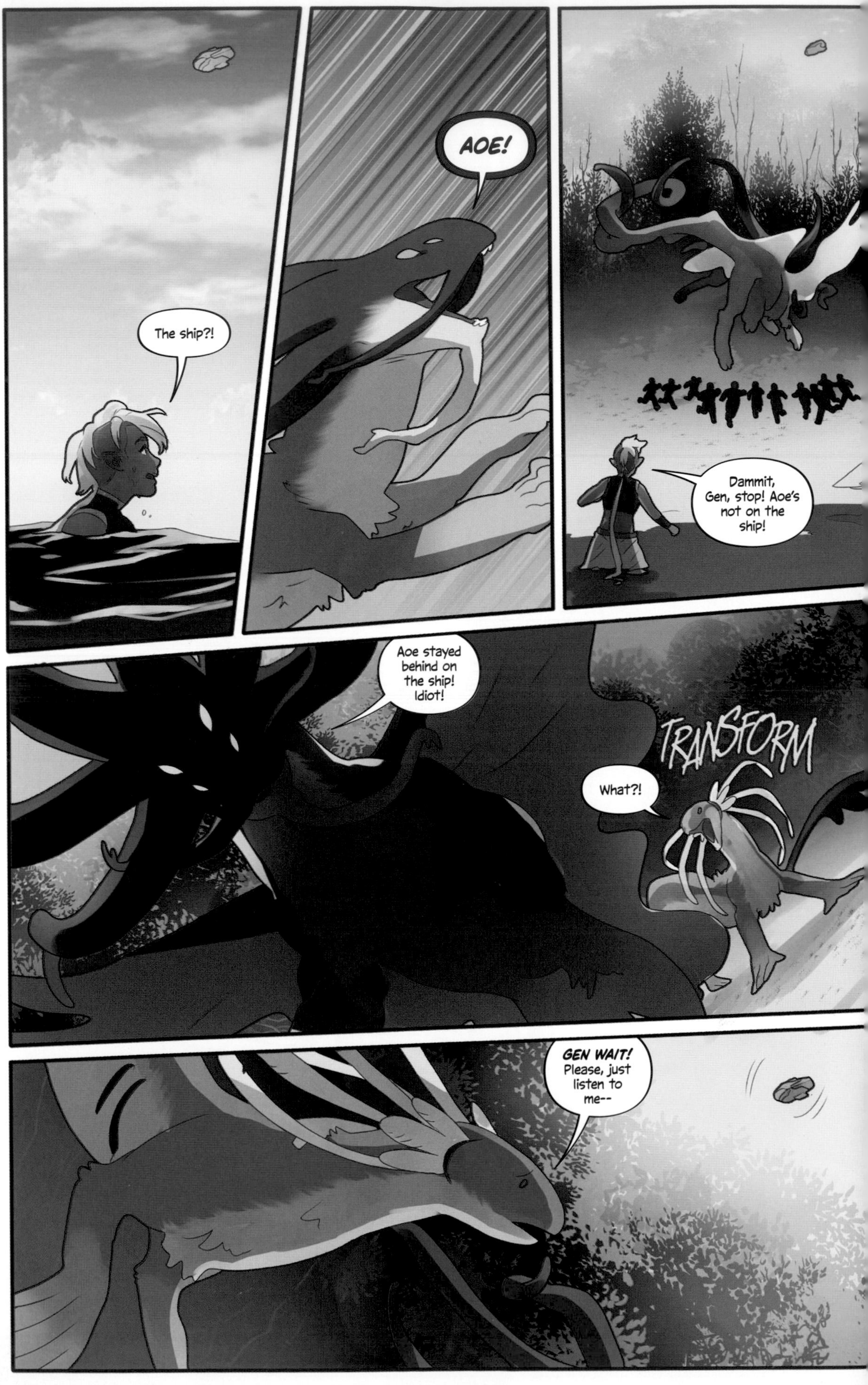
The ship?!
AOE!
Dammit, Gen, stop! Aoe's not on the ship!
Aoe stayed behind on the ship! Idiot!
TRANSFORM
What?!
GEN WAIT! Please, just listen to me--

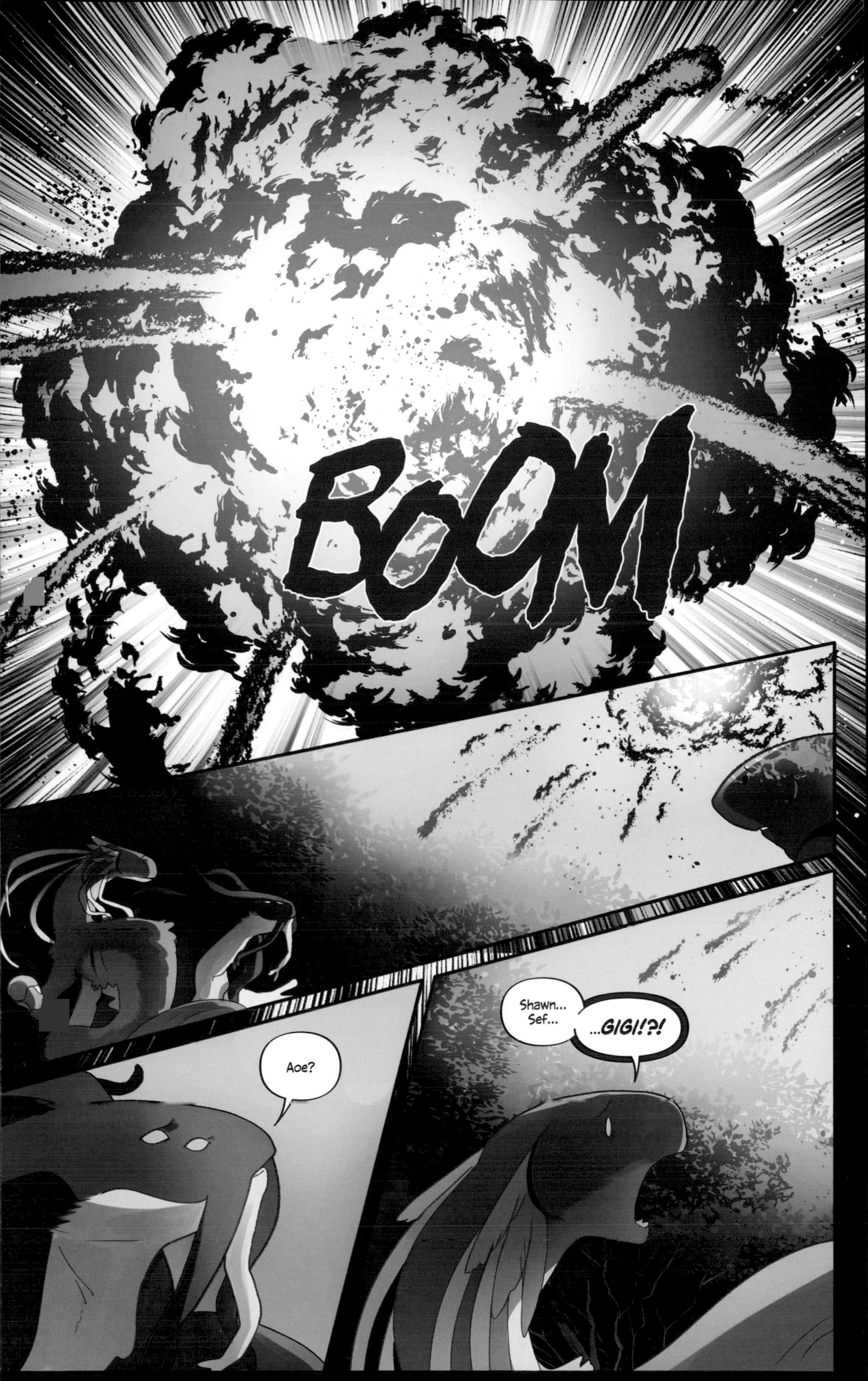
BOOM
Aoe?
Shawn... Sef...
...GIGI!?!

SAVE YOURSELF! #3 MAIN COVER BY

KELLY & NICHOLE MATTHEWS

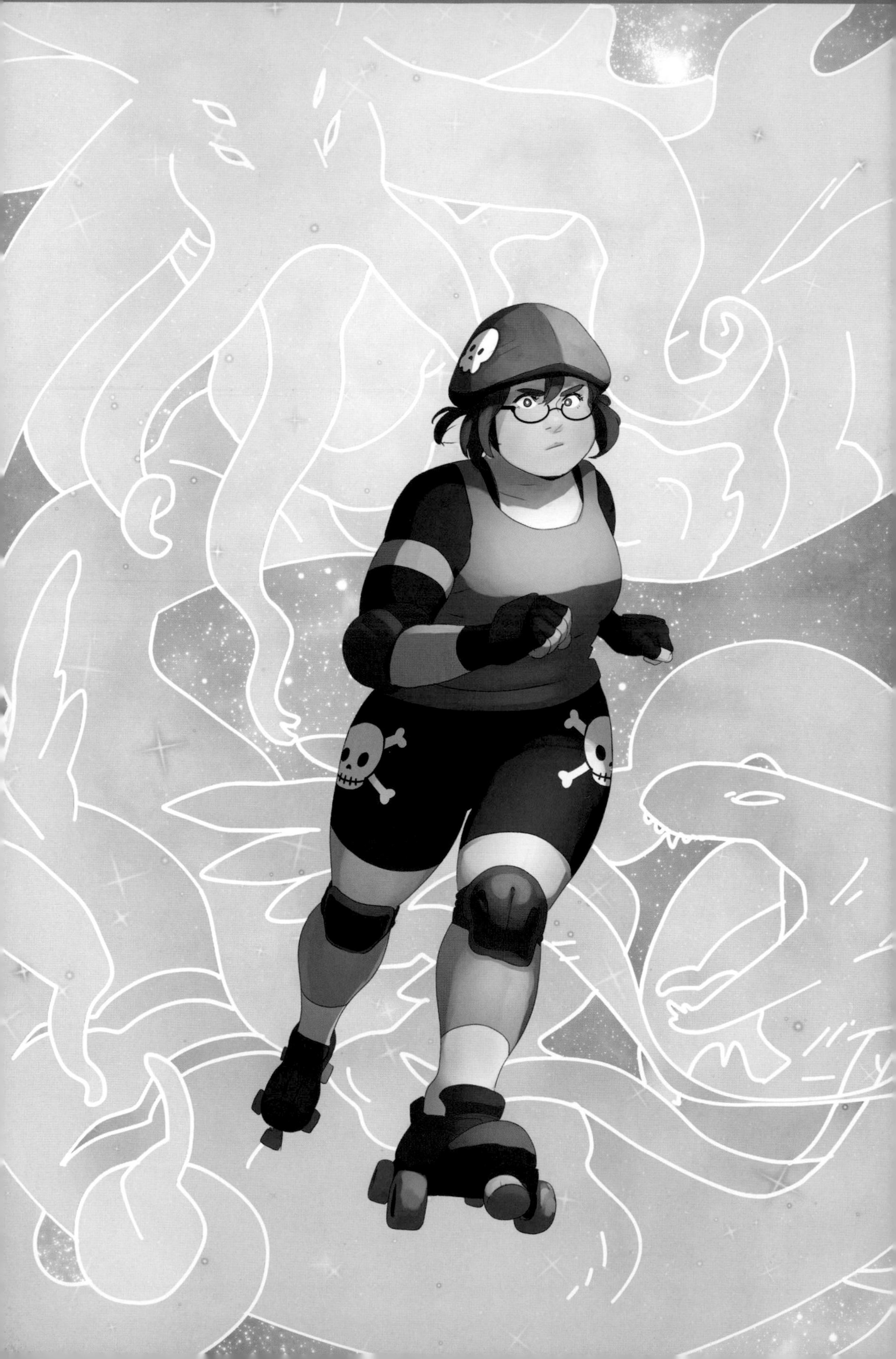

CHAPTER
FOUR

SAVE YOURSELF! #4 MAIN COVER BY

KELLY & NICHOLE MATTHEWS

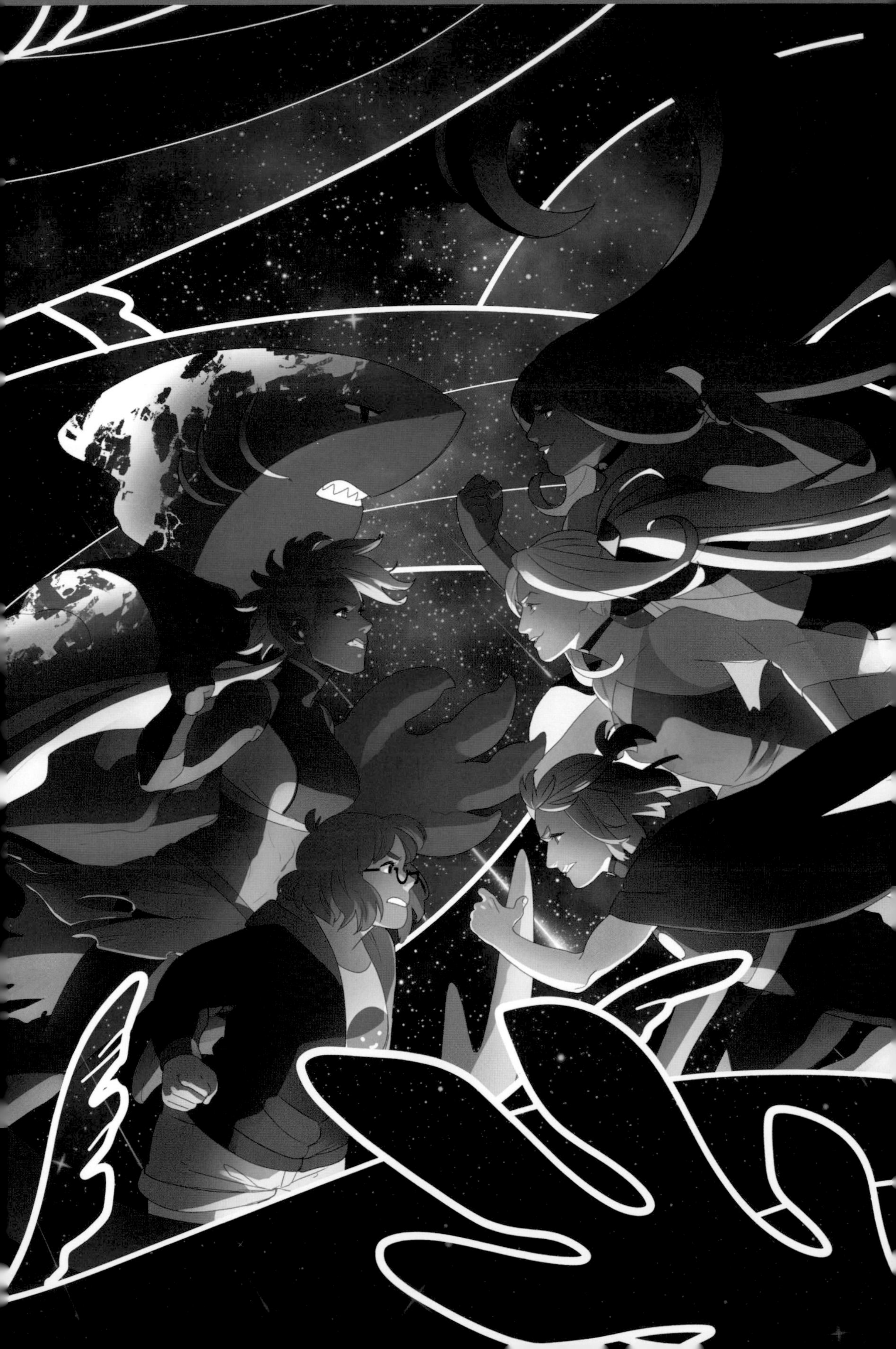

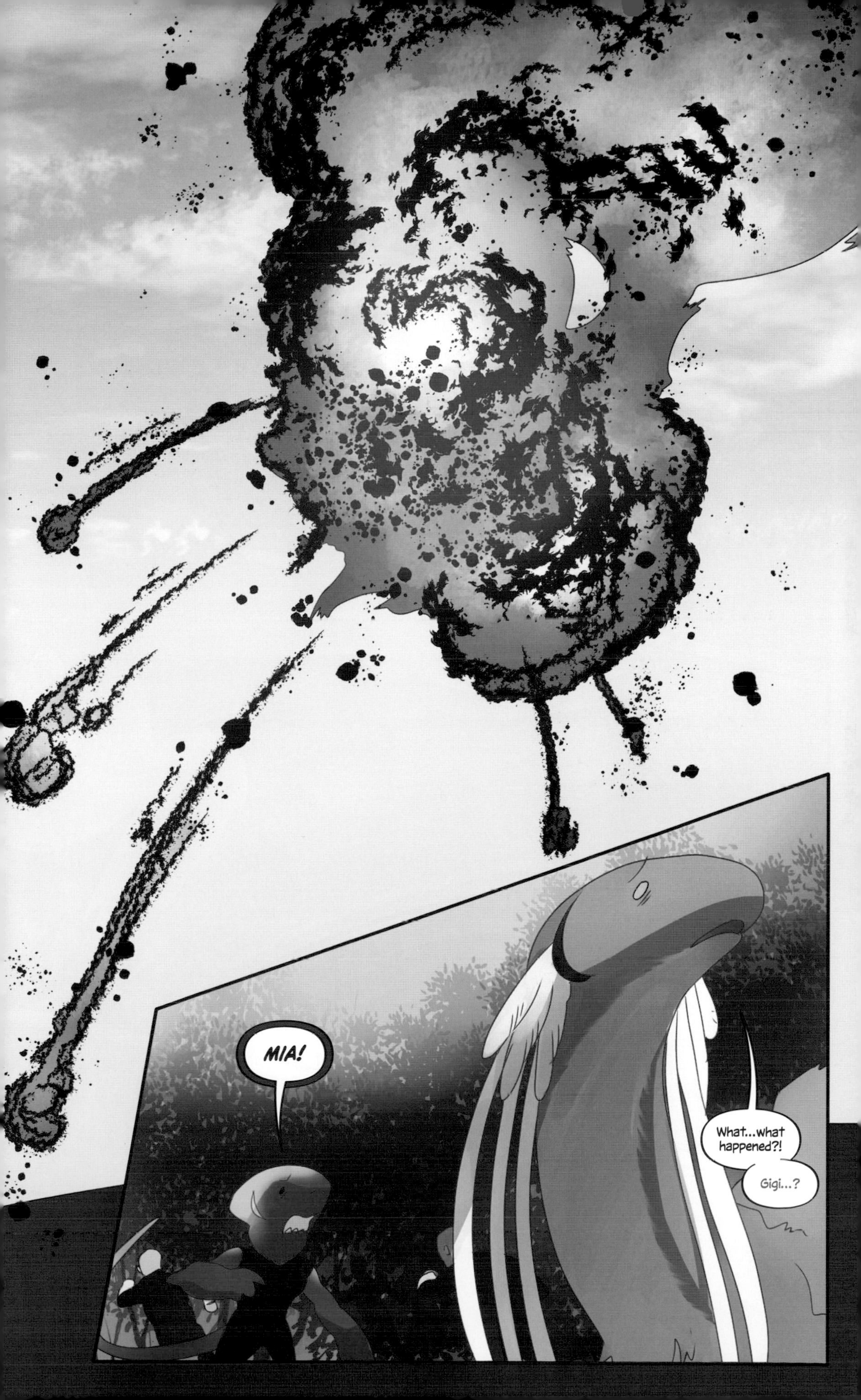
MIA!
What...what happened?!
Gigi...?

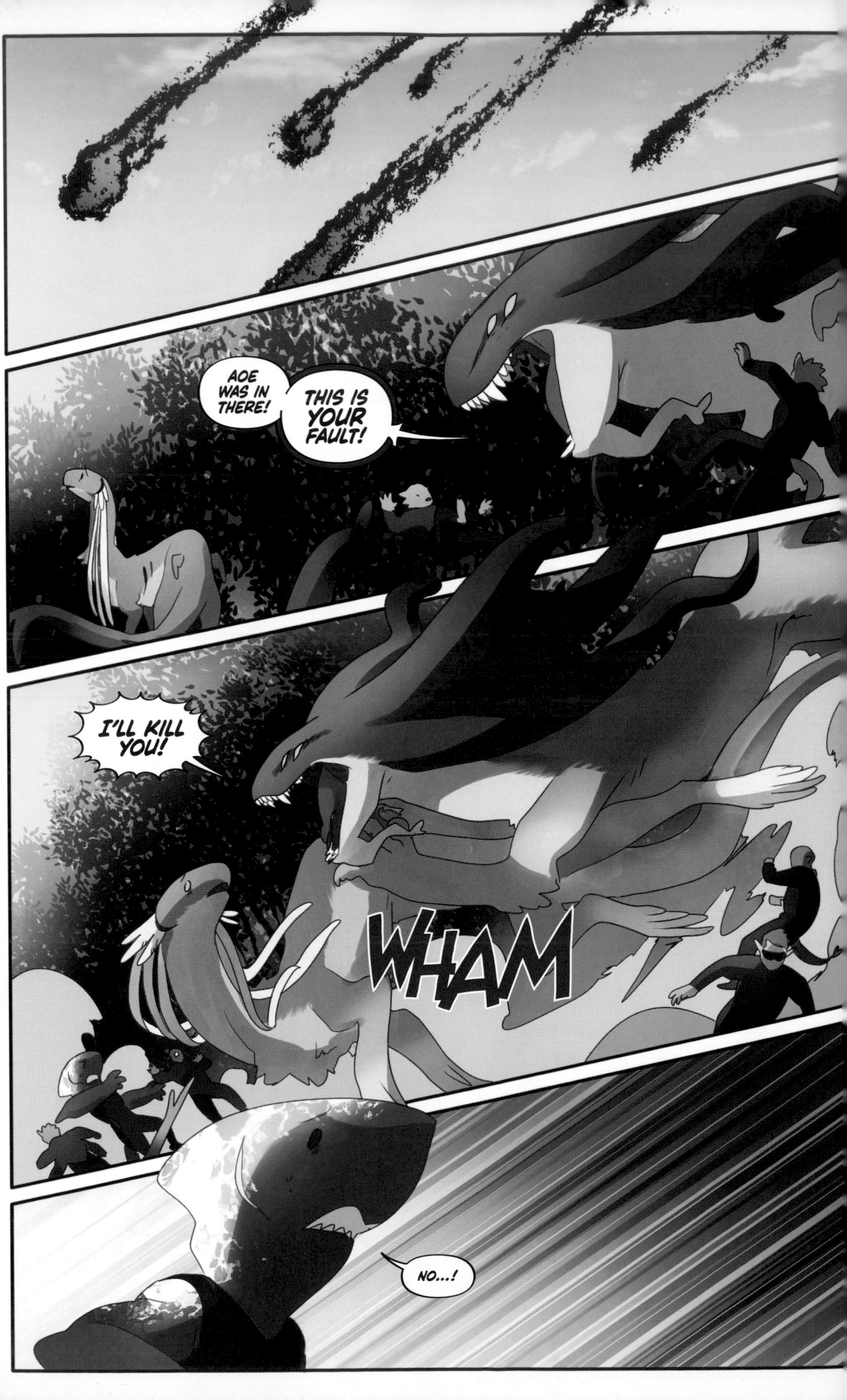
AOE WAS IN THERE!
THIS IS YOUR FAULT!
I'LL KILL YOU!
WHAM
NO...!

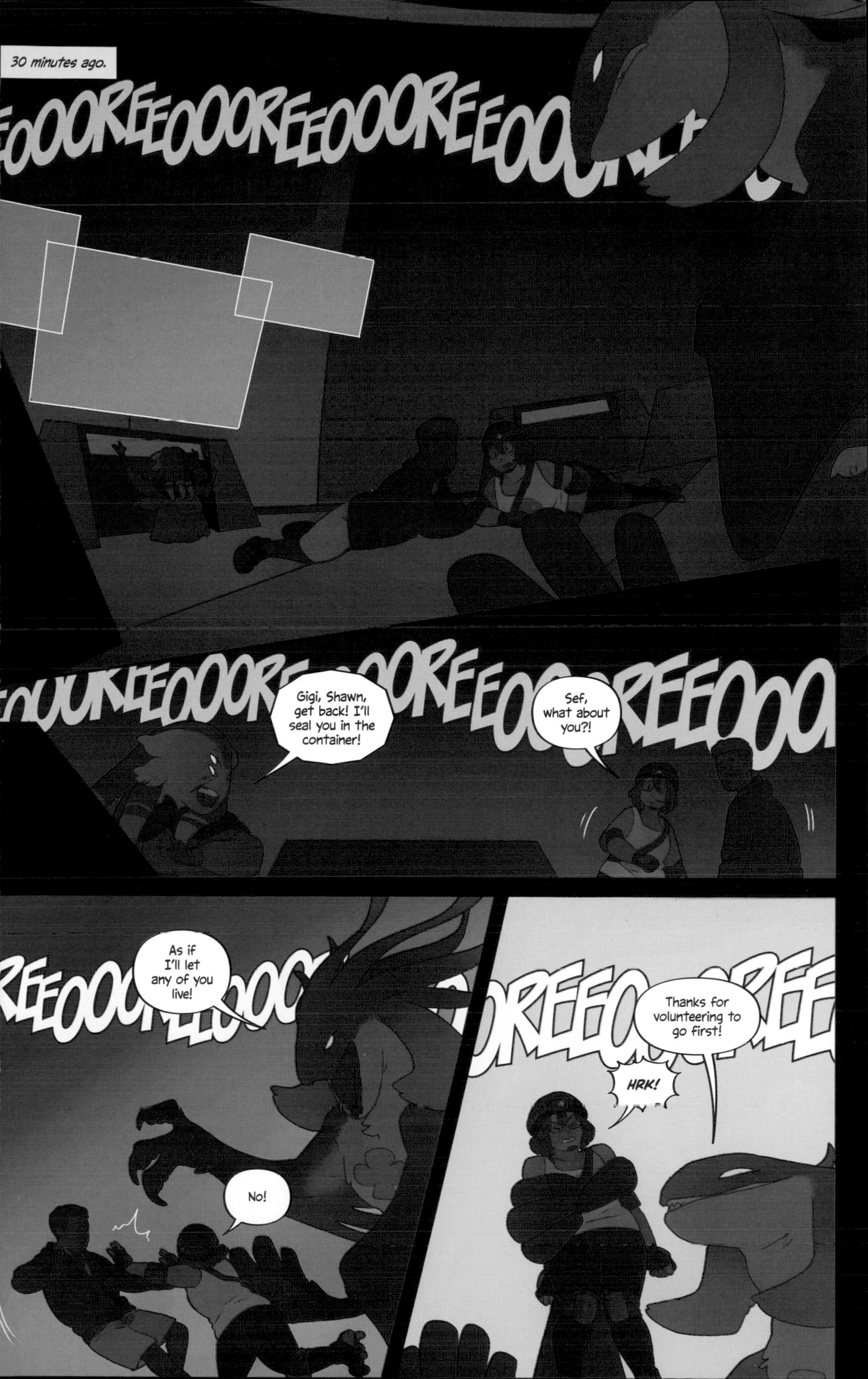
30 minutes ago.
Gigi, Shawn, get back! I'll seal you in the container!
Sef, what about you?!
As if I'll let any of you live!
No!
Thanks for volunteering to go first!
HRK!

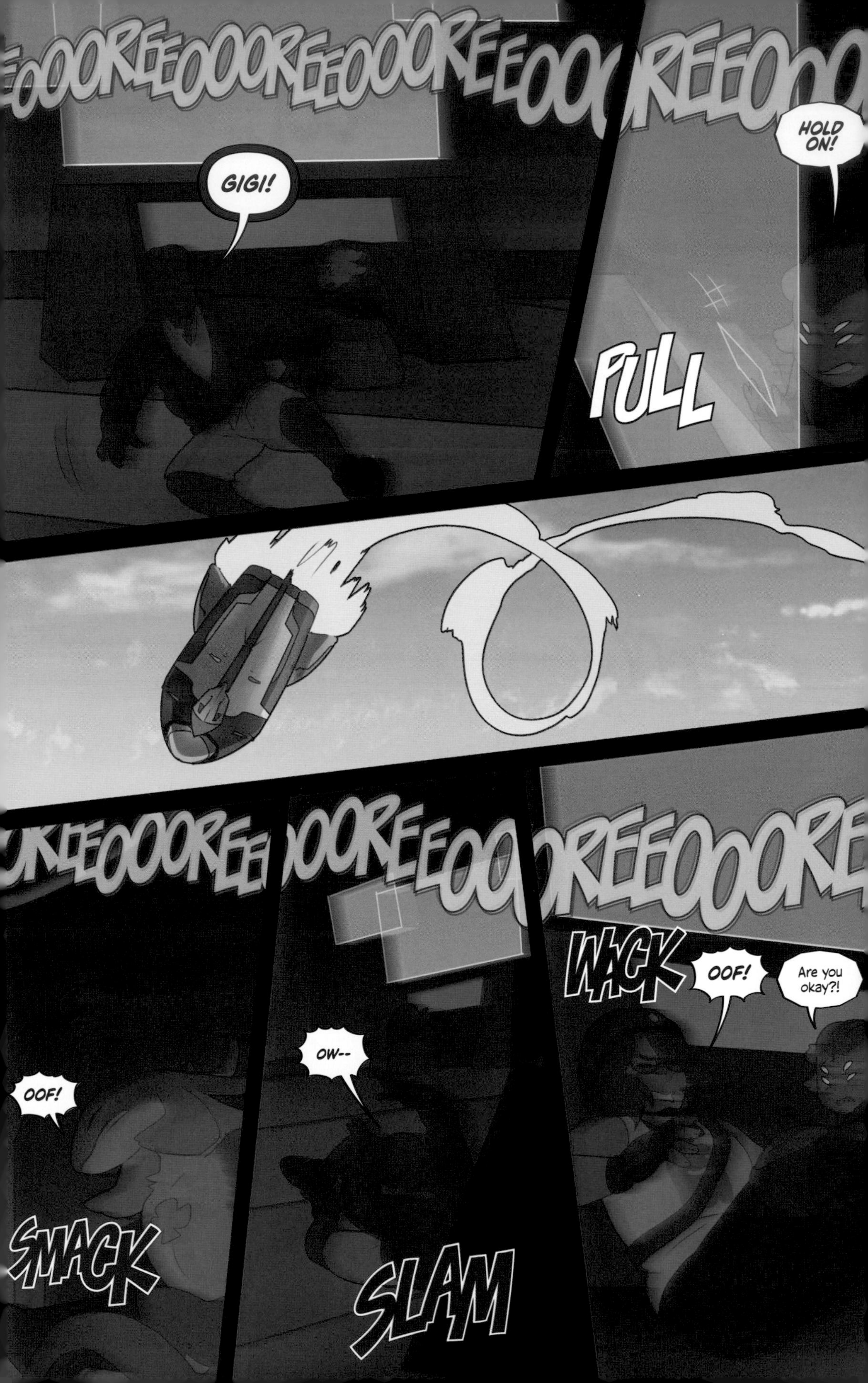
EEOOOREEOOOREEOOOREEOOOREEOOO
GIGI!
HOLD ON!
PULL
OREEOOOREEOOOREEOOOREEOOOREEOOORE
OOF!
SMACK
OW--
SLAM
WACK
OOF!
Are you okay?!

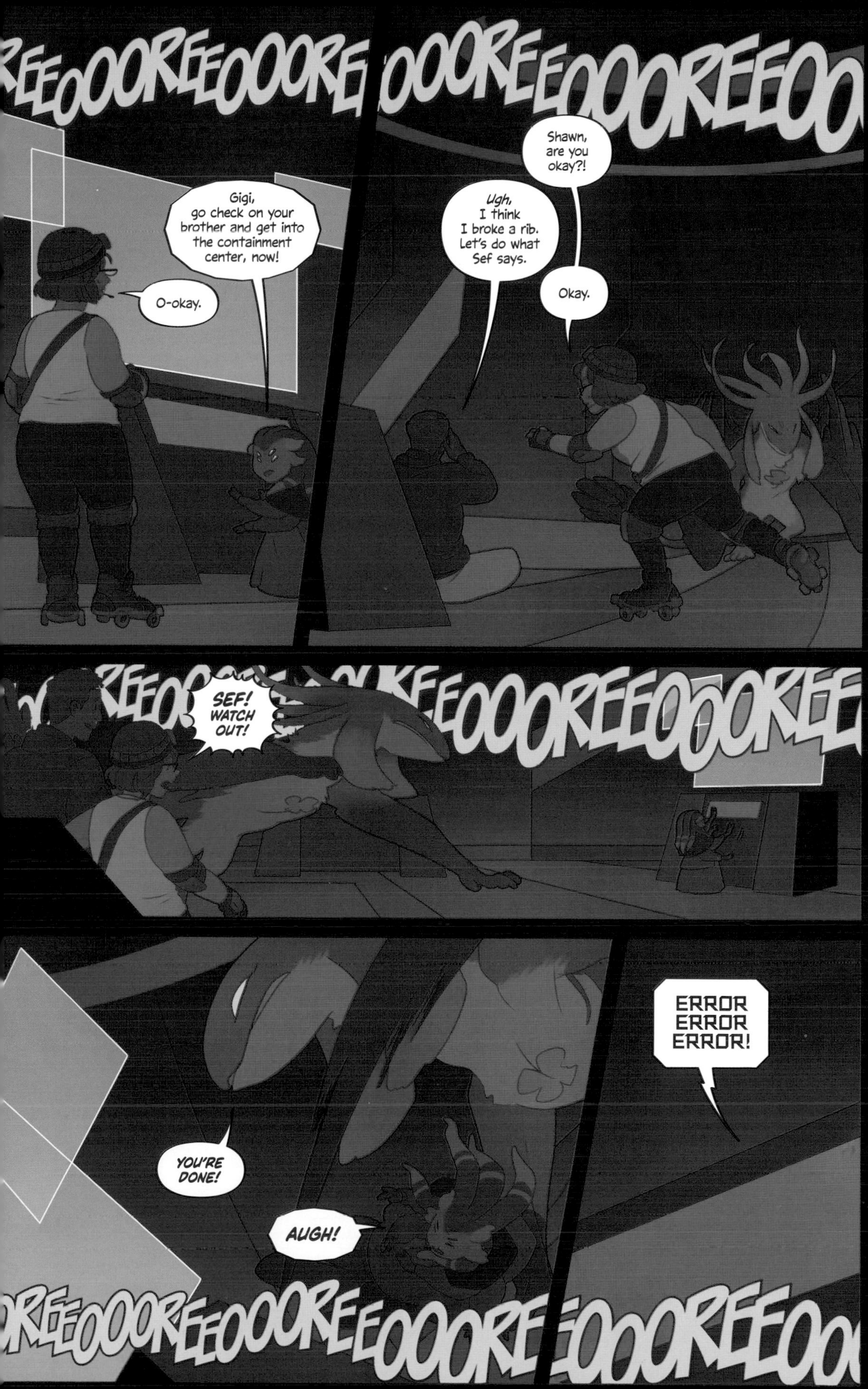
REEOOOREEOOOREEOOOREEOOOREEOO
Gigi, go check on your brother and get into the containment center, now!
O-okay.
Shawn, are you okay?!
Ugh, I think I broke a rib. Let's do what Sef says.
Okay.
SEF! WATCH OUT!
YOU'RE DONE!
AUGH!
ERROR ERROR ERROR!
REEOOOREEOOOREEOOOREEOO

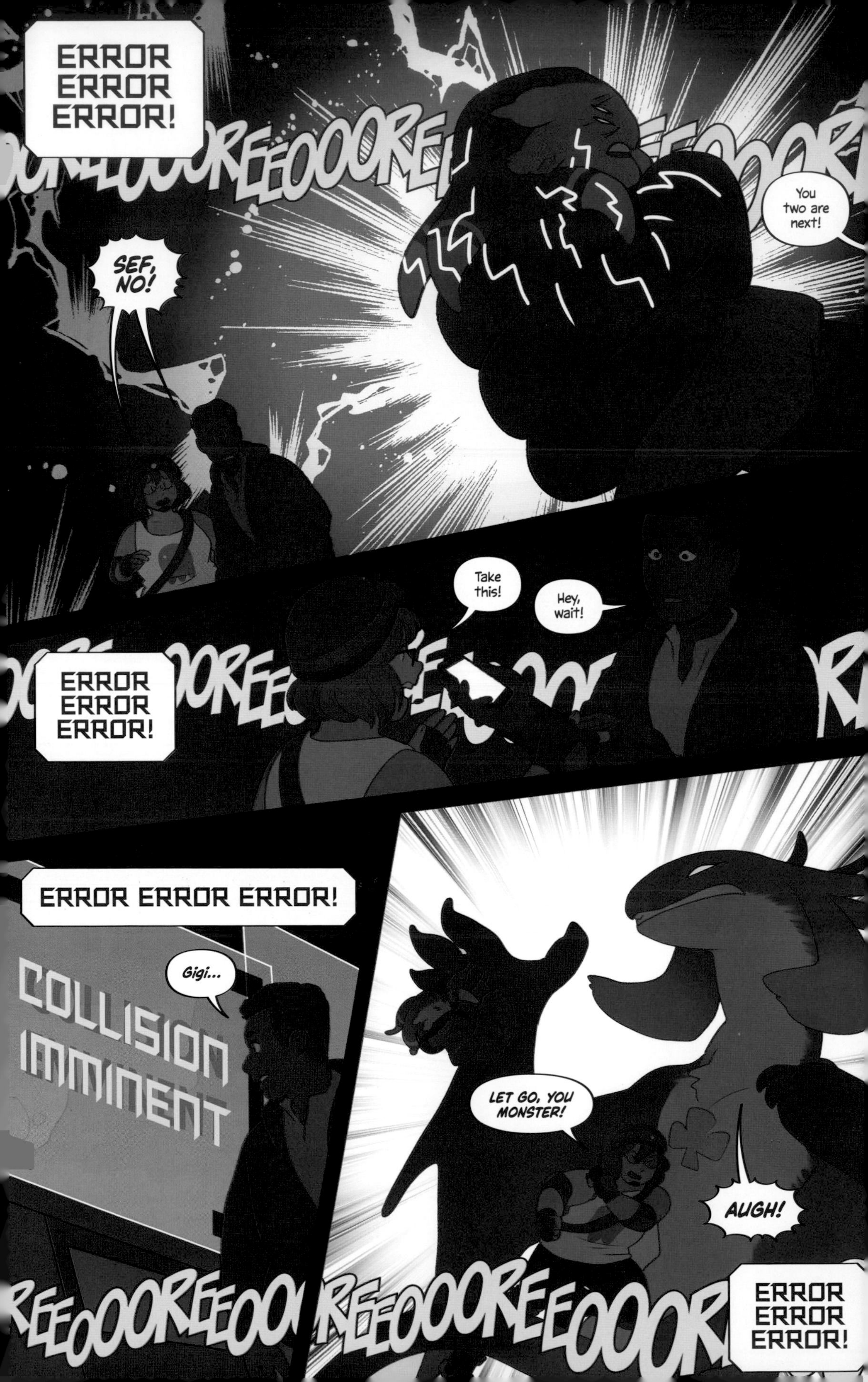
ERROR ERROR ERROR!
EEOOOREEOOOREEOOOR
You two are next!
SEF, NO!
Take this!
Hey, wait!
ERROR ERROR ERROR!
ERROR ERROR ERROR!
Gigi...
COLLISION IMMINENT
LET GO, YOU MONSTER!
AUGH!
REEOOOREEOOOREEOOOREEOOOR
ERROR ERROR ERROR!

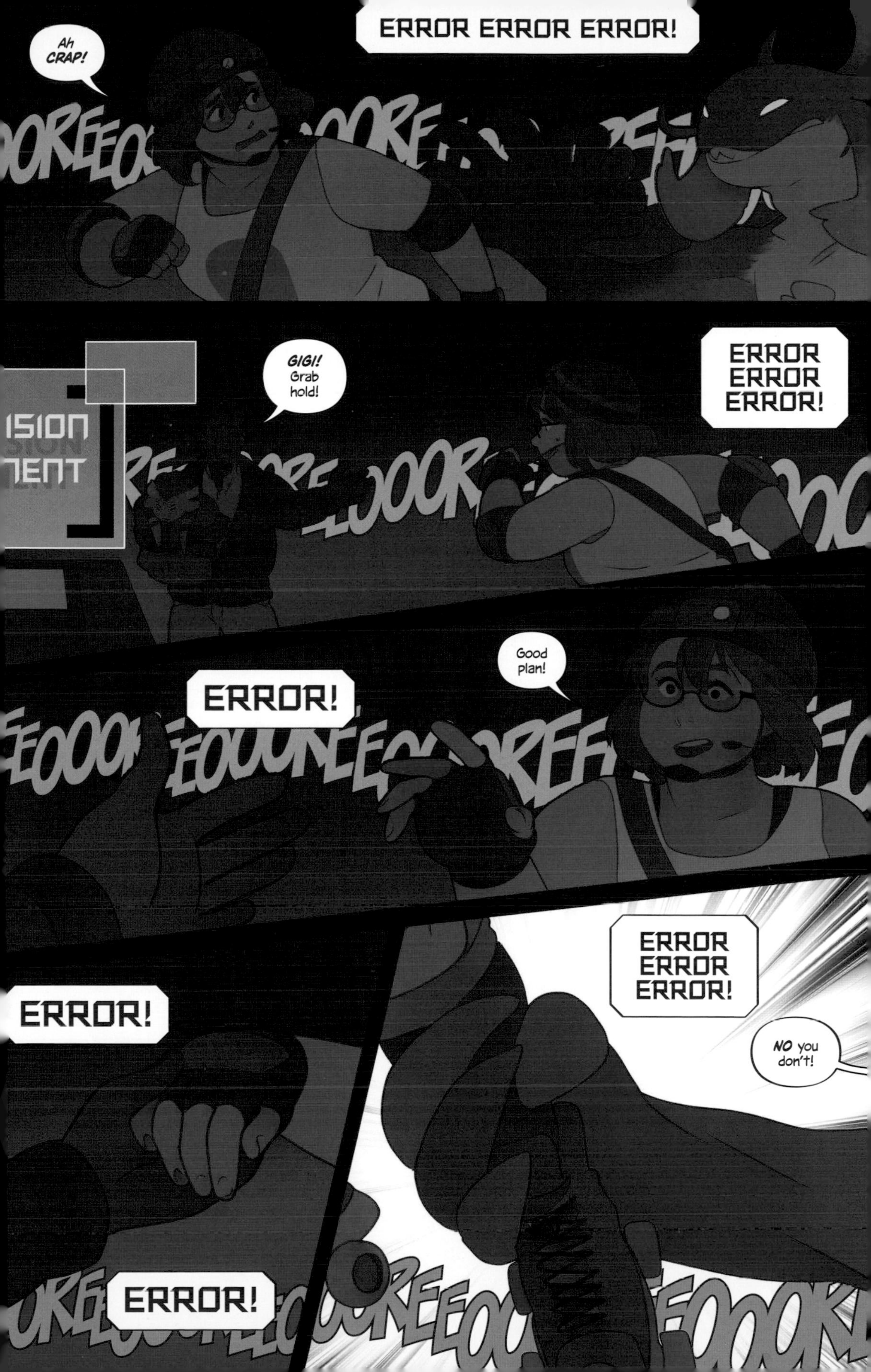
ERROR ERROR ERROR!
Ah CRAP!
GIGI! Grab hold!
ERROR ERROR ERROR!
ERROR!
Good plan!
ERROR!
ERROR ERROR ERROR!
NO you don't!
ERROR!

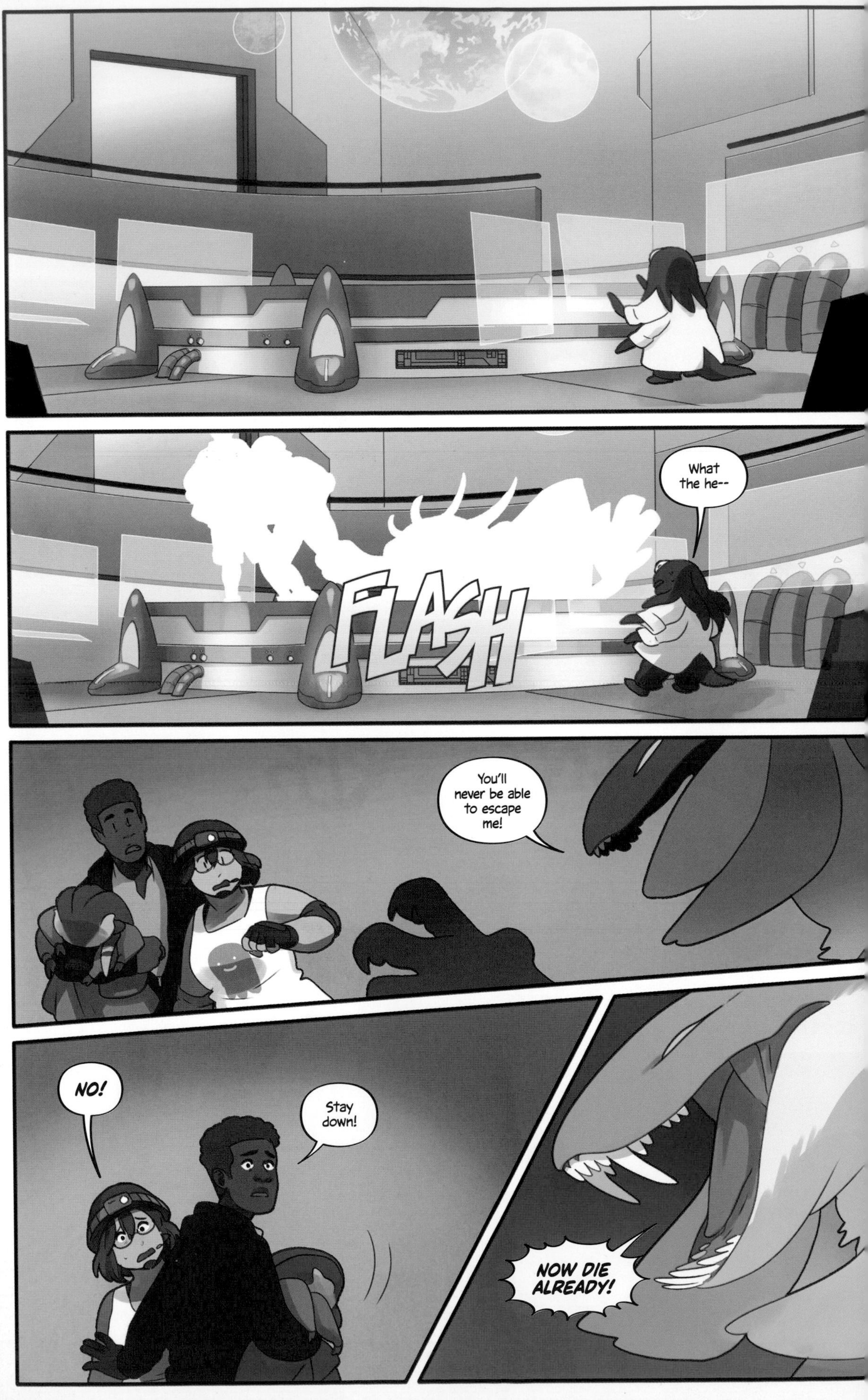

What the he--
FLASH
You'll never be able to escape me!
NO!
Stay down!
NOW DIE ALREADY!

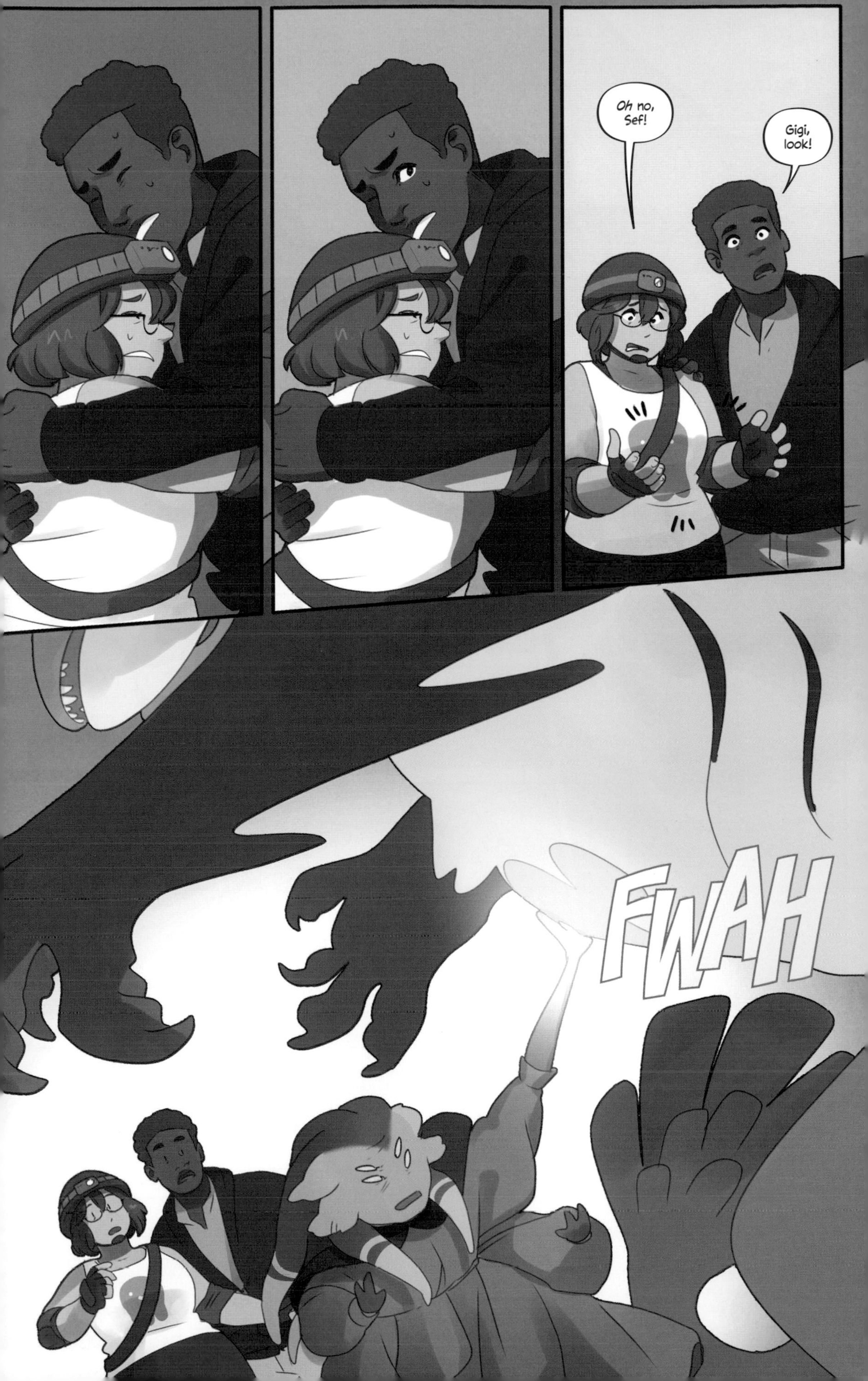
Oh no, Sef!
Gigi, look!
FWAH

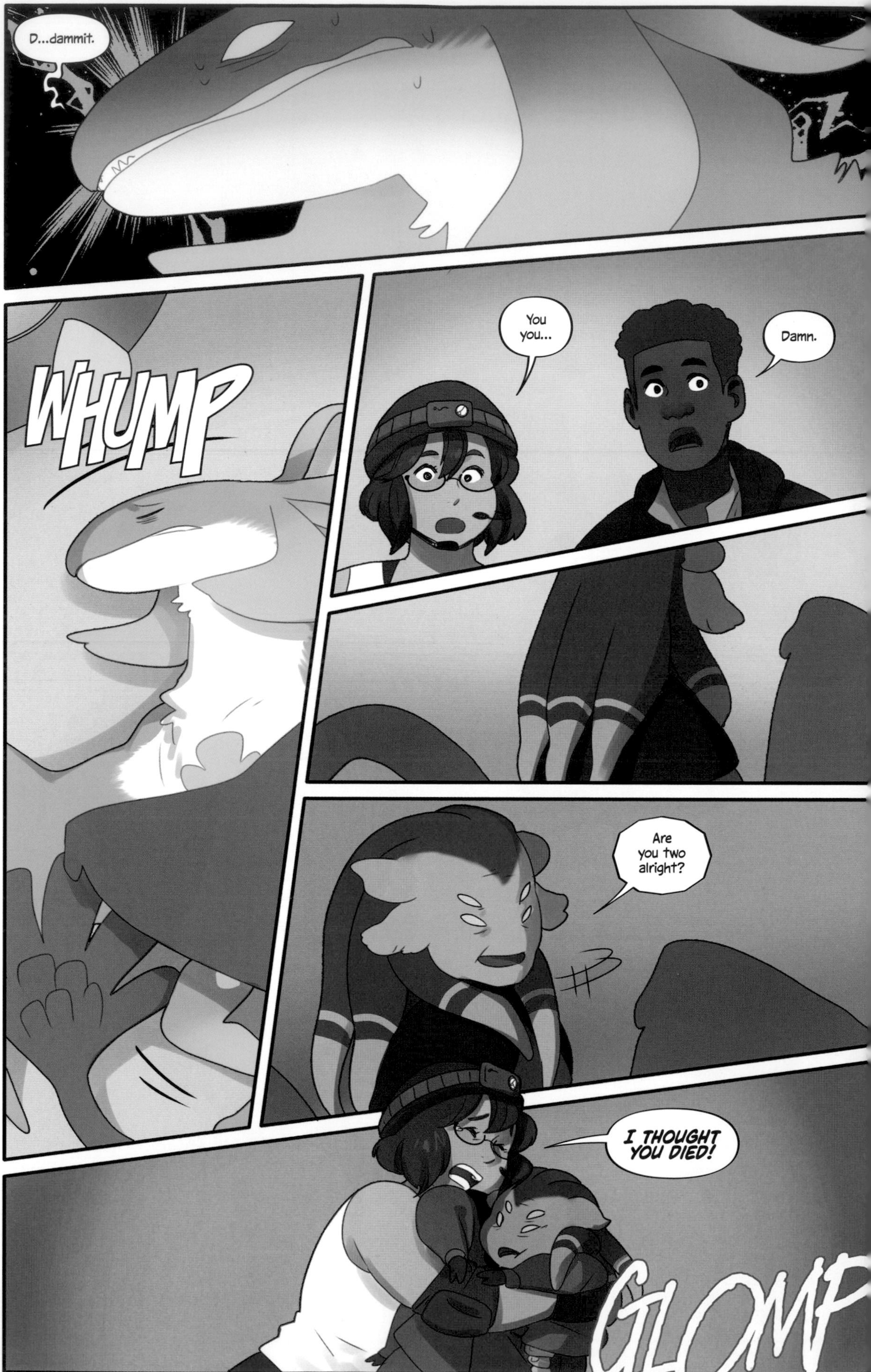
D...dammit.
WHUMP
You you...
Damn.
Are you two alright?
I THOUGHT YOU DIED!
GLOMP

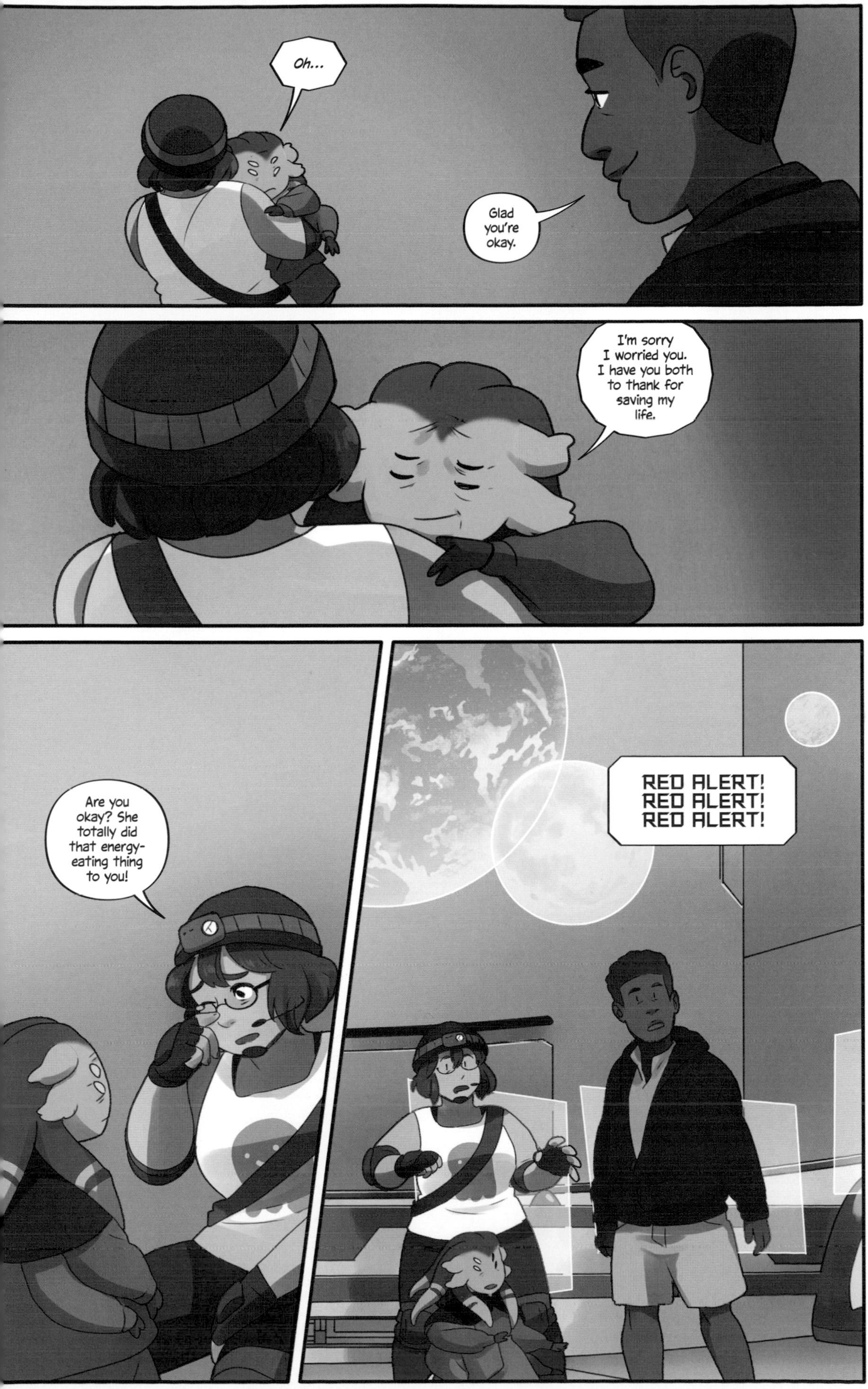
Oh...
Glad you're okay.
I'm sorry I worried you. I have you both to thank for saving my life.
Are you okay? She totally did that energy-eating thing to you!
RED ALERT! RED ALERT! RED ALERT!

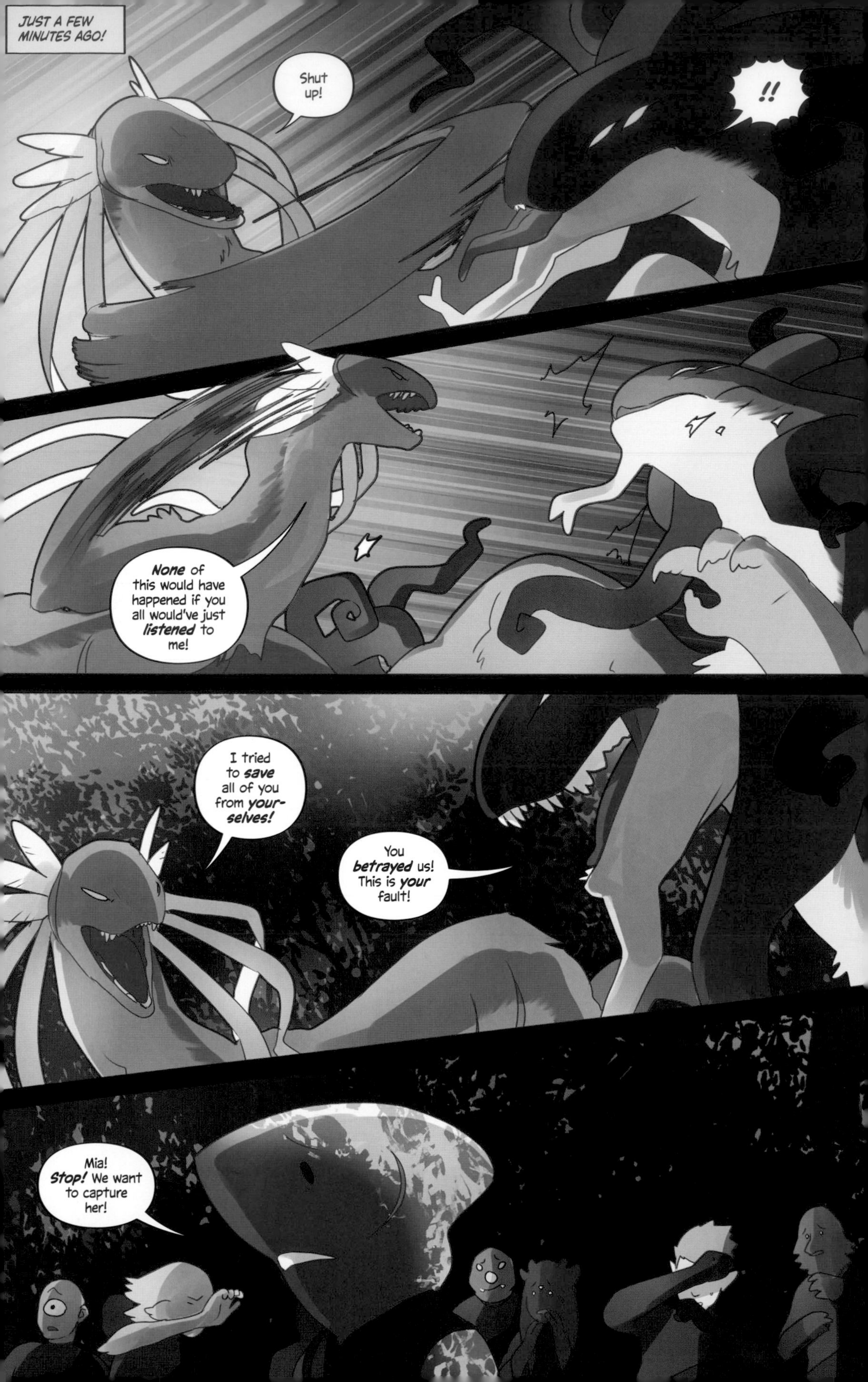
JUST A FEW MINUTES AGO!
Shut up!
!!
None of this would have happened if you all would've just listened to me!
I tried to save all of you from your-selves!
You betrayed us! This is your fault!
Mia! Stop! We want to capture her!

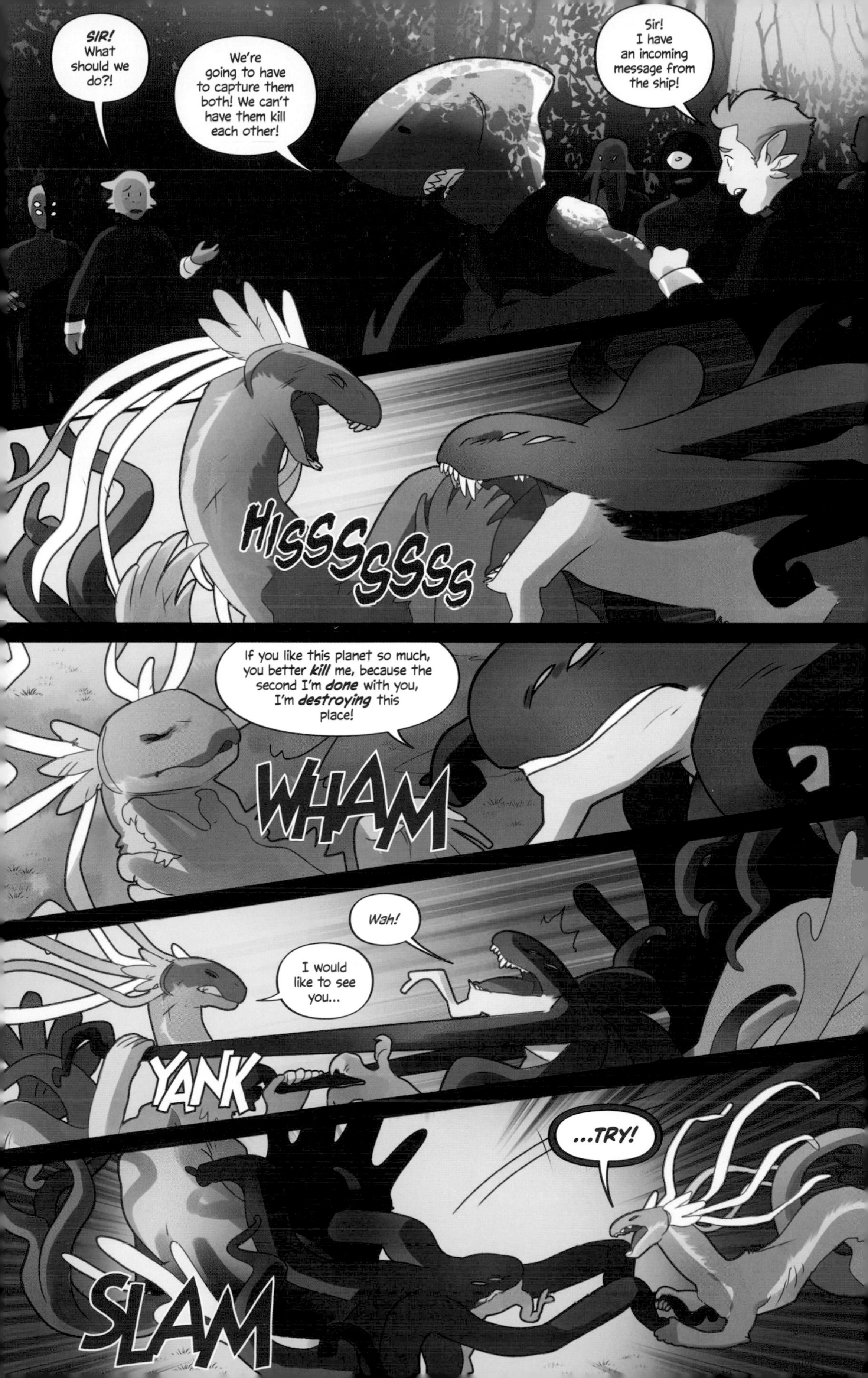
SIR! What should we do?!
We're going to have to capture them both! We can't have them kill each other!
Sir! I have an incoming message from the ship!
HISSSSSSSS
If you like this planet so much, you better **kill** me, because the second I'm **done** with you, I'm **destroying** this place!
WHAM
Wah!
I would like to see you...
YANK
...TRY!
SLAM

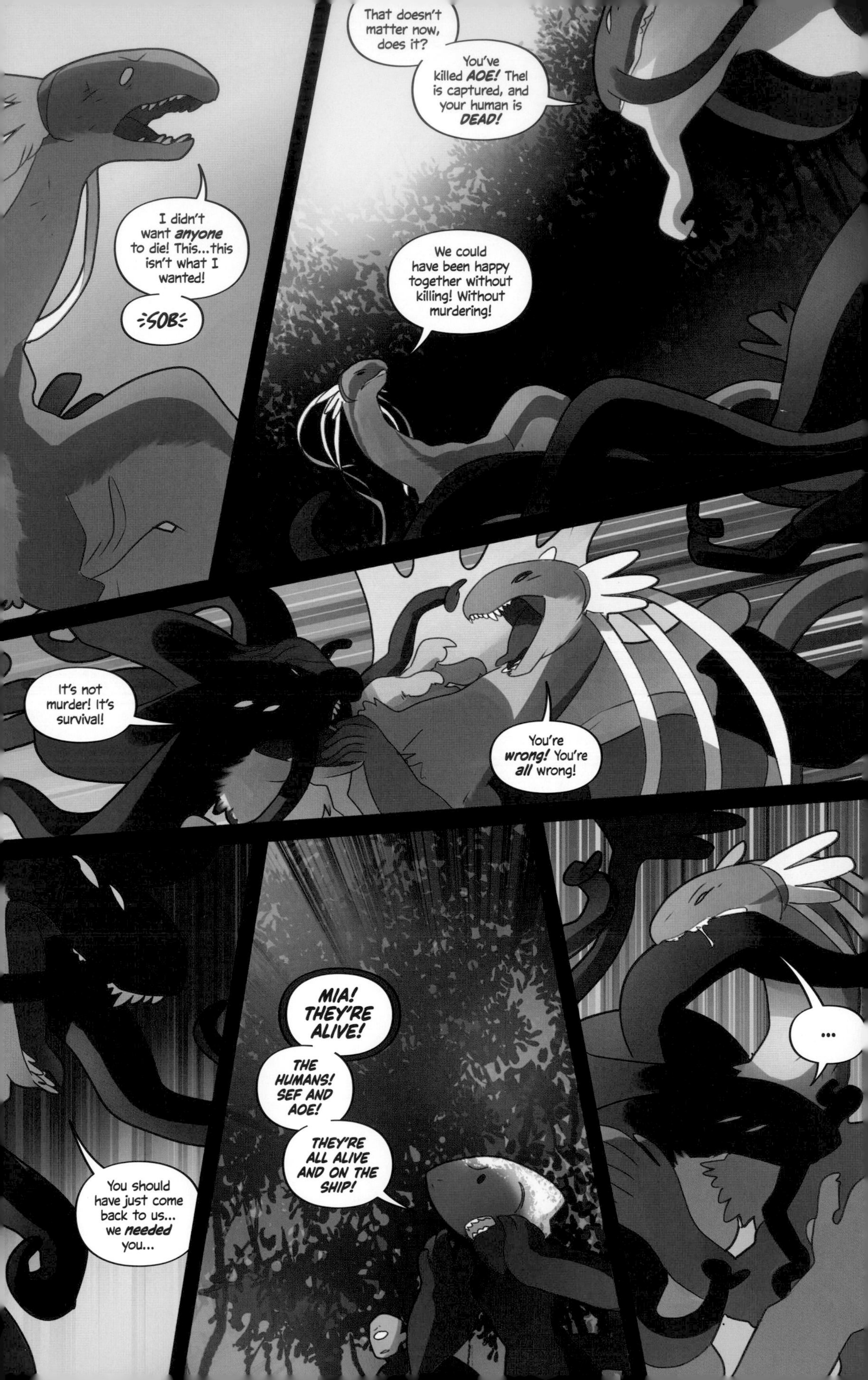

That doesn't matter now, does it?
You've killed AOE! Thel is captured, and your human is DEAD!
I didn't want anyone to die! This...this isn't what I wanted!
SOB
We could have been happy together without killing! Without murdering!
It's not murder! It's survival!
You're wrong! You're all wrong!
You should have just come back to us... we needed you...
MIA! THEY'RE ALIVE!
THE HUMANS! SEF AND AOE!
THEY'RE ALL ALIVE AND ON THE SHIP!
...

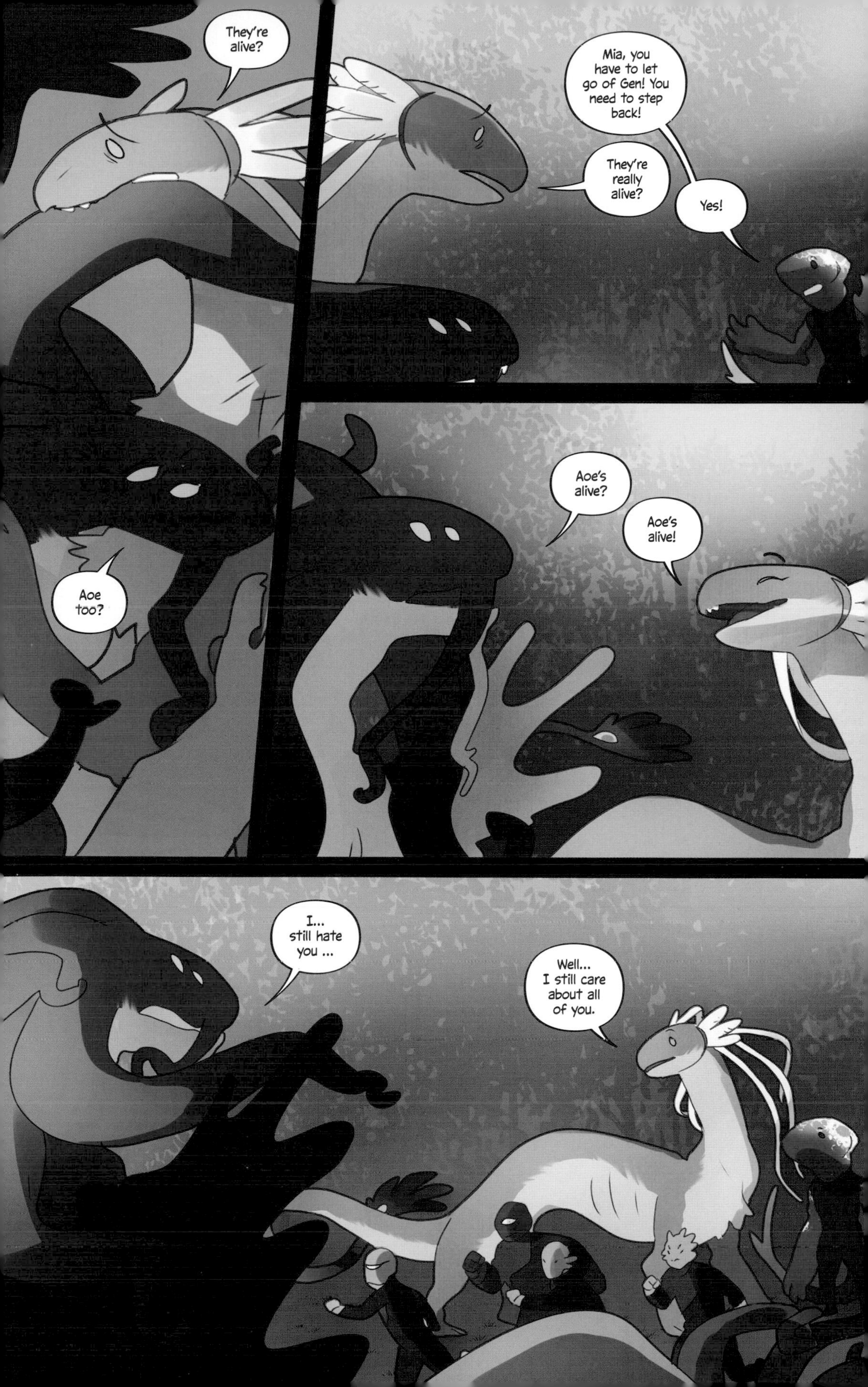
They're alive?
Mia, you have to let go of Gen! You need to step back!
They're really alive?
Yes!
Aoe too?
Aoe's alive?
Aoe's alive!
I... still hate you ...
Well... I still care about all of you.

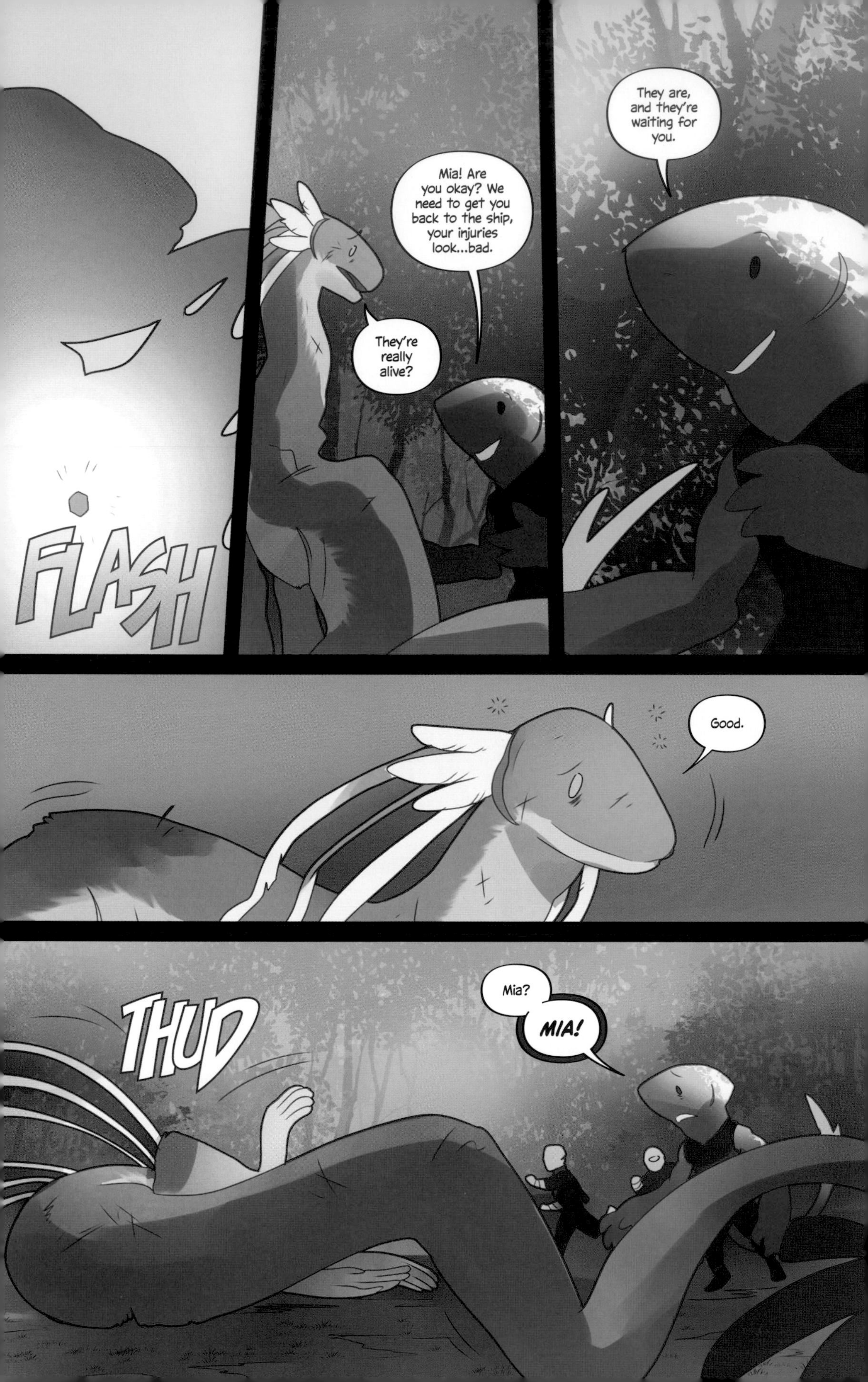
FLASH
They're really alive?
Mia! Are you okay? We need to get you back to the ship, your injuries look...bad.
They are, and they're waiting for you.
Good.
THUD
Mia?
MIA!

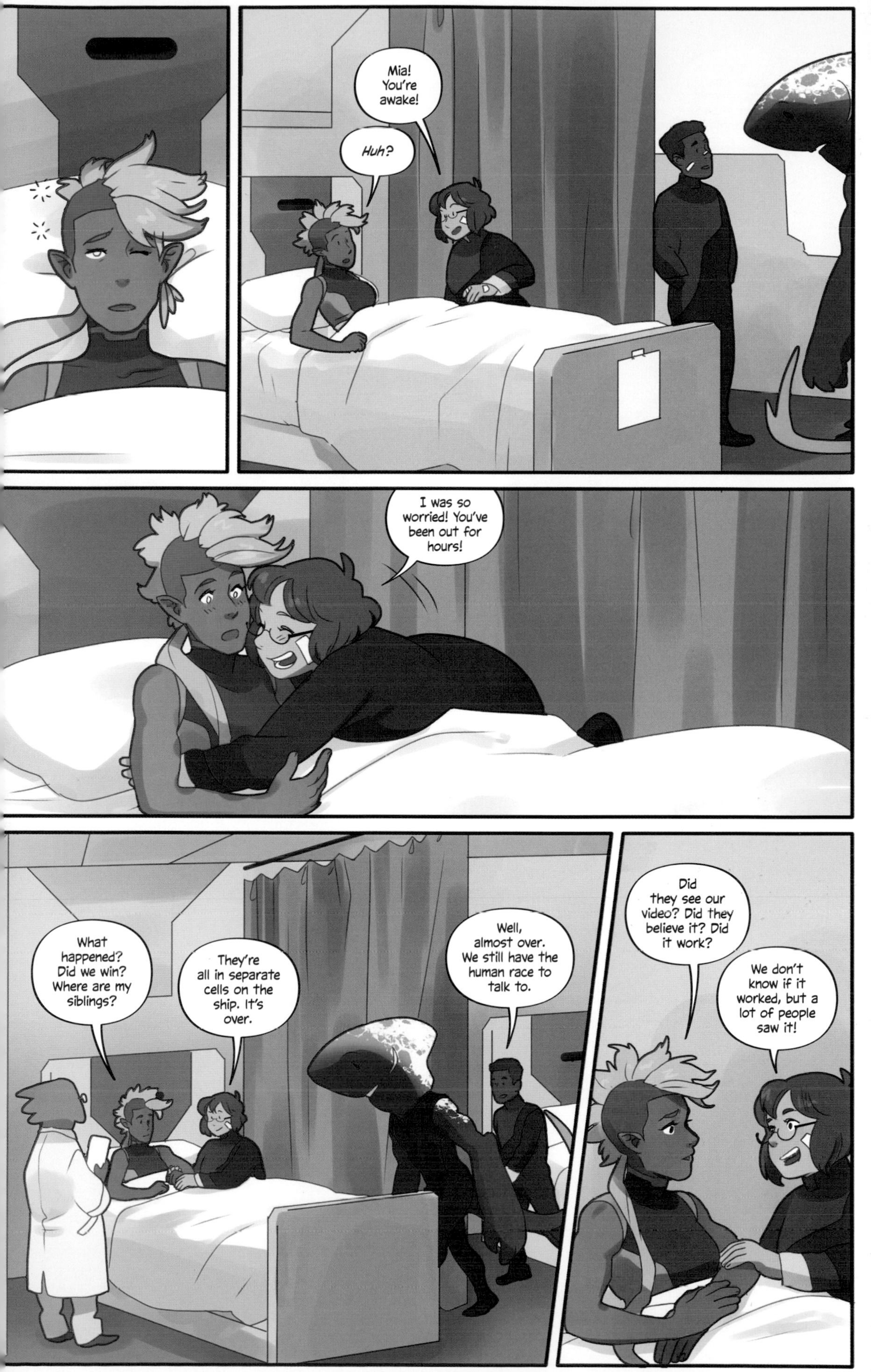
Mia! You're awake!
Huh?
I was so worried! You've been out for hours!
What happened? Did we win? Where are my siblings?
They're all in separate cells on the ship. It's over.
Well, almost over. We still have the human race to talk to.
Did they see our video? Did they believe it? Did it work?
We don't know if it worked, but a lot of people saw it!

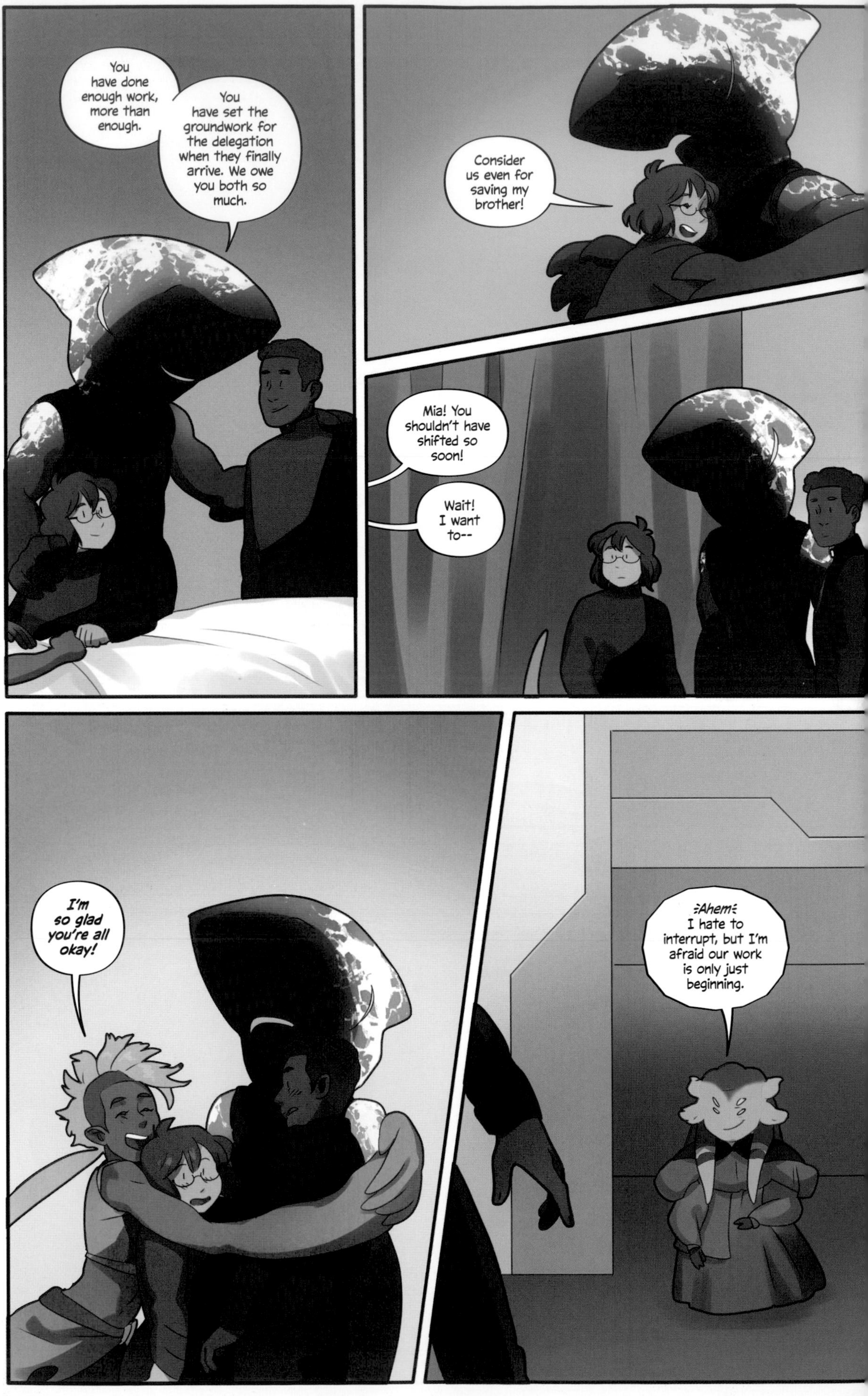
You have done enough work, more than enough.
You have set the groundwork for the delegation when they finally arrive. We owe you both so much.
Consider us even for saving my brother!
Mia! You shouldn't have shifted so soon!
Wait! I want to--
I'm so glad you're all okay!
Ahem
I hate to interrupt, but I'm afraid our work is only just beginning.

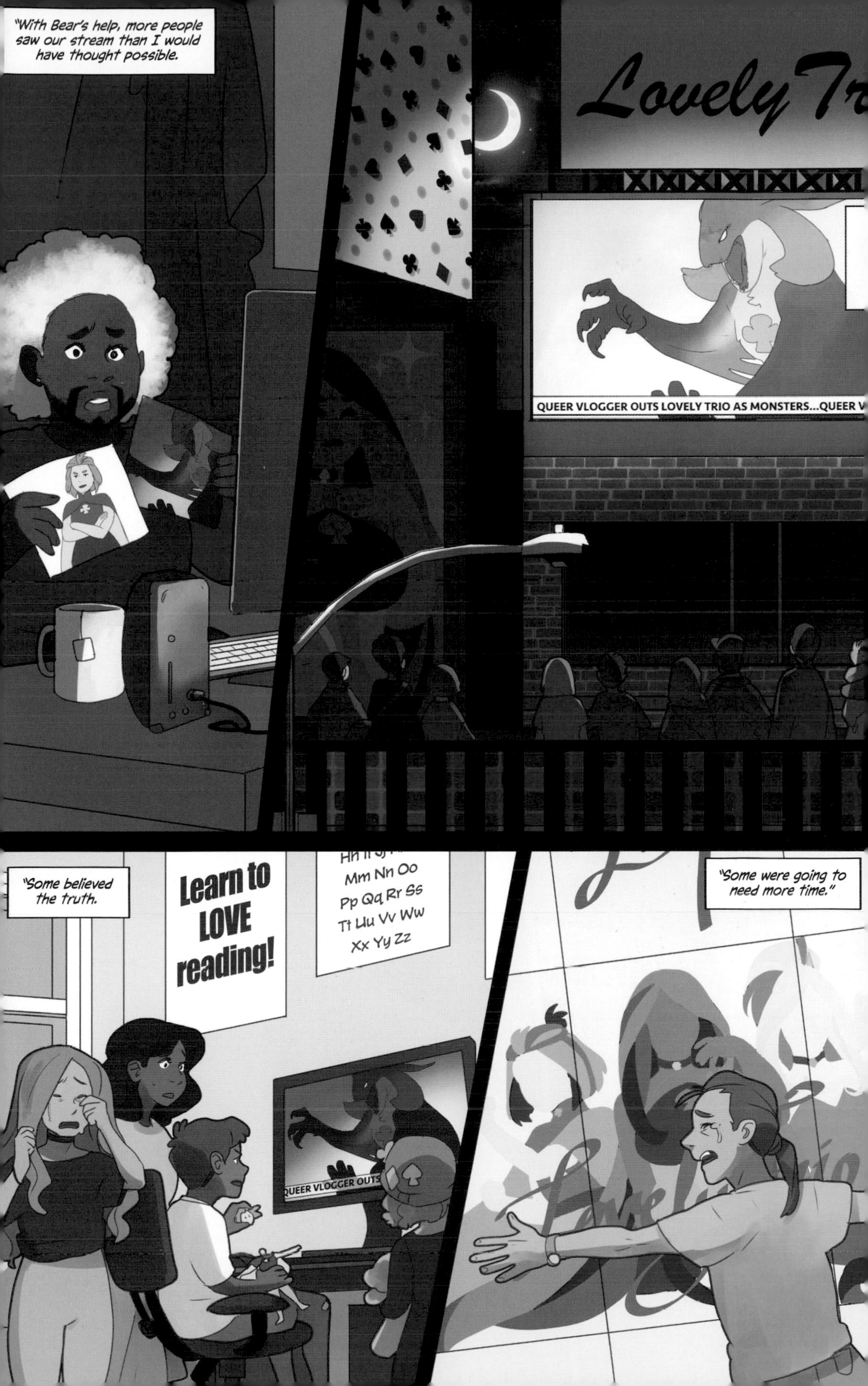
"With Bear's help, more people saw our stream than I would have thought possible.
Lovely Tr
QUEER VLOGGER OUTS LOVELY TRIO AS MONSTERS...QUEER V
"Some believed the truth.
Learn to LOVE reading!
Mm Nn Oo
Pp Qq Rr Ss
Tt Uu Vv Ww
Xx Yy Zz
QUEER VLOGGER OUTS
"Some were going to need more time."

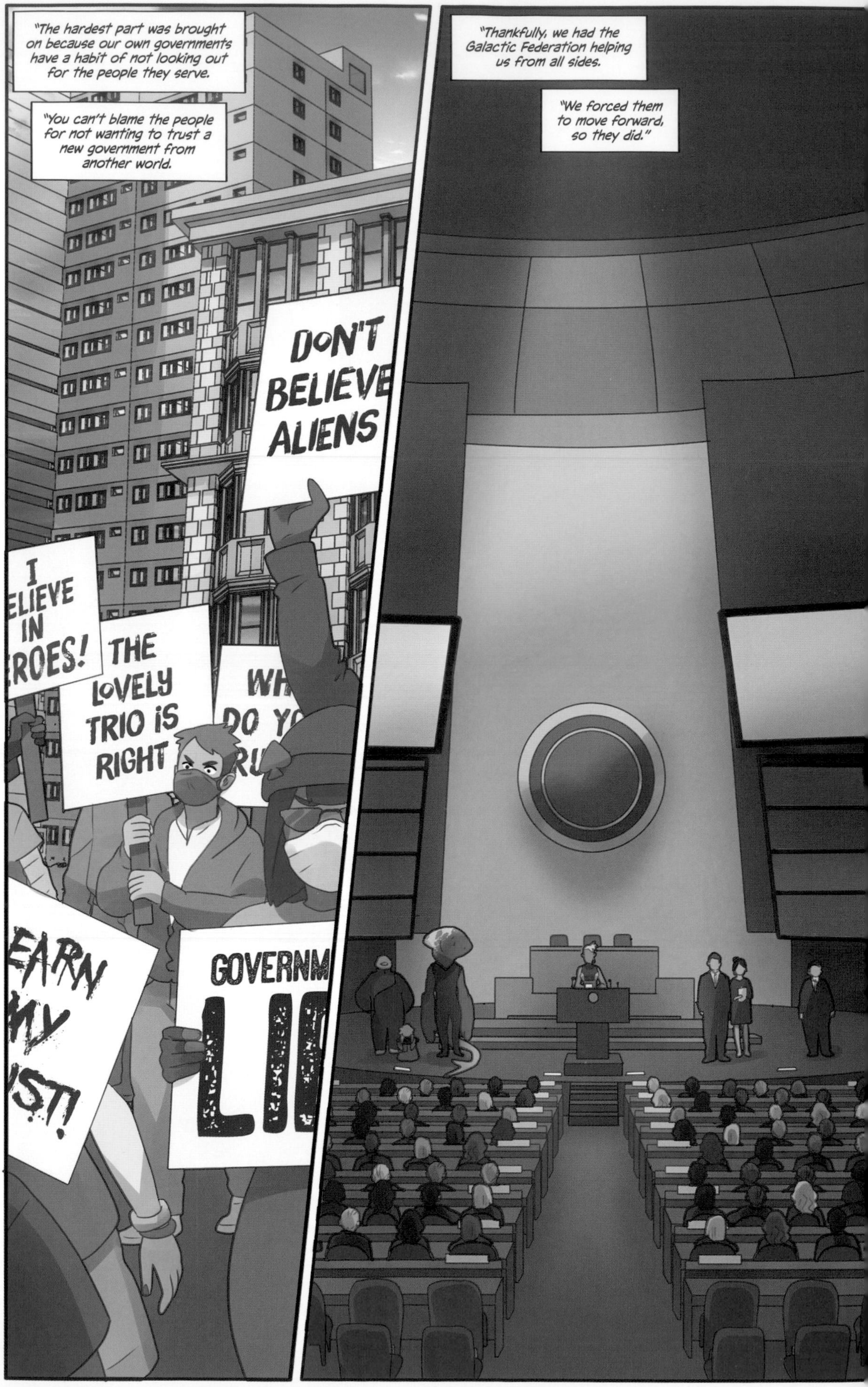
"The hardest part was brought on because our own governments have a habit of not looking out for the people they serve.
"You can't blame the people for not wanting to trust a new government from another world.
DON'T BELIEVE ALIENS
I ELIEVE IN EROES!
THE LOVELY TRIO IS RIGHT
WH DO YO RU
EARN MY UST!
GOVERNM LI
"Thankfully, we had the Galactic Federation helping us from all sides.
"We forced them to move forward, so they did."

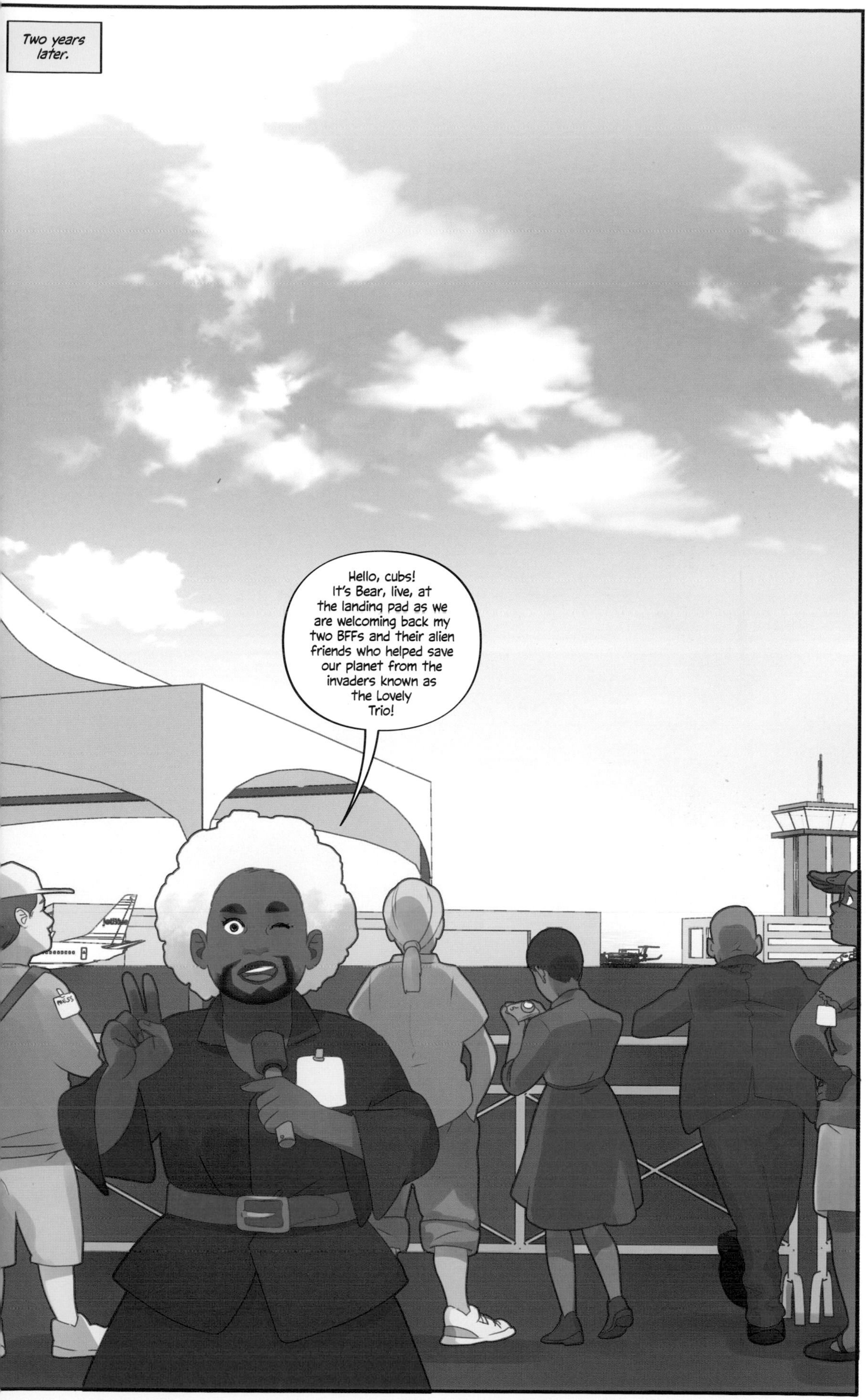
Two years later.
Hello, cubs! It's Bear, live, at the landing pad as we are welcoming back my two BFFs and their alien friends who helped save our planet from the invaders known as the Lovely Trio!

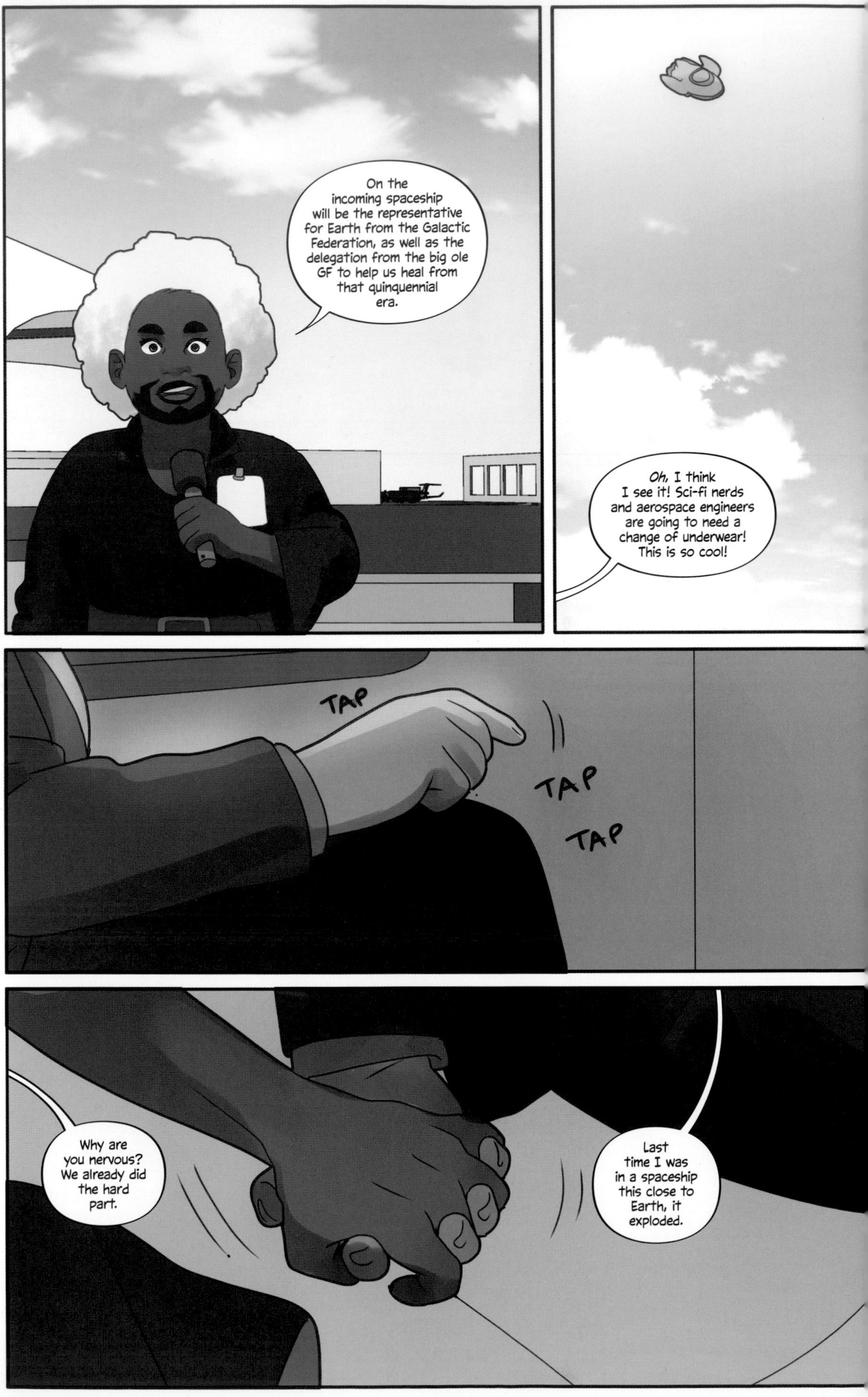
On the incoming spaceship will be the representative for Earth from the Galactic Federation, as well as the delegation from the big ole GF to help us heal from that quinquennial era.
Oh, I think I see it! Sci-fi nerds and aerospace engineers are going to need a change of underwear! This is so cool!
TAP
TAP
TAP
Why are you nervous? We already did the hard part.
Last time I was in a spaceship this close to Earth, it exploded.

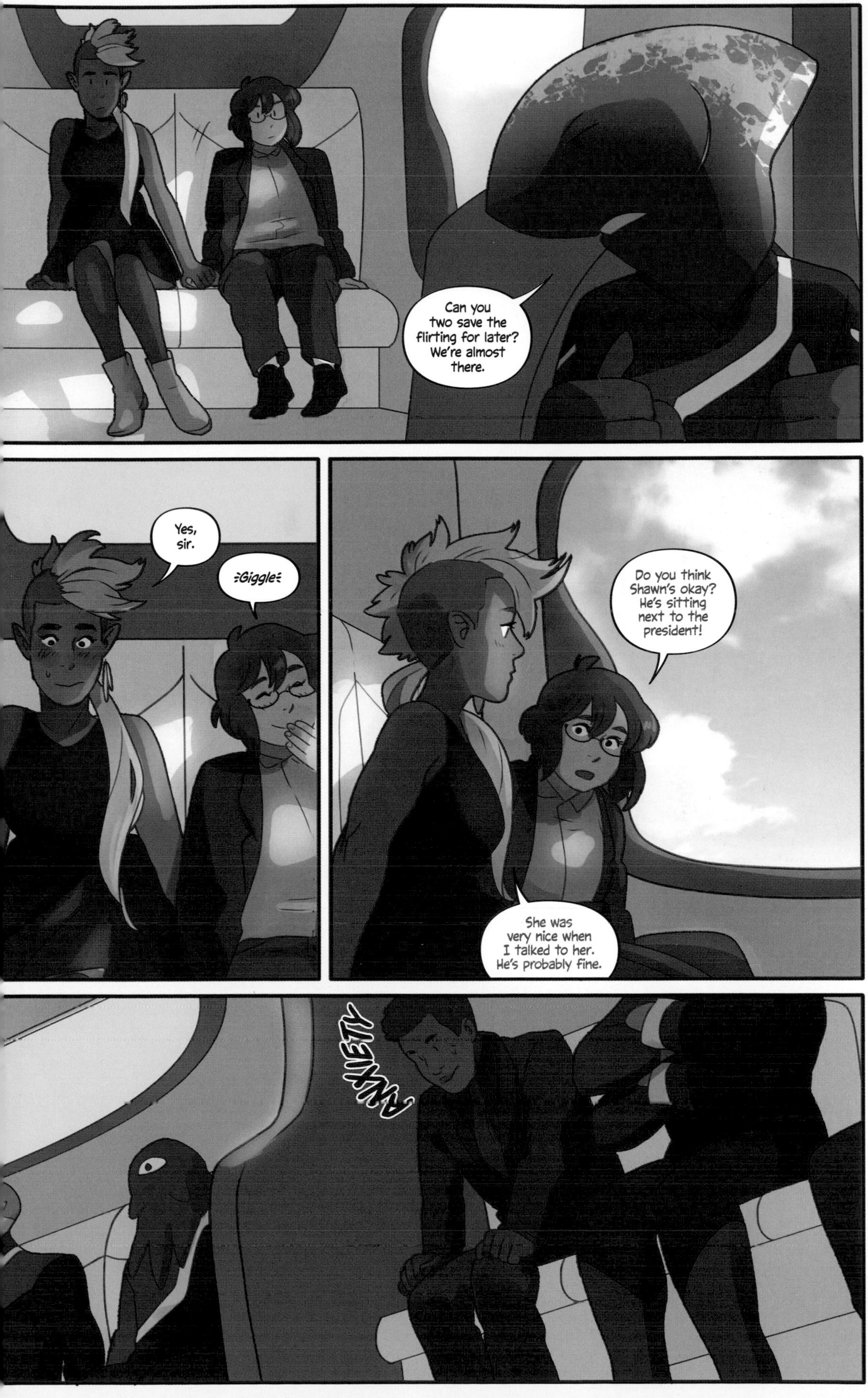
Can you two save the flirting for later? We're almost there.
Yes, sir.
Giggle
Do you think Shawn's okay? He's sitting next to the president!
She was very nice when I talked to her. He's probably fine.
ANXIETY

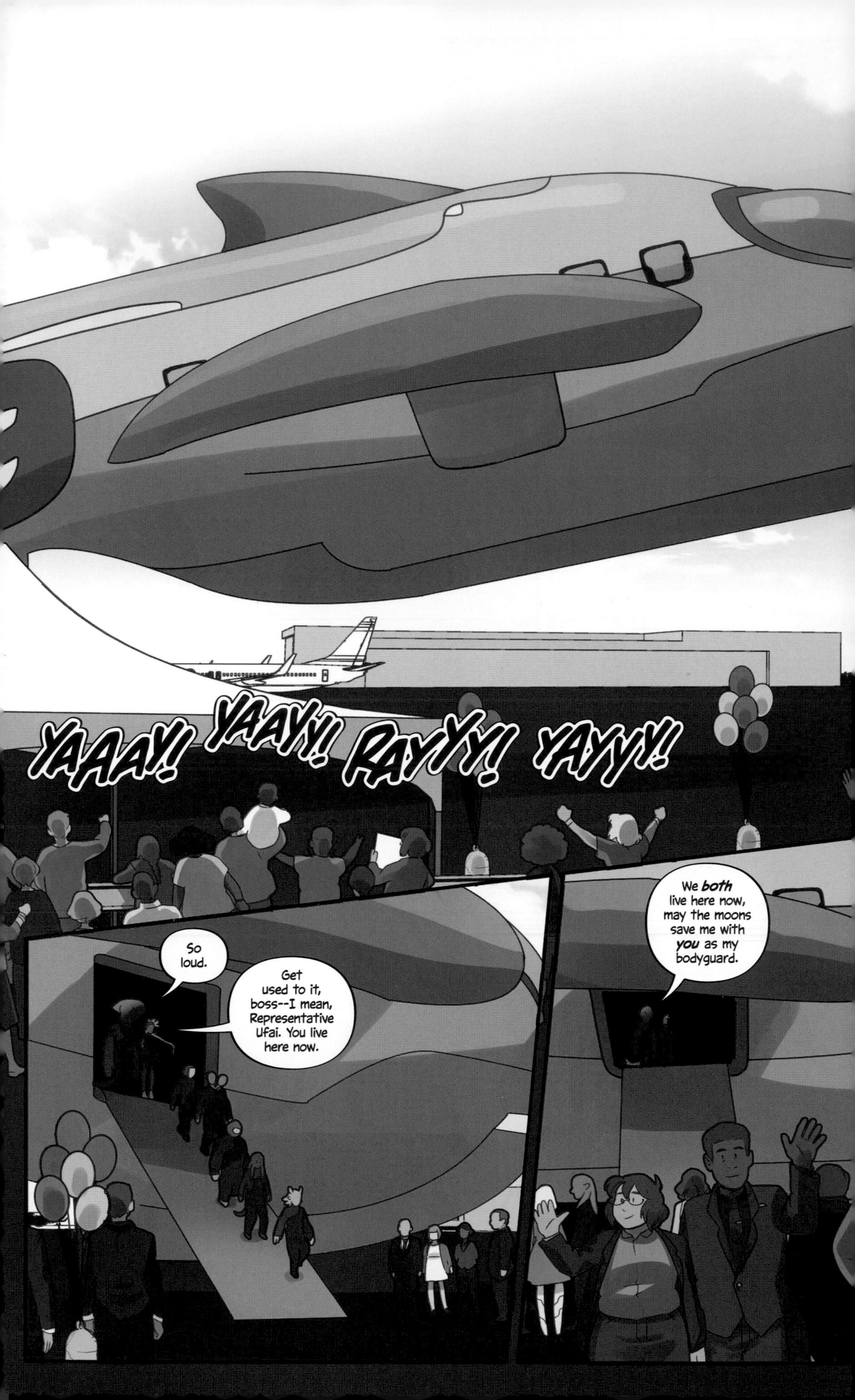
YAAAY! YAAYY! RAYYY! YAYYY!
So loud.
Get used to it, boss--I mean, Representative Ufai. You live here now.
We *both* live here now, may the moons save me with *you* as my bodyguard.

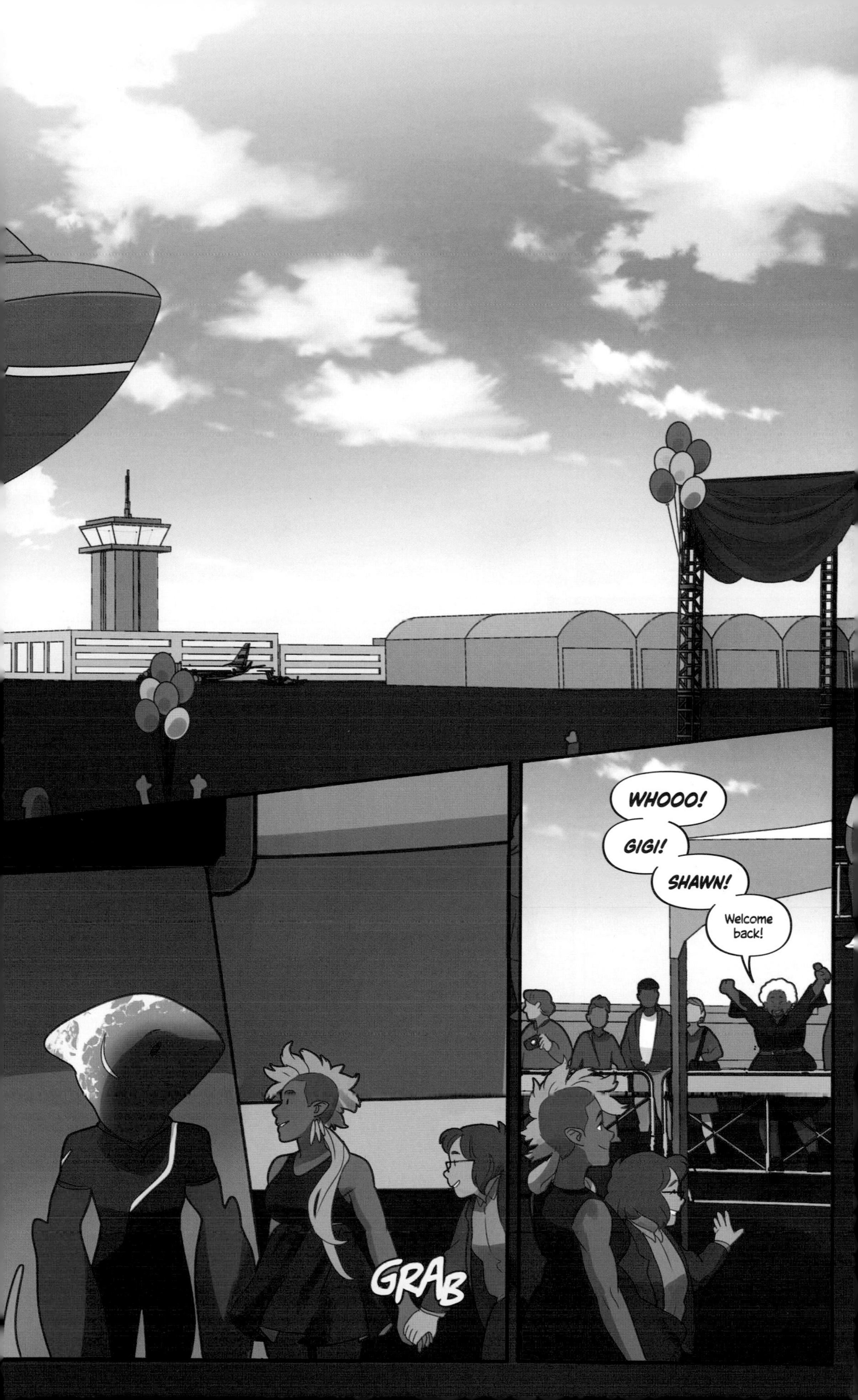
WHOOO!
GIGI!
SHAWN!
Welcome back!
GRAB

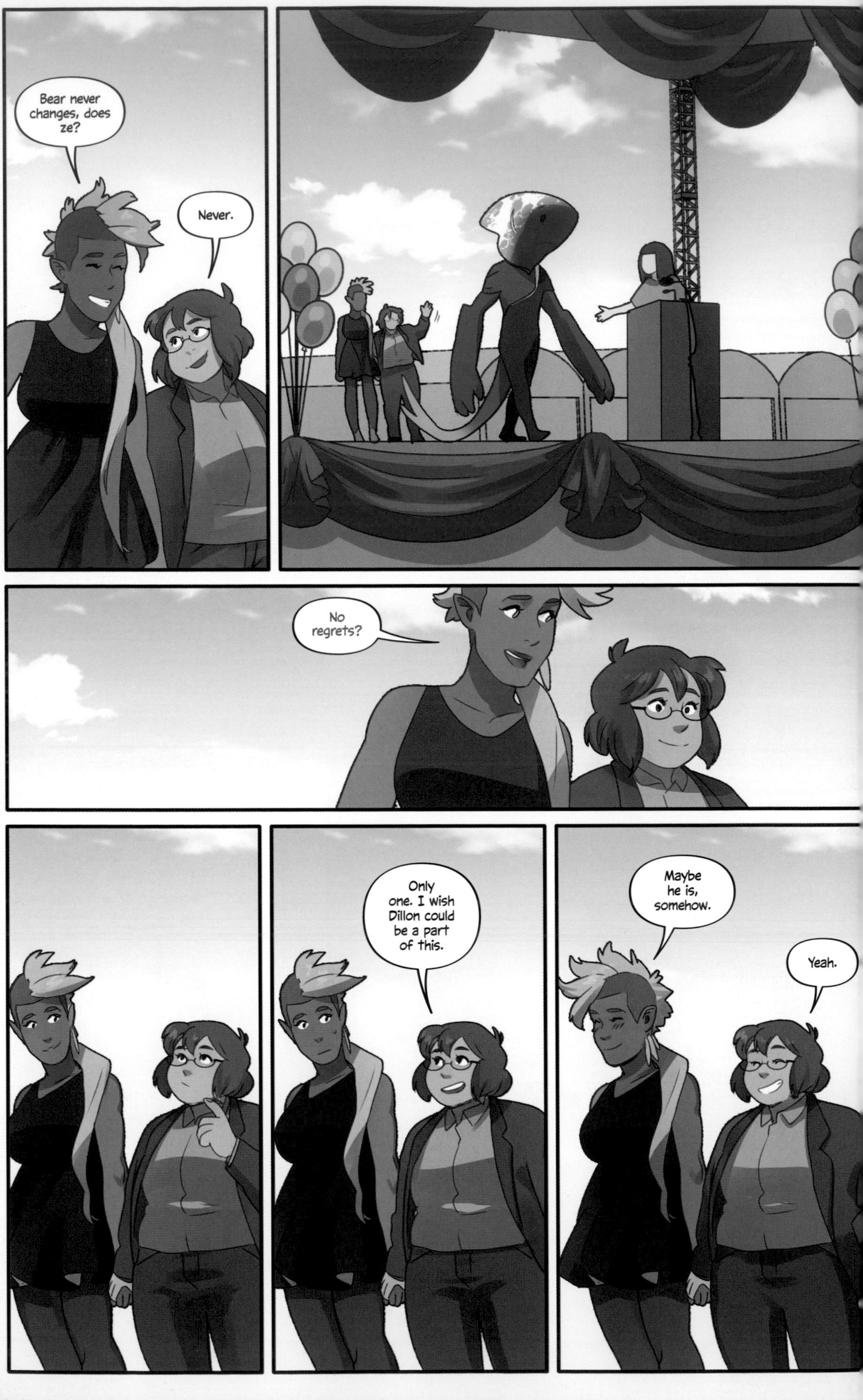
Bear never changes, does ze?
Never.
No regrets?
Only one. I wish Dillon could be a part of this.
Maybe he is, somehow.
Yeah.

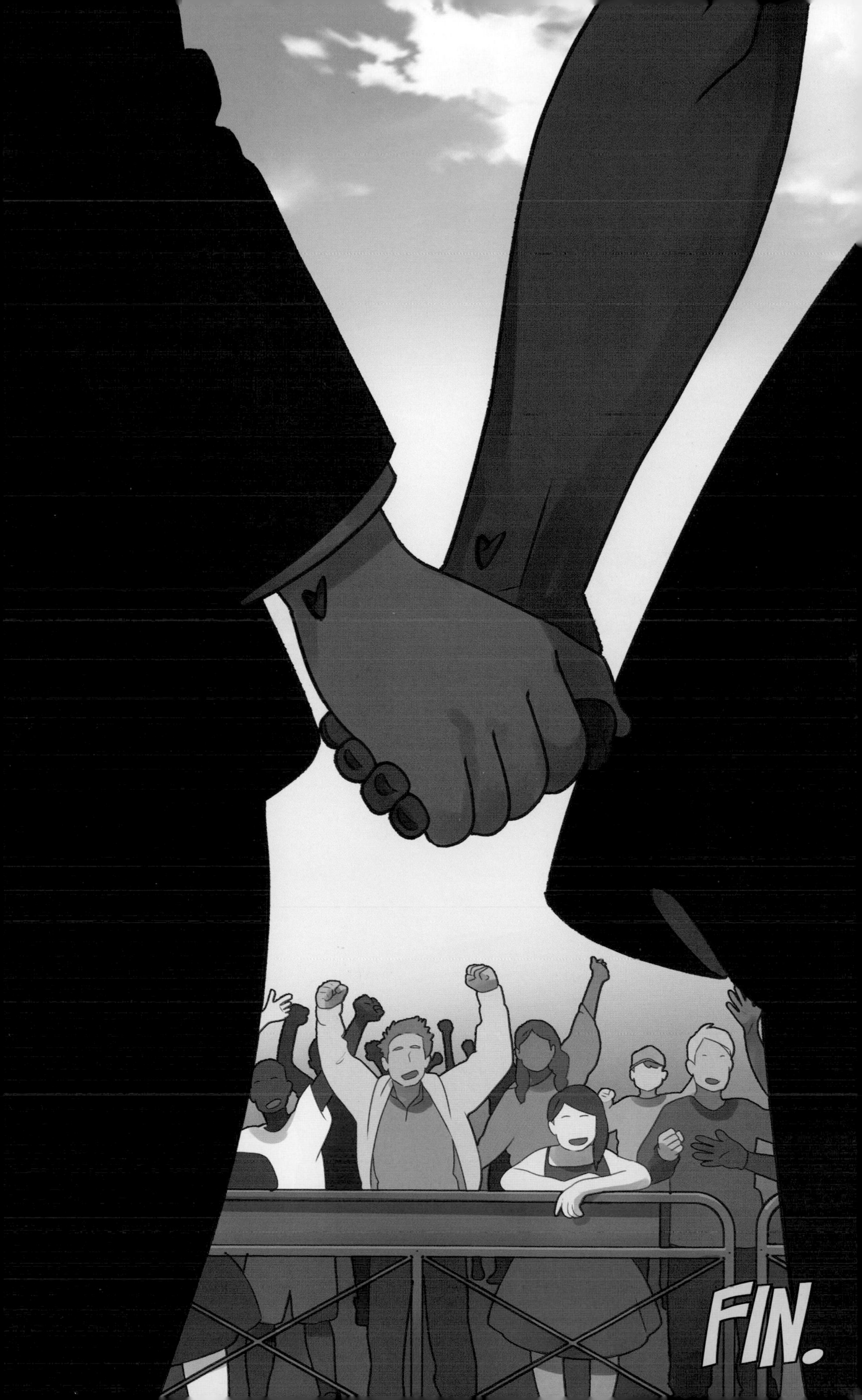
FIN.

SAVE YOURSELF! #1 SECOND PRINT COVER BY

KELLY & NICHOLE MATTHEWS

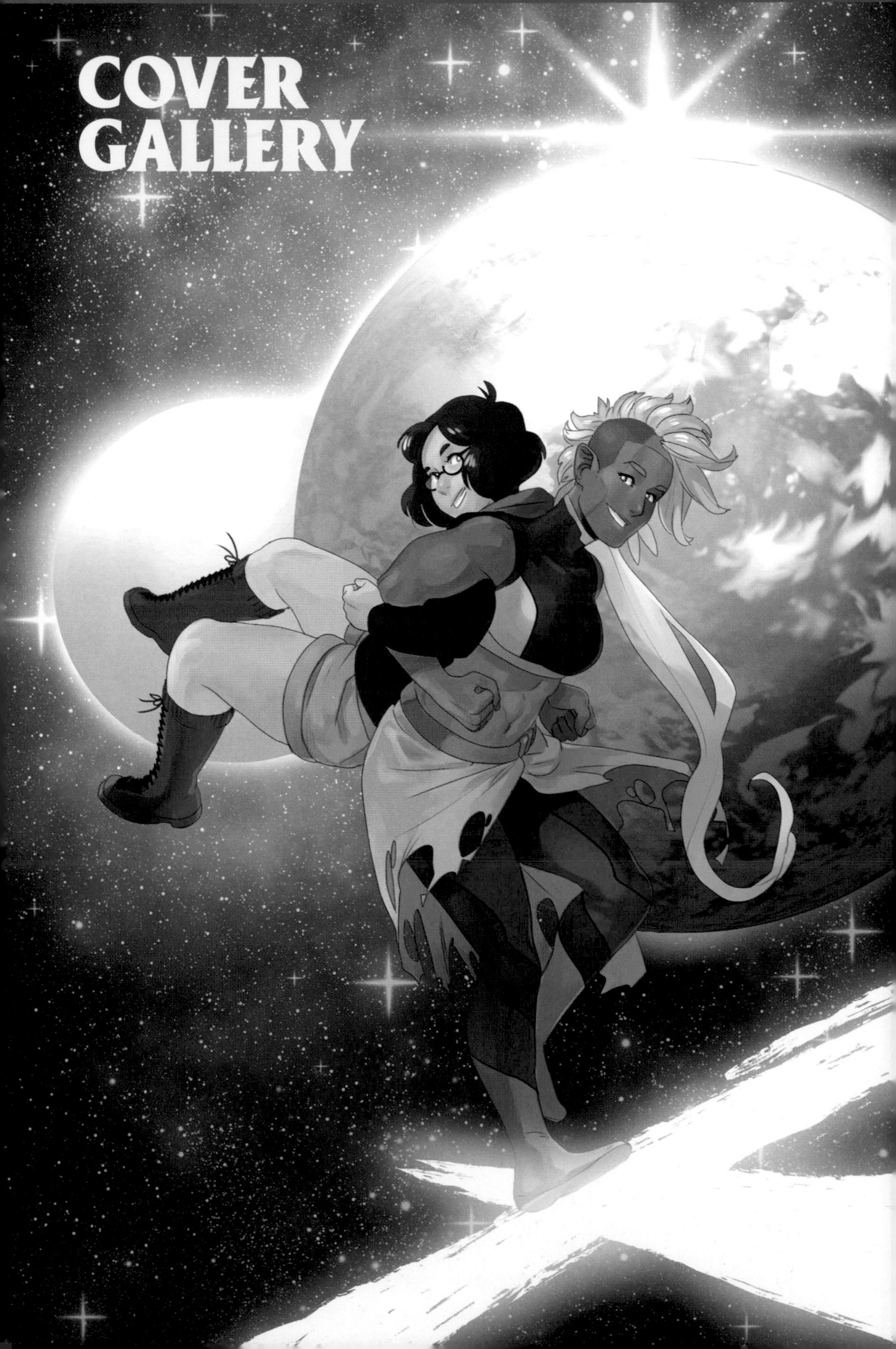
COVER
GALLERY

SAVE YOURSELF! #1-#4 MAGICAL GIRL VARIANT COVERS BY

STEPHANIE GONZAGA

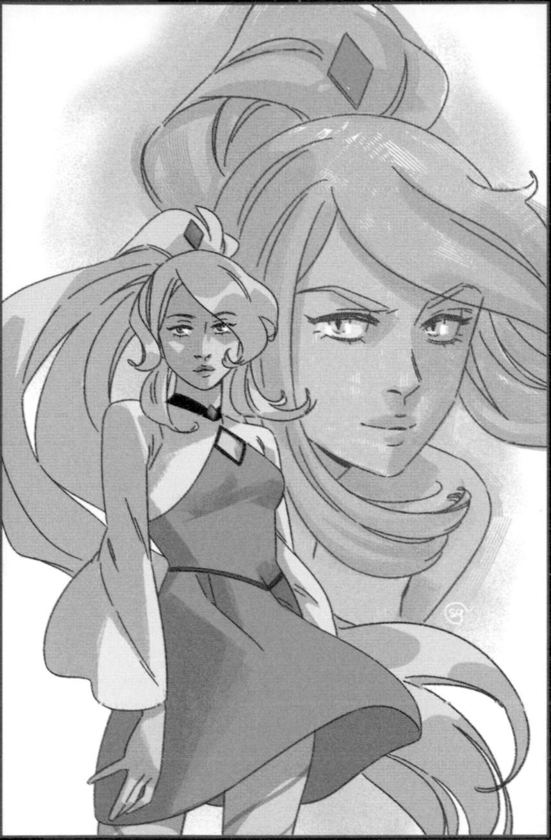

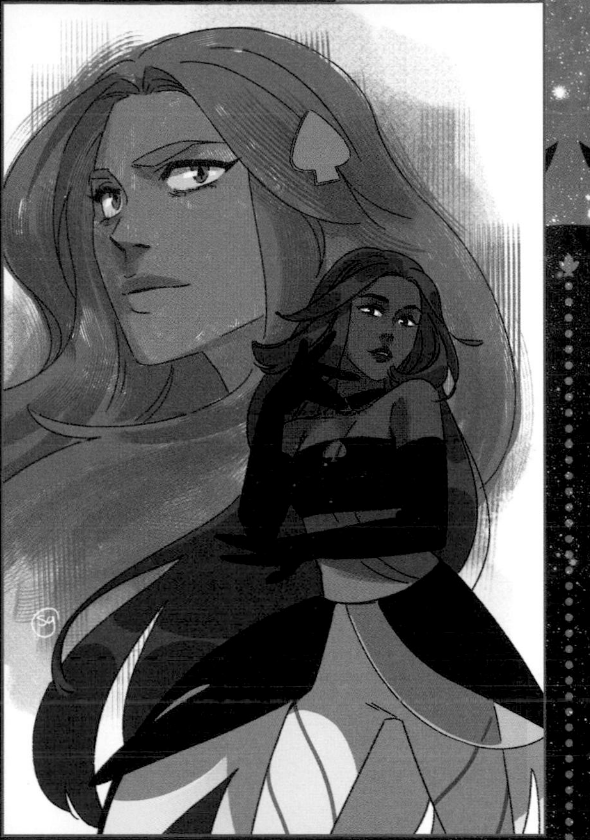

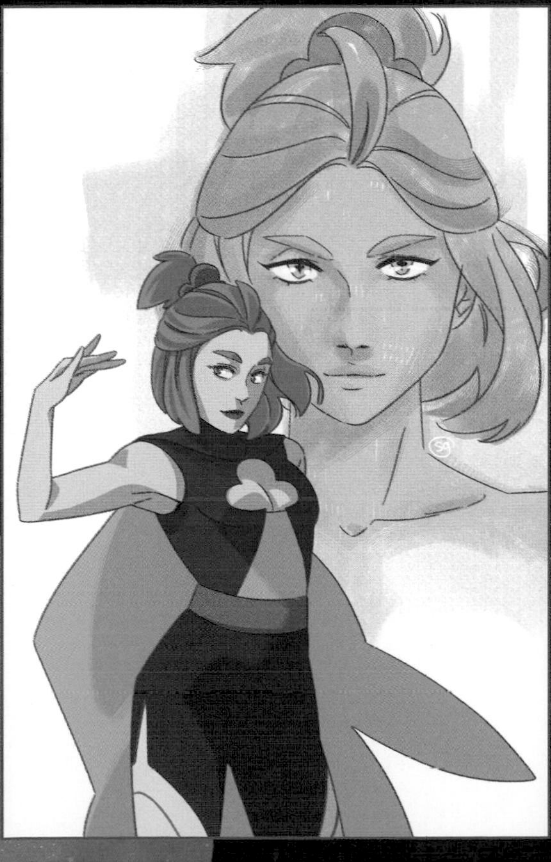

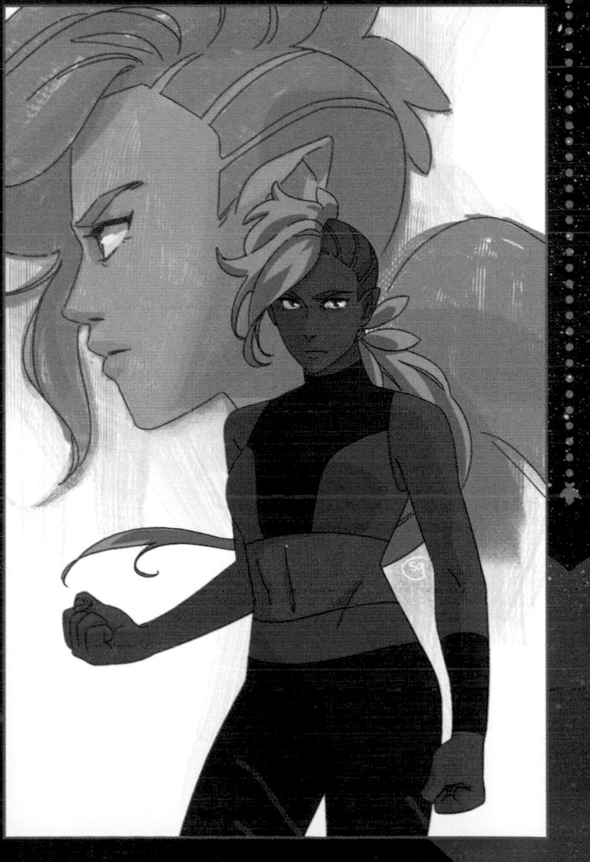

SAVE YOURSELF! #1 VARIANT COVER BY

KEVIN WADA

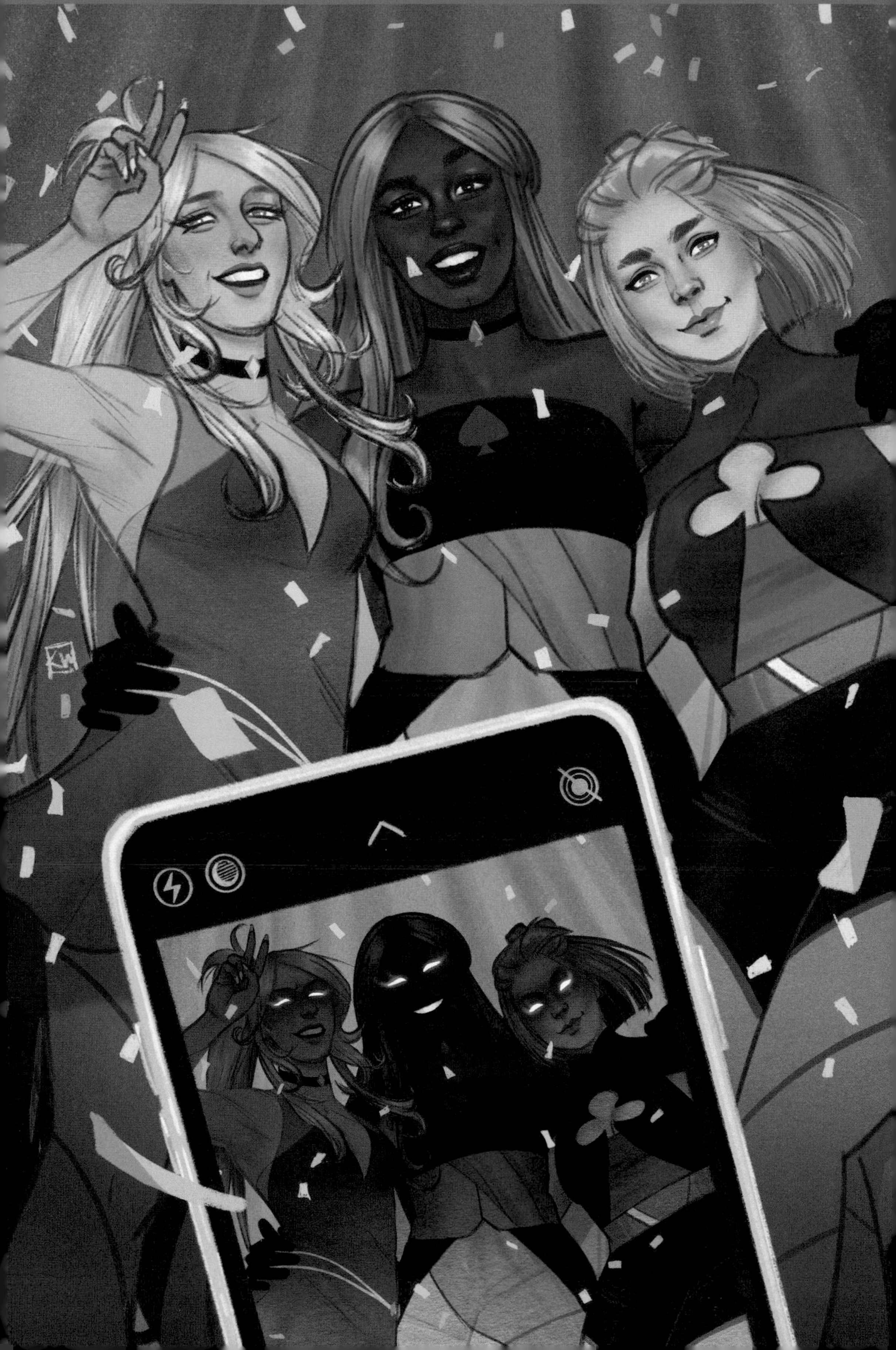

SAVE YOURSELF! #1 BOOM! STUDIOS EXCLUSIVE COVER BY

JORGE CORONA

WITH COLORS BY SARAH STERN

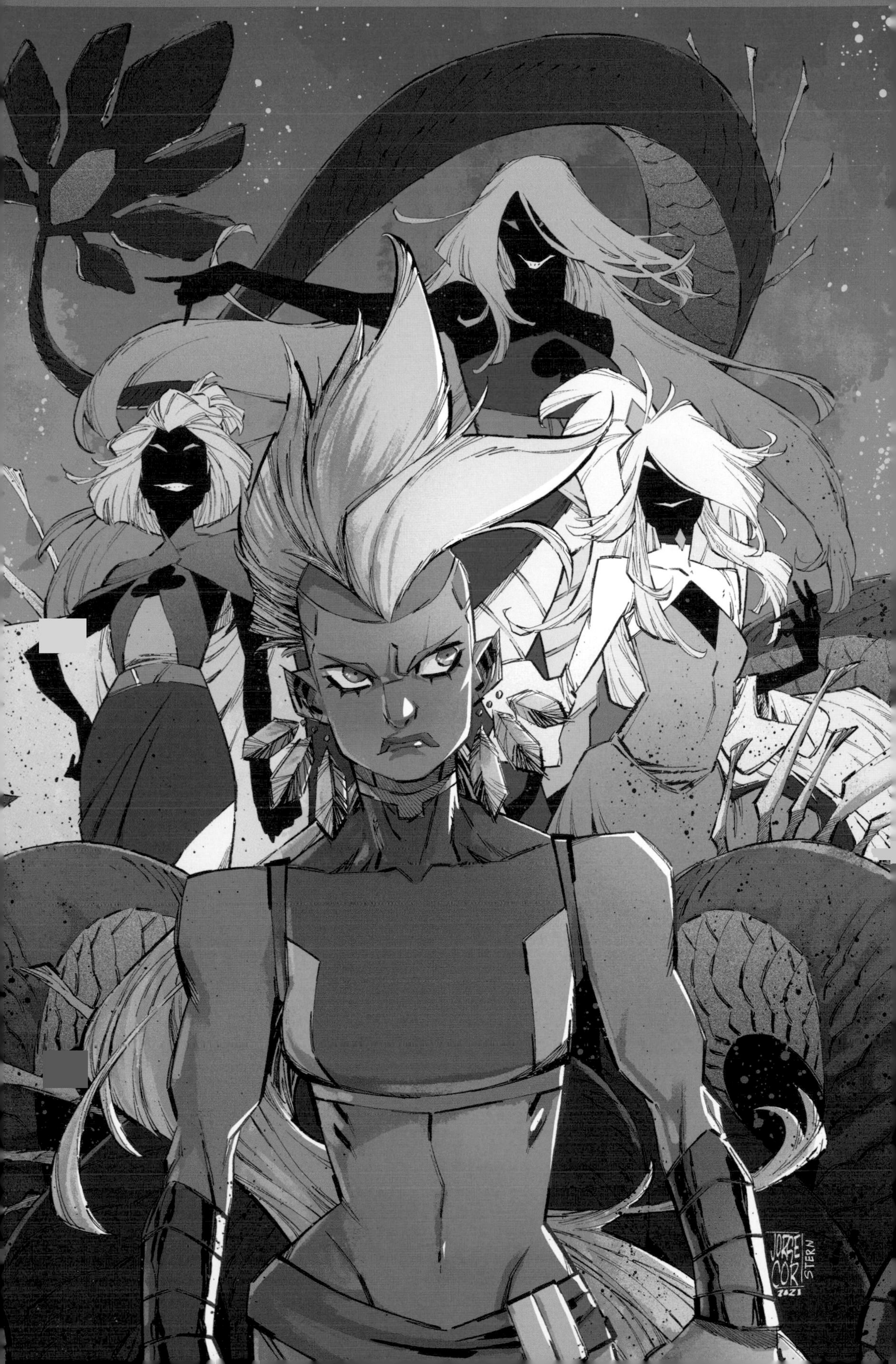

SAVE YOURSELF! #1 FRANKIE'S COMICS
EXCLUSIVE VARIANT COVER BY
RIAN GONZALES

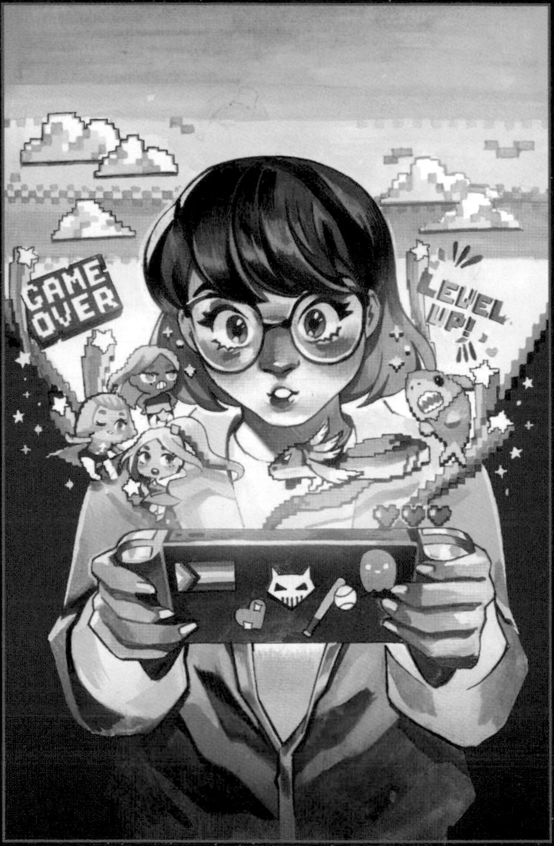
GAME OVER
LEVEL UP!

SAVE YOURSELF! #1 COMIC VAULT LIVE
EXCLUSIVE VARIANT COVER BY
DJ KIRKLAND

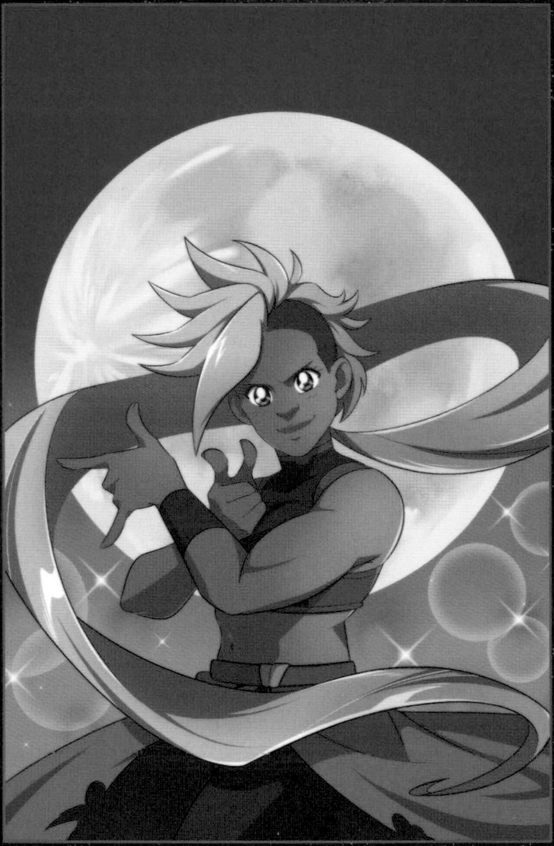

ORIGINAL CHARACTER DESIGNS BY
KELLY & NICHOLE MATTHEWS

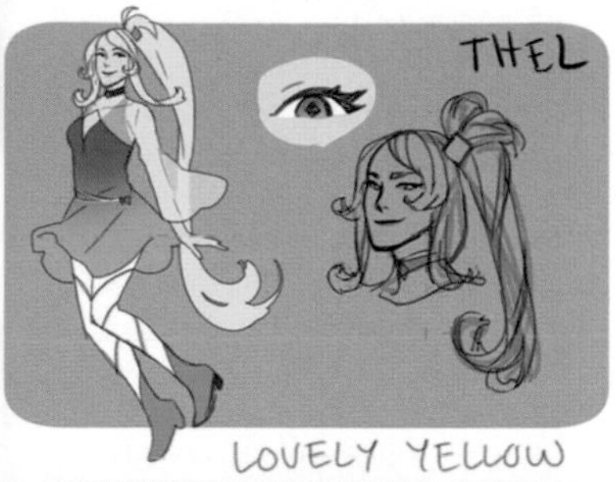
THEL
LOVELY YELLOW

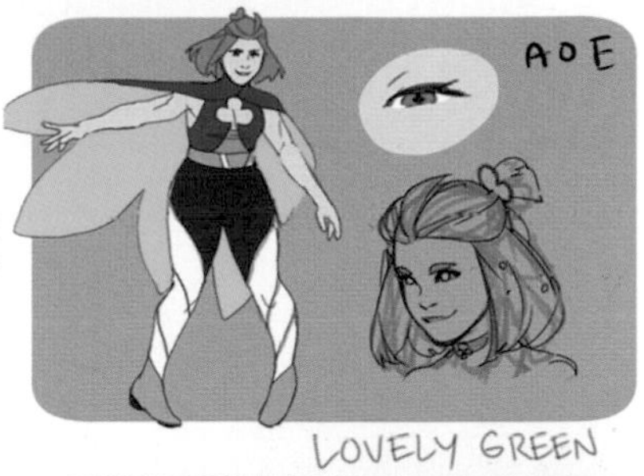
AOE
LOVELY GREEN

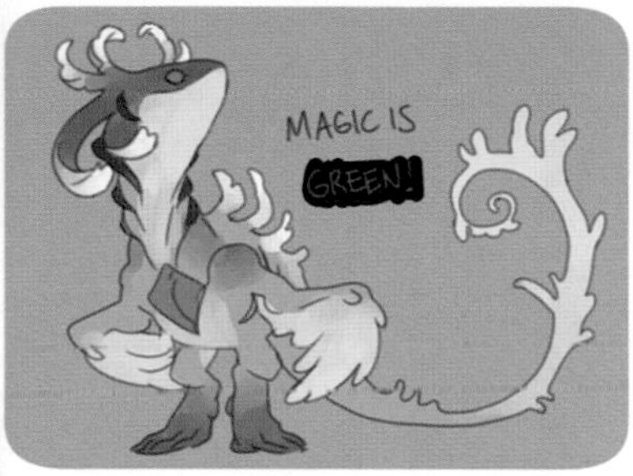
MAGIC IS
GREEN!

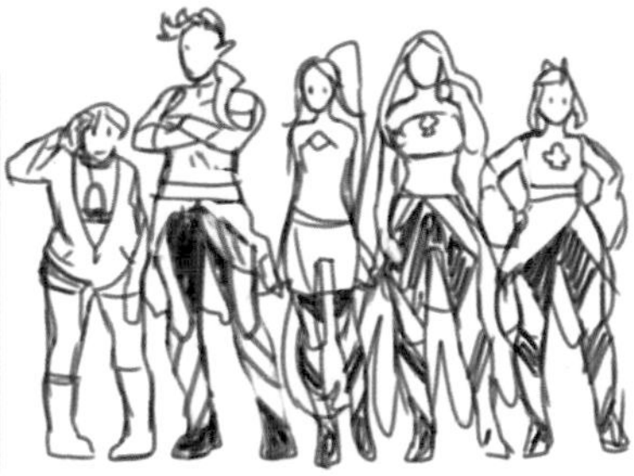

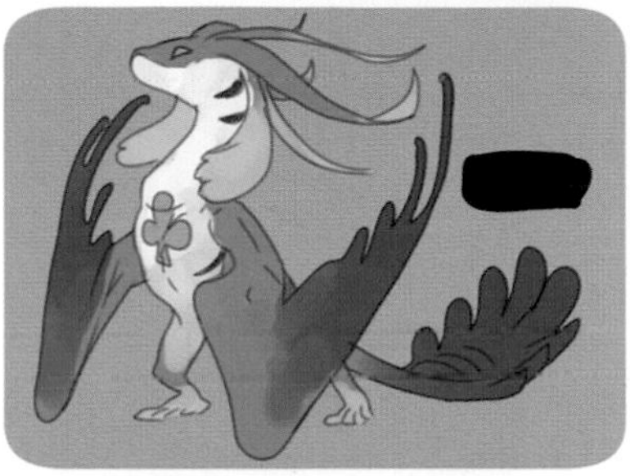

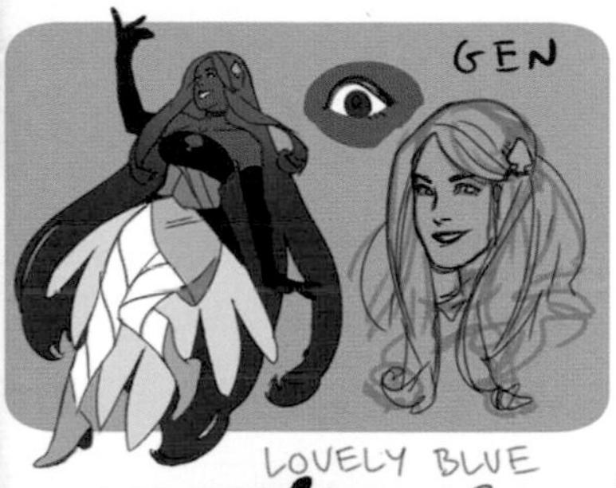
GEN
LOVELY BLUE

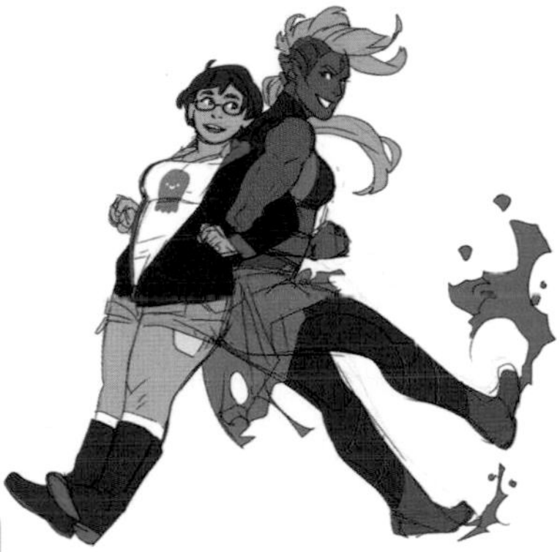

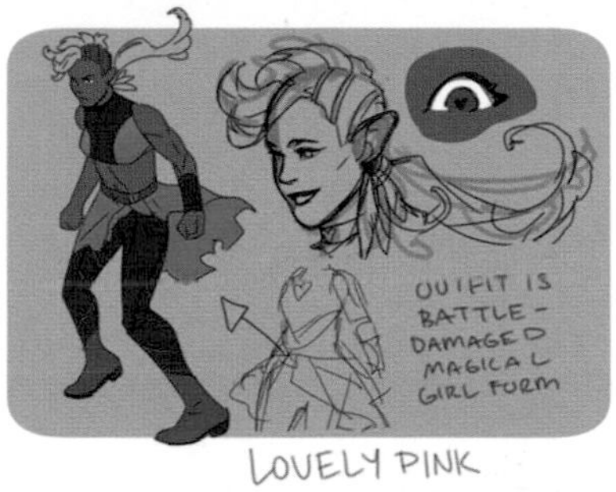
OUTFIT IS
BATTLE-
DAMAGED
MAGICAL
GIRL FORM
LOVELY PINK

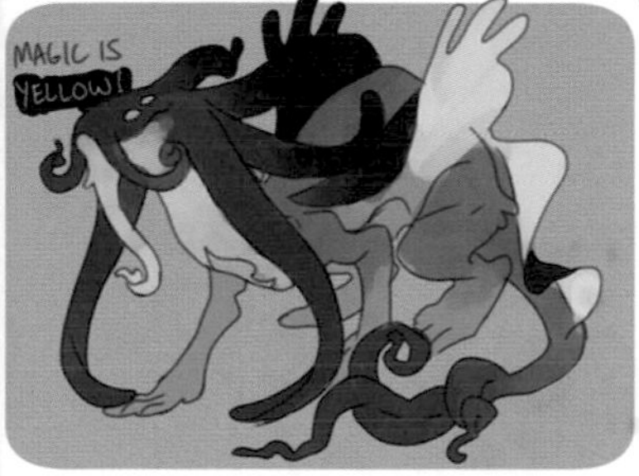
MAGIC IS
YELLOW!

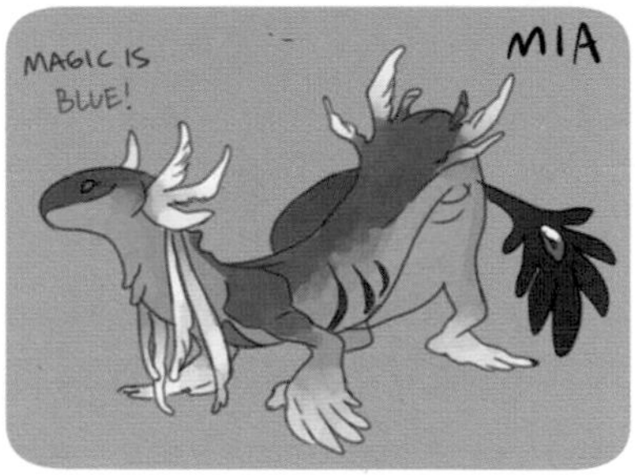
MAGIC IS
BLUE!
MIA

ORIGINAL CHARACTER DESIGNS BY
BONES LEOPARD

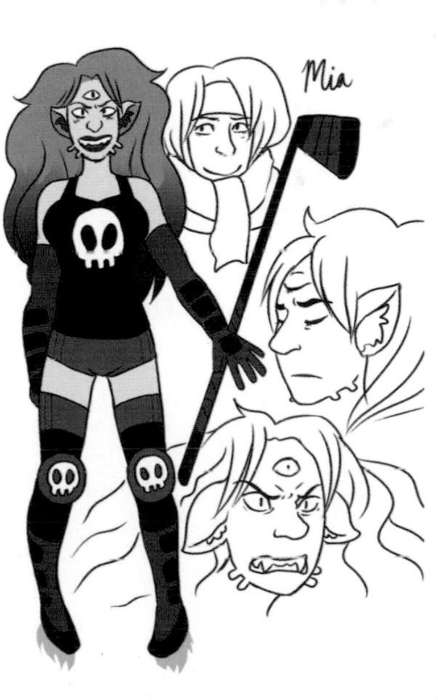
Mia

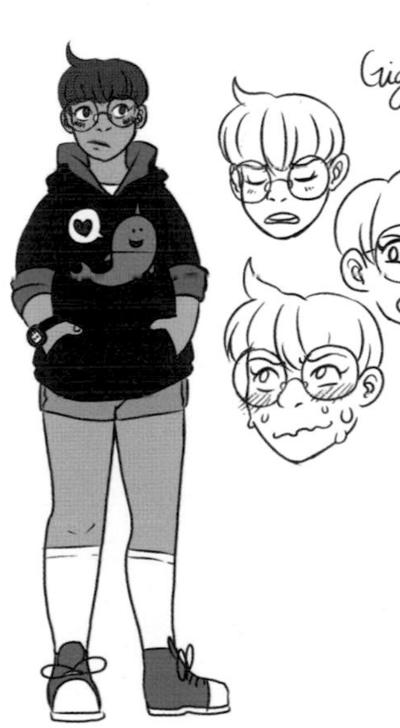
Gigi

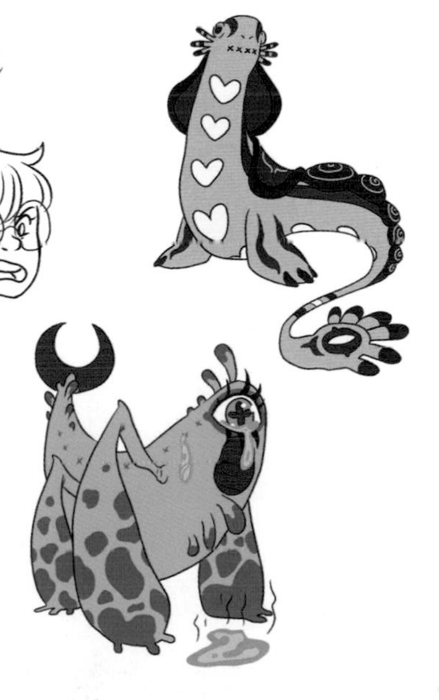

DISCOVER
ALL THE HITS

STEVENSON • ELLIS • WATTERS • ALLEN
LUMBERJANES
BEWARE THE KITTEN HOLY
NEW YORK TIMES BESTSELLING SERIES

Allison + Treiman + Cogar
GIANT DAYS
VOLUME ONE

From a writer of Disney's Moana
RIBON • FISH • PEER
SLAM!

Hope Larson • Brittney Williams • Sarah Stern
GOLDIE VANCE
"Scoot over Nancy Drew..." —Los Angeles Times
Volume One

JAMES TYNION IV • RIAN SYGH • WALTER BAIAMONTE
THE BACKSTAGERS

TYSON HESSE'S
DIESEL
IGNITION

BOOM! BOX

AVAILABLE AT YOUR LOCAL COMICS SHOP AND BOOKSTORE

To find a comics shop in your area, visit www.comicshoplocator.com

WWW.**BOOM-STUDIOS**.COM

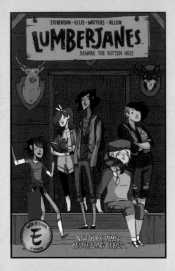

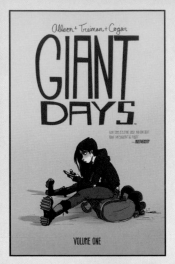

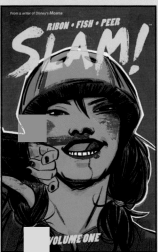

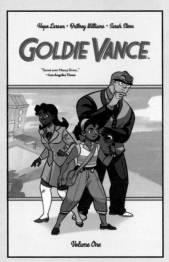

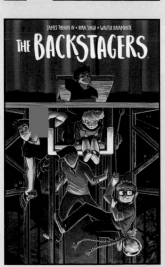

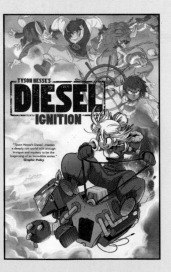

Lumberjanes
Noelle Stevenson, Shannon Watters, Grace Ellis, Brooklyn Allen, and Others
Volume 1: Beware the Kitten Holy
ISBN: 978-1-60886-687-8 | $14.99 US
Volume 2: Friendship to the Max
ISBN: 978-1-60886-737-0 | $14.99 US
Volume 3: A Terrible Plan
ISBN: 978-1-60886-803-2 | $14.99 US
Volume 4: Out of Time
ISBN: 978-1-60886-860-5 | $14.99 US
Volume 5: Band Together
ISBN: 978-1-60886-919-0 | $14.99 US

Giant Days
John Allison, Lissa Treiman, Max Sarin
Volume 1
ISBN: 978-1-60886-789-9 | $9.99 US
Volume 2
ISBN: 978-1-60886-804-9 | $14.99 US
Volume 3
ISBN: 978-1-60886-851-3 | $14.99 US

Jonesy
Sam Humphries, Caitlin Rose Boyle
Volume 1
ISBN: 978-1-60886-883-4 | $9.99 US
Volume 2
ISBN: 978-1-60886-999-2 | $14.99 US

Slam!
Pamela Ribon, Veronica Fish, Brittany Peer
Volume 1
ISBN: 978-1-68415-004-5 | $14.99 US

Goldie Vance
Hope Larson, Brittney Williams
Volume 1
ISBN: 978-1-60886-898-8 | $9.99 US
Volume 2
ISBN: 978-1-60886-974-9 | $14.99 US

The Backstagers
James Tynion IV, Rian Sygh
Volume 1
ISBN: 978-1-60886-993-0 | $14.99 US

Tyson Hesse's Diesel: Ignition
Tyson Hesse
ISBN: 978-1-60886-907-7 | $14.99 US

Coady & The Creepies
Liz Prince, Amanda Kirk, Hannah Fisher
ISBN: 978-1-68415-029-8 | $14.99 US